THE ACCIDENTAL HERO
THE REAWAKENING
BOOK 2

ANDREW RYLANDS

ANDREW RYLANDS

Copyright © Andrew Rylands, 2023

The moral right of the author has been asserted.

978-1-914505-04-1 – (Ebook edition)

978-1-914505-05-8 – (Paperback edition)

No part of this book may be reproduced in any form or by any electronic or mechanical means, including information storage and retrieval systems, without written permission from the author, except for the use of brief quotations in a book review.

www.andrewrylands.com

For Alex

CONTENTS

Prologue	1
1. Acquaintance Renewed	5
2. A Visit	14
3. The Vow	32
4. Prague	35
5. Theft	47
6. Escape	58
7. A Security Upgrade	69
8. The Giant in the Cave	74
9. The Watch	89
10. Agent 73	95
11. STUBBINS	107
12. A Proposition	110
13. A Commission	112
14. Treacherous Moonlight	118
15. Anja	130
16. Lunch	138
17. Healthcare	150
18. Captured	159
19. The Oracle of Acheron	170
20. Betrayed	177
21. A Journey in the Dark	183
22. A Stranger Abroad	191
23. Following a Cold Trail	194
24. Deserted Village	200
25. Freddie	210
26. No Escape	216
27. Haldred and the Wolves	222
28. Dream Twister	226
29. Deposit	233
30. The Wolf Queen	236
31. Interrogation	240
32. Mykonos	254
33. Decision Time	261
34. Moon Carver	269
35. God of Ecstasy and Terror	278

36. Adrift	281
37. Night Club	284
38. A Resolution of Sorts	294
39. The Note	302
40. Secrets of the Urdabrunnr	307
41. The Apartment	321
42. The House on the Lake	325
Free Prequel	335
Acknowledgments	337
About the Author	339

MAILING LIST

Welcome to The Reawakening. To keep up to date with news about the series as it evolves, and download a FREE PREQUEL, sign up to my mailing list.

You will find the links at the end of the book.

Happy reading.

PROLOGUE

The smith toiled at his forge. A long day of dull routine – fathoming base metal into ploughshares, scythes and other farm equipment for the villagers who lived along the valley and beyond – was drawing to a close. Another wasted day to add to the lengthening list as his life dwindled to nought in this long-forsaken place. As work goes, it paid; enough to get by. But it had no hold over his heart. He longed to test himself once more; to fashion exotic and beautiful objects in gold or silver with nothing more than the power of his imagination and the skill of his hands. Precious metals and gemstones spoke to him like nothing else. To touch them was to inflame the craftsman's calling that burned deep in his heart. He could bring life to those exquisite materials; imbue them with his cunning, his ingenuity and his art. Then spin them into marvellous objects of veneration and desire.

The thought of it quickened his heart. His reputation had been great in the days before. Now, thanks to his flawed and feckless family, he was exiled to this cold, far-flung place on the outer edges of the world; grim and embittered, the victim of his family's misfortune: the golden curse. Even his brother, for so long his ally, declined to visit him in this dreary country; a land shorn of joy and laughter.

It was winter, and the days were short, but that bothered him not; the heat of the forge delivered warmth enough. Alone in his cottage beneath the mountain's wall, he could still dream of his halls of old, decked with gold and precious artefacts aplenty. In those days he'd been someone, had counted for something, before his brother's foolhardy scheming. He paused, staring into the glowing coals, seeing instead the ornaments and other devices of intricate manufacture that adorned his old home. They would catch and reflect the candle's glow, magnifying it, illuminating the rooms and transforming them into something wonderful and alive; a palace that danced with sparkling light. Yes, the product of his skills had once burnished his reputation indeed, and brought him a life of luxury, fame and influence.

But it hadn't been enough.

The latest batch of pitchforks was nearly done. Just a few handles to be fitted, and he was finished. He glanced up to see a stranger on the road, staring at him. The man was tall but stooped, as if bent by the relentless north wind. His features were obscured by the shadow of his hat, but beneath its brim the smith caught the glint of deep-set eyes.

The smith waited for him to continue on his way, but he remained outside the forge, as if considering, then entered.

"A master jewellery maker lives in these parts, I have heard. 'Tis said that no woman who ever lived could renounce a gift wrought by his cunning hand."

The smith regarded the stranger, his interest kindled. "You have heard right. That much is so. There is none other who can create aught fairer that might adorn a lady's breast or arm or hair."

The stranger gave him an appraising look. "Brave words, dear Smith. Yet if that is so, why do you eke out a bare living here, on the forsaken edge of the world, far from your kind, far from your former home? To the eyes of this passer-by, it would seem thou liv'st in circumstances so poor that a man might question that bold claim, or ask if it still stands true. Does there remain any remnant of skill to back up your strong words, or is it naught but hot breath on a cold wind?" His eyes sparkled beneath his broad-brimmed hat, reflecting the forge's glow.

The smith bridled at the slight, and in his pride, his retort caught something of the heat from the furnace below. "My skill has never been equalled. Nor will it falter before your challenge, old man."

The stranger gave him a sidelong look. "But time is an enemy of all skills, 'tis said. Time is the grinding wheel that erodes all our dreams and hopes. I reckon your art, if indeed it was as good as you claim, is naught but a shadow of what it once was."

The smith stood up straight and looked the stranger in the eye, his ire rising. "There was never a woman in creation who would disavow a gift from my hand, and no one as gifted at the craft. There are plenty out there who would vouch for my skills, though they be my mortal enemy or not."

"No woman in creation, you say? That is a bold claim indeed." He glanced around the workshop with disdain. "Why, from circumstances like these, I doubt you could manufacture a trinket pretty enough to fool my daughter."

"My necklaces have adorned the necks of queens. If it's evidence you want, first let me have sight of your money. Then, maybe, we can make a pact."

The stranger drew closer, his voice turning sly. "Perhaps your hands have more cunning and are quicker than your mind. Take care lest your tongue outrun your skill."

With temper rising, the smith's grip tightened on the shaft of his hammer. "You have no cause to doubt me. Not even she who doomed fair Baldur could spurn a gift from my hand."

There was a long pause, the silence broken only by the

crackle of the burning charcoal, and somewhere in the dark, at the back of his thought, a sliver of doubt crept into the smith's mind.

The stranger took out a purse, weighing it in his hand, as if considering. "Let me test your skill, then. Here are thirty gold coins. Make a necklace pretty enough that my beloved girl cannot but desire it to adorn her throat, and I will acknowledge your greatness, and all the wealth and power that a mighty king commands will be thine for the rest of your days. You shall live in a palace amid a mighty citadel by the sea and command armies and navies to make your enemies tremble. Your kingdom shall have no equal north, south, east or west."

The smith looked at him, cautious now. "Or?"

The stranger met his eye. Shrugged. "Or if you fail, I ask naught other than you do my bidding, as and when I ask, unto the end of your days, and live at my command. Should you carry out my instructions, I will see you rewarded well enough. I am not an ogre." He stopped. Waited a beat. "Do we have a wager?"

On any other day the smith might have softened the edge of his sharp tongue and damped his hasty temper with cool words. But with his ability questioned thus, and his pride at stake, there was no drawing back. He spat into the palm of his hand and held it out. "Deal."

The stranger's mouth curled into a twisted grin, and he extended his hand, and when palm met palm, the unbreakable bond was sealed.

CHAPTER 1
ACQUAINTANCE RENEWED

Athena was speechless. Odin: a name bearing only the faintest echo from a distant past now-forgotten. He had no place in her life, and no place in her time, she hoped. He was an anachronism. Why was he here? And how come he too was a cat? He wasn't part of her original plans.

Myriad questions floated around her mind as she sat, staring stupidly at the computer screen. Athena adjusted her paws minutely, every fibre focused on the black-and-white cat on the screen in front of her. From the small room at the back of Lieutenant Samaras's house, she communicated with Cat Intelligence HQ, in Geneva; an outfit she'd discovered a little while previously, seemingly by chance, and which appeared to dovetail perfectly with her own intelligence-gathering mission.

The computer was acquired and set up at her insistence by her housemate, the lieutenant. She operated it by a sophisticated voice synthesiser attuned to her special artefact: the item painstakingly recovered from the nearby archaeological dig. Athena's re-emerging mental powers did the rest, connecting her to the new electronic networks humans had so cunningly devised in recent years.

For the moment, Athena said nothing while Odin rumbled on, though she found herself increasingly distracted by his multicoloured glass eye.

"I have been observing you for some time. In fact, I established this network for that very purpose," Odin continued.

An outrage: that was her idea. Who did he think he was, this Odin? Athena was affronted at the thought her new contacts might not have arrived entirely because of serendipity. Her thoughts continued to bubble while he went on.

"I wanted to track down others of our kind before they succumb to the weariness and final indignity of old age and creeping senility. Time crushes everything, I'm sure you'd agree. Even beings like us." He paused and stared into the lens, as if trying to reach through the camera.

Establishing a network of cats across the country to act as her remote eyes and ears on the ground was a first step in Athena's wider project. She had recently used the artefact to show herself, or rather a facsimile of her former self, to Lieutenant Samaras, intimidating him to the point where he was at least nominally onboard. Using information she had fed him, he had solved a case that uncovered a sizeable international criminal network, and as a result had been promoted. As her first protégé in many years, Athena had plans for him. Importantly, he provided her with access to a wealth of data that might be useful for her search for the tree and possibly other mythical items that she sought. Her attention returned to the animal on screen, who had resumed his monologue.

"Originally, I came to the opposite conclusion as you. I thought it best to hide; to stay in our gilded enclave beyond Bifrost, and beyond this troublesome world. But ultimately it proved an unwise choice. Boredom is a poor companion, and sadly there are those among my extended family who persist in meddling, as far as they are able." Another pause. Odin looked to the side, allowing her to study his profile. Scar tissue was visible below his ear; an old battle wound, she guessed.

Athena wondered how much to reveal. Did he know who she was? She gave, rather than took, instruction. But she knew she might have met her match, and remained silent.

Across the connection in Geneva, the Norse god tilted his head and looked directly into the screen once more. His multicoloured eye glinted as it caught the light of some lamp off camera, giving her the briefest impression of a rainbow. As she tried to catch its light, it vanished.

The transformation into the body of a cat was something she had come to regret. She had persuaded all of them – the whole pantheon – to change en masse into feline form, to ride out the fallow years when they were no longer worshipped or wanted. But over time, some had retired into senile domesticity, and others had simply disappeared, while humanity careered down a path to seeming apocalyptic disaster. Something had to be done.

The first step was to discover a way of reversing the change, allowing her to recover the power she had lost in her transformation.

Developing a network was a recent idea. At face value, her Cat Intelligence Team had been recruited with a mission to protect the cultural heritage of Greece as she sought to develop her partnership with the police through the lieutenant. But her real goal was to find clues to the whereabouts of the object that had got her into this mess in the first place: the tree that she and her colleague Demeter had devised so long ago. When she found it, she hoped it would enable her to reverse the change that she had, in hindsight, so hastily decided upon and persuaded her colleagues to pursue.

So far, there was no sign of it.

Her search had alerted her to the existence of another

feline presence on the internet. The more the merrier, was her first thought, followed by suspicion. But then she realised that animals in far-flung places, evidently part of some interspecies communications experiment devised by humans, could be useful. She established contact and began to get to know them. Then this large black-and-white cat had appeared, uninvited and completely unexpected. Odin.

"But you're a cat," she said at last. "Like me."

Odin stared at her for a moment. "Yes." He hesitated, as if deciding whether to share details. "For a long time, I observed the world below, seeking news of unfolding events. But, increasingly concerned at the reports that reached my ears, I intervened. My usual disguises seemed ill-suited to this modern age, so I pondered the alternatives. Then one of my ravens told me of some unusual events in Athens and I took note."

"But you're a cat," Athena repeated.

"Is there a patent on this form of transformation?"

"How did you do it?"

"I should imagine similarly to you." Odin waited for a while, which merely added to Athena's sense of discomfort.

She changed the subject.

"I meant, *why?*"

It was Odin's turn to reflect. "I heard news that made me uncomfortable. News that was, frankly, disturbing."

"Go on."

"My brother..." It was as if the word had to be prised out of him "He is causing trouble. Stirring things up. I don't like the implications."

At last, they were discussing something Athena understood. Family was always trouble. She realised that she knew nothing of Odin's relatives, however.

"Who?" she asked.

Odin returned a curious look. "I would have thought it

was obvious." He looked aside, apparently lost in thought. "I'd hoped he was sleeping for now, but apparently not."

"So, you need to speak to him? Challenge him?"

"I fear we are long past that juncture." He looked directly at the screen again. "If I were to challenge him now, I fear it would merely presage a war, and one that I am not yet prepared for."

A long-forgotten memory rose in the back of Athena's mind. "I thought you were always preparing for a war."

He narrowed his eyes for a moment and stared into the screen as if trying to read her thoughts. "Well, yes. That's the plan. According to the Tapestry of Fate spun by the Norns, deep among the roots of the World Tree, everything we do leads inexorably to that far distant day. But I don't think any of us want to bring the date forward. That is what I am trying to avoid."

Another pause. With eyes downcast, Odin continued. "He is stirring up trouble, renewing old acquaintances, re-establishing former bonds, extending his reach and spreading his malevolence far and wide. He seems to be searching for something."

"Searching?" Her ears pricked; the black-and-white cat commanded her full attention.

Odin looked up once more. "Yes. That is what I deduce. But what it is he seeks is presently beyond me."

"But why bother? If you're so certain this tapestry is correct, why not just wait it out? Let what will happen, happen?"

He gave her a curious look. "Fate is a strange thing, is it not? Certain, yet uncertain. It is not set in stone. It lives and breathes with the movement of the world. If the balance tilts sharply and irrevocably; if some of us are removed from the board, and all looks lost and the outcome long foreseen comes with insurmountable odds, then the Norns might reconsider their work, unpick their threads and make it anew. They are the daughters of probability and chance, after all. I merely seek to maintain the balance we have. That is all I can do to preserve the future that comes after the future."

Athena didn't believe in fate, or her opposite number's idea of a cosmos, and gave him a dismissive glance of her own. Odin and his strange family, with their doom-laden predictions, were of no concern to her. They could get on with their little dispute in some private realm far away, for all she cared. She settled down on her crimson cushion and thought about cutting the connection. Rude as that might be.

"That's your affair, I'm afraid. Nothing to do with me."

Odin's head turned towards her sharply, his appearance changed. With a backward tilt to his ears, a wild look came over his face. Athena noticed the whites of his eyes and when he spoke, it was with fangs bared. Despite the distance, she felt her throat constrict. His rasping voice seemed to travel on the sharp breath of the north wind. Loud and bitter, it surrounded her.

"My affair? You think my quest trivial? You think you can avoid it, and its implications?" He paused, daring her to challenge him. "The events unfolding affect us all. You cannot hide." His chin rose and he stared at her down his nose. "I am a god of war. The time will come when I weigh Gungnir in my hand again and clasp the wild madness of battle to my heart like a brother long missed. That day I shall answer the call of Heimdall's horn and stride the plain in search of my doom. It will be a red day, a blood day. A day of black and crimson, of darkness and hope. It will not be forestalled forever."

As she looked into his eyes, she stood on a desolate plain beneath a starless sky laden with layer upon layer of dark clouds shedding cold, black rain. A dim red light coloured the horizon; the only illumination in this pitiless place. Hope shrivelled in her heart as, in the distance, she heard the clash of spear on shield. The ground shook with the tramp of ironclad feet and the air vibrated with the unearthly roar of unseen, monstrous foes in numbers uncountable.

The vision faded as suddenly as it had arisen, leaving Athena with a queasy sensation in her stomach.

Slowly, Odin's features softened. His eyes resumed their normal appearance, and his snarl receded. "That day is long foreseen and will be my last. But the outcome, despite what is written, hangs in the balance and is subject to influence. This, I fear, is what he aims to do; to unpick the threads and have them re-weave the tapestry to his own ends. Unless he is forestalled, it will indeed become a day without hope. A day to presage the return of darkness forever. And from that you cannot run."

Athena swallowed. This god on the screen before her danced a fine line between civility and madness. Within him, she detected a blood lust that was truly alarming. But she too was immortal and tempered by battle. She knew only too well the visceral, primitive sensations of close-quarters combat, and above all, she knew when to keep those urges at bay and maintain a cooler head. Yet experience told her it would be better to have Odin on her side than ranged against her. His enemy must be foolhardy or equally unhinged. The thought was alarming.

His emotions under control once more, Odin resumed the conversation.

"To return to your earlier point, if it were merely internal family bickering, I'd have to agree, but I suspect my estranged blood brother is trying to manipulate fate on a wider scale."

She sat up a little straighter. "How?"

"It is difficult to say at this stage. My information is far from complete. I had hoped to speak to one of your relatives who might, I suspect, know more."

Athena held her breath. What did he know of her and her relatives? "Who?"

"The one we know as Hyperborean Apollo."

Athena's eyes widened. "Hyper…?"

"Hyperborean, it's a Greek word, meaning—"

"I know, I know." She couldn't keep the irritation out of her voice. She didn't need a lecture on her own language from a stranger, no matter who. "What do you want him for?"

Odin scratched an ear absently. "He knew us of old. We knew him. I think he might have some information I'm looking for. I'd value his opinion. I presume you've seen him recently and know where he is? Will you ask him to get in touch?"

Annoyed at her ignorance, but more so at being out of the loop, Athena cut the connection. She stretched and circumnavigated the compact room, then scratched deep grooves into the thin carpet. Needing air, she exited via the cat flap to walk through the nearby woods of Filopappou Hill, to think. Her eyes were fixed on the ground ahead, but her progress was automatic, her attention focused on what she had learned from Odin. His familiarity with Apollo was a shock. How come they seemed to know each other, and what did he want to discuss?

She veered towards denser foliage, to remain unseen, while her thoughts raced. Perhaps she should have persuaded Apollo stay in Athens longer, so she could have spent more time trying to reconnect. His visit had been far too brief. What did he really want when he breezed through the city on his mission to save his lover? Was that really the sum of it? He certainly brought a host of trouble in his wake, even if he had removed her main rival, Kratos, from the scene.

Perhaps it was better that he'd gone; Athens may have proved too small to contain both of their egos. Hermes and Ares she could deal with easily enough, but with his volatile nature, Apollo always needed to be handled with care. Could she really trust him? She thought she knew him, but now she wasn't so sure. How much of his past life was unknown to her? How many other alien deities did he know?

Athena paused and lay down among the dappled sunlight and shadow beneath the trees. She was not yet ready to meet her followers who lived in this urban wood. She needed to think. Something Odin had said bothered her.

"I should imagine similarly to you."

She was certain he would not have partaken of the fruit of the tree. That begged urgent questions. If he had transformed, presumably he could change back? Did the same apply to his peers? She and Demeter had never thought of other pantheons all those years ago; their consideration had only been Hellenic in extent. That was no longer the case. Athena nurtured a growing horror that she had been premature in her thinking. The sensible move might have been to do nothing. In the light of this conversation, the need to recover her old powers assumed a much greater urgency. Of one thing, however, she felt certain. Whatever his motives, this Odin had made a mistake. There was no chance that she would pass any such message on to her wandering cousin, even if the fate of the world hung by a thread.

CHAPTER 2
A VISIT

For a vertigo sufferer, owning a penthouse apartment overlooking Central Park was a perverse choice, but Haldred had to admit the night-time view across Manhattan from the mezzanine floor of his duplex condo was captivating. The towers sparkled amid velvet black, each window a tiny prick of light. They looked like a slew of stars at the heart of the galaxy, or a spray of diamonds in a dragon's horde. It made a strange retreat for someone scared of heights, but that was only one of the many contrary aspects of Haldred Schmidt.

A successful, yet publicity-shy art dealer said to be worth hundreds of millions, if not billions; a socialite able to move smoothly within the exalted circles of New York's elite, yet never truly part of them; a part-time recluse, often disappearing from public view for months at a time. And according to a now dated and largely forgotten *Time* magazine cover, the world's most successful man under five feet tall. And that was only what could be discerned from the publicly available sources. To an extremely select few, he was also a deadly assassin, accomplished burglar, ruthless terrorist and expert bomb maker. The full list of his crimes, none of them solved, dated back centuries, and was known to only two others, neither of them inclined to comment.

Haldred was certainly different. His actual height was around four feet ten, but his body was well proportioned. Barrel chested, and powerfully built, he had the kind of ruddy face usually associated with a life lived outdoors, rather than the air-conditioned interiors of artists' salons, galleries and auction houses. Genteel and effete he was not, despite his expensive wardrobe. He was, though, articulate and softly spoken, with a mid-Atlantic accent. A large beard – oiled, forked and platted for the evening's event – hid most of his face. In the part that was visible, two deep-set eyes sat beneath unkempt brows and a bulbous nose. His hair – black, flecked with grey – was long and hard to tame. Tonight, he'd pulled it back into a ponytail, for reasons of convenience as much as style. Some would describe his demeanour as shrewd and calculating, and it is true he had cemented many excellent deals over the years. Excellent for him, in particular. But beyond deal making, he had a directness rarely found in the commercial world of art, and that was far more important to his success. However, the long-forgotten magazine profile was inaccurate in one important respect; Haldred Schmidt was not a man. He was a dwarf.

Standing in the entrance hall of his apartment, Haldred couldn't bear the view for long; even at this distance it made him feel dizzy, and the closer he came to the large picture window the worse it got. Merely the thought of standing outside on the terrace, no matter how high the restraining wall, made him nauseous. He had bought the apartment only to follow social etiquette. It was useful for entertaining; he could impress his contacts within the rarefied ranks of New York's high society with the wide rooftop terrace and the stunning view, even though he could barely glance at it himself. He coped by keeping his back to the windows as far as possible. If Haldred were to follow his natural inclinations, he'd live deep underground, in a glittering, bejewelled palace among a labyrinth of caverns, shaped and sculpted to his own design, just like the one he'd been forced to flee from so long ago.

Beside him, the girl finished her wows, although she'd probably been in dozens of places like this before. She gave him an arch look and her hand wandered across the back of his head, playing with his wiry hair.

"Let's get comfortable. How about you pour me a drink?" She was well practised at putting her clients at ease.

Haldred returned a glassy smile as she glided down the curving stairs towards the living room below, draping herself across the sofa like an expensive throw. He followed, making his way to the drinks cabinet at the opposite side of the room, and fixed a couple of large vodka martinis while she kicked off her shoes and waited. He glanced over his shoulder, admiring her curves, as ice clinked into the crystal tumblers. She looked more at home than he felt. As he mixed the drinks, his thoughts drifted.

What am I doing here?

The nagging ache at the back of his mind was stronger tonight. He could sometimes set it aside for days, but it always returned, lurking on the edge of consciousness: a feeling of displacement, helplessness and dread. That sense of a fish so far from his ocean. Behind him, he heard a squeal of delight.

"Is that a van Dyck?"

Her question interrupted his gloomy train of thought. Haldred halted, a glass in each hand, and followed her gaze.

"Yes." He declined to elaborate, not expecting an agency escort to be well versed in old masters.

Flushed with success, she rewarded him with a beaming smile and began to peruse the room in more detail.

"Ooh, that's not a Raphael, is it?" She twisted around on the sofa, staring at a portrait of a young Renaissance prince on the far wall. Haldred handed her the tumbler, a feeling of unease spreading. The last thing he wanted was some amateur sleuth cataloguing the content of his walls. Perhaps he'd been reckless displaying them here. Maybe he and Yuri had gone too far.

"You seem to know a lot about paintings."

She turned back towards him, still wide-eyed with wonder. "You must have…" She glanced around the room, noting three further small portraits in different nooks, and a large landscape above the mock medieval fireplace. "You must have ten million or more's worth of paintings just in this room."

"Yes, well, I like to collect as well as deal." Haldred wanted to get back to business of the carnal variety. The last thing he wanted was to have to discuss his collection. For years he'd taken malicious pleasure in taunting visitors from the art world with the paintings in his apartment. For all their expertise, none had ever questioned the provenance of these supposed lost masters. Provoking them and exposing their ignorance was one of his little jokes. How many could identify an elaborate copy? To date, no one had come close to discerning the reality: they were all fake. Indeed, this young woman was ahead of many of them, he suspected. At least she recognised the original artists.

"But, how did you… Sorry, not my business." She corrected herself and took a sip. Haldred glanced around the room, as if to check the paintings were all still there. He felt a slight thrill of misgiving. The escort filled the silence, trying to explain herself.

"I majored in art history at Columbia. I love the Renaissance period, and the Romantic movement. This place is a treasure trove. Do you ever lend any of them out?"

This was one young lady who wouldn't get a second invite to his pad.

"No." Haldred took a gulp, desperate to steer the conversation back to matters of a more sensual nature. That was what he was paying for, after all. At the back of his mind, he made a note to speak to Yuri about copying someone more obscure in the future. Perhaps an unknown abstract Impressionist. In the meantime, he coughed. Fortunately, she took the hint, dropped her voice an octave, and adopted a more seductive tone.

"Well, I like to feel a connection with a client. It makes it all a bit more real, don't you think?" She shuffled closer and placed a hand on his chest, teasing a button open. Haldred placed his glass on the floor by his feet, and with mouth suddenly dry, then took her hand and guided her to his bedroom, hoping against hope she wouldn't remark on the undiscovered Gainsborough facing the bed. He was in luck; she was as committed to getting down to business as he was. He began to relax and steered his thoughts towards a more serene course.

It took more effort than he hoped. The nagging dread that haunted him wouldn't let go.

The exhibition had gone well. Sales were good for an opening night, and the artist was more than satisfied. As gallery owner, Haldred was pleased. He'd made fresh connections and reinforced existing relationships. It had been a success on every measure, which had led to him asking the agency for one of their most accomplished assets to round off his evening. He deserved to celebrate with champagne and caviar, and the most acquiescent female company. But he couldn't. The urbane persona he'd adopted in this city was cracking under prolonged strain, and Haldred's nerves were fraying. The reason? The darkness that shadowed his every waking hour, encroaching on his consciousness. The old familiar feeling had returned; a sixth sense that presaged another unwelcome call to action from his master. The commands were separated by decades, but Haldred dreaded each new one, and knew he couldn't refuse. With every fibre of his being, he wanted out. But the insistent whisper in his head wouldn't let him go.

With a feeling akin to desperation, he stood by the bed while she undressed him. He said nothing while she caressed, trying to get him aroused. It was more difficult than he'd expected, and he began to fret. What was wrong with him? She was very attractive. Why couldn't…? With eyes closed, he tried to shut out the world beyond the room and focus his thoughts. He'd performed this ritual many times before and never had a problem, no matter how brief the acquaintance. But something else was chilling his soul this evening; something he knew intimately but dared not name.

A conspiratorial silence grew between them; him standing naked, her lounging back in expensive silk lingerie. "Here," she said, handing him a condom. She misread the look on his face and her voice softened. "Do you want me to put it on for you?" Dark, exquisitely made-up eyes looked up at him. Glossed lips pouted, sensuously.

"No, I don't like the things. They get in the way."

Her eyes hardened. "You wear it, or I walk."

Haldred looked her in the eye, hesitated, and gave in. With a sigh, he tore open the wrapping and put it on, but all semblance of intimacy had evaporated. She strove to reconnect, but the act felt mechanical and gave him little pleasure. Afterwards, he lay on his back, staring at the ceiling while she dressed in silence. With a last glance over her shoulder, she picked up her coat and left.

As Freya stepped into the luxuriously carpeted corridor, a cat wrapped itself around her legs, head raised up. She looked down and smiled, then made her way to the elevator. "Dwarves," she murmured to the animal at her feet. "They're all the same."

· · ·

For Haldred, it was a relief to hear the apartment door close. When the darkness took him, it was better to be alone. Lying on the bed, he looked out of the windows once more to the distant, sparkling skyline, and tried to quieten the voices in his head.

The temperature in his apartment dropped. The windows juddered, then rattled in a wind that appeared from nowhere. Haldred sat up. Could this be it? He grabbed a gown and stepped into his living room, scanning the horizon through the wide picture windows that led to his terrace, and shivered. The early summer warmth had disappeared, replaced by a late bite of winter from the deep freeze.

The Jotun came from the northeast in a curving path that swept across Queens and Central Park; an obsidian shadow against the dark sky. A bitter blast of arctic cold preceded it; cold that also bore the faint scent of carrion and decay. As it drew nearer, its shadowy wings seemed to span the entire sky from horizon to horizon, blotting out man's lights and the stars above with an unnatural darkness, blacker than midnight. Haldred braced himself and tried not to flinch, but every meeting with Corpse Swallower filled him with dread, almost as much as meeting his master.

The mighty giant in eagle form landed on the broad stone parapet and folded its wings. Its huge head and dangerously curved beak loomed above Haldred. Light from the city below crept back into Haldred's peripheral vision. A sharp, beady eye pinned him where he stood, and an ugly, grating voice spoke.

"You have a fresh instruction."

Haldred hardly dared ask. "What is it this time?"

The eagle's feathers ruffled in the wind. Its massive head turned, giving Haldred the benefit of a glare from both eyes.

"Your master wants you to retrieve an item of interest to him. His request is of the utmost urgency."

"Retrieve something? Steal it, I guess. Is that all? What's the catch?"

"You make light of this? Don't be so insolent. I can pluck you from this roof and hurl you to your doom in an instant."

"You wouldn't, though, would you? Who would do his bidding then?"

Exasperation drove Haldred's belligerence, but it was a dangerous sentiment, with demons like this one around. Corpse Swallower continued to glare at the dwarf.

"Are you such a fool as to believe you are the only servant at his command?"

Haldred bit his tongue. The thought of being side-lined was almost as unpleasant as a place at the heart of the storm, and probably came with a shorter life expectancy. The eagle continued.

"You are to deliver it in person, before the next full moon."

Despite himself, Haldred's heart leaped. An audience: a chance to plead his case. It was more than a century since he'd last had the chance. None of his recent tasks had required an in-person report. He'd received no pat on the back nor personal congratulation; merely a generous deposit into his Swiss bank account. Haldred had begun to think a face-to-face meeting would never happen again. Even though he dreaded every encounter, Haldred knew he would need a cool head and well-rehearsed argument if he were to be successful and finally have this endless contract terminated.

"So, what is it? Where do I find it?"

The bird spread its wings and a shadow darker than night enveloped Haldred once more. With a freezing blast of air that almost knocked the dwarf off his feet, he took to the sky.

"Wait. Where do I find this object?" he shouted.

The eagle circled above him. "The territory known as Greece."

"Greece? Where in Greece? I need details."

"Further instructions will be delivered in Prague. Tonight. Don't be late."

Haldred stared at the receding speck as the Jotun left. Warmer air replaced the sudden cold, but he barely noticed; his mind was racing. Tonight? Prague? What the… This was one appointment he didn't dare miss, but Prague was a long way away, and given the time difference, it was, by his reckoning, already dawn. He had perhaps fifteen hours? A countdown had started and Haldred was already in a race against the clock.

He swore, spun on his heel and hurried to his office, any thought of sleep banished. These days, with significant wealth accumulated and spread among many bank accounts, booking a seat on a private jet would be straightforward, but anxiety knotted his stomach as his search returned no available planes he could commandeer.

In desperation he started phoning, but most of the airlines diverted calls to recorded message services at this hour, and neither of the two answered by real people in some far distant call centre could help. They were suitably apologetic, blaming logistical problems, unexpected aircraft maintenance requirements, scheduling issues, unanticipated demand, and more. But none of that was any help. The flights that were departing had no spare seats. There was simply no availability on flights to Europe for the next twenty-four hours.

Haldred felt like tearing his beard out. With increasing desperation, he checked out regular airlines, fumbling his way through their interminable timetabling and booking systems, but with the same result: there was nothing. Throat constricted, he was close to panic. He turned back to private jets; there must be something, surely? In anguish he scrolled once more down the list, checking off those companies he'd contacted: no availability, no flights, flights cancelled, no available planes. Finally, his eyes alighted on one he hadn't contacted; he must have missed it in his haste. Dale Aviation. He called the number, expecting another failure.

"Hello, this is Dale Aviation. How may I help you?"

"I'm looking for a flight to Europe. Prague, or anywhere within a few hundred miles. I need to get there this afternoon, local time." Haldred held his breath. The pause was interminable. Sweat formed on his brow. He wiped it away.

"Yes, we have something for you. Leaving at 8 a.m. It does call in London first. Arrives Prague at 9:30 p.m., local. Is that okay? I can see if there's anything for tomorrow that's direct."

"No, that's fine. I'll take it. Great." Haldred glanced at his watch. Nearly 5 a.m. There was time, even accounting for rush hour traffic.

"Good. Let me take some details."

Haldred gave the necessary information and read out his card details, all the while his pulse rate slowly subsiding. He would be okay; he was going to make it. The telephone operative gave him final confirmation, and the call ended. He flopped back in his chair, drained. For a minute he stayed still, eyes closed, while his heart rate returned to normal, then he made for the shower. He was exhausted, and he hadn't even left his apartment.

In the shower, Haldred closed his eyes and leaned his forehead against the tiled wall, letting the water run over him while he tried to corral his thoughts. He would be okay. Everything was going to be alright. He'd be on time, and then, with the right attitude and a positive outlook, he'd request an audience and put his case for retirement. Permanent retirement. The servitude he'd endured had worn him away and shredded all sense of wellbeing. He'd dangled on the end of a frayed rope above the abyss for so long; he couldn't take it anymore. Each task an ordeal, each one carrying a greater risk of failure; and, in his case, failure meant oblivion. His nerves were shot. It might be a decade or more since his last assignment – a political assassination in a small Middle Eastern country to stimulate another violent spasm in its ongoing civil war – but the fear of the next always played on his mind, and it became worse.

What would he be required to do now? Another act of terrorism? Yet another assassination? An impossible heist? He'd had enough. Last time round, he'd barely escaped the heavy security contingent that always accompanied Mr Big. It had left him badly injured, as they shot out the tyres of the car he was driving, and it skidded from the twisting coastal road. Somehow, he'd been thrown clear before the tank ruptured.

His pursuers had expected the resulting explosion claimed his life, but they were wrong. Barely alive at first. It took him seventy-two hours to crawl to somewhere he could call for rescue. Seventy-two hours of pain and anguish to contemplate his fate, followed by months in a discreet private clinic undergoing rehabilitation, all the while expecting dreadful revenge to be exacted, despite the care he'd taken to cover his tracks. It took a lot longer for mental equanimity to return.

He couldn't go through that again. He needed to be released, but for that to happen, he had to plead his case. In person. The thought filled him with dread, but there was no alternative. If only she'd said yes. The thought, unbidden and unwanted, popped up again, like a demon from the deep. No, he would not be trapped in that cycle of despair. He had his pride, still.

Shower finished, he gobbled some toast and threw a few clothes into a backpack as he waited for his car to arrive. From the rear cabin, behind smoked glass, he left messages for his gallery manager. She was an able deputy, more than capable of taking care of things until his return. He made another call to his PA to clear his diary for the next few weeks, and he was free. Free to contemplate his journey, and what might await him at its end. Free to return to servitude. Dare he hope for a final severance? Reward for long and successful service over so many years? The thought almost choked him. The opportunity might never come again.

Dale Aviation's unassuming office occupied a far corner of the private jet terminal at JFK. It scarcely looked as if it belonged in such august company. Haldred spent several increasingly fraught minutes walking back and forth, before he found it, and after the unexpected delays on the turnpike, he was in a fragile mood by the time he crossed the threshold barely twenty minutes before departure. Slightly breathless, he handed over his passport and credit card for confirmation, then made his way to the small but comfortable departure lounge behind the front desk. It wasn't as luxurious as those he'd become used to in recent years, but it would do. He just wanted to get onto the plane and relax, as far as possible, for the next few hours.

No sooner had he settled into a chair than the flight was called. Haldred stood and made his way to the door leading to the apron, and the jet beyond, arriving simultaneously with a tall man in an immaculate fawn suit. He stepped back to let Haldred past, smiling. It wasn't his size that took Haldred by surprise, so much as the fact he was carrying a large black-and-white cat. Haldred gave it a suspicious look. The cat stared back in curiosity, its eyes never leaving him.

With a grunt of acknowledgement, he presented his boarding pass, pushed through the door and walked to the plane. Inevitably, he had company on his trip, given the struggle to find a flight. But he still suppressed a sigh. In normal times, he'd pay a hefty supplement for exclusivity.

Onboard, he threw his pack on the seat facing him, settled into his own, and clipped his seatbelt shut. Across the cabin, the tall man, who appeared to have no luggage, settled down, with the cat curling up opposite, apparently going to sleep.

The flight attendant swooped by, smiling, and took Haldred's pack to stow it away. He leaned across, nodding at the cat.

"Shouldn't that thing be in the hold? In a crate, or something?" As if in response, the cat half opened a multicoloured eye, and stared back with unmistaken hostility. Haldred tried to ignore it, and focused instead on the man, who seemed unconcerned. He looked up from the magazine he was reading and met Haldred's challenge with his clear grey eyes set above a long, straight nose and beneath a crop of fair hair, expensively styled. He looked amused at Haldred's intervention.

"Oh, he's okay. He's quite used to flying."

Haldred wasn't ready to give in. "Yes, but it's not just about him, is it? What about us? What if we hit turbulence, or he panics? We don't want that thing hurtling around the cabin. He could do some damage."

To Haldred's irritation, the man looked disconcertingly pleased at the prospect. "Oh, yes. He could certainly do some damage." He sounded almost proud of the fact. Seeing Haldred's face, he went on. "Don't worry. It'll be fine. I'm sure he'll behave himself." The man flashed a reassuring smile which did nothing to calm Haldred's annoyance, but he had no choice but to sit back, defeated. Why should he care if the thing got broken, smashing into a bulkhead or onto some sharp corner? Across the aisle, a low growl from the puddle of black and white fur gave the impression it was reading his thoughts. Haldred's travelling companion leaned across and held out a hand.

"I do apologise. I should have introduced myself. I'm Mr Valley, by the way. Pleased to meet you."

"Schmidt, Haldred Schmidt. Likewise."

Haldred sat back once more, hoping for some peace and quiet. He didn't feel like making conversation. Unfortunately, he was out of luck.

"I believe you're going to Prague. Nice city. Do you have business there?"

"Yes, well, something like that." He was in no mood to elaborate. Instead, he shut his eyes, hoping his fellow traveller would pick up the signal.

"I do like the Old Town Square, don't you? And that quirky old bridge. The one with the statues."

"Charles Bridge." Haldred didn't open his eyes.

"That's the one. Yes. Charles Bridge. Great views. Mind you, last time I was there it was foggy. Fall, as they say over here. Couldn't see a thing. It was all a bit spooky, really. Ghostly, you might say."

Haldred hoped that was the end of it. The plane finished taxiing and moved onto the runway for take-off. As the engines roared, the force of acceleration pushed him back onto the luxurious leather padding, and he tried to sleep. A few minutes later they reached cruising altitude, and Valley piped up again. Haldred fought to suppress his frustration.

"I believe you're in the art world."

Haldred opened his eyes in astonishment. "How did you know?"

"Oh, don't worry. It's nothing sinister. I looked at the flight schedule when I arrived at the terminal." He caught Haldred's mystified expression. "I'm a shareholder, you see. In fact, the main shareholder, so I like to take an interest in our guests. I did a quick Google. I hope you don't mind." His expression was open and friendly, with the hint of a smirk touching the corner of his mouth. When he continued, he sounded a little more circumspect. "Mind you, there's not much out there about you. You're a difficult fellow to pin down, given your prominence."

Haldred was momentarily lost for words.

"Yes, well, I'm quite a private person." He looked out of the window at the Connecticut coastline below.

"Of course. Of course. And quite right, too. Everyone

should have the right to privacy in this day and age. There's far too much information manufactured around celebrities, don't you think? One doesn't know what to believe." He sounded reflective. "Far too much. It's quite alarming, really. I mean, where will it all end?"

"Dale Aviation," Haldred cut in. "Valley. Of course. Very clever." Vacuous small talk about even more vacuous so-called celebrities had no appeal, but he could put two and two together.

"Excuse me?" said Valley.

Haldred repeated himself, feeling rather pleased with his deduction. "Your company. Dale Aviation. And you're called Valley. It's a nice play on words. Very clever." He sat back and regarded the man. The cat's eyes opened to a slit, as if studying his companion's reaction. Valley seemed lost for words, but soon recovered.

"Well, yes, I can see that, if you look at it from a Nordic perspective." He stroked his chin as if contemplating the connection for the first time. "But wide of the mark, I'm afraid. My business partner is Dale Stephenson. He founded the airline."

Haldred grunted. He'd been pleased with his reasoning. Now he felt deflated. He studied the cat.

"What happened to his eye?"

Valley contemplated the animal for a moment. "I'm not sure."

"You don't know?"

"It was before my time."

"What do you mean? How old is he?"

Valley's grey eyes sparkled in amusement as he looked across the aisle.

"Oh, I've only had him for a short while. He must have had an accident when he was younger." He glanced back at the cat, who was now paying close attention to his companion. Valley continued the conversation while looking at the cat. "Yes, he's a bit of a character. Almost wild, you might say. But he can be quite affectionate occasionally, when the fancy takes him. He makes a good companion, though. Keeps himself to himself when we're at home."

"Home?"

Valley looked up. "I live near Geneva. That's where we're based. Our European hub, and operations centre. It's a good location. Lots of international corporations, intergovernmental organisations, the UN, FIFA, and many more besides. Between them, they keep us pretty busy."

There was silence for a while. The flight attendant brought them drinks and refreshments. It reminded Haldred how hungry he felt. Perhaps a bite to eat and a gin and tonic would help him sleep. He'd need it; in Europe it was already early afternoon.

"So, what brought you to the art world?" Valley questioned him again.

"Circumstances." Haldred looked down into his glass, watching bubbles fizz around the ice cubes. "I appreciate beauty in things that are made by hand, that are crafted. I started in jewellery." He looked at the man, a glint in his eye. "I used to be a jewellery maker." His chin raised just a fraction.

Valley's eyebrows shot up. "How interesting. As a hobby? Or for commercial purposes? So many successful dealers have only a narrow skill set, don't you think? They seem to have interest only in buying and selling. They don't give a fig for the quality of the art itself."

Haldred leaned towards him, suddenly engaged. "I made some of the most beautiful pieces ever created. There have been few able to match me. Carl Fabergé, maybe." He stopped, realising he was in danger of saying too much.

Valley sat back, an appraising look on his face, flattery in his voice. "Well, I am impressed. Honoured even, to be sharing a flight with you." His eyes narrowed. "Might I see some examples of your work anywhere?"

Haldred looked down and frowned. "Well, nowhere that I can think of. Most are in private collections. Or lost." He cleared his throat. "Anyway, the thing is, you don't want to get too attached to pieces you like, things you've poured so much of yourself into. Otherwise, it's hard to let it go. I could have started a museum with the art I'd like to have kept over the years."

"But you must have retained something you liked, surely? After so long in the business, surely something crossed your path that you couldn't let go?" Valley's expression was open, querying.

Suddenly Haldred felt the man could see right through him. A sliver of ice pierced his heart. He looked away and said nothing.

After a pause, his companion continued. "Maybe not. I can see the problem. It must be even more difficult with something you've made yourself. To have to give it away after all that effort has been expended. Once you've poured so much of yourself into it?" He gave Haldred a questioning look. The dwarf avoided his eye.

"Yes, well… It's difficult."

Valley changed tack. "I came across something recently that might be of interest. It's not jewellery but it is a fascinating object, and of great antiquity. Quite remarkable, really. I'd strongly urge you to take a look."

"Very kind, but I don't deal in antiques. It's really not my ballpark."

"Quite. I totally get that." He frowned, suddenly intense and serious. "But I think you'd find it illuminating. Enlightening, even. Particularly for someone like yourself. A real craftsman and lover of precious things. A creator." Valley let the word hang. "It's an ancient kettle. So old, in fact, that it's virtually impossible to date. There's said to be some mythical associations. Of course, these things are easily dismissed in this day and age. It's probably only old wives' tales, but…" He leaned forwards, a glint in his eye. "They say it has magical properties. Those who drink from it are said to gain great wisdom. It can reveal insights hidden, even from farsighted Odin." He leaned back, smiling once more. "I'd recommend you take a look."

Whatever nonsense he was spouting, he'd clearly bought into the story, Haldred recognised. What a fool. He glanced at the cat. It stared at Valley intently, its tail twitching.

"Where is it?" He felt obliged to respond, even though he had no interest in this object, whatever it was.

"Trondheim. A little out of the way, granted, but my friend would be delighted if you'd drop by. She's been really keen for an expert opinion; someone with connections. Someone like you. I'm sure you'd find it a useful trip." Mr Valley took a small leather-bound notebook from his inside pocket, and scribbled an address, then presented it to Haldred with his most engaging smile. Haldred glanced at it, and put it in a pocket, safely out of sight and soon to be out of mind. He began to feel sleepy, the stress of last night finally catching up with him. From the corner of his eye he felt, rather than saw, the cat looking at him.

"What's his name?" he asked, struggling to keep his eyes open.

Valley looked at him. "The cat? Oh, he's called…"

Haldred was asleep. Valley sighed and picked up a book.

CHAPTER 3
THE VOW

"*I hereby pledge to help preserve and protect the cultural integrity of Greece, including its historical artefacts, art and treasures, as a loyal member of the Cat Intelligence Team, Hellenic Chapter.* What do you think?"

"Don't be ridiculous. That's far too long. Who do you think we're dealing with? We're not recruiting Plato; these are ordinary animals."

"They need to know what they're being asked to do and know how it helps. That's how to encourage positive engagement."

Hermes looked sceptical. Athena was in full execution mode, and he already felt exhausted. The two cats, the white and the grey, sat in the shade of a cypress tree in a quiet spot on Filopappou Hill in central Athens. It was early spring, but even at this time of year, the sun's rays held a surprising power.

"So, what would you suggest?" she asked. Hermes detected the irritation in her voice. He thought for a while.

"Well, you've got to think about the recruits," he said evenly. For once, he was in no mood to antagonise her. He knew only too well that she was far better at strategising than detail, and when anyone picked up on that she could quickly get grumpy. Of course, the scope for winding her up was enormous, and the temptation huge, but he decided to resist it and play the long game.

"Most of them are likely to be around one or two years old at most. Maybe we'll get some of the more active four- or five-year-olds or even older. But no matter how experienced they are, hardly any of them will know what all these long words mean. 'Preserve and protect'. 'Cultural integrity'. I mean, get real." He looked away, dismissive. "It's way too difficult. You've got to keep it short and simple."

"So, what should I cut out? They need to have some idea what they're doing. All of it is important. Very important. I've already removed the part about 'apprehend and capture'." She studied him intensely. Hermes reached forwards with a hind paw and scratched his neck, then diverted his gaze into the shadows beneath the trees.

"You can get rid of all the stuff about artefacts and treasures for a start. They won't know what that means. And as for calling them a chapter, well, it's all just gobbledygook to them. No, keep it simple."

"Such as?"

"*I pledge to help.*"

The grey cat was incredulous. "What, that's all?" Before she could protest, he cut across her.

"Yes, that's all. They won't know much about history or culture, but hopefully the ones you select will be an honest bunch, and willing to help. For a fee."

"A fee?" Athena was almost lost for words. Surely preserving the honour of Greece was sufficient reward, and what greater feeling could there be than protecting the legacy of the past? Their names would live for... well, they'd be doing the decent thing, at any rate. What more did they need?

Hermes anticipated her likely train of thought.

"Times have changed. It's not that they're any more

mercenary." He didn't dwell on the point; perhaps they were. "But the fact is, many of our recruits will probably live off their wits and mostly be concerned about where their next meal is coming from. Provide them with an easy and regular source of food and they'll probably be falling over each other to join."

Athena stared into the distance, determined not to give him the satisfaction of acknowledging he was right. But he spent a lot more time among ordinary mortals than she did, confined as she usually was to this hill and woodland, and the nearby Agora with her select band of followers – and grudgingly she thought he might have a point. Agents in the field would be little or no use if all they thought about was empty stomachs and nothing else. She needed them to be vigilant, and not just for potential theft or cultural vandalism; they had a far more important role.

Athena focused on recruiting a contented workforce. Not fat or lazy, but not worried or fretful, either. With a few carefully concocted words in the correct ear, food could be arranged, and maybe a health plan, she thought, returning to what she liked most: solutionising. She stood up and looked him in the eye, still not entirely convinced.

"I pledge to help?"

"Nailed it." Hermes stared back, unreadable as ever. Athena turned away, looking into the distance, planning her next steps.

"Right, that's settled then. That was useful. I'll get onto it." Without a backward glance, she set off down the hill.

The white cat stared after her.

CHAPTER 4
PRAGUE

Haldred awoke during the final descent into Heathrow. Mr Valley's eyes flicked up from the book he was reading, but to Haldred's relief, he refrained from conversation. They landed and disembarked while the plane was refuelled for the shorter onward flight to Prague. The afternoon was already well advanced, and chilly drizzle draped the airport. Haldred shivered as he made his way to the portion of the terminal devoted to private jet passengers. As he left, Valley shook his hand.

"Be sure to look her up. It's by the dwarf in Trondheim. I'm sure you'll find it illuminating."

"By the dwarf?"

"Um, did I say that? Slip of the tongue. Wharf. By the wharf, in Trondheim. You can't miss it. *Secrets of the Urdarbrunnr*. Silly name, I know, but well worth your time. Good day." With a brief nod, he turned and smoothly walked away.

Haldred nodded, grateful to see the back of him. He grimaced at the paper that had been thrust into his hand, crumpled it up and threw it in the nearest bin. *Trondheim? What would I want to go there for?* He spent the next few minutes scrolling through notifications on his phone until he could get back on board for the next leg of his journey.

From the private jet terminal at Prague, it was a short taxi ride to his apartment block in the Old Town. The building certainly matched the description, having been built in the nineteenth century, but it still carried a whiff of the former Communist era with its dark and forbidding lobby and gloomy stairwell. The contrast to his penthouse in New York was acute.

With a heavy tread, Haldred ascended to the top floor – fortunately only the fourth – and the apartment he held on a long-term lease. A sense of foreboding increased with every step. At the door, he paused, key in hand. Must he really enter? The Grand was just around the corner. He could easily afford a luxury suite, but that would screw any planned rendezvous, of course. His heart sank. What if he could just escape? Freedom? No chance; the thrill of escape would be fleeting and he knew he'd be tracked down and made to pay. His nemesis had more servants that slither and creep than fly and walk, and Haldred had an acute fear of being caught like a rat in a trap. Instead, he set his face to the door with a look of grim determination and entered.

The apartment was the same as ever: sparsely equipped and furnished. He had never intended to spend much time here. He threw his pack on a chair and searched the cupboards for glasses and something to drink. He always needed strong liquor here, to dull his senses and ease the pain. Fortunately, he still had half a bottle of vodka. Good. He knocked back a stiff one and poured another. This time he sipped; it wouldn't do to be drunk for his visitor, whoever that might be. But as he drank, he noticed *it* once more, like a nagging toothache that no painkiller would ease; always in the background, always impossible to ignore. A constant unceasing muttering, no words ever audible, but it left an indelible mark on his subconscious, a nagging unease. It even invaded his sleep, unless he was sufficiently inoculated with drink.

More than once he'd tried to throw it away, but somehow it always returned, driven by the terrible curse she'd placed on it. The only solution he could devise was to seal it into the strongest box he could manufacture and place a charm of his own devising on the lock, then leave it here, in a place classified as nominally his, and stay as far away from it for as long as possible.

With an effort of will, he ignored the incessant call and turned on the TV to provide some background noise. He tried to focus on the mystery task. Retrieve something, the eagle had said. How hard could that be? Haldred was reasonably proficient in circumventing modern security systems, his brother better still. This sounded like a task for Karrig, so it might be sensible to get him onboard. They usually worked together, so really this would be little different, perhaps safer, than their last few capers.

Capers? How to trivialise his crimes. His missions had been anything but easy or enjoyable, just ask his victims. Not that they were alive. But without Karrig, he probably wouldn't be, either. Karrig was another item to tick off his list. Their relationship was difficult, but symbiotic; neither could succeed without the other. Haldred needed his brother's help to achieve his tasks. Karrig relied on the generous bounty his brother sent his way in compensation. Haldred knew he just frittered it away on parties, booze, recreational drugs and women. He had long held a deep resentment of his sibling's frivolous, hedonistic lifestyle; the opposite of his own. Haldred kept himself to himself and only socialised for business purposes. Even then, he felt like the perennial outsider, uncomfortable and alone, even in company.

He snapped back to the present. How would his instructions be delivered, and who would be the messenger? Surely no one too outlandish? Whenever he met one of his master's servants, his skin crawled. Inevitably, he had an urge to wash afterwards. Would it be a ghoul, demon, or some other kind of monster he'd yet to encounter? A knot of dread settled in the pit of his stomach. Why put himself through this again? He had millions in the bank; enough to buy or build a hideaway wherever he wanted. But he couldn't flee far or fast enough to escape the inevitable retribution that would pursue him. It wasn't the act itself that worried him, but what would come after. Haldred was one of very few for whom the phrase "a fate worse than death" held real substance.

If that wasn't enough, he was also tied, as if by some invisible umbilical cord, to that thing in his strongbox. He took one last swallow and stared out of the window. Beyond the rooftops opposite, the spires of the Church of Our Lady before Tyn reached up, and beyond them the steeply pitched, tiled roofs of Prague's medieval towers. But he wasn't taking any of it in; his thoughts were locked into a loop, wondering how his instructions would be delivered, and what kind of monster would be the messenger this time?

The doorbell rang, loud and shrill. He hated the sound, but not enough to bother changing it. He paused, licked his lips. Then, as if waking from a dream, he went to open the door.

A short figure stood on his threshold, dressed in a scruffy brown duffel coat. He was scarcely taller than Haldred, bald but with a bushy ginger beard, his face adorned with horn-rimmed spectacles and an earnest, worried look. He cast a frantic glance over his shoulder, then pushed past the dwarf and into the flat, as if desperate to get out of the stairwell.

"Yuri?"

Yuri pushed past him into the cramped living room, then paced up and down. Haldred cast a glance down the stairs, closed the door, then tried again.

"Yuri, what's wrong? What are you doing here?"

His visitor finally paused in his pacing and looked Haldred in the eye. He chewed his lip, apparently working out what to say. Haldred noticed his hands clenching and unclenching. He fidgeted, pushing his glasses up his nose, taking them off and staring at them, replacing them; then pacing backwards and forwards again, unable to keep still. Watching his discomfort, Haldred's mouth felt dry.

"Yuri, what do you want?" He glanced at his watch. "It's late, and I'm expecting a visitor."

"Thank god you're in. I took a chance. I couldn't wait. I need to talk to someone." Yuri continued his pacing. He swallowed and made a visible effort to slow his breathing. Haldred sighed.

"What is it?" The fact that painters rarely knew the time of day, or day of the week, no longer surprised him. But what had spooked Yuri enough to persuade him to take a spur-of-the-moment five-hour train journey from Bratislava on the off chance Haldred would be home? Haldred had known Yuri for decades; his friend's particular skills gave him an entry into the international art scene in the first place. He knew Yuri wasn't easily intimidated.

Finally, his visitor formed a coherent sentence. "I've had a request." There was a pause. What was unusual about that? Yuri lived off commissions.

"A new commission. So?"

"Well, no. Not as such. Just an instruction, really. A demand."

Haldred sighed. "What do you mean?"

"I can't do it. I just can't. No way."

"Can't do what?"

"I've been told to get a painting. From Greece. Not paint one. Get one."

Haldred's mouth went dry, his mind racing. "What do you mean, 'get'?"

"Have you got any vodka? Slivovitz? Anything? I need a drink. Man, I need a drink." Yuri passed a trembling hand across his brow, then resumed his pacing, his eyes downcast. Haldred looked around. What little alcohol he kept in the flat he'd just finished. He grabbed his friend by the arm, picked up his jacket from the sofa where he'd thrown it and marched towards the door.

"Come on, I know a bar nearby. It'll be quiet there."

With a grim determination, he led his friend down the stairs and along the street.

It was midweek, and the bar was quiet, its interior dimly lit. Haldred found a discreet alcove at the rear and ordered a couple of doubles. He sat opposite the forger and waited.

"What happened? Tell me from the start."

Yuri looked up from the scratched and graffitied table top and met his eye for the first time. Haldred saw bewilderment, the furrow in his friend's brow, a bead of sweat trickling down the side of his face. Yuri's voice trembled.

"He said he'd destroy me. I mean really destroy, as in eliminate. Not kill my business, he said he'd *kill* me. No. That's not it; he said he'd unmake me. Destroy me and kill my immortal soul." Yuri's voice rose an octave. He was almost sobbing. He took a gulp of vodka.

"Calm down. Pull yourself together, man." Haldred's breath caught in the back of his throat. "Right. Start at the beginning." There was a pause while Yuri gathered his thoughts.

"I can handle threats. I've had dealings with some pretty rough people, even worked for some. You know the type. The ones that arrive in the limos with the blacked-out windows and the heavies in the accompanying four-by-four. You know where you stand. Provided you don't get out of line, they're okay. I can handle them. But this guy was different. I just felt... No, I can't describe it. I've never been so... It was horrible. It was... No. No. And then he..."

"What?"

"He had a smell. About him. He smelled of death. That's the only way I can describe it. He smelled like death. Unnatural. Not like anyone I've ever met." He said nothing for a while. Haldred could tell he was lost in recollection. He ordered a couple more drinks.

"I mean, I didn't know I had an immortal soul. I've never really thought about it, but..." He looked up again, searching Haldred's face. "Have you ever met anyone like that? It wasn't like he was unhinged. Far from it. He was totally calm. That was the scariest part." He took another swig. "Do you think there's someone new on the market? Have you picked up vibes?"

"Are you sure that's what he said?" Haldred asked. Yuri nodded. "So, what did he want you to do?"

"Well, that's just it. It's vague, isn't it? I mean, he must have known I'm a painter. I like Greek medieval art, of course. Some of it's really beautiful; the craft can be amazing, but I don't 'get' it. I recreate it. I don't steal stuff."

"Turn the request down. Tell him no." Haldred's heart raced.

"I can't."

"What do you mean?"

"I just can't refuse. I can't explain it. It was a feeling. In my core. I felt him, somehow, but he never laid a finger on me. I just know that if I fail, he'll..." His voice trailed into silence.

Haldred couldn't dismiss his friend's story. Judging by his own experience, it held more than a grain of truth. Haldred knew well that feeling of supernatural dread when in the company of a major deity: the feeling that at a command your entire being could simply unravel. He shuddered and tried to focus. Had the messenger made a mistake? Had this been meant for Haldred? Perhaps Yuri was supposed to pass it on. The more he thought about it, the more that sounded right. The messenger must have embedded a deep fear in the hope it would encourage him to take it seriously. The thought felt callous, but Haldred began to feel that he was the intended recipient, and Yuri the go-between. Perhaps this was why it was so important for him to be in Europe? On the other hand, why use Yuri as the intermediary? The forger couldn't be part of his network? There were certain aspects of his master's plans he'd never understand. A thought came to him.

"Why don't you just do what he wants?"

"I can't. Just can't. It's inhuman."

"What is?"

"Asking me to climb up there. I can't do it. Not to save my life."

"Climb up where?"

Yuri was lost on another rant. "What's he think I am, a fucking spider? How am I supposed to get up that thing, and in the dead of night? It's impossible."

A knot wove into Haldred's stomach. He didn't like the direction the conversation had taken. "Climb what?" he insisted.

"Up to the monastery. Varlaam Monastery. It's in Greece. I mean, have you seen it? It's on the top of a fucking pillar of rock. The sides are sheer. It's a hundred metres. There's no way up."

Haldred swallowed. "Where?"

"Middle of Greece. Place called the Meteora. Monasteries on stupid pillars of rock. Doesn't he know I'm a painter, not a bloody mountaineer?" Yuri passed a hand across his brow. He was babbling again, his voice rising.

Haldred leaned forwards. "Shush. Calm down. What are you supposed to do after you've climbed up to this monastery?"

Yuri gave a strangled laugh. "I'm only supposed to go and

steal a painting. In the pitch-dark. In the middle of the night. Waking no one." He sounded almost delirious.

Haldred's heart was in his throat. "Which painting?"

Yuri didn't seem to have heard him. He gave a manic giggle and began another unhinged rant. "Scamper up a vertical rock face and nick a priceless medieval icon. Just like that." He snapped his fingers and giggled again. Haldred moved forwards and grabbed his companion's head, forcing him to look at him.

"Which painting?" he said, forcefully.

Yuri paused, as if noticing him for the first time. His eyes clouded in thought. "Saint Nick something. I think." He sounded delirious again. "Nick Saint Nick, Nick Saint Nick." Haldred slapped him and grabbed him more tightly. A look of shock and anger flashed across Yuri's face, followed by apology. "Sorry." He tried to concentrate. "Nicklas, Nicolas, Nicky... Nikita. Yes, that was it, *Nikita*." His brow furrowed as he contemplated the name. "Yes, I'm sure it was Nikita. Nikita the Martyr. I remember now. 'Don't be a martyr,' he said. He was threatening me, you see. 'Steal the painting and don't be a martyr.' He was reinforcing it. Nikita the Martyr. It exists; I've tracked it down. It's in the Monastery of Varlaam. That's the problem. I'm not a climber. That rock is sheer. There's no way I can get up there, and even if I did, how would I get away again?"

Haldred's thoughts raced. An idea came to him. "Why don't you copy it? Like it was a commission? Would he ever know?"

A cloud passed across Yuri's face once more as he considered it. "He didn't say it absolutely had to be the original." He swallowed, trying to convince himself. "He just said he wanted it. For his collection." Yuri forced a weak smile and focused on Haldred's face for the first time, summoning the false confidence of the self-deluded.

"Who?" demanded Haldred. "Whose collection?"

Yuri's brow furrowed once more. A stammer entered his voice. "I don't know, that's the trouble. Thing is, I don't want to know." He paused. "It was another case of a man in a limo. I didn't get to see his face. Just his servant. Guy in a dark overcoat with a gun. So unoriginal." For a moment, he sounded dismissive. "Boss was in the back." Yuri's eyes unfocused as he searched his memories. "I never got to see him. Just feel his presence. Feel him there. I swear I've never been so scared in my whole life. And I've met some pretty bad characters."

"How do you mean, scared?"

"It was like there was a smell in the car. A stench. Of dead things, rotting. And a feeling of decay. And pictures in my mind. Visions of chaos. War without end. Parts of bodies littering the ground. Famine, pestilence, plague. All of it. Strange monsters tearing chunks out of each other and ripping people apart. Biting their heads off." He shuddered. "And it was like I had these images going round and round in my head the whole time I was in there. Like I said, I've never been so scared."

"And what else?"

"He said he'd destroy me. If I didn't deliver. Destroy me utterly. Erase me like I'd never existed. His voice was... just awful. Deep, but oily. I felt it rather than heard it." He stopped and looked away. Haldred sat back.

"He doesn't sound like an expert or a dealer. Just a murderous thug. Make a good enough job of it and he'll never know it's not the real thing."

"But if there's no word of any theft, he'll know, won't he?"

Haldred gave a reassuring smile. "I think I can help there. Leave that with me." He signalled to the barman for more drinks, grateful to have received his instructions. His master had chosen a different conduit this time, sure, but that wasn't so bad. He started to make a mental note of the things he had to do. First, he needed more information about these monasteries of the Meteora, in particular Varlaam, the supposed location of the painting of Nikita the Martyr. The deadline popped into his thoughts again. How long did he have until the next full moon? Who used lunar cycles anyway? He began to make a mental note of the things he'd need. First item on the list was his brother.

Further along the same street, a young woman dressed entirely in black, her styling bearing elements of both steampunk and goth, entered Haldred's building and made her way up the stairs, cursing under her breath that her contact had to live so high. Beneath her pale make-up, the last thing Anja needed was her face to redden with effort, although at least there would be none of her acquaintances around to see it. At the door to his flat, she paused to allow her breathing to steady, then pressed the bell. There was no answer. She leaned on the button and pressed for longer. Still no response. Her purple-painted lips pursed in disapproval.

Behind her, a door opened and a tall man stepped out, fumbling with a large set of keys. The girl looked over her shoulder, silently dismissing his normcore styling: jeans, trainers and a light-coloured casual jacket. Another clone; a nobody. She confronted the door again as he locked up and brushed past her on his way downstairs.

"Think he's out."

She glanced at him, catching his unruly mop of straw-coloured hair. He looked younger than she'd expected. "Do you know when he's going to be back?"

The man paused on the first half landing and looked up. For an instant their eyes met, and Anja caught a fleeting image of grey northern skies above a stormy sea. She paused. Perhaps he'd look good in leather, she mused. A vintage biker jacket. With drainpipe jeans. And he should definitely grow his stubble.

The tall man shrugged. "Might be a few hours. Might be months. You can never tell." He resumed his descent.

Frustrated, she glared at the door and considered her options. It looked straightforward enough to pick the lock, but what was the point? And she'd now been spotted by a neighbour. Ah well, it was his loss.

As she descended, she pondered her next move. Irritatingly, she'd have to make a detour to let her handler know that the delivery had not taken place. There would, she felt sure, be consequences; she just had to make sure that none of them would fall on her.

In the end, exhausted and drunk, Haldred led the short walk back to his apartment. He'd agreed to let Yuri sleep on his sofa. It had been a long day. Sitting on the side of his bed, he tried to work out how many hours had passed since he'd last slept, or since his conversation with Corpse Swallower, but gave up. He could scarcely think straight.

He lay down. Why the interest in Greece? His master had made a strange, convoluted choice of messenger, but when had he ever been straightforward? In the end, the instruction was clear enough. He'd got his target. Tomorrow he would get to work on the logistics. As he drifted to sleep, the chattering, hissing voice cut through with greater clarity than before.

"Releassse me."

Never, he thought.

CHAPTER 5
THEFT

Deep, comforting dark surrounded him as he woke. A brief glance at the clock confirmed the time: 2:45 a.m. Father Zakinthos swung his legs over the side of his narrow bed and rose to his feet, his back complaining as usual. A brief stretch did little to ease the ache, so he tried to ignore it, and fumbled for the light switch, then poured some water from the pitcher into the basin on the stand in the corner of his small cell. Plunging his face into the cold water banished the last remnants of sleep and sparked his senses into life. He dressed quickly, then left his cell and scurried as hastily as was seemly to the church to prepare it for the nightly vigil.

As he hastened through the compact knot of buildings that comprised the monastery, perched on the summit of this pulpit rock, he muttered the prayer that underpinned every waking hour of his life, over and over. It had long since become a background mantra to every act he performed, a fundamental part of his daily contemplation and a form of meditation. "Lord Jesus Christ, Son and Word of God, have mercy on me."

A half-moon cast its pale light on the cloister next to the

church and partly illuminated the antique, slightly warped door. Pushing it open, Father Zakinthos remembered once more that he should set about repairing it. The lower panel was cracked and chipped and bore a split that was becoming more pronounced; the result of generations of monks applying a little extra pressure with their feet to open it when it stuck on the stubbornly raised floor tile beneath. It was another job to add to the lengthening list that hovered at the back of his mind. Once inside, the thought vanished once more, as it usually did. He stood for a moment, closed his eyes and breathed in. Beeswax and incense, candles and floor polish mixed with a hint of dust. The scent never changed and always lent a kind of peace. This moment was always precious to him, here alone at the start of the day. A fleeting moment of communion with the Almighty, and a chance to soak up some of the history of this venerable place. A brief connection with the ghosts of the past. How many more had stood in this exact spot, at this same time of night, before him?

Father Zakinthos opened his eyes and returned to the present, hurrying forwards to prepare the church for the vigil, a nightly ritual that had taken place for centuries. It was 2:54 a.m. now; he was behind schedule.

He made his way to the alcove by the altar screen where the candles lay, reaching for the box of matches in the drawer beneath, pausing to cross himself before the main altar panel. He made his way from station to station around the narthex, lighting candles. With each lit candle, the ancient building returned to life, the flickering light reflecting from the frescoes of the Lord and Holy Family that adorned the walls. Before the altar was the iconostasis, the wooden screen that separated the sanctuary from the nave, richly carved and adorned with precious icon paintings, neatly arranged in rows, leaving scarcely any blank space. Its ornate beauty almost overwhelmed the senses. Before it was a lantern containing more candles to be lit.

Father Zakinthos stopped, rooted to the spot, staring at a blank rectangular space on the lower part of the iconostasis to the left-hand side. The screen should have no blank space. Something was wrong. Had an icon been removed for conservation work? He'd have known. Where there should have been an image of the smiling serenity of a saint, secure in his secret sacred knowledge, there was only bare wood. He stared. Which one? Shock froze his brain. Frantically, his mind's eye scrolled through the familiar images around him that formed the backdrop to everyday life, but the missing icon wouldn't come.

The bell! He'd forgotten the bell. A quick glance at his watch informed him it was 2:59 a.m. He'd left no time for the summoning.

Father Zakinthos scurried to the rope at the rear corner of the church and unwound it from the double hook. In his haste, he fumbled, his hands betraying his scrambled thoughts. Even as he fretted, he returned to the comfort of his prayer.

Lord Jesus Christ, Son and Word of God, have mercy on me.

Eventually he had the rope free, and tugged it, relieved to hear the distant muffled sound of the bronze bell high above. A form of calm returned and his heartbeat slowed. *Don't fret*, he thought; *it's only a painting*. Only a painting. But it wasn't only a painting. It was a burglary; an intrusion into a sacred place.

The irony. A House of God should be open to all, including sinners. But not if they steal. Surely not them? The profane greed of the sinful exterior world had pierced the heart of holiness on this rock.

The other monks arrived and made obeisance, several sharp looks darting in his direction. His tardiness had been noted, but it made little impression on Father Zakinthos. His jumbled thoughts were still focused on the theft. Should he alert his colleagues to their collective loss? None of them had noticed. For a moment, Father Zakinthos agonised about what to do. Would the extra hour help catch the thief? Probably not. It was far more important to maintain the tradition of the years; to hold vigil through the middle of the night and pray for the sins of humanity. Material things, no matter how precious, no matter how beautiful, should always play second fiddle to God. Satisfied with his reasoning, he took his place among them as they formed a little knot around the multi-sided lectern and began to chant the sacrament. The nightly ritual had begun: an hour of collective rhythmic chanting of the gospels mixed with periods of silent contemplation. There was comfort in routine, after all.

Once the service was over, free to assume secular responsibilities once more, Father Zakinthos conferred with his colleagues, then hurried to the office. There must be some record in the footage recorded by the security cameras, they felt. The system had been installed years ago and never required until now. He prayed it would provide the information he needed, and that the thief or thieves would be apprehended before they could sell or pass the painting on. Yes, the video recordings would hold the answer. They wouldn't get away with it.

The monk threw himself into the chair behind the desk in the cramped administrative office that formed the secular heart of this tiny religious community, perched atop its sheer-sided rocky pillar. He grabbed the mouse and swished it from side to side to awaken the elderly computer. The fan at the rear of the base unit whirred into life, fluttering some papers pinned to the corkboard behind the desk. He should telephone the police straight away, but something told him it would be better to give them some evidence to go on; a rough picture of the thief, so they could start setting up road blocks right away.

Father Zakinthos clicked on the security system icon and the log-in page opened. He stared at the screen in exasperation; he could never remember the damn password. The complexities of the catechism presented no problem; he was word perfect. But a simple password escaped his clutches.

A minute passed while he sat in agonised silence, racking his brains and trying to remember if he'd written it down somewhere. He rummaged through desk drawers until, finally, it came to him. In relief, he punched it into the grimy keyboard, his fingers pounding more firmly than usual. A new screen opened, and he scanned the menu of camera positions, first selecting that for the main church, then scrolling back to what he guessed would be a likely time. All he saw was white noise; the static of an untuned television. As he stared at the screen, his mouth opened and closed silently as he struggled to find any words to match the confusion in his head. What had gone wrong? He closed his eyes for a few seconds to centre his thoughts, then clicked on another camera position and found the same result, then a third and fourth. All the cameras appeared to have suffered the same blackout. Jaw set, he began a more systematic investigation, viewing other periods along the timeline. Finally, Father Zakinthos established that all the cameras lost their picture just after midnight, and the problem lasted until 2:55 a.m. He glanced at the clock on the wall, horrified at how long his detective work was taking him, and picked up the phone. It was time to get the experts involved.

The police arrived within half an hour: a bleary-eyed detective accompanied by a young constable who looked like he should be off to do his paper round the moment they were finished. His uniform looked at least one size too big.

Father Zakinthos showed them the main church, needlessly gesturing towards the obvious rectangular shadow on the wall where the icon had hung, then ushered them into the cramped office to demonstrate the lack of camera footage. The detective took notes, said little and told him not to disturb anything while he called for reinforcements, specifically a forensic team, to examine the crime scene.

The detective wandered outside and around the tightly knit complex of interlocking buildings on the summit of the rock, looking for ways in or out, with the monk trailing behind, keen to assist, but not called upon. Other than the winding staircase that ended at the main gate, there were no entry or exit points; a fact Father Zakinthos could have pointed out himself, were he asked. He supposed the policeman needed to satisfy his own curiosity on the point. Apart from climbing the sheer sides of the rock, or descending from the heavens, the stairs and door were the only way in or out. The monk kept his thoughts to himself and waited for questions.

The detective concluded his tour of the buildings, then, to the monk's alarm, stepped over the wall and onto the remaining bare surface of the rock.

"You're not allowed…"

The detective returned a withering look and carried on, regardless. Father Zakinthos followed, muttering a prayer under his breath. Death held little fear for one so devoted to the holy scriptures and who had lived on this exalted summit for years, but he worried about laypeople. The last thing he wanted was the demise of a policeman on his conscience. Alongside the loss of a precious icon, that would be the mark of a terrible night indeed.

Varlaam differed slightly from the neighbouring monasteries; its complex of buildings occupied approximately seventy percent of the summit of its rocky column. Most of the others covered every inch of theirs. The remaining area was uneven, and riven with several deep cracks that split an otherwise even, convex surface which, ever steepening, fell away into the void below. The policeman, apparently having no sense of vertigo, flirted with the point of no return. The monk wondered idly whether he would have time to catch him if he stepped too far, and if so, whether he was strong enough to pull him back, or whether he would be unable to halt the fall and end up going over the edge with him in one last desperate tumble into the abyss. Would such a sacrifice absolve him of the sin of neglect? He hoped the Lord would have mercy on his clumsy, forgetful soul.

His thoughts turned to secular matters. In just a few short hours, they would have to open up to tourists. Would the police be finished by then?

"When will the forensic team be arriving?" he asked.

"Soon. We'll see them from here," the detective told him. It was true; the road at its nearest point stopped only a hundred metres away on the horizontal plane, but from this vantage point, you could see it rising from the broad river valley, winding in and out of the hillside as it made its way up, and no vehicles were yet in sight. At this early hour, with the sun just creeping over the horizon, their headlights would mark them out even more. Once at they'd arrived at the car park, visitors had to descend into the narrow defile below, then climb the one hundred and forty steps carved into the rock pillar itself, up to the monastery's narrow entrance gate to request entry. He would have plenty of time to prepare for their arrival.

"Of course. It's just that we open to visitors at nine." Father Zakinthos considered the options. "Perhaps we could delay…"

The policeman turned to look at him over his shoulder.

"That shouldn't be necessary. We've got plenty of time."

The monk looked about him at the buildings emerging from shadow in the pale early light. It seemed churlish to point out, but he begged to differ. Unless the forensic team arrived soon, there was no way they could admit tourists at nine. In his mind, he drafted and re-drafted a notice to pin on the information board down in the car park. Visitors needed to be informed before they began the climb; he could imagine the reaction if they arrived at the gate to find it locked. Perhaps he or one of his colleagues should be stationed down there to head off the tourists in person.

As he pondered, he tried to picture the monastery from below. The flat-topped pillar rose sheer on all sides, separated from the plateau behind, by a deep chasm. It presented a formidable obstacle: an island shorn of its sea, as the land around descended to the broad valley of the Pineios. There were several others like it. Not all of them had a religious house on their summit, but several did, and all of them would present a challenge. How had the thief gained entry? There was only one plausible answer: he climbed. The thought sent an involuntary shiver down his spine.

A more ungracious thought followed: why Varlaam? Why not steal a painting from one of the other monasteries in the district? As the sky brightened, he looked across, to the Convent of Rousanou, and the Holy Trinity beyond. Either of them would have been a shorter ascent. Easier. Father Zakinthos shook his head and admonished himself for such an unworthy idea, then let his thoughts wander back to the thief. How had he scrambled the camera system?

A sudden movement from the detective started him from his reverie. He appeared to have seen something. The policeman looked past the monk to his young colleague lingering on the terrace behind them, and whistled to attract his attention. He beckoned the young man over.

"See that crack? There's something in it, something reflecting the sun. See it?"

Something was wedged in a small crack in the rock, to which a short loop of what looked like metallic rope was attached, on the end of which dangled a clip. The constable followed his pointing finger, but said nothing.

"I think that's where he fixed his abseil. We'd better get it."

The constable looked at him, his face visibly paling. It was horribly close to the edge of a drop of perhaps 200 metres. Retrieving it looked suicidal. The detective saw the look on his face and relented.

"Just hold my legs," he instructed. He took a pair of latex gloves from the inside pocket of his jacket and put them on, then, crouching down on the surface of the rock, edged head first down towards the precipice. The constable also flattened himself on the rock and gripped his superior's ankles as he edged forwards. The detective got hold of the clip to try to work it loose, but the irregularly shaped blob of metal on the end, wedged deep inside the crack, was stuck fast. Swearing, he edged even closer to the drop, perilously close to the point of no return. Despite the tug of gravity, he finally worked it free. Behind him, the monk gave a silent prayer, relieved to see him begin to venture back towards safety. As the detective clambered to his feet, Father Zakinthos realised he'd been holding his breath.

Pleased with his efforts, the detective produced an evidence bag from another pocket and dropped his prize into it. As he held it up, the three of them examined the object through the clear plastic. It comprised a metallic wedge into which a cable was looped, with the other end attached to a clip. Despite knowing nothing about rock climbing, Father Zakinthos guessed it would be easy to lock a rope into the clip to enable descent. It was clearly manufactured. Probably such devices were commonplace in rock climbing circles. The monk briefly speculated on the ingenuity of humanity and the variety of bizarre secular pastimes people pursued. He snapped back to the present, as the detective began giving instructions to his junior colleague. Then he turned back to the monk.

"If you don't mind, Father, I think I'll have that coffee now."

"I didn't offer you one." Father Zakinthos looked confused.

"Perhaps you'd be so kind?"

"Coming up."

Father Zakinthos hurried away over the wall and into the heart of the monastery, relieved to have something to do.

Shortly afterwards, a couple of forensic specialists arrived from Larissa, the nearest major town. They set about dusting for fingerprints and examining the main church for evidence. After showing them the likely entrance and exit route, and giving them the equipment he'd retrieved, the detective left them to it and sat in the office with the monk, sipping his coffee.

"Tell me about this painting," he said, studying the monk's face.

Father Zakinthos gathered his thoughts. He sat back, hands together, fingers steepled below his chin, frowning.

"It is an image of a martyr, Saint Nikitas. He was a Goth by birth. High born. Noble. Came from somewhere near the Danube, I think."

"Why here?"

The monk looked up. "He is revered within the Orthodox faith. He defied his oppressors and was tortured for his beliefs, then thrown into a fire. Such loyalty and devotion to the Lord should never be forgotten." He gave the detective a stern look. "I don't know if any of the saints captured in art came from around here. Where they were born or died doesn't matter. What is important is the example they set, and their sacrifice before God." Lecture over, he sipped his cooling coffee and asked the question closest to his heart. "Do you think you'll find it? Find the perpetrators?"

"Forensic science has advanced considerably in recent years," said the detective. "We have every chance." He smiled in a way Father Zakinthos found unconvincing. "But given the specialist nature of this crime, I think we'd better call in the experts." The monk raised an eyebrow. "The Department of Heritage and Antiquities Crime," he added. "Let's see what the cultural and forensic boffins can discover."

He nodded to the monk and went outside. Father Zakinthos followed a moment later, but paused at the doorway when he heard the policeman speaking into his phone. Eavesdropping was another sin to add to this morning's mounting toll, but the monk couldn't help himself.

"It's an icon theft, so right in your domain. But if you ask me, it's a shame to drag you all the way out here. It's most likely an inside job. Someone tampered with the security system. There's only five monks perched on this God-forsaken rock. It shouldn't be too difficult to unmask the culprit."

CHAPTER 6
ESCAPE

Haldred waited, his fingers drumming a tattoo on the steering wheel. This part – boredom set against a background of nagging tension – he always hated. He had confidence in his brother's ability, annoying as he was, and they had planned this heist as meticulously as possible, but the tight deadline left him feeling anxious. He'd much rather be out there, actively involved; but on this occasion, it made no sense, so he fretted in this rust-bucket of a getaway car, ready to drive them away as soon as Karrig appeared.

It was difficult to keep still. He stopped tapping and twisted his signet ring around his finger, a knot of tension sitting where his stomach should be. Once again, he checked his watch. It was approaching 3:15, and the streets of Kalambaka were silent, but he felt exposed. What if a police officer strolled by on patrol? Did they do that here? It's not exactly a crime-ridden inner city, so probably not; he shrank down in the driver's seat anyway, even though the place he'd chosen to park was a dead-end street and had been carefully selected so as not to be visible from any nearby houses.

Another check of the mirrors, and then his watch. Two

minutes had passed since he'd last looked. It wasn't usually like this. He'd always kept cool before; a professional detachment, even in the run-up to an assassination or other disruption, like blowing up those oil wells. This was small-scale stuff by comparison; so why was he on edge? He struck up a different rhythm with his fingers, puffed out his cheeks and noisily exhaled. *It's always him,* he thought. *Karrig's always late.* He was even late the night they'd fled from... No. That was a furrow he had no desire to plough. Exile rankled still, even after all this time. It was because Haldred had always been in control; he had always been the leader and main actor. Pulling the trigger, detonating the bombs, stealing the diamonds. He'd never had to sit and wait like this before. If he didn't suffer from vertigo, he wouldn't have to now.

Having to rely on his brother like this was annoying, even though they usually worked well together, with Haldred, the older of the two, calling the shots.

His thoughts turned to Karrig. It was a long time since he'd seen him – two and a half decades – but nothing had changed. If anything, he found him more irritating down the years, with his smooth confidence and wide circle of friends. Haldred knew it was only from his payouts that Karrig could afford his luxury lifestyle. His master might be terrifying, but at least he rewarded his subjects well.

Time moved fast here in Midgard, but that was about the best thing that could be said for it. No matter how many years passed, Haldred always felt out of place. It had taken a monumental effort of will to enter the art world, and establish himself as an eminent dealer. Thankfully a chance meeting with his forger friend Yuri had secured that passage, first via commissions for underground connections, later through contacts with those characters who operated in the grey area between legitimate and illegal dealing, and finally through embracing the above-board gallery scene and investing in one of his own.

book was comprehensive, with a contact in almost every city, but very few on speed-dial.

A competent craftsman, he did not share his brother's creative gift, and was never more than adequate as a smith, but he possessed an innate understanding of machinery and had become a skilled mechanic. He was also an extremely competent part-time thief, inevitably called on to provide the help or skills his brother required.

Another look at his watch, and Haldred muttered a curse under his breath. He glanced in the rear-view mirror once again, and to his relief saw a short figure hurrying towards him out of the shadows, from the path that led down from the strange hills behind the town. He resumed his drumming on the steering wheel while Karrig opened the trunk and deposited his pack inside; none too carefully, he noted. It had better not be damaged. His brother clambered into the passenger seat, bringing with him the scent of fresh vegetation and sweat, and slammed the door. The sound, amplified in the still night air, made Haldred wince.

"Call yourself a burglar? I hope you were quieter up there." He turned the key in the ignition, and the ancient Dacia stuttered into life. "Anyway, did you get it?" He glanced across, looking for a sign. Karrig maintained a mournful expression for just a few seconds and shook his head. But he couldn't keep it up, and his face cracked into a grin.

"'Course I did. It was fine once I'd got past the overhang. The handholds were pretty good, considering, and once you're up there, it's easy. These monks have no security at all. They're hopeless." He paused, thinking. "Well, there were a couple of antique cameras, but they were decades old. No proper night vision capability by the look of them. Maybe some basic infra-red. That simple jammer was enough to fool them." Haldred suppressed the niggle of doubt at the back of his mind. He put the car into gear, and slowly drew away, heading out of town to the west on the E92, and keeping well within the speed limit. He felt exposed with so few vehicles on the road, and desperate not to do anything that would draw attention to them.

"Let's hope it's the last time." He could sense Karrig giving him a sharp look in the dark, trying to read his expression.

"Do you mean that?"

Haldred paused and focused on the road. "Yes, I do. I really do. I'm tired. I want out. I'm going to tell him."

There was silence as the kilometres passed. To the east, the sky shaded from black to deepest blue, and the silhouettes of the mountains slowly emerged. It was Karrig who broke the silence, as if talking to himself.

"He won't, you know. It's for life. He'll never let you go."

Haldred shuddered. It was his deepest fear, and one he tried to suppress. "I've done good service. Paid my penance. It's time. It's more than time." Beside him, his brother grunted.

"You should have thought of that before you—"

"Oh, shut up. We're not raking over that again." He gripped the steering wheel tighter. The conversation was closed. For the next hour, each of them kept his thoughts to himself, but the silence in the car screamed of bitter rage.

Karrig had initially ended up in Midgard because of their father's misdeeds, which he'd supported. After his misadventure, life in Nidavellir became impossible and he'd barely escaped with his life, but his wife… his wife… An image of her floated in his mind's eye, her face twisted in helpless fear as her hand slid from his grip as she dangled above the abyss.

Long years of sorrowful penance followed, but just as a rapprochement looked possible –along with forgiveness for the sins of his father, his brother sabotaged everything by committing the crime that damned them both forever. Even in Midgard, he was exposed and vulnerable as the Dread

Queen's agents arrived seeking revenge. The wider family he'd left behind were no support; they readily pointed them in his direction, so initially he hid, and later became grateful for the protection extended by his brother's patron.

In the car, thankful for the dark, Karrig shut his eyes and took several deep breaths. Meditation was his best relief, but right now he struggled to clear his mind of negative thoughts.

Exile under the protection of Haldred's patron might have been the only practical solution to his woes, but as the years passed, his resentment grew until he could barely stand to be in his brother's company. But no matter how much he wanted to, he could not ignore him. The two of them became enveloped in a poisonous symbiotic relationship that both of them resented, but neither could break.

By the time they reached Ioannina, the sun had not yet risen, but was casting a rosy glow over the horizon behind them. They took a twisting country road north, towards Albania. The border was not far away. Even on a winding road like this, they would reach the crossing point in little over an hour: far too early. A few kilometres out of town, Haldred pulled onto a patch of gravel by the side of the road and turned off the engine.

"What are you doing?"

"We're too early."

"We need to get away."

Haldred sighed. An element of sarcasm entered his voice. "You're the logistics expert. You're supposed to understand the value of planning. It's not open twenty-four hours. We have to wait."

Karrig grunted his assent, reclined his seat and closed his eyes. Haldred looked at him, marvelling at his ability to switch off. In contrast, he felt like a coiled spring. He just wanted this mission over so that he could deliver the goods and plead his case for retirement. Despite what his brother had said, he felt he had a case. He'd given loyal service for more years than he cared to remember, but he wanted out. He'd had enough. The strain seemed to get worse with each new mission, and he felt stretched in every way.

He was getting old. But not old enough, perhaps.

What had been done to him? His kind were long-lived, and had grown to expect a long and relatively healthy life. But this long? And all the while enduring the perpetual stress that the lifestyle brought? This job had been easier than some, but he still needed his brother's help. He couldn't have made the climb, and unlike Yuri, he hadn't the skill to forge a replacement. The knowledge that he needed such support frayed his nerves even more. Without Karrig's skills, he knew he wouldn't have survived so long.

What if he was instructed to do something beyond their combined ability? What then? In this game, failure wasn't an option.

Haldred felt mentally exhausted. This time it was worse than usual, but it had been building for years.

The interior of the car suddenly felt airless. He had to get out. He stepped into the quiet of morning. Birdsong was all around and a refreshing breeze blew from the southwest, bringing a hint of the sea. Later on, it would fade, and the heat and humidity would rise. But for now, it was perfect. He set his back to the car and closed his eyes, trying to shut out the noise in his head and find some elusive inner peace.

The early sun warmed him. After a while, Haldred opened his eyes and took in the view. The road climbed into mountains, following the contours and rising slowly. He was surprised at how high they'd already ascended from the valley below. The vista before him, clear in the early morning air, was stunning. In the distance, he felt sure he could see the sea. And was that Corfu?

The sound of an engine straining against the gradient

pierced his reverie, and he crouched down behind the vehicle, unwilling to be seen. A small van rattled past, the engine over-revving in too low a gear.

Change up, you idiot.

He stood and watched as the van disappeared around the bend ahead, the engine straining. Finally, just before it went out of earshot, the driver selected a higher gear, and Haldred almost felt relief. He put it from his mind and looked at the mountains ahead. But instead of taking them in, he fretted once more about his state of mind. Was he becoming paranoid? All his senses seemed to be on high alert. *It's just the cargo*, he reasoned. *Get the job done, and it will ease.*

He performed a few neck rolls to ease the tension in his shoulders. To pass the time, he perched on a nearby rock and threw pebbles at a crushed and faded Coke can, poking out from beneath a bush.

Finally, it was time to go. The border would be open. He got back into the car and turned the key. Karrig came to beside him, scrambling for the lever to bring his seat upright once more.

"Thought we were early?" Haldred chose to ignore him, for once failing to rise to the bait. Forced to endure each other's company for more years than was natural, the brothers had long ago resorted to needling each other in an endless points-scoring exercise, where nobody kept a tally. They'd long ago given up on small talk.

Instead he stared at the road ahead and slowed down even more. Another hour passed before they approached the crossing point. A short line of vehicles lay ahead of them, waiting. Haldred groaned.

"You did put it in the secret compartment, didn't you?"

"I forgot. Look, it won't be a problem. It never is."

Haldred glared at his brother, speechless with rage. Karrig returned a broad smile, mocking his fury and raising it several notches. Sometimes his confidence smacked of complacency, but there was nothing he could do other than silently fume over his brother's slapdash idiocy. Karrig was the one who'd adapted the car, constructing a secret compartment beneath the floor of the trunk, big enough to hide their prize. Why had he not remembered it until now? *Moron*. He continued muttering under his breath as they edged to the front of the queue.

"Stop fretting," his brother instructed, in a tone of voice that could have been genetically engineered to wind him up even more. As if to underline his point, Karrig whistled tunelessly, while taking in their surroundings. "Relax."

"Shut up." Haldred struggled to keep the tension out of his voice.

They reached the front of the queue. As if trying to annoy him more, Karrig gave the female customs officer a beaming smile, but she ignored him, took the passports from Haldred, gave them a dismissive glance and waved the pair through. Fifty metres further on, her Albanian counterpart glared at the documents as if willpower alone would enable him to detect hidden codes within the printed page beneath its plastic veneer. He was forced to give up eventually, and handed them back.

They were free to continue.

Haldred stalled the engine. Flustered and reddening, he turned the key once more, hoping against hope that he hadn't flooded the carburettor. He pumped the gas pedal and turned the key again. Beside the car, the border guard waved them on, yammering at them for holding up the queue. For an agonising moment, the starter motor struggled, but then engaged. Karrig sniggered as Haldred flashed the guard an embarrassed smile and set off.

As he drove away, he tried to ease the tension in his shoulders by letting them drop. It was barely eight o'clock, and he felt shattered.

"Stupid bastard," Haldred spat. "I thought you'd serviced this heap of junk? Are you trying to get us arrested?"

"It's fine. It's in perfect condition. I think you'll find the problem is the driver." Karrig looked away from his brother and out of the side window and began to whistle once more. Haldred suppressed the urge to swing a fist in his brother's direction. Instead, he tried to take his mind off him, and for the next few hours at least, relax. They had left Greece, the scene of the crime. There had been no sign of pursuit. He wasn't sure if the Albanian police were connected to their colleagues across the border, but he suspected the relationship wasn't close. Now they were here, they could take a little time to plot the next move. Haldred could deliver the object to his patron, and Karrig could return to one of his various homes in exile, after he'd been paid. Once delivered of his cargo, Haldred looked forward to taking a long break from his annoying sibling.

CHAPTER 7
A SECURITY UPGRADE

T he message that arrived in the abbot's inbox was polite, but to the point.

As a philanthropist and a keen defender of our shared heritage, my attention was drawn to your unfortunate recent loss. I extend my heartfelt sympathy. To lose a treasured icon in such unfortunate circumstances is, I can see, a blow to your revered institution as much as to your faith. Furthermore, it represents a shattering blow to our collective memories; the foundation we all share. Its loss is deeply felt by all of us who prize art and culture. Without seeking to over-dramatise the event, this theft is a dastardly stab to the heart of all that we hold dear: our shared values, and our collective inheritance.

I would like to assist you, in some small way, to preserve and protect the incomparable collection that remains within your custody, and in doing so, help secure it for future generations. Please allow me to offer some practical assistance in this endeavour. With your permission, I am willing to donate, at my own expense, a discrete but powerful security system that will, at least, help to strengthen your defences against any future attempted theft. What I propose will be a significant upgrade to your existing equipment, which I understand to have been found wanting. Through my contacts, I can provide your institution with new infra-red motion detectors, the latest generation of digital camera and image capture equipment. All wirelessly connected, unobtrusive and discreet. In summary, a state-of-the-art security system. It will provide a direct connection to your local law enforcement agencies, and as such, allows officers to be on the scene within minutes of an alarm being triggered, if such an unfortunate event were ever to occur again.

If you are willing to accept this meagre offering of practical assistance, even though, sadly, it is too late to be of any consolation regarding your recent loss, I will be happy to arrange installation at your earliest convenience, and at no cost to yourselves or your wider organisation. All the above will be done entirely at my expense. Please accept this offer as a gift. In view of my relatively high public profile, I would prefer to keep my identity private, but please rest assured, my representative, whose telephone number I provide below, has full authority to conduct this task on my behalf. I urge you to contact him to finalise the details and make all necessary arrangements.

With kindest regards,
A well-wisher.

The abbot read and re-read the email several times, all the while pondering its implications. He hadn't expected news of their loss to remain secret for long, but scarcely twelve hours had passed since the theft, and the news had not yet made the local or national bulletins. He stroked his chin. The message was too prompt. How had news of the theft leaked? He searched for a sinister motive behind the offer of help.

It was unfortunate that the outside world intruded on their little community like this. The abbot sighed. He would like to believe the sender of the message was genuine, but was that naïve? The plain fact was that the monastery's current security system was woefully inadequate, and as the events of last night had proved, easily bypassed. He considered his response. His initial inclination had been to firmly, but politely, turn it down. This was a religious order; the monastery was a House of God, not an art gallery. Secular matters and objects, even those of veneration, were of little significance when set against the institution's sacred duty to save the soul and pray for the salvation of all humanity. The maintenance of holy scriptures and imagery was of huge importance, but his order's primary purpose was to serve God and observe the Will of God.

Then again, if genuine, the offer in the email was extremely generous, and as theirs was an order cemented by vows of poverty and obedience, could it be interpreted in some obscure way as a sign of God's will? To summarily dismiss it as the ramblings of a crank or do-gooder might be churlish and inappropriate. The monastery, and its peers, collectively held a trove that was of value beyond measure to the faithful; but there were also many among the secular community who valued the art and craft of the long-lost past, and who revered their treasure on its artistic merits alone. He reconsidered. Perhaps it would be wise to seek council. A consultation with his fellow abbots might be prudent, at least.

A brief round of telephone calls revealed that every monastery in the district had received a similar offer, all sent to private email addresses known only to members of the church hierarchy. The offers were unexpected but seemed genuine. With the request for discretion, it certainly did not appear to be a publicity stunt. Once again, the abbot wondered how far news of the theft had spread. Presumably it must have come from somewhere in the police force, or its forensic agency? He found it hard to accept that a senior cleric would spill the beans; they would have little or no motivation. It seemed there was no option but to call the number and speak to the representative of the mysterious philanthropist.

His call connected almost immediately. The voice at the end was polite, male, and had an accent that was difficult to place, but definitely not Greek. It should not have come as a surprise, as the most affluent members of society were surrounded with multinational staff from all around the world. The contact, who called himself Antef, seemed genuine enough.

No, he was not the scribe of the email. Yes, he was familiar with its content, but could not shed any light on the identity of the sender other than to reiterate that this was a serious offer from a well-intentioned, extremely wealthy and high-profile individual. News of their involvement would bring unwelcome attention to all parties, so discretion was both important and required.

He reminded the abbot that the purpose of making contact in the first place was to protect the cultural integrity of the monastery, and the others within the area, and of course to protect the artistic treasures they held for posterity and for future generations, including future generations of monks and priests who would inhabit the buildings and maintain their traditions long after the present generation had moved on to their eternal resting places. The abbot promised to call back.

As he returned the handset to its cradle, he reviewed the conversation once more. There must be a catch. A second opinion would be useful. He picked up the handset and dialled the number for the Monastery of Great Meteoron, the largest of their neighbours, to speak to his counterpart, Abbot Kokkinos.

"Dear Reverend Father," he said, sticking to the formalities, "I seek your advice on a delicate matter."

"Have you spoken to him as well?"

The abbot shouldn't have been surprised, but he was,

nevertheless, taken aback. "Yes. I called the number given in the email."

"So did I." Abbot Kokkinos seemed too enthusiastic for his liking. "If you're wondering, I told him 'yes' – we'd be delighted to take up his offer." There was a pause which the abbot assumed was supposed to be his opportunity to agree. He remained silent. Kokkinos continued. The abbot detected a slight air of exasperation in his voice. "This has every indication of being an act of selfless philanthropy. You don't want to look such a gift horse in the mouth, do you?"

"Well, quite…" the abbot demurred, his thoughts drifting to other horses Greeks have given in gift. He sought to frame his concern. "It's just that he, well, how can I put it, he didn't sound like one of us? Necessarily?"

Another brief pause. "Now, look, let's consider the facts. He came across to me as a serious individual. His responses to every question I posed had a ring of credibility, and his offer of help sounded genuine. To reject such an offer out of hand seems irresponsible, given the fragile condition of our finances."

Thus chastised, the abbot put aside his doubts and concluded the conversation before his peer began to think him surly and ungrateful. The offer was most likely genuine, he reflected, and would certainly help take a weight off his mind. Every form of assistance that eliminated, or at least distanced, the problems thrown up by the chaotic outside world was to be welcomed. Nothing should, after all, distract his small religious community from their main calling: devoting every hour possible to the worship of the Lord.

CHAPTER 8
THE GIANT IN THE CAVE

Haldred made his way through the vast tunnel complex with ease, a spring in his step. Cavernous subterranean depths lent a sense of deep satisfaction that always lifted his spirits; he felt at home in places like this. The interlocking caves were dry, the route mainly level, circulating around stalagmites, detouring past stalactites, and navigating through fields of crystal and gemstones the sun never saw.

Now and then, he would reach one of the interconnecting passageways that linked the vast cave complexes together. They were not natural features; they had been mined and tunnelled, and to improve communication, most had recently been upgraded and modernised to make them wide enough for vehicles to navigate. A network of electric car depots and charging points had been established throughout this underground realm and the modern infrastructure sped up his journey considerably. In the old days, he'd relied on chariots drawn by wargs.

A brief exchange of hisses and grunts with the demonic figure guarding the rental vehicle park gave Haldred the keys to a newish car, and from there it was only three or four hours' drive to his destination: the cathedral-scale cave at the heart of the system.

Halfway there he was brought to a halt by a short figure brandishing a stop-go sign. Haldred shrunk back in his seat and suppressed a groan. Forced to a halt, he checked the locks on the doors and wished the windscreen were opaque. The figure standing in the middle of the road stared right through him, bored and disconnected. Behind him, Haldred caught sight of other dwarves labouring to unload a crate from the back of a truck. The sight made the hair on his neck stand up. Well-justified paranoia had long made him shun others of his kind. Being recognised might be bad for his life expectancy.

He looked to each side for a potential turning place, but the road was too narrow. To his left he saw yet more dwarves resting on picks and shovels, others carrying pneumatic drilling equipment. They were preparing a place for whatever was being delivered. With horror, Haldred watched the dwarf with the stop sign approach to the side of his car, apparently wanting to speak to him. He opened the window a crack, and avoided eye contact.

"Sorry 'bout the delay. Won't be long." The working figure peered at him. Apparently expecting a response.

"Er, no problem." Haldred waited for him to move away, but he didn't. He tried to think of something to divert attention from himself. "What are they doing?"

The dwarf leaned on his sign, and gestured behind him. "Geothermal generator being delivered. We've got to fit it into the alcove over there, then plumb it into the pipework beyond." He nodded towards the alcove Haldred had spotted. "We're putting in some more charging points all down this route. Part of the wider Sub-Midgard Transit Infrastructure improvements." He turned back to Haldred, suddenly taking an interest. "How far to your destination? How much charge you got left? Is your trip urgent?"

"I'm okay for two hundred clicks." He didn't elaborate

further, hoping the workman would take the hint and clear off, but he didn't.

"Well, that's okay if you're wanting somewhere central. If you need to carry on to, say one of the East Baltic entrances, you'd be well short."

Haldred was as aware of the fact as anybody, but suppressed a comment. Better not get into a longer discussion; he just wanted to arrive at his destination and deliver the goods. Above all, he didn't want to be recognised.

He peered ahead, and saw the truck driver clamber back into his cab. The engine grumbled into life, emitting a cloud of dense black smoke. Clearly, not every vehicle down here was environmentally sound. He glanced up at the workman.

"Am I clear to go?"

The dwarf had been admiring his car. He turned and watched the truck move off.

"Yeah, okay. Off you go." He stepped back, bowed and waved his arm in an unnecessarily elaborate fashion. Haldred nodded and set off again, relieved to be moving.

It had taken him less than a day to get here from the entrance he'd discovered in the Albanian mountains, and a mere forty-eight hours had passed since their audacious theft. By far, the most challenging part of the process had been tracking down the entrance portal in the first place. He had no local contacts, and internet connectivity in their location had been slow and prone to service outages. Still, Haldred felt pleased with himself. The job had gone smoothly, because of his excellent planning and preparation, and he'd navigated and interpreted a ridiculously hard trail of clues. Now, with his prize on the seat beside him, he had the confidence of an A-grade student delivering a winning thesis. His master's delight would give him the opening to raise the subject of his release from endless servitude. He couldn't wait to be free.

Haldred parked the vehicle in a marked bay at the end of a long, wide passage and nodded to the attendant in the booth opposite. A short distance ahead, in an alcove, was a large iron-bound wooden door that looked like it had blocked this passage since the dawn of time. Dark and battered though it was, his critical eye was drawn to the iron hinges; they were so old, they looked in need of replacement, but perhaps they were the key to the structural integrity of the door. Remove them and the wood behind might crumble to dust.

He realised his thoughts were rambling to distract from the idea of what, or who, lay beyond.

Haldred clutched the strap of the bag draped over his shoulder. He knocked and waited, his mouth dry, a familiar tightness constricting his stomach. Once more, in his mind, he rehearsed the arguments he planned to use.

The scraping sound of a rusty bolt being drawn back echoed in the passageway, followed by the creaking complaint of hinges made to work against their will. Inside, an enormous armour-clad figure carrying a spiked club held the door open. The dwarf shuddered; the guard was nearly three times his size, and his knotted brows and sunken eyes offered little welcome.

"Password."

Haldred's resentment at being asked rose to the surface once more. Why the ridiculous security? Surely by now he was known as a trusted servant. Overcoming an almost teenage reluctance, he gave his answer in a monotone. It was not the time to argue otherwise, and he didn't feel like taking on one of these meatheads. Not without a proper weapon, at least. Preferably a long one with a sharp point. Or a gun. On reflection, he couldn't be sure the memory span of these trolls lasted beyond a couple of hours, so probably the welcome wasn't personal.

With a glare at the sentry, Haldred entered a vast cavern, its ceiling high enough to accommodate most of Earth's major cathedrals with room to spare, and long enough for two of them end to end, but with a very different atmosphere. During the several minutes it took to walk to the far end, his dread grew. For such a large space, it seemed hot and airless; he never felt he could breathe deeply enough to fill his lungs, while all the time the knot that filled the space where his stomach should be grew, hardening and fossilising with every step.

A large stone bed dominated the far end of the cave, close to the rock wall although in this vast underground space it looked small and insignificant. On it lay an enormous male figure, at least five metres from head to foot, broad shouldered, lean and well muscled, and restrained by stretchy ropes that adapted to his movement. They were the most sinister ties Haldred had ever seen: organic, almost alive. Elastic ropes of a pinkish hue. They flexed when the figure moved, and the moment he relaxed, tightened again, as if taunting him.

Haldred wondered, as he always did when he approached across the vast empty floor, about his captors, and whether they hadn't been too vindictive. Was the victim really such a threat to them? How dangerous would he be if free? In Haldred's opinion, he was as dangerous when bound as he had been when he walked the earth; perhaps moreso, he now had a purpose. The closer he got, the more the giant's malevolent power bore down on him, latent and brooding. As he approached, dread encircled his thoughts and the hairs on his forearms stood out. It was always like this, and it always scrambled his brain, making coherent thought difficult.

A rogue thought crossed his mind: awed as he was by the power of their imprisoned victim, what would he feel if he stood before his gaolers? Was it wise to get on their wrong side? It was too late to worry about that: the die had already been cast.

His master's imprisonment had occurred soon after his contract began, but it hadn't meant his release. Instead it made the prisoner more reliant on his services in the early years, and the apparent injustice dealt out by his captors eased Haldred's conscience for a while. Their idea of punishment had been unfair, in his opinion, but with a grimace he recognised his opinion of fairness probably differed from theirs.

Time seemed to stretch as he walked across that endless floor. With every step it seemed harder to advance, as if Haldred were pushing against some invisible weight. The air felt thicker, and sweat pricked his brow. It was a long time since he'd last been permitted to approach, and he'd somehow forgotten the raw power the prone figure emitted. A force that filled this place, waiting for release.

The figure beneath the cords was still, as if sleeping or meditating. At his head sat a large female figure – a giantess – silent, bored and sullen. She held a large cup into which an amber liquid dripped; each drop dangling from a protrusion of the rock above for a tantalising moment before falling, marking out time in this dismal place. How long it had been going on for? Haldred didn't like to think. The years of his master's imprisonment also marked a large proportion of his own seemingly endless bondage.

As he approached, he mused on the crime that had led to Loki being bound here, and failed to come up with anything sufficiently horrendous to warrant it. Surely there must be some time limit on his sentence? That said, he had little love for the Norse god, but in his presence, fear banished any sense of injustice about his own entrapment; he just wanted to get as far away as possible, and in one piece. Once away from this place his grievance would return and nag at his waking thoughts, but here, in Loki's presence, dread and awe held sway and a desperate desire to survive the encounter was his only motivation.

Still, he needed to conquer his dread and somehow find a way out of this stalemate. As he reached the end of the hall, next to the prisoner's head, Haldred paused and stood still, hardly daring to breathe. The figure on the stone bed opened his eyes and turned his head. A sharp nose, dark eyebrows, and worst of all, the power in those dark hazel eyes hit him with a force that was almost physical. He struggled to organise his thoughts.

"Well, where is it? Show me." For a figure so large, his voice was mellow, and high in pitch. Haldred opened the bag he'd been carrying over his shoulder, and carefully extracted the object his brother had so painstakingly stolen: the treasured painting. Nerves led to clumsiness, and he struggled to remove it from the bubble wrap he'd used to protect it during his journey. In the process he shuffled sideways, struggling to prevent his bag from falling off his shoulder. With face reddening, he realised he must look foolish and wished he'd put it down first. Finally, Haldred held up his prize for inspection, like a nervous child presenting homework.

"Lift it up properly, man."

He held it above his head and moved closer. His master's eyes narrowed and tried to focus.

"As you requested, sir. *Saint Nikitas the Goth*, also known as *The Martyr*." A sudden surge of pride in his achievement led him on. "Carefully and professionally stolen to order, just as you requested."

There was silence. The prostrate figure squinted at the painting. His expression turned sour.

"I'm so disappointed in you. I thought I knew you better."

The dwarf lowered the painting, deflated and not a little worried. Automatically he glanced at the ties restraining his master, as if fearing they may not be strong enough to hold him. They seemed alive, almost. Even as he observed them, they flexed and tightened as if reading their victim's moods and anticipating his movements. The gigantic figure continued, addressing his words to the high ceiling, as if in discussion with himself, with Haldred a mere afterthought.

"Maybe my expectations were too great. Perhaps it was all too difficult." A pause for internal reflection. "Maybe he's just not up to it. Outlived his usefulness." The voice boomed around the open space, and Haldred's spirits sank further. He swallowed. His host's disappointment appeared to have given way to more sinister sentiments, even if mildly expressed. The head turned back to the dwarf, the eyes penetrating. Haldred fumbled for something to say; anything to justify his worth. With a humourless grin, the prone giant observed him.

"Apparently it is not only my instructions that go astray; even my conversation can no longer hold your attention. Instead, you admire my bonds?" The dwarf could only stare back, his mouth working, but no words forming.

The monologue continued, soft and deadly. "Cunning, are they not? Designed with care and forethought that few would have suspected their designers capable of. Obviously, they were not as dim-witted as they appeared. I misjudged them." The face darkened, the brow furrowed, and the figure strained against them, testing their strength. Suddenly, the floor vibrated with a powerful tremor, and a deep and disconcerting rumble shook the rock and earth around them. Boulders of various sizes dislodged from the rough cavern ceiling high above and crashed down, littering the ground. Amid the turmoil, the giantess at the figure's head struggled to retain her balance and keep her bowl level, and some of its contents spilled over the edge, the drops hissing with acidic venom as they splashed on the floor. Haldred jumped back from them, managing with some effort to remain on his feet. The tremors subsided, and the figure on the stone bed lay still once more. The face turned back to the dwarf, calmer now, but the bitterness behind his words was clear.

"They are good, aren't they? These bonds that hold me? Did you admire the way they stretch and contract with my every movement? Clever, isn't it, the way they do that? Do you know what they're made from?"

Unable to look away, but suddenly overcome with dread, Haldred could only shake his head.

"*My son*. They're made from Narfi, my son." The giant figure laughed, a sound both fey and wild that made the air vibrate. Haldred stood rooted, dumb with shock. "Yes, they killed him in front of me, then gutted him and used his entrails to bind me here."

There was a pause. With his mouth dry, Haldred could only stare. Loki's face was unreadable, his voice, for a moment, conversational.

"The ties that bind us, eh Haldred? Never let it be said that I do not keep my family close." Then he looked up to the roof, and the air shook as he shouted in his anguish, challenging those who would never answer. "Release me, you fools! You think yourselves so virtuous, so caring, so fair? Release me, and look me in the eye once more, you cowards." The shouting subsided. A momentary silence fell. Then the head turned to face Haldred, more reflective now. "But they won't, will they? They dare not. Instead, they hide up among the clouds, crouching in fear behind their walls: Odin the sly betrayer; one-handed Tyr, brave fool that he is; strong and stupid Thor; Freya, the promiscuous slut, and all the others. Faceless cowards, too terrified to even show their faces in the world above these days. They will deserve what they get." Loki studied the figure before him. "And what they get, my dear dwarf, is the revenge I am preparing." He paused, intent upon his visitor, who, eyes like saucers, was paying full attention. "And that revenge, so slowly and painstakingly assembled and planned, will depend on every component, no matter how small and insignificant, being properly compiled, and every piece completed. And that means no more fuck-ups, am I clear?"

Haldred swallowed hard. He nodded and strove to find

something to say, but his thoughts were scrambled. "I… I'm sorry, Lord, if I misunderstood your orders." He bowed low, hoping to deflect the piercing stare, anything to dig himself out of this hole. The eyes refused to release him, but now the voice was quieter, more potent.

"I specifically sent instructions for you to steal the painting of Saint Nicholas of Myra. Something I shouldn't have thought beyond your capabilities. I'm sure I've set you harder tasks before." Haldred looked down at his feet and mumbled another apology.

"The research was… Maybe I misspelled it…"

"I'm not interested in excuses. Excuses are for failures." The voice became so quiet that Haldred had to strain to hear. "I don't tolerate failure. I'm sure you are aware of that fact. I'm sure you know also that, though given a gift of long life, you and that fool of a brother you apparently can't operate without, are still mortal." Haldred's mouth felt drier than ever. He had no words; he could only nod like a marionette with invisible strings. Loki observed his reaction, then continued. "You were foolish beyond my expectation in thinking you could win the affections of my daughter, or worse still, control her thoughts." There was a deadly velvet in the voice now. It hypnotised the dwarf. His master had never previously spoken of the fateful bet. Haldred had hoped it was all but forgotten, but after all this time it was not, and his worst nightmare was still fresh. The threat was as real now as the day it was made; the dreadful day it all happened. "Remember, dear Haldred, that should you fail; should you try with what feeble wits you possess, to deceive me; should you make any idiotic attempt to rob me of my prize, you will find a welcome in her domain that is far worse than the fate of death itself, and certainly more hideous than anything I can conjure up. I'm sure I do not have to elaborate."

In the deadly silence that followed, Haldred could only nod to acknowledge he'd understood. He trembled with fear and inwardly cursed once again the naïve stupidity that had put him in this position in the first place. The reach of the captive figure on the stone bed, from deep in this underground prison, was long and deadly. The only payment he could expect from another failure would be swiftly delivered and fatal, but it was what would come after which left him quaking at the knee. To date, he'd avoided such a fate because of his diligence and application. He could scarcely believe he'd become so careless as to get this last mission so badly wrong.

Apparently, Loki had dispensed with threats. He became business-like. "So, we have a renewed understanding? Good. Time is, of course, of the essence. You'd best begone and get on with your planning."

Haldred hesitated.

"What is it?"

"Where will I find this painting, my lord?"

An exasperated sigh greeted him, which deepened his sense of unease. The self-reflective musing tone returned and the face turned to the rocky ceiling once more.

"Should I give the frivolous answer or the serious one? I'm tempted by the former, which goes like this: I don't know and I don't care. Work it out." He glanced at the dwarf, who by now was shuffling from foot to foot. "However, if I left it at that, you'd probably get it wrong. Again. And I'd be forced to recruit someone with an ounce of ability, and that takes time. So, here is the longer answer. The painting I desire, of Saint Nicolas of Myra, can be found in one of the monasteries in the Greek province of Thessaly, at a location known colloquially as the Meteora. I do not know which one. That I leave to you. But it is important to me. I want it. And I want it to be brought here sooner rather than later. Is that understood?"

Haldred dared look up. "Perfectly. Thank you." He thought for a moment, and before he could stop himself, said it out loud. "Why do you want a painting of a Christian saint?" Shocked by his audacity, Haldred covered his mouth and prepared an apology. Instead, the figure on the stone bed gave a short laugh.

"Incongruous, isn't it? Why, indeed? You ask a good question, master dwarf. Why should I, of all people, want an image painted, according to my own timescale, quite recently, yet more than ten centuries ago, of someone who would fail to acknowledge me, even if he were standing where you are now? Indeed, he would probably condemn me and even try to exorcise my spirit from this place. Strange, isn't it?"

He turned once more to the dwarf. "Well, that is something I will have to leave you to ponder, Haldred. You can reflect on it as you plan and execute your crime. Perhaps I have taken a collector's fancy to early Christian iconography, you may think." He glanced at the bare walls of the cave. "Or perhaps not. However, I shall just have to leave you with the thought that it is for me alone to know, until the time is right. Suffice to say that my plans have many threads, and the full web is unlikely to be visible to those working on any one strand. Of course, it is also the case that there are clues and information that I discern from certain objects that are beyond your wit to comprehend. Finally, you might care to understand that it is none of your business."

Haldred took this as a dismissal, bowed once more and made to leave. "Sorry. I understand. I'll get onto it straight away." He turned to walk away with whatever dignity he could muster.

"See that you do, lest your impertinence lead to impermanence, if you catch my meaning." As he left, the voice pursued him down the cave. "I am counting on you, Haldred. And rest assured, I will be taking great interest in reports of your progress. Don't delay."

. . .

As he reached the exit, Haldred realised he was still holding the painting. He laid it against the wall of the cave and headed out the door, grateful to escape. With dread churning in his gut, he retraced his steps to the car. The attendant, still absorbed in his magazine, barely acknowledged his passing. He climbed behind the wheel, relieved to be going somewhere, anywhere, but realised immediately that there was nowhere far enough to escape the threat hanging over him. His hands shook. He closed his eyes, gripped the wheel tight and tried to slow his breathing, but found it too difficult. The last thing he wanted was to suffer a panic attack here. Perhaps driving would help; he needed to put some distance between himself and the cave.

With dismay, he realised he was going to have to inform his brother of the mistake. Haldred could imagine his reaction. A meeting with Karrig was the last thing he wanted, but he couldn't put it off; time was of the essence. First, though, he had to get away from this place to somewhere quiet where he could get his head down and sort through the problem. How could he get in Loki's good books once more? Stealing the right painting was the immediate way, but even that wouldn't solve his long-term predicament. He was as tightly bound to Loki as the day he'd lost the wager and he'd be on the hook permanently unless he could find some way to get the threat annulled? But how? Who could help?

One thing at a time. He pressed the start button and pulled out of the parking lot, then at the meeting of passageways, selected the one that provided the shortest route home.

A few hours later, Haldred deposited the car at another parking lot, this one deserted, and exited through an inconspicuous steel door to the rear. It led to the foot of a deep shaft, at the base of a heavy wooden staircase. Looking up, the top was invisible; the stairs vanished into distant gloom.

With a deep breath, he began his ascent. It was good exercise, but inevitably, halfway up, he needed to pause for breath, and found himself wondering once again whether it was time they put in an elevator.

Finally, legs and lungs aching, he arrived at another heavy wooden door, and this time produced a large key from a deep pocket. To his relief, this door swung open silently, its hinges having been recently oiled. Emergence back into the so-called real world always unnerved him to a degree. He stepped into a short corridor.

Navigating the rabbit warren of passageways, cellars and staircases, he finally arrived, three floors higher, in the better-populated corners of the subterranean labyrinth.

Nobody paid him any attention as he strode confidently past; a courtier on an important errand. One last flight of stairs, polished stone this time, took him to ground level and out, blinking, into daylight via a little used door that opened onto a silent courtyard. A few further changes of direction and connecting passageways took him out through the main entrance of Prague's citadel, Hradcany and into the large square before it.

It was nearly midday, and tourists thronged the district, hoping to catch sight of the changing of the palace guard, a favourite ritual at any time of year. For once he welcomed the crowds. They conferred annonymity. Dodging past a woman fiddling distractedly with an antique bracelet, he made his way into the maze of narrow streets nearby. His apartment was just a short walk away, but with a sinking feeling, he realised getting home would bring no relief; not while that thing was there.

Walking across Charles Bridge, Haldred fumed at the missed communications that had led to him stealing the wrong painting. He wanted to wring Yuri's neck, but instead he began rehearsing what to say to Karrig. He was in no mood to apologise; the stakes were too high, and in any case,

Haldred was certain it hadn't been his fault. He might grovel before a god, but his brother was a different matter. The instructions had been too opaque, the conduit – Yuri – too garbled and terrified. His master had clearly set him up to fail, to reinforce his debt and ensure his continued service. What other explanation could there be? One thing was certain; there could be no more cock-ups. His life depended on it.

CHAPTER 9
THE WATCH

Freya placed a large plate of freshly baked scones in the middle of the table, delicately plucked the topmost, and sat. She put her feet up on the chair next to her and pulled her silk kaftan across her legs. At the other side of the broad oak table sat Vali, smartly casual in chinos and an open-necked shirt, not a hair out of place. He eyed the plate suspiciously, then selected a scone from the edge of the pile and took a bite, frowning at the crumbs that spilled down the front of his expensive-looking shirt.

"What do you think he's going to do?" Freya asked, knowing that trying to guess Odin's mind was futile.

Vali ignored the question and asked one of his own. "Is there any coffee on?" She nodded back towards the kitchen.

"Over there. Help yourself. Mugs on the top shelf."

A full percolator of freshly brewed coffee that Vali hadn't previously noticed sat at the far end of the polished granite worktop in Freya's open-plan kitchen.

"Can you bring me one?" she added, as he made his way over.

He selected two large mugs patterned with elaborate runic

designs and filled them close to the brim, then returned to the table.

"Anybody's guess, really, " he said, returning to her original question.

Freya observed him place his mug down with careful precision and study it, rather than meet her eye. "The dwarf certainly interests him."

Freya shrugged acknowledgement and took a sip. "I don't know why. He's nothing special." She ruminated for a while. "Got some nice paintings, though."

The door swung open and Odin stepped inside, once more in human form. His lank grey locks drooped across the shoulders of an ancient fisherman's sweater that had seen better days. A ragged goatee adorned the chin of his craggy face, but it was his disconcerting multicoloured glass eye that drew Freya's attention, as always.

As was his wont, the Allfather had dressed down for the occasion, his sweater looked two sizes too large, with sleeves that almost covered his hands, and was holed in several places. Beneath it, Freya noted, he wore old, shapeless jeans with a pair of stained and musty moccasins on his sockless feet.

Across the table, she was amused to see the avenger god sit more upright in his chair. She couldn't help but smirk at the brief look of disdain that accompanied his sideways glance at Odin's attire. Odin took a place at the head of the table. He pushed his sleeves up his forearms, placed his hands on the wooden surface and glared at them.

"Our fears are confirmed."

Freya and Vali exchanged wary glances. Odin looked from one to the other, awaiting a response. Vali broke the silence.

"Can you be absolutely certain?" Freya sensed he found it difficult to hold the Allfather's stare. Odin nodded.

"The dwarf's movements confirm it, and my other spies have given me rumour that networks of agents are being recruited. He is becoming more active by the week. The question now is, what is he after, and why?"

Freya brushed crumbs from her hands and lowered her feet from the chair next to her. She leaned forwards, more business-like now. "Isn't that obvious? He needs an army. Beyond the foresworn cast of monsters and misfits that will assemble at the end of days, I mean. A proper army of foot soldiers and captains, if he is to mount a serious challenge. I don't see any sign of that suddenly materialising." She frowned. "To be honest, I don't yet have the feeling that we are approaching the end game."

Odin nodded. "We are not at that stage, I agree, although the world becomes more chaotic by the year." He stared at the table, deep in thought. "No, I don't think we're at the stage of his mass mobilisation, and if he were, there is no way he would chose to put that dwarf in charge of anything. Like all his kind, his only interest is himself. No, there's got to be something more at play. That's the puzzle: why is he so interested in this Haldred character? What has he tasked him to do?"

Vali shrugged. "Does it matter? We know what is going to happen in the end. It's already woven."

A sharp look from Odin silenced him. "Is that the case? The weavers are diligent, it is true, but alongside the golden thread of fate are countless others, and the patterns they create can always be unpicked."

Vali was indignant. "Not without enormous power and influence. The Norns yield to no one. They are impervious to reasoned argument. Maybe you, alone, could persuade them? They would not take *his* guidance."

Vali stared at Odin. Odin held his eye. Freya remained silent, observing them both. Odin closed his eyes, as if meditating. When at last he spoke, his words came slowly.

"Not just me. In the beginning, beside me were Vili and Ve, my brothers."

Vali leaned towards him. "But they are dead. Gone, lost in the void, imprisoned deep beneath the nine worlds…"

"That just about covers it," murmured Freya, leaning forwards to select a second scone. She pushed the plate towards Odin. "Take one. They're freshly baked."

He glanced in her direction, but ignored the plate. "Not dead, I don't think. Lost maybe, or in some place I cannot see." He sat back. "Anyway, they're probably not inclined to ally with Loki. Not knowingly. There are other ways he can seek an edge."

Freya and Vali exchanged another glance, both baffled now.

"Through alliance," Odin said with a degree of exasperation. "With others like ourselves."

Vali opened his mouth to speak but struggled to find the words. Having silenced his companions, Odin continued. "I have opened a channel to our Greek friends." He paused. "Our associates, you might say. As a courtesy. To alert them."

"Alert them?" Freya was less than impressed. "Since when did we need their help with our dirty laundry?"

Odin returned a long look. "When the fate of the world is at stake, it is not so much to ask."

"But they disappeared," she added. "Nothing has been seen of them for… ages. I thought them gone."

"Gone where?" Odin asked. "For better or for worse they are trapped here just like us."

The kitchen descended into silence once more as the three Norse gods considered their long-term fate. Odin placed his hands flat on the table. Freya suppressed a smirk as she saw the look on the fastidiously tidy Vali's face as he watched the unruly sleeves of his father's antique sweater creep down his arms.

"The fact is," the Allfather said, "the more resources we can throw at the problem, the better. And as you are aware, the Eastern Mediterranean represents a major hole in our surveillance capabilities. Loki is up to something and the indication is that he's searching there. For what? We don't yet know."

"They won't like it if we encroach on their turf," Freya said.

"Which is why I reached out." Odin looked from one the other. "Come on, think. We have to be strategic in this. Consider the bigger picture."

"But our resources are few." Vali was stating what they all knew. Odin cast him a look that bordered on self-satisfied, Freya thought.

"Which is why I've taken some steps to help plug the gap," he said, then raised his hands, palms out, as if to deflect questions. "I won't say more at this stage. It's still evolving, but hopefully, before long we won't need the Greeks. Or anyone."

Freya looked at Vali for clues, but was pleased to see he was as baffled as she. Each of them tried a question, but Odin would say no more on the matter.

"In the meantime," he said, "we have the assistance of our Mediterranean friends. Such as they are." He sighed. "There is a problem, though." Quizzical looks from the other two. "They're all cats."

Freya leaned forwards, unsure she'd heard correctly. "Cats?"

"Yes, cats." Odin gave a shrug. "They took some kind of collective oath. More than a thousand years ago. Perhaps only Ratatosk knows why."

Vali sat back looking thoroughly baffled.

"Yet Ratatosk has never mentioned it," Freya murmured.

Odin leaned forwards once more, hands clasped before him in a business-like fashion. "Anyway, although in diminished form and circumstances, they are still on the scene. We will have to work with what we've got."

Vali was still coming to terms with the news. "Why would

they do that?" He spread his hands in exasperation. "Now they see what's happening they will surely have to change back and stop playing games."

"You'd like to think so, but…" Odin was not yet convinced.

Freya shook her head, and sat back, laughing. She clapped her hands, lost in mirth. "Cats! Fabulous. I wonder if they want a go with my chariot?"

Vali confronted her. "Come on, this is serious."

"I know," she replied, wiping her eyes. "But you've got to admire the absurdity of it." She sat up straighter, and made a conscious effort to calm down. It does mean we're probably screwed, though."

"What do you mean?"

"Come on, you know the Greeks." She leaned across the table, looked deep into his eyes, amusement still etched onto her features. "They always operate through a hero. They love a hero."

Blank looks were returned from both of her companions. She spread her hands. "Where are they going to find one now? Athens cat rescue?"

CHAPTER 10
AGENT 73

The car park was the heart of the small black cat's universe. He was familiar with every square metre of cracked, uneven asphalt and the fading paintwork that delineated parking spaces. Each hollow and pothole – whether empty or filled with grit, dirt, cigarette butts and the temporary detritus of transient humans – was his domain. That and the valley beneath. It provided a haven of lush and fertile vegetation sloping down to the wide river flats below, which could be glimpsed in the gaps between the sandstone towers. Tall, sheer-sided and seemingly unconquerable, the towers resembled the stripped-clean bones of a giant after the body that once coated them had decayed and rotted away. Many of their flat summits housed clusters of buildings perched precariously above the void, and he knew that some humans chose to live there. Oh, well. To each his own.

The cat had never visited them. They didn't interest him, but they were part of the landscape he called home. It is said that home is where the heart is, but his nine-month-old heart was typically set on the next morsel he could scavenge from a malleable human who would fall for his youthful feline charm; ragged and flea-bitten though that was, although the competition from his peers could be brutal.

"You never knew your mother, scrawny string of gristle that she was, otherwise you'd never show your face round here." The taunts were worse today.

"That's not true."

"Oh, isn't it? What colour was she then? Tell me that, smart arse?"

"And why didn't she even leave you a name?"

It hurt. He couldn't pretend otherwise. The barbs stung, and he had no answers. He had no real recollection of his mother and her markings, or anything about her. The small black cat was well used to the low-grade taunts and bickering among his colleagues who staked out the car park, but he hadn't been the brunt of their collective anger until now. The others seemed more resentful of their lot than ever, and it seemed they wanted to pin the blame on him. What was worse, they were backing up their hard words with actions, viciously edging him out of the daily contest for titbits from the humans; the meagre scratchings that passed for a diet in this tourist hotspot. The marks on his nose and nips on his neck told the story.

Tourists. They all lived off the tourists, swarming around them like bees around bougainvillea, grateful for any morsels that fell in their path. The visitors brought cash to feed the local economy, but crucially, from the resident feline population's point of view, food. It didn't matter if it was indigestible, already half chewed, or inappropriate for their digestive system; as long as it was edible, they were trading. They were hungry, most of them little more than a skeletal frame held together by a thin coating of membrane and muscle, covered with tightly stretched skin and fur, and most of them displaying the sores and marks of their maltreatment of one another and the diseases that accompanied their precarious lifestyle. None of them had an ounce of flesh to spare. They lived off their wits and by pushing each other out of the way to get the best handouts from their benefactors.

Here was another car: a big black SUV. The small black cat saw the blue and white quartered logo, and recognised this was a posh one. He didn't know the name BMW, but inhabitants of such badges were either aloof and ignored them entirely, or were quite generous with their gifts. There wasn't much in between. Stealthily, so as not to arouse too much attention from his peers, he positioned himself next to the passenger door and looked up. *Be quick*, he thought; *if you wait too long, the others will be here*. Sure enough, a scruffy-looking tabby sidled up, gave him a dismissive look, and sat down. From the corner of his eye, he spotted a third cat walking slowly in his direction.

The door above him opened, and a leg appeared. The human it belonged to saw him, cooed in that irritating fashion they had and stepped out, as did a smaller version from the rear of the car.

The cats mingled as close as they dared, jostling for position. Meanwhile, the smaller human made appreciative noises and broke off part of the thing it was eating: cured ham. Gold dust. The little black cat pushed as hard as he could for prime position and caught the human's eye as she dropped the meat before him. It was his!

But even as he jumped, the larger tabby barged him sideways and sent him rolling in the dirt. The treasure fell to the ground between them, tantalisingly close. He could still get it, but a new arrival squeezed between him and his prize, and was engaged in a tug of war for the meat with the tabby. While they each grabbed a mouthful, the black cat got nothing and peered up to see if there was any more. Couldn't they recognise the injustice of the scrap? Surely there was something more for him?

The smaller human had consumed the last of its sandwich and started peeling a banana. Seeing the black cat's reproachful look, it broke off the end and offered it to him. He sniffed it suspiciously, and the human dropped it before him. He sniffed again, unimpressed. It smelled disgusting; inedible. Why did they try to fob him off with something he couldn't eat? None of his peers were interested either, which told a story of itself. He swallowed his hunger and irritation and slunk away beneath a nearby car, pretending to ignore the smug glances from the two victors. He couldn't afford to let them see his resentment, so acted as if nothing had happened and ignored the rumble in his stomach.

It was nearly always the same. He was no match for the others physically and, being younger, he wasn't as streetwise or ruthless. If he had anything going for him, it was that he was slightly less flea-bitten. And he was quick. But often that wasn't enough. Sometimes the humans seemed to relish and encourage the bouts of gladiatorial combat between the cats of the car park, throwing food in their midst rather than to anyone in particular, to see how the real hunger games played out. Unless a prize landed close, the small black cat inevitably lost the contest. This latest incident proved that even when it was in mid-air heading towards his mouth, he had no guarantee of success. Life was tough in the car park.

Without the tourists, he didn't know what he would do, or how he would survive. The little black cat's hunting skills were, by his own admission, pathetic. Maybe, if all else was lost, he'd have to rely on them, and on some latent native instinct. But he dreaded the thought. Instead, like so many others, he flocked to these car parks beneath the monasteries, dodging the wheels and the trampling feet in pursuit of a mouthful of something to satisfy the permanent gnawing hunger pangs.

The two-legs didn't really give a shit. Some of them oohed or aahed at him and his like; but what did they know or care about their existence? Nothing. They were little more than four-legged poverty porn for these god-like visitors who, from the small cat's perspective, might just as well come from outer space; the gaps between the stars. They had it all, of course; in particular those fancy magical cars in which they travelled. He occasionally fantasised about what they were like inside. They must be palatial, and comfortable, and full of things to eat. Just look at how fat many of them were when they clambered out; some of them could barely walk. They must do nothing else inside other than stuff their faces, surely? What a life. He fantasised about what it might be like to feast all day until you got fat. It must feel good. If only.

They all came to see these strange buildings that their ancestors had built, or so he'd overheard from the elders. Yes, the fantastical monasteries that perched on the hilltops, clinging to the rocks by some kind of magic or maybe just collective willpower. It still seemed incredible to the small black cat that the two-legs had built them, from what he'd seen of their limited physical capabilities. Why did they build them in such inaccessible places, and how? He couldn't begin to guess. Perhaps they only had a few buildings like these, and that was why they attracted others of their kind to see them. Maybe they were special. Or maybe there was something up there that the two-legs liked. Special food. It was useless to speculate. He would never understand their motives.

Their behaviour was also baffling. Despite the difficulty, he tried to understand it, as far as he could. Knowing something of their body language might just be a lifesaver. Humans, to give them their posh name, were unpredictable. No two were the same. They veered from wild and angry to lazy and lethargic and everything in between. He saw all such emotions and more, expressed in the car park each day. The bottom line was that all the two-legs could prove dangerous.

When the day was quiet, with few visitors about, he sometimes wondered if there might be a better way to survive; but his limited imagination didn't spread far beyond the edge of the tarmac, and he had no comprehension of any alternative lifestyle. Instead, he was stuck here, in an endlessly repeating diorama beneath the cliffs which housed the monasteries. Were there any other creatures better inclined to his kind, or animals in general? Someone who could ease them out of this dull monotony? A better, kinder species of guardian? Such speculation got you nowhere. The small black cat could not conceive of such beings. If they did exist, they were probably gods of some kind, and he had heard about them from the storytellers, as he crouched in the shadows on the fringes of their gatherings in the evening gloom.

If he got too close, he'd be shooed away. But even at the edge of the group, straining his ears and concentrating, he could sometimes hear the stories, and they all amounted to the same thing: gods were bad news, and very bad for those who got close. They were dangerous to know, and no friend to ordinary cats like him. Geniuses they may be, but they were inherently unstable; Greek gods, especially so. He hoped he never met one.

Today, however, was different. Today his life would change; he just didn't realise it as he watched the silver Nissan reverse into the space alongside the car he was sitting beneath. From his vantage point, the arrival of another small, somewhat battered hatchback was not remarkable. He gave it a cursory glance, noticed the thickly layered dust which did its best to conceal its silver colouring, spotted the dents in the front wing and passenger door and the cracked brake light cover at the rear – the signs of a careless driver – and saw the human handprints in the dust on the rear hatch where the occupant opened and closed it.

A man climbed out of the door on the far side and walked to the back. He had few distinguishing marks from the young cat's point of view, other than dark hair flecked with grey, and that untidy-looking facial hair so many of them sported these days. Here, it looked as if he hadn't scraped it off for several days. Why did some humans scrape away the fur on their faces? They had so little to begin with. They did some funny things with the fur on their heads, to be fair, but despite his curiosity, he was no connoisseur of hairstyles and fashions in grooming. This morning, he had nothing better to do, so he continued watching as the man opened the large back door and spoke to whoever was inside.

"Right, we're here. So please take care. I presume you won't get lost." The black cat could hear no response as he continued. "Are you sure it is a good idea to follow me up there?" He glanced at the monastery complex perched on the summit of the sheer rocks. Again, there was no audible response. "Come on, then," he added, and reached inside to release some kind of catch. To the young animal's surprise, a large, immaculately groomed grey cat jumped down from the rear of the car. His eyes widened, and he stiffened, prepared to fight if necessary should this interloper want to do anything stupid like claim territorial rights. It was his car park, and he was prepared to defend it.

The other cat glanced dismissively in his direction and stalked off towards the monastery. The human retrieved a briefcase from the car, locked it and hurried after her.

The small black cat watched them leave and tried to work out what had just happened, but failed.

An hour later, the odd couple returned, the man looking hot in his crumpled and discoloured jacket. He paused at the far end of the car park to speak to two other humans. The black cat recognised them; they parked here every day for a while, keeping an eye on things. But most other humans ignored them. They always seemed to wear the same dark uniform, perhaps to identify each other, but they never seemed interested in the monastery. Instead, they just came to look at the other people, then after a few hours they went away. Maybe the recent arrival knew them. It would be a first. The grey cat, however, left him to it. She strolled across the tarmac towards the car she'd arrived in, then veered off between a couple of parked vehicles and jumped onto the low, flat-topped wall that marked the perimeter. She was now very close. The small black animal repositioned himself at the other end of his vehicle so he could keep a discrete eye on her.

"Were you here last night?" she asked, looking out across the valley and back to the monastery. His head jerked towards her. He didn't think she'd spotted him.

"Mm, yes," he mumbled. Why did she care about his movements? He reprimanded himself for answering so promptly. It would have been better to pretend not to hear, at least until she'd introduced herself. He attempted to look uninterested, but she threw another question in his direction.

"When?"

"Last night."

"What time last night. Roughly?" She glanced at him, and for the first time, he got a glimpse of penetrating green eyes and the urge to respond. He thought quickly. It already seemed a long time ago. When was it exactly? What had he been doing? He'd wandered off after sunset, down into the valley below the rock towers, looking for rodents and, as usual, failing to catch one. He had practised some stalking through the gorse bushes on the hillside, then sat for a while enjoying the crescent moon and the stars. He slept a little, then did it all again. Later, he saw the human walking down the cliff. Then it was time for a quick nap before the sun came up and brought more hunting opportunities.

"After moonrise, for a while."

She waited, just looking at him. It wasn't even a threatening look, but to fill the silence he gave her some details of his evening. His eyes narrowed and he averted his gaze, aggrieved at having to explain himself to this stranger. Did she go round interrogating every animal she met? A modest feeling of outrage formed at the back of his mind.

"How did they walk down the cliff?"

He hadn't been expecting any follow-up queries. "Haven't I told you enough?"

"It's important." She spoke with exaggerated patience, as if he were a kitten. It needled him further; she was hard work. Why didn't she just hop into the back of that car and drive off? He wondered if he should walk away, but something made him stay. Looking around for distractions, he saw the dishevelled man saunter in their direction. Good. He turned back to find her staring at him.

"I don't know," he mumbled. Then another memory emerged. "He had some string," he said. "Like a spider, but thicker. He was on a thread, coming down the cliff face."

"Abseiling," she said. "I might have guessed. Did he have a bag with him? A backpack, something like that?"

"What's a bag?"

She muttered something he couldn't hear, then more loudly… "A thing they keep stuff in. They usually carry them over their shoulder."

The smaller animal pondered for a moment; the human approached his vehicle and opened its rear hatchback door, looking expectantly at the grey cat. Getting no immediate response, he opened the front door, took off his jacket and threw it inside along with his briefcase, then climbed in and wrote something in a notebook.

"Well?" The grey cat waited for an answer. The black cat racked his brains again.

"I think so. Maybe. But it was dark."

His interrogator seemed happy enough with the response. She looked away again.

"Do you fancy a job?"

"What's one of those?"

"Helping us. Helping me. You could be a hero."

Immediately, he was suspicious. What did she want now? He was keen to see the back of her. She asked far too many questions.

"We are trying to stop people stealing works of art," she continued. "Historical artefacts, that sort of thing."

Her words meant nothing to him. He had no idea what art was. All he wanted most of the time was his next meal and if he had to steal it, so what? He looked at her blankly.

"You'd be helping me. Helping Greece."

Helping Greece?

"Would you like to be a hero?" The way she put it, how could he refuse?

"No."

She pretended she hadn't heard. "And of course, there'd be rewards for you."

"What kind of reward?" His bullshit detector was on red alert.

"Food," she said, simply. "You'd never go hungry again."

He tilted his head and, without thinking, let out a small chirrup of excitement. This sounded almost too good to be true, but immediately his suspicions returned. Before he could say more, she went on.

"There's a place down in the town. It's on this side of the main street. There's an alley that leads to a quiet neighbourhood with some of the nicer houses they live in. The first one you come to will have food and water set out in the garden behind the shed. There is a calico cat who lives there, but she's friendly. You can use it any time, as long as you agree to help me." He was still suspicious.

"What do I have to do?"

"Keep watch. Let me know what goes on. Get word to me the moment anything strange or unusual happens."

"How do I do that?"

"As I said, there's a large calico cat called Freddie who

lives at the place I mentioned. Tell her and she will get word to me. If it's really urgent, tell the nearest owl."

He blinked. Owl? How the hell was he going to find an owl in a hurry?

"Okay."

"Good. Right, I'd better induct you."

"What?"

"Enrol you. Repeat after me: *I hereby pledge to help preserve and protect the cultural integrity…*"

"What's a hereby?"

She gave him a withering look and collected her thoughts. "Let's try again: *I pledge to help.*"

This time, he repeated the words, although he wasn't sure why. The grey cat jumped down. The interview was apparently over. As she walked past the car he was sitting under, she paused and lowered her head to look at him.

"What's your name?" she asked.

"I don't have one."

"What, no name?" She sounded shocked, but her voice softened. "We'll have to see about that. In the meantime, you will be known as…" She did some quick mental arithmetic. "Agent 73." She set off again, only to pause once more. "Oh, I almost forgot. There's also a healthcare plan." Before boarding the car, she turned to him again. "One last thing. Let me know about any unusual trees you might come across, particularly if they have a black trunk, and silver and grey leaves. It's important." With that, she performed a neat hop into the rear entrance and disappeared from sight.

Lieutenant Samaras emerged from the front seat to fasten the lid of the cat's travelling compartment and close the rear door. He climbed in behind the steering wheel. The grey cat settled down to get as comfortable as possible among the rugs lining her travel space. Before he turned the key, the lieutenant looked at her in the rear-view mirror.

"I've just got the lab report from the forensics team," he

said. "The findings are odd. They got some DNA samples from that climbing chock that the thief used to anchor the abseil." The cat stared at him. "It's not human." He started the engine while the cat continued to stare back. "It may be a fault with their equipment. They're going to re-run the analysis." He adjusted the mirror and drove away.

Agent 73 watched the departing vehicle, struggling to take it all in. Today had been unlike any other he'd known. He reviewed the conversation. Out of the blue, he had a purpose, a job, and something even more exciting. *I have a name*, he thought. He turned it over in his mind again and again. *Agent 73*. It felt good. It felt important. He felt like sticking his little chest out and telling the world: "I'm not just a cat. I'm a number!"

On the surface, nothing had changed. The landscape was the same, the day scarcely any older. The sun still beat down, baking the asphalt with its daytime glare, but one of the local inhabitants, one of the tiny chess pieces on this infinite board was just a bit different.

CHAPTER 11
STUBBINS

Antef proved extremely efficient. Within a few days, workmen arrived on site and spent the morning installing an upgraded camera system operated via Wi-Fi. The abbot spent most of the morning tracking their every movement to make sure no unnecessary holes were drilled in the ancient walls. He hovered in the background, tutting disapproval and watching out for unsightly wiring or chipped masonry. The high-pitched screech of the drill was an unnatural torment in this holy space, piercing not just his ears, but his heart. He satisfied himself that the work was a necessary test of his commitment to the monastery's future, but in a place of peace and tranquillity it was akin to sacrilege. To calm himself the abbot cast suspicious glances in the direction of Father Zakinthos, as if to judge by his reaction whether he, too, felt the torment. When the last camera was in place, he let out a sigh of relief.

Once everything was set up and tested, the systems engineer gave the abbot and a couple of his monks a brief lesson on the system's capabilities and how to use the software.

"STUBBINS has a really simple interface," the engineer said. The abbot smiled, but privately demurred. Despite the daily tourist invasion, theirs was a secluded community, set apart from the ways of the modern world. He doubted there was any such thing as an interface simple enough to prove foolproof. The engineer looked up, expectantly. With his smile lingering perhaps an instant too long, the abbot pondered possible questions, not wanting to appear a complete ingenue. Father Zakinthos saved him by asking how to switch the view from one camera to another, and querying the value of the infra-red display. The abbot, grateful for the intervention, began to fret about his colleague's newfound enthusiasm for technology, and considered whether to recommend a few days of solitary contemplation.

"Why's it called STUBBINS?" he asked, emerging from his reverie and cutting across the discussion.

The systems engineer faltered.

"It stands for Secure Technologies Ultimate Broadband Intruder Negation System," Father Maxwell informed him. "Or so it says in the literature." He pointed to the user manual the engineer had deposited on the desk. The abbot met his eye. Of course the American would know. Despite the strong foothold Orthodoxy held in that country, the abbot still distrusted Americans and their technical know-how, can-do attitude and new ideas. It all reeked of modernity.

"Thank you, brother," he said, nodding in acknowledgement.

The lesson continued, but the abbot's eyes glazed over and his thoughts drifted. It would be a relief to see the workmen depart and a degree of normality return to their small community.

"It's just one *B*," he said.

"Hmm?" The systems engineer paused once more in his walkthrough, and looked up, frowning. Fathers Maxwell and Zakinthos turned towards him.

The abbot smiled and adopted an airy tone. "Broadband. It's one word. It should just be one B, surely?"

The monks looked at the engineer for explanation, eyebrows raised. For a moment, he floundered.

"Umm… marketing," he came up with, eventually. "They needed something to fit. Probably came up with the name first." He grinned at them but was met with silence. The abbot indulged him with a smile, satisfied to have made his point. The instruction continued.

From its many, well-positioned vantage points, STUBBINS unpacked the relevant security algorithms and undertook an extensive set of systems checks, including testing both local and remote alert systems, and their responsiveness. Once satisfied that all appropriate viewing angles were covered and there were no dark spots, it set about constructing a meticulously detailed 3D map of the internal and visible external environment of each monastery, then photographed and catalogued their entire collection.

"It is a relief that our treasures are now secured, is it not?" prompted Father Maxwell, beaming in the direction of the abbot. The abbot returned the briefest of nods.

"Indeed. Yet we should remember that the true worth of God's works lies in our hearts and our minds," he replied.

Father Maxwell nodded. "Of course." The abbot couldn't help but notice the look that passed between the other two monks. He chose to ignore the insubordination and turned to the engineer.

"Nevertheless, we should pay thanks to our benefactor and his servants for the service they have wrought on our behalf to ensure the future security of this place." He smiled once more and gave the startled man a gracious bow, then, secular matters settled, he departed, relieved to be returning to affairs of a spiritual nature.

CHAPTER 12
A PROPOSITION

Sitting at his kitchen table, Haldred's mood darkened. The nagging headache had returned, and worry clouded his thoughts. Once again, he returned to the discussion in the cave. It was something the Trickster had said. The name of the monastery? Was Yuri to blame? In his scrambled brain, he must have picked up the wrong name. There couldn't be another explanation. He skipped the fact that he might not have been as thorough in his research and planning as usual. The circumstances were different; he'd been given a tight deadline. But at the same time, he'd been convinced he had the right target. The pain behind his eyes got worse, and he massaged his temples with a finger, trying to ease the pressure.

It was clear. It was all Yuri's fault. All along he'd been following the wrong lead because the forger had been so spooked his brain was scrambled. Despite their friendship, at that moment, Haldred wanted nothing more than to shoot the messenger.

He searched his bare cupboards for paracetamol, all the while continuing to brood on the matter. All plans for retirement lay in tatters, unless he could redeem the situation and get back in his master's good books. This time it needed to be perfect; there could be no further mistakes.

A large bowl of pasta later, he pored over his laptop once more. All the bookmarked sites were just as he'd thought. All confirmed the location: Varlaam Monastery, Greece. Karrig wouldn't like it, but they had no alternative; he had to revisit the scene of his previous crime. It broke all the rules of common sense. Haldred sat back and stared at the ceiling, picturing the painting in his mind's eye. Karrig must have passed within a few metres of it at most. Why did Loki regard it as important? He frowned and looked at the screen once again. The only image he'd found was grainy and quite small. Enlarging and examining it in greater detail revealed little; he struggled to find anything Loki might find significant. Haldred checked the caption again, re-read the accompanying text, and all the other snippets he'd tracked down. He studied the biography of Saint Nicolas of Myra. All sources repeated pretty much the same information, and they all contained the same curious omission. The saint and the stylised image of the fortified town to his right were relatively straightforward, but nowhere could he find an explanation for the cave depicted beneath it. Curious. But why didn't Loki just get someone to take a photo for him? What could he glean from the original that he couldn't get from a blown-up high-definition photograph?

Unable to come up with any answers, Haldred went back to work, a nugget of anxiety worming around in his gut. Once he had the outline of a plan, he phoned his brother and arranged lunch. They needed to talk.

CHAPTER 13
A COMMISSION

Haldred hung up abruptly. Sitting at the wheel of his car, Karrig frowned at his phone, as if it would provide the answer. His brother had sounded on edge. Karrig was used to his mood swings, and he was a miserable bugger at the best of times, but this time seemed different. He didn't really care what Haldred felt. Having to spend a tedious couple of hours in his company trying to keep his temper over grilled monkfish or similar was bad enough, but his biggest concern was when he was going to get paid. He had expenses, trips planned, parties to go to, events lined up. Those Wimbledon tickets weren't cheap.

He was still ruminating on the matter when the passenger door opened and a sharply suited man got in.

"Hey. You've got the wrong…" He fell silent as he stared at the snub nose of a pistol.

"Just act normal and keep your hands on the wheel and your eyes looking ahead." As if reading the dwarf's mind, the suited man reached with his other hand to move the rear-view mirror. A moment later, Karrig heard the rear door open behind him as someone else climbed in. His mouth felt dry.

"I don't know what you want, but I have no money," he lied.

The man with the gun gave a humourless laugh.

"We don't want your money. Please don't take us for simpletons."

"Then what…"

"My friend has a proposition to put to you. We just want you to listen."

There was a strange scent in the car; a strong musk odour, cloying and stupefying. The cologne worn by the new arrival, perhaps? It clung in Karrig's throat.

Then everything went dark.

He came to on a flat, featureless plain beneath a starry sky. There was a faint red line along the horizon to what he assumed was the east; a desert in the hour before dawn. The land in every direction was flat and barren, littered with small boulders and football-sized rocks. No sign of life.

Slowly, Karrig turned around, scanning for any clues as to where he was, and where there might be habitation or shelter, but as he turned full circle, he stopped in shock. A figure stood in front of him, much taller in stature than a man. He was silent and still, like an ancient statue. Where had he come from?

Karrig looked at the new arrival. He wasn't human, that much was clear. He was far too tall, and his head was all wrong. It was like nothing he'd ever seen. Was it a hat? An elaborate mask? He peered at the disturbingly still stranger, statue-like and inscrutable, craning his neck to get a proper look at the inhuman face. He jumped as it spoke.

"I am Set. God of Chaos and true Pharaoh of Egypt."

"Karrig, son of Hildingr, son of Hanarr," he replied, recovering his wits, and bowed, as seemed appropriate.

Set regarded him for a moment. Karrig stared back, feeling

way outside anything that could vaguely be described as his comfort zone. The name was faintly familiar to him, but only at the outermost fringes of his consciousness. He'd never given Egypt a moment's consideration in his entire life. He'd never needed to. Until now. The god before him appeared like a man from the neck down, but bore the head of an animal. Karrig wasn't an avid viewer of nature programmes; all those David Attenborough documentaries left him cold. But he was fairly sure that this head was unlike any animal that had ever lived. The snout was long and had a downward curve, and resembled that of an ant-eater, but the ears were sharply angled, large and pointed, rising far above the crown. Around Set's shoulders and descending over his breast was an ornate golden collar inset with blue and black stripes that looked both extremely heavy and stunningly crafted, and to a connoisseur of fine jewellery, beyond price. Other than that, he was naked to the waist, wearing only a loincloth covered by a long linen skirt and sandals. On his wrists were jewel-encrusted amulets, and he held a spear in his right hand.

"Where am I?" said Karrig.

The god moved for the first time and looked around. "Does it matter?"

"What am I here for?"

Set faced him once more, and gave him a long, appraising look. "I need a thief. You fit the bill."

"I am extremely busy. I am already contracted to another."

"Break it." The command sent a shiver down Karrig's spine. The thought of breaking an oath had never seemed so thrilling or so dangerous. Think of the chaos he would unleash. The fury of his brother. The idea was delicious. He also knew it was suicidally stupid.

"I can't. It's unbreakable. I have my reputation to think of."

"*Break it.*" This time, the command was louder and more insistent. It held almost physical force. Karrig took an involuntary step backwards. Wild thoughts and images crowded his mind like a swarm of angry wasps.

"They'll kill me."

Set remained silent, watching. The moment stretched until the silence became uncomfortable. Then, with long-practised martial skill and precision, the god whirled the spear about and around his body until Karrig could no longer see anything but a blur. Set switched his grip and stance and made a thrust towards the dwarf. The spear tip halted a centimetre short of his left eye.

"I can kill you now, if you prefer."

Karrig swallowed hard and stood frozen. Images of darkness, strange beasts, jackals and hyenas, carrion birds and bats invaded his brain, sucking at his thoughts. He could barely breathe.

"Okay," he said slowly. "Can I think about it?"

The spear tip never wavered.

"Do not double-cross me. If you do, I will pursue your soul across every underworld, known and unknown, until I find it and break it and cast it into the eternal void. Is that clear?"

A cold fear descended on him. "No, no. I'd never do that." Desperately, he tried to think of some way out. Could he do two jobs simultaneously? "What is it you want?"

To his intense relief, Set withdrew the spear and moved from the warrior's crouch to a relaxed upright stance once more.

"I want a painting."

"What painting?" A scintilla of doubt nagged at the edge of Karrig's consciousness.

"An image of a Christian. Saint Nicolas of Myra. The job is identical to the last one you performed, and in the same area. The ground is already laid out for you. The target item's location has been pinpointed and identified. There will be no mistake. Not like the last fool I recruited."

"If you know that, you must realise that it's a highly risky job. The location is likely to be in a state of heightened alert. They've already upgraded their security, I understand. It will take careful planning."

"They are technologically illiterate, and haven't got two shekels to rub together. The new security system they have been gifted will present you with no problems. You will be easily able to evade it with the jamming device you will be given. Your main area of concern will be shaking off your former employer's puppies and getting the item to me. That is where you should devote your planning activities."

"Puppies?"

Set remained silent. Karrig tried again. "Why can't you take it?"

The cold black eyes surveyed him dispassionately. "You ask too many questions." Karrig couldn't help but feel a thrill of fear down his spine. Had he gone too far? To his surprise, the god continued. "It is in a land that is less than welcoming to me or my servants. There are still forces that I prefer not to antagonise at this stage. I am not yet ready to reveal myself."

None of this made any sense to Karrig. He tried to focus on practicalities. "Where do I deliver—"

"My servant will leave instructions via an application that will be inserted into your phone, attuned to your biometrics and therefore only accessible to yourself. Keep the device with you at all times. It is the means by which further instructions will be delivered."

Karrig came to, slumped in the front seat of his car. Opening his eyes was painful; his head ached and the afternoon light hurt his retinas. He dared a sidelong glance, then peered over his shoulder. Thankfully, he was alone. He breathed out slowly and shut his eyes once more, trying to let the tension ease from his body. What had just happened? Was it for real?

Gradually, his physical symptoms improved, but he retained a vestige of nausea. He drove home cautiously, but arrived without incident.

His home, this one at any rate, was a secluded country house in rural Bohemia. It was modest in scale, but with its own grounds and set back from the road it provided a sense of security. Karrig had never been more grateful to be back there.

He parked at the side of the house and looked down. On the passenger seat lay the black slab of a brand-new phone. Karrig viewed it suspiciously; it felt expensively heavy in his hand. As he looked at the blank face, an Egyptian ankh symbol flared into life in the centre of the screen, orange against black. It faded as the screen lit up.

Karrig suppressed a shudder. So the meeting had been real. He couldn't pretend otherwise.

Apart from the wake-up screen, the configuration looked like his old phone. Instinctively, he reached in his pocket, but there was nothing there.

A slither of unease grew. Karrig patted down his pockets, then searched the car, rummaging in the glove compartment, all the other receptacles and beneath his seat, but to no avail. His old phone had gone. The slither in his stomach knotted as he picked up the new device once more and watched it come alive in his hand. He tried opening the mail and address book, the photos app and browser. His contacts and data seemed as normal, but on the third screen was a new app, also bearing the ankh symbol. He opened it and viewed a message which simply said *WELCOME*. Karrig stared at it, then returned to the home screen, pocketed the device and retreated indoors. He felt himself being watched, and glanced over his shoulder, but could see no one lurking in the undergrowth. Yet he felt exposed and vulnerable. Above all, he felt trapped.

CHAPTER 14
TREACHEROUS MOONLIGHT

Apollo made his way north. Now wise to the possibilities of bus travel, he brazenly boarded northbound services, strangely ignored by drivers and most of the passengers. In this way, he reached the town of Arta, safely bypassing Delphi. From there, he ventured on foot, travelling mainly by night to avoid the prying eyes of Zeus' many spies.

He stuck to the forested mountainsides, away from villages and towns and human activity, heading ever north and west. His journey was not without purpose. He had a goal in mind: the river Acheron, where it emerged from the Underworld to wind its way westward towards the Ionian Sea. There were many strange stories woven about this river. Beneath ground, it was said to wash away the sins of the dead. Would it work for creatures such as himself? Perhaps bathing in the cool green waters of the River of Pain might at least help him gain some absolution for the sins that had accumulated on his paws. He needed to find some way out of this endless misery encircling his soul.

As he travelled, Apollo reflected on recent events. He wasn't sorry for killing Kratos, but the fact he'd resorted to such elemental savagery was unnerving. Could he ever free himself from such psychotic rage? He still carried an underlying sense of dread that was impossible to escape; there was something fundamentally wrong with him, like the flaw in a diamond. But rather than emphasise perfection, he feared it would split him apart. And then again, he missed her: Daphne, the focus of his dreams. Deep in his immortal heart, he recognised that she'd turned away from him and chosen another; but surely not forever? The iron grip of unrequited love held him firm, and he had not yet found a way to release himself. In fact, he barely understood it at all; this complicated, multifaceted thing called love. How could something so intangible be so powerful? Powerful enough to support, embrace and invigorate, yet also torture, destroy and debilitate? Even for one so old, he still had a lot to learn. But he was little inclined to consult with his colleague Eros. The god of matchmaking, as he dismissively referred to Eros' calling, was an intellectual lightweight; he would get little sense from him. If enlightenment was unattainable from that source, he would stumble on in search of some other form of absolution until he could work it out for himself.

Trapped in these circular thoughts, Apollo plodded on through the forests and across the mountains, until one moonlit night he glimpsed a silver-white movement from the corner of his eye, over to his right. He paused, readying himself for the chase, but whatever had caused that mysterious flash of pale light disappeared like a will-o'-the-wisp into the night air. Every nerve-end tingling, the ginger-and-white cat inched forwards, his eyes scanning left and right to seek the deepest cover he could find. In his head, a flash of annoyance was offset by surprise that it had taken her so long to find him. He'd been expecting her for some time now, particularly after venturing so far into some of her favourite haunts.

There it was again, to his left now; but the moment he

looked, it vanished once more. He studied the place it had been, his senses on full alert, but deep in the woods his ears and nose were more use than his eyes. Was that the rustle of a dry leaf? A twig dislodged? She wouldn't be so careless, would she? But there it was, behind the scent of moist earth and damp foliage, the faint aroma of honeysuckle and myrtle. Yes, it was her, but where exactly?

Sudden movement to his left alerted him; something heading in his direction, fast. He fled, away and up the slope ahead, darting past tree trunks and beneath low-hanging boughs, but she was quick, this one. Right on his tail.

A surge of adrenaline lent him extra speed as he raced through a narrow gap between tumbled boulders and turned sharply downhill into the narrow ravine of a mountain stream. He leaped across the water and flew up the far bank to find her waiting for him. He tried to change direction, but she pounced and caught him in mid-air, and they fell, tumbling and crashing through the undergrowth, paws entwined, mouths seeking purchase on a neck or, better still, a throat. But not with real intent. After a while they parted, each panting and warily studying the other.

"Well met, brother."

"What took you so long?"

The moonlight, so bright in the little glade, seemed to give the white cat a silver glow, but the effect didn't extend to Apollo. His ginger-and-white markings looked dull by comparison, but there remained a light in his eyes. Artemis moved towards him slowly, nuzzled his neck and rubbed her body along his flank. He stood still to let her, making only a slight gesture in return.

"I wondered when I might see you."

"You know he's looking for you?"

"Of course. What are you going to tell him?"

They broke apart, and she looked into the shadows behind him. "I haven't decided yet."

"But you must have an idea."

"I wanted to hear your side of the story first."

He studied her face. She was alone, of that he was certain. He knew his twin would allow none of Zeus' spies to observe her, especially when she was involved in her favourite pursuit: hunting. Artemis had an intense dislike of anybody spying on her, of course, as several unfortunate mortals had found to their cost in the past. Apollo didn't say anything; he just watched as she moved around to face him.

"Come on, tell me," she said. "I want to know everything."

Thoughts and emotions tumbled through his brain. She wanted to know everything? Just like that? Their first meeting in, how long, 800 years? It was as if she read his thoughts.

"Starting from the beginning, of course," she said brightly. "Not just the exciting stuff from the last few weeks." She lowered her eyes and gently butted his cheek with her forehead, encouragingly. "You haven't forgotten how impatient I get?" Self-mockery suited her, he thought. It just about got her out of the hole she'd started digging.

"You know these parts better than me," he said. "Let's eat first and then I might tell you something. But first things first. I'm hungry."

"You want me to catch something for you? Have you run out of slaves?"

He caught the gentle sarcasm in her voice. It was like old times again. "Well, seeing as you're so good at it…"

"Ha. You'd better see if you can catch me first!" With that, she darted off into the undergrowth. He followed, just about able to keep pace; but he knew that here, in her element, he could not match her skills. She relented a bit and led him to more straightforward hunting grounds where they both could find and catch prey. Finally sated, she led him to the shores of a small mountain lake, its calm surface reflecting the moon and stars above. Her stature seemed to grow in the pale light.

"He's furious, you know."

"I guessed he would be." For a while, Apollo was wrapped in his thoughts. He felt a strange reluctance to explain himself, particularly before his sister. They had always been close, but he knew she was one of Zeus' favourites. He stirred, trying to organise his thoughts.

"You have to talk to him sometime. Why not get it over with?"

"No." Apollo was adamant. He looked at her. "What would it achieve? I have no desire to apologise, and I'm not going to atone via some new punishment or whatever he comes up with. I'm satisfied with what I did. He deserved it." They both knew it wouldn't be the first time he'd have had to explain himself to their father. Artemis looked across the lake, for a moment everything forgotten as she enjoyed the silver light playing on the surface as a breeze ruffled it. Apollo looked up. There were plenty of clouds scattered across the sky, but none of them seemed to intercede between the moon and their location.

"He won't let it rest."

"Maybe. But what can he do? His wings are as clipped as any of us. Perhaps more. He may still rustle up a storm, but he can no longer conjure a typhoon, or bring down a bitter blizzard from the north, such that the sea might freeze with even Poseidon powerless to stop it. Nor can he order Helios to scorch the earth and burn their crops like before, or reduce a city to rubble with his terror weapons. The thunderbolts, are gone."

Artemis said nothing for a while. "He is still our leader," she said. "He still has that authority." Apollo gave her a sharp glance. Her loyalty to their father surprised him and was beginning to grate.

"What authority? By what right does he deserve our respect? If he is our leader, he leads best by staying out of the way."

"Still, you should be careful."

Apollo sighed inwardly. He knew she was right, and that beneath Zeus' capricious exterior lay a will of iron. When he spoke again, he sounded reflective. "I was there when Kratos briefly discovered some of his powers. For a moment, he grasped at some things we all used to take for granted. Being on the outside, with no real means of defence, was terrifying." He paused, recalling the horrible realisation of how powerless he'd felt and how inadequate. "In just a few minutes, he wrought damage such as none of us have done for millennia. I witnessed it from the other side for the first time, from the position of a mortal. They were bewildered. They didn't realise what was behind it. All that sudden destruction. It just seemed random to them. And it was. He was just flexing his mental muscles. A stretch to see what worked after all this time. There was no plan; it was a reflex. This is Kratos, after all."

He studied Artemis' face for her reaction, but she gave nothing away.

"But imagine if there was. What destruction could he wreak if he did have a plan? In the end we were lucky that it was him. If it had been someone else, Poseidon say, or Zeus himself, think what damage could be done? And what would it be like if we all wielded these powers once again? With a real purpose." He left the thought hanging and stared out across the water. Suddenly restless to be on his way, he looked at her once more. "Those days are gone. The world is better without us. We should stay out of the way."

The look Artemis gave him was difficult to read. "You do not speak for everyone."

Apollo heard the impatience in her voice, the yearning to feel, once again, the tingle of real power beneath her fingertips or hovering just below the threshold of her thoughts. Power sufficient to tilt the balance of fate and affect the future. Now those fingertips were gone, hidden beneath this sleek but sometimes clumsy body. Paws and claws were poorly formed for delicate work, unless it was gutting a mouse or climbing a tree.

He felt saddened but not surprised. They had not spoken or interacted for centuries. How could he expect her to snap into lockstep with his thinking after such a long time apart? If he had the time, he was sure he could talk her round. But he had an itch to be on his way. Zeus' powers might be reduced, but Apollo still felt the urge to stay out of his sight for as long as possible, and he wasn't entirely certain that his father's abilities were as limited as he had just declared. These days, Zeus was an unknown quantity. Nor was he certain, as he once would have been, that his sister would keep their conversation to herself.

"Athena has it, then?" Her question jolted him out of his reverie.

"The artefact? Yes. But I trust her. I don't think she'll misuse it."

"She has her own agenda, and she is far more measured than Kratos. If she can bend it to her will, her actions might be equally dramatic. She likes to meddle in the affairs of humans, after all. It's sport for her. She won't be able to resist. Leaving it with her was a mistake."

Apollo looked her in the eye, trying to work out where this line of thought was leading. It seemed the ancient rivalry between Athena and his twin was as alive as ever. Once it manifested as an occasional contest for the love of their worshippers, or a test of their loyalty, what more did they have to prove?

"I trust her," he said simply.

It was Artemis who broke away first. "You always did like to see the best in people."

Apollo couldn't fail to detect the thinly veiled contempt behind her words.

"I haven't got time for this. I have to go." He stood,

casting a glance towards the shadows beneath the trees, searching for the best path.

"Has she told you about the trees?"

He turned back sharply, eyes narrowed. "What do you mean?"

Artemis gave him a cool, steady look. "Have you forgotten what brought us to this state?"

Apollo stared back, unsure what to say. "I heard about it…"

"Heard? Were you so lost that you have no memory?"

Apollo's face was blank. Why couldn't he remember the moment of transformation? It was as if that chapter of his life had been erased. Until now, he'd never given it any thought.

"It happened. So what?"

Artemis got up and stretched, then took a step closer until her nose was almost touching his. She stared deep into his eyes, as if searching. Her voice sounded distant. "Perhaps you really have forgotten. What else has been wiped from your memory?"

Doubt and uncertainty, those familiar friends, wrapped themselves about him. His eyes narrowed. "What do you mean?"

She turned away and gazed across the lake, enjoying the interplay of moonlight and shadow. "What did she tell you?"

Apollo hesitated. "Only that she doesn't know where it is. Nobody does."

"It? She only mentioned one?"

"Yes. What do you mean?"

Artemis glanced at him over her shoulder. "Interesting. Do you think she really believes that?"

Apollo wondered what she was getting at. What was he missing? Rooted to the spot, he felt ill-informed and hated it. "What's behind this? Are you jealous of her? Do you want the object for yourself, is that it?"

The silver-white cat turned away to look across the

moonlit water once more. With a soft splashing sound, tiny waves broke upon the stony shore by her feet.

"Demeter took a cutting, you know? Athena's precious tree is not unique."

There was a sudden tightening in his chest. Artemis walked slowly by the water's edge towards the nearby trees. He called after her. "So, you know where it is?"

"No. But I know at least one more exists."

"But…?"

She stopped and turned towards him, her eyes narrowed. "Where might it be? I've spent many a year pondering that, dear brother, searching for it, while you slept on your cosy hillside."

Apollo tried to work out the implications, but Artemis wasn't finished.

"Of course, it raises so many questions; not just what she did with her cutting, and where she planted it, but for what purpose? Why did she need another? Was one not bad enough? Does the second tree reverse the actions of the first or amplify it? Maybe its fruit will reduce us to mere mortals?" She gave him a long, stare. "Or does it engineer some different change entirely? Perhaps it is truly deadly poison that will kill us instantly? Then there are the actions of our dear aunt herself. Did Demeter partake of the fruit of the second tree, and is that why no one can find her? Maybe she's truly dead? Forever. A victim of her own experiment."

He didn't move a muscle; just followed her with his eyes. He felt unable to breathe, as if the entire future hung on her next response. "How do you know about this other tree?"

Artemis slunk back and forth by the lake shore, as if considering what to say.

"Unlike most, I didn't leave the grove in the immediate aftermath of transforming. I stayed close by, trying to come to terms with what had happened, desperate to reverse it. I tried to warn the others: the latecomers, all the nymphs and driads, the satyrs and the others. None of them deserved to suffer like we had. But all to no avail. No one could understand a word I said. One by one, or in small groups, they all went happily along to their fate. And as I watched, I grew more and more angry with Athena. She saw what we went through, but there was no remorse. I began to hate her; to despise her stupid plan."

Apollo could only stare. His sister gave him another glance. "Demeter, though. She was different. She began to empathise. She saw how we struggled with the pain. I watched her growing doubt, saw the uncertainty on her face; she no longer believed in the plan. They argued, but Athena remained true to her conviction. It was the only path. For all of us. Transformation or nothing. She wouldn't be moved."

Apollo cast his eyes to the ground, absorbing the news, but wondering why he had no recollection of the event at all. He had been more proficient at erasing his memories than he'd realised. It was more than disconcerting; he felt numb.

"So, it came as no surprise when she cracked. One morning, while her partner was otherwise engaged, Demeter passed quickly along the terraces and through the gardens of the sanctuary. I followed her until she arrived at the courtyard with the tree and watched as she took a cutting. Carefully, she wrapped it in her apron, then she left. I don't know where. I couldn't catch up with her. I didn't see her again until the following day, when the next batch of innocents arrived to suffer and twist and shriek for Athena's entertainment."

"What sanctuary? Where did all this take place?"

His sister paused. For once, she could not meet his eye. "That's the problem. I've forgotten." There was a note of anguish in her voice. "Everywhere looks so different now. They're tearing up our world. There's hardly anything left."

He stared at her, unable to think of a response. He needed to think, to reassess. "I have to go."

Artemis threw him another look over her shoulder. "You

haven't fallen into her trap, have you? You're not helping her?"

"What do you mean?"

She turned once more to face him. "You have, haven't you? You're helping her. Joining her quest to rediscover the whereabouts of her precious tree? I can't believe you've sunk so low."

"What do you mean? That's what you want, isn't it? To find the tree and rediscover what you used to be." It was apparent that it was not; the fur along Artemis' spine was standing on end in betrayal of her emotions. She glared at him.

"I only want to find it to destroy it. It's poison. It's a god-killer, and she's damn near eliminated us. Another dose and she'll finish the job. If she finds that tree again, it will be the end for all of us. But if there is another one, and it reverses the process so that she gets all her powers back, before the rest of us…"

The moonlight shone on her coat, making it glow in the still night air. Pale white beams reflected about the lake shore. Anger intensified her aura.

"No. I'm sure it's not like that…" He had no real answer. He was just groping for words. Was that really Athena's plan? Apollo needed to think, but beneath the piercing light of the moon in this peaceful glade, nothing made sense. He turned on his tail and made his way into the shadows beneath the trees.

In a matter of a few strides, he plunged into darkness and became entangled in dense undergrowth. Thorns and brambles stabbed and gashed his flanks, and wound around his legs. The clear path they'd followed to the lake shore was nowhere to be seen. Instead, the ground was uncertain beneath his feet. He fell into gullies and scrambled his way over loose dirt and forced a path through tangled thickets of vegetation that seemed near impenetrable. With every step, his irritation grew until it shone in a faint golden aura about his body. It was a while before Apollo found a way back onto more open ground. He raised his snout, sniffed the air and watched the stars. Then he sped away, north.

CHAPTER 15
ANJA

Anja looked as if she'd escaped from a monochrome world, and couldn't adapt to her new surroundings. Black hair, long and straight, tumbled across her shoulders and down her back. The black top hat she wore had aviator goggles on its rim. Beneath her long coat her T-shirt bore the logo of Beyond Belief, her favourite band – from their world tour to promote their latest album - *Everything You Know is Wrong*. A shorter black skirt finished above tall black boots with an unfeasible number of buckles up each side, sporting a thick crepe sole. Her outfit was accessorised with fingerless lace gloves, also black, and an assortment of bangles and bracelets. Dramatic make-up completed her look, but the attitude which brought it all together was all her own.

Anja didn't smile. She was here in Bratislava on business. That her mission coincided with a stop on her favourite death metal band's European tour was a happy coincidence. Nobody paid her the slightest attention as she strode through the busy streets.

She'd been recruited quite recently, having been discovered via various underground channels and anonymous sources, and her willingness to contemplate the unthinkable made her a valuable asset. Joining the movement was not accidental; she'd sought them out. It had taken a little while, but hanging out in the right clubs and bars, being seen, making an appropriate response in a seemingly innocuous conversation with a roadie, and meeting other, better-connected people, had led eventually to a brief meeting with a shady character in the back room of a Bergen nightclub. Her handler was Ron, coincidentally the manager of her favourite band. He was a wiry man of indeterminate age, with bow legs, heavily gelled thinning hair, and a 1950s rock and roll style that jarred, she felt, with the artists he was promoting. He took her credentials apparently on trust, but she possessed enough insight to know that in the background, others would be checking up on her, trailing and speaking to any contacts, and tracing her past movements. It amused her to contemplate how far they'd get with that.

Anja had felt the calling years ago when she was very young, but in her suffocating early life such rebellious thoughts could not be acknowledged without ridicule or reprimand. So, she kept it to herself, nurturing her animosity to the wholesome light, and gravitating towards the welcoming dark. Once she was of age, there was no way she was going to remain in Aelfheim, confined in their shallow, cosy little world. The vast majority of her kin leaned towards the light and followed respectable and virtuous pursuits, but Anja revelled in her difference, and began to hate everything they stood for. It became impossible to continue living among them; not because she was persecuted – they didn't have the guts – but because she despised them. Instead, she sought a refuge in Midgard, among other worshippers of Loki, the deity she adored.

She wanted control over her destiny. She wanted chaos. She wanted disreputable fun. She wanted sex with strangers.

Not goody-two-shoes cosy intimacy, and fretting about this year's apple crop, and *was the glacier retreating just a little more*, coupling they practised back home. No, she wanted real, hot, fleshy, wet, dirty, tongues out, panting, roll-on-the-floor, sweaty, all-in fucking. Wherever. Whenever. With whomever she fancied. It's what drove her here, to this alternative life. This real life of booze and cigarettes, hard music and soft drugs, risk and excitement, and dangerous encounters. In the dirty, grimy dark at the back of the most disreputable clubs, she felt more alive than she'd ever done in Aelfheim.

Originating from a particular version of Iceland, Anja was an elf, and she grew up well versed in all the perverse nature of Nordic lore. Her people lived in a separate fold of reality that overlapped and simultaneously occupied the same geographical space as the Midgard equivalent. This twist in the fabric of space-time allowed them to hide in plain sight and remain unseen, should they so wish. But by following the correct paths, once you knew their start points, it was easy to cross between worlds. Their realm, Aelfheim, had a vast hinterland that stretched far beyond Iceland's rocky shores to many exotic distant realms. But in that land, the two worlds overlapped, and that provided her means of escape.

The only trouble with Midgard was that she found most of the inhabitants unutterably stupid. Most of them didn't seem able to cope with her mix of passive-aggressive barbs and sarcastic come-ons. Some were as dumb as those she'd been so desperate to flee. At first she was frustrated, struggling to connect. But gradually her familiarity and knowledge grew until she found a few like her, then eagerly she sought others. She spent time with them and became accepted. Through the underbelly of heavy, heavy music she found her tribe and her confidence grew.

As an insider, she learned how to manipulate and steer the others, and persuade them to do her bidding. Gradually, she became better known on the underground circuit. In some ways, it remained disappointing that there were so few who were like her, but the air of exclusivity was appealing, and slowly their number grew, and being an early follower held kudos. Through them she cultivated deeper lying connections, and gained admittance to trusted inner circles, and tasks began to come her way. Simple at first, to test her appetite, then more difficult, and more challenging, to test her boundaries. They were delighted to find she didn't have any, and she became a trusted operative.

To date, Ron was her most senior contact, but she knew he'd only be a small cog in a far larger machine. For the moment, he would have to do, even though every minute spent in his company made her skin crawl. Tall and slender, she towered over him, but he had a shiftiness that always put her on edge. His eyes continually darted around the room, never lingering on her, or anyone else, for more than an instant, as if he was always checking for an escape route. Even so, she took him seriously. He had the air of a seasoned street fighter and his lined face had the scars to match and she suspected he always had a flick knife to hand. More importantly, he was the centrepiece of a web of underground connections that was her route into the organisation: drug dealers, crime gangs, people smugglers, equipment suppliers, safe house owners and more. Within this web, he was the spider that pulled the strings; but as far as spiders go, Ron would be quite a small one in the wider web of individuals that led back to the Norse god of mischief himself.

The thought was exhilarating. She'd become part of the ever-expanding corps of agents, servants, foot soldiers, assassins and spies that collectively advanced the plans of a dark, and at present hidden, criminal mastermind. Someone with the vision to plan on a truly epic scale. Ron was just a stepping stone. Anja's life mission was to work her way up the hierarchy and worm her way into her lord's affections, one crime at a time.

That, and to shag the drummer of her favourite band, the band that, if it wasn't for her work, she'd follow around the world. As far as her sex life went, to date it hadn't lived up to expectations, but she knew that would change. If only he'd look at her, take her seriously, get to know her.

Walking through Bratislava's Old Town with a look that brooked no challenge, Anja carried a hard-shell briefcase in one hand, and pulled a wheeled suitcase with the other. She was on the way to pick up the keys to the apartment she'd rented online. Her target was on the move, and likely to arrive in the city any day now. The only intelligence lacking was when and where in the city she could find him. It was her job to ensure that this time he did not leave.

To prepare the ground, she had found a cheap flat in the rundown area near the river to use as her base. Furnished, the agency had said, but looking at the stained mattress and chipped and creaking chairs and table she wondered at the description. There was an armchair – she supposed it could be called that – but she dreaded to think what she might catch from actually sitting in it, so she set off in search of disposable covers, or as a last resort, plastic sheeting, plus a sleeping bag and other basic items. It was a little dispiriting, given that she'd paid three months' rent in advance.

Once settled in, she set about her hunt. Anja preferred to work alone once a job came through, but this mission had come with very little background information, as if there were still some doubt whether the client actually wanted it to go ahead. Her target had been spotted near the railway station, but some time ago. That was all she had to go on. The informant didn't even say if he was arriving or leaving.

She sat at the table and opened her laptop and its dark-net browser, then pointed it to a little-known site, suttungr.net, a chat server for many would-be rebels and wannabe members of the dark side. Among them were many fans of the bands she liked, together with a lot of conspiracy theorists and other dissenters. There were even a few genuine agents of chaos among them, lurking in the shadows. It took her a few minutes sifting through the labyrinthine structure of message boards and chat rooms to find the one she sought, and pose her question. Within seconds, she had a reply. *"Embrace that which is twice fake. The non-dark will lead you to your answer."*

Why could she never get a straight answer? Obscure riddles with multiple interpretations preserved deniability, she supposed, and put others off the scent, perhaps, but it was still irritating. Anja didn't dwell on the possibility that the other side may know of her or even be tracking her. He was dismissive of their abilities. Their innocence would prove their undoing. They were no match for the ever growing armies of darkness.

She put aside her meandering thoughts and tried to concentrate. She had work to do and solving enigmatic riddles was part of the process.

Anja shut the computer and considered the message, dissecting it to try and extract meaning. She parsed it into smaller phrases, then further down to syllables or letters. Was it an anagram? Was it in code? What other interpretations were there? After she'd exhausted every angle she could think of, she gave up, frustrated, but with a lingering feeling that she was missing something obvious. It was a call to act, not a cryptic crossword clue. There had to be a straightforward interpretation. Twice fake? Non-dark? The phrases echoed in her head, but still she couldn't come up with an answer. Eventually, she decided to get some air and clear her head.

Walking by the Danube, ostensibly exploring the city as any tourist might, her thoughts were elsewhere. By early evening, hungry and tired, she made her way to the Old Town in search of a supermarket en route back to her temporary home. With only a vague idea of the direction she needed to take, Anja got lost in the warren of streets; none were familiar from her previous exploration. Local people streamed past on their way home from work, but despite her unusual looks, she attracted no attention. There was a chill in the air, an early precursor of autumn, driven on a thin north-easterly wind. The people pulled their jackets and coats closer, but her northern roots in far colder climes lent her resilience; her homeland would be far cooler at this time of year.

A dwarf scuttled past her as her thoughts turned to food. What would she pick up this evening? A stray thought snagged at the back of her mind.

Short. Bearded. Ginger. Dwarf?

She spun on her heel and searched back along the street for the retreating figure. There he was, huddled against the cold, heading back the way she'd come. In stature, he looked about right. Maybe a centimetre or two too tall? But in all her experience of that devious species, she'd never come across a ginger one. As she followed, Anja revisited her previous experience of dwarves. All those she'd known sported dark wiry hair, usually unkempt, but she supposed there was nothing to stop some of them being ginger in colouring. Bald was new as well, but at least he was bearded; that fitted the mould. A fake dwarf? She hastened her step, her interest aroused.

The figure twenty metres ahead now commanded all of her attention. He was hunched into his coat, and clutched a plastic carrier bag, bulging with provisions. She slowed down as he turned into a narrower side street. There were few people on the sidewalks, and less cover. At the corner she dawdled, pretending to study her phone while watching him from the corner of her eye. Halfway along the street he turned into a building and disappeared from sight. She walked up to the entrance: a recessed door, metal framed with frosted glass panels and pushed it to check that it was locked. On the wall at the side there was an entry PIN pad, and below it a set of brass buttons with name spaces alongside where the inhabitants could identify themselves. Some were happy to remain anonymous. Those that were filled in meant nothing to her. She took a photo with her phone then left. She had her first clue.

CHAPTER 16
LUNCH

The bar his brother had chosen for their meeting was far too close to the tourist hotspots of the Charles Bridge for Karrig's liking. He preferred the more anonymous hostelries, further out, that locals frequented. They were more authentic, and certainly a lot cheaper, and in any case, with a new and deadly patron, it would have been better to start planning out his new mission rather than suffer a couple of hours in his brother's company.. Still, Haldred had been insistent, so he came, if only to find out when he would get paid.

The late summer's day was warm enough for a T-shirt, so he felt conspicuous in his quilted jacket. Unlike the inexhaustible supply of human females he befriended, Karrig never seemed to read the weather properly. Red-faced and sweating, he turned away from the main drag leading up towards the citadel of Hradcany, and instead entered the meandering streets of the Male Strana, growing more irritable with each step.

On another day he might have enjoyed idling in the bars and restaurants around here, flashing his charm and cash around; the life and soul of the party. But today's meeting was a distraction he could do without.

His destination lay behind a high wall through an arched entrance. Karrig crossed the small courtyard packed with tables and crowded with tourists hiding from the sun beneath red umbrellas, and into the warm darkness beyond. It took a moment before his eyes adjusted, and he spotted Haldred perched on a bar stool, his legs too short to reach the footrest. He was staring into a glass of beer, apparently lost in thought. Karrig watched him for a moment. The trouble with being their height in this world of men meant everything was a little too big. The way his legs dangled was reminiscent of something a human child might do, but that was the extent of any resemblance. The straggly beard and craggy features spoke of a different experience entirely.

Watching him from across the room, Karrig wondered when the change had happened. As what point had a meeting with Haldred become such an ordeal? He suppressed a sigh and walked across. Haldred gave a grunt of welcome and gestured with his eyes to an empty table in an alcove by the wall. Karrig got there first, eased himself onto the bench seating and plucked a menu from behind the pot of condiments and cutlery by the wall. It was useful to have something to peruse while reading his brother's mood. If he was fractious, as he tended to be these days, it could be a short meeting.

"I need your help," said Haldred.

"Hello," Karrig said, looking up sharply. "Lovely to see you. How are you?" He stared at his brother to emphasise the point and was met with a derisory snort. Haldred put his beer down and squeezed behind the table. Short he might be, but his girth was definitely increasing; testimony to too many hours spent soothing the egos of art dealers in the expensive restaurants of Manhattan. He waited.

"Fancy something to eat?" Haldred browsed the menu.

Still, Karrig said nothing. A waitress approached. Haldred looked at her and Karrig noted the leer on his face. She held a tablet and stylus and waited for them, bored.

"What's the special?" Haldred asked.

"Roast duck with dumplings, red cabbage and seasonal vegetables." Her reply was automatic, as her eyes scanned nearby tables. Haldred looked her up and down, deliberately lingering on her breasts.

"Only, it's my birthday," he said. "I could do with something special. I bet we could cook up something special between us this afternoon, eh? You and me? What time do you get off?"

She gave him a humourless smile. "We don't have any vacancies in the kitchen today, sir."

Karrig dived in, anxious to head off the next lewd remark from the imbecile opposite. "I'll just have the burger. With onion rings on the side."

"What sauce do you want with that?"

"Barbecue."

"Fries?"

"Yeah."

She gave Haldred a look that could curdle milk. He returned his most lascivious smile and surveyed the menu. Karrig felt like ordering for him, but knew that would be a provocation too far. He felt tired of all this; of the embarrassment of being with him when he was in this kind of mood. His resentment grew.

"I'll go with the special after all, given your glowing recommendation." Haldred stared up at her with a moonstruck expression. She tapped in the order and turned to go. Before she moved, he slapped her bottom, a stupid grin on his face. Karrig groaned and put a hand over his eyes. The waitress turned back, smartly.

"Try that again and I'll have you thrown out." She glared at them both, then retreated. Karrig leaned across the table.

"What did you do that for? Are you stupid?"

"I'm bored. Thought I'd spice things up a bit." His eyes wandered after the waitress. "She didn't mind, really. Probably quite likes a bit of attention, that one."

Karrig followed his gaze to the back of the bar and saw her in conversation with the barman, who was drying glasses with a towel and frowning in their direction. He didn't look pleased. Karrig turned back, wondering if his brother was drunk.

"She doesn't seem all that impressed. Anyway, what did you want to see me about?"

Haldred said nothing for a moment. He just stared at the table. "I need some help."

"Already? We've only just completed one job for him. What does he want now?" He leaned across the table. "Has he paid us yet, by the way?"

"Me. Paid *me*, remember? You've never been on the payroll."

Karrig glared at the figure opposite, hating him. But he couldn't deny the truth: he existed on the generous payments his brother granted. With his mouth feeling suddenly dry, he reached for his beer and took a long swig, trying to calm his feelings. His remuneration, generous though it was, had always felt demeaning. Being reminded of the fact made his hackles rise and soured his mood further. But things were about to change. He had an ace up his sleeve; a new benefactor.

"Wanna see how far you get without me?" Karrig took satisfaction from his brother's inability to look him in the eye. He sat back and cast a critical eye on the dwarf opposite. How much did he keep for himself? Karrig had never been naïve enough to believe he split the payments equally. How much was his brother worth, and what satisfaction did he get from it? He obviously didn't spend it on his appearance, or his wardrobe, by the look of the tattered T-shirt he wore and the ragged old fleece he'd thrown on the seat beside him. "What is it this time?"

Haldred looked up from beneath unruly brows, a glint in his eye. "The same job as before, but done properly this time." He seemed agitated, anger brewing behind the frown.

"What do you mean?"

Haldred leaned closer, lowering his voice. "We screwed up. Or should I say, Yuri screwed up."

Confusion clouded Karrig's thoughts. There had to be a mistake. "Bullshit. I tracked it down to that monastery in Greece, up on its perch. *Nikita the Martyr*, just like you said. You verified it."

"Yeah, well, the message was wrong. Somehow. Someone got in the way. Confused it, corrupted it, I don't know. Right now, I feel like killing him."

"Yuri?"

Haldred nodded. Karrig's brows furrowed. His eyes darted around the dark interior of the bar, as if the answer was lurking in the shadows. "How come? You seemed so sure. Are you telling me you made me risk my life for some kind of sick joke? Is this a wind-up?" Haldred said nothing. Karrig continued to vent his fury. "So that was all some wild goose chase? Is he trying to make us look stupid? Is he playing games with us? Does he want me dead? Where were we supposed to go? Spain? South America?"

Haldred spoke, keeping his voice low. "We were close. The message must have been garbled. You went to the right place, but it was the wrong saint. That's all."

The revelation did nothing to improve Karrig's mood. "Wrong saint? We got the wrong saint? Are you kidding me?"

Haldred leaned closer. "It was Nicolas. Nicolas, not Nikita. And Myra as in Myra, not Myra as in Martyr." There was a pause while they locked eyes. "Like I said, we were close."

For an instant, they remained still, each staring at the other in fury. Karrig was aware of nothing but his brother's ugly face. The desire to give Haldred a black eye danced at the front of his thoughts, but behind it there was doubt. His brother had never made such an obvious mistake before. It couldn't be him, could it? Was he finally losing his touch? Was his memory going? He sat back, a slow grin spreading across his face.

"Seriously? The wrong saint? So, all that was for nothing? You must have been popular." He felt like laughing. His brother's voice cut into his thoughts.

"It's no laughing matter, idiot. This is serious. We're in deep shit if we get this wrong."

Anger replaced incredulity on Karrig's face. He leaned forwards, his finger stabbing the air between them. "You mean *you're* in deep shit. Your projects are nothing to do with me. I just came here to lend a hand. I'm the sub-contractor, remember? You're the one on the hook, and don't you forget it. You can keep your trouble with him far away from me. I'm not interested." The longer he spoke, the more irritated he felt. It was the release of decades of frustration. His eyes narrowed. "Just what do you make from him? How much am I getting? Not fifty percent, is it?" As Karrig's anger began to mount, Haldred just stared back, his face unreadable.

"Fuck off! Just fuck right off. You get more than your fair share. I'm the one who takes the risks. It's me who has to deal with him. I'm the one who has to visit him down there, with his nightmare pals. You don't understand." Haldred ran a hand across his brow. Karrig was disconcerted to see it tremble slightly, but it did nothing to assuage him. "You just get to come along for the ride. You get your rewards."

"Rubbish. We're only here because of you and your stupid bet. You've done more than enough to screw up my life, both of our lives, for centuries. If it wasn't for me, you'd never have survived this long. You'd be long dead." Karrig had never aired his slow-burning resentment, but at this moment, all his restraint had gone. He leaned forwards, his voice lower now. "Don't dare tell me I don't understand. Not after everything that happened."

Haldred's face reddened. "What do you mean, 'because of you'? It's your fault we got stuck here in the first place. You and that bloody gold. If you'd stayed out of it, we could have gone back once it had blown over."

They glared at each other across the table as the barbs struck home, their dispute teetering on the brink of blows. The waitress appeared and slammed a couple of plates down in front of them with scarcely concealed contempt. Haldred looked up at her, taking advantage of the interruption.

"A beer, please." He flashed a wan smile, attempting to soften her mood.

"Make that two." Karrig didn't look up, just continued glaring across the table, but he sounded calmer. The waitress left without a word.

For a few minutes, neither of them spoke. The arrival of food gave them an excuse to sort out cutlery and begin to eat. Slowly, the tension dissipated. Finally, Karrig spoke again, his temper finally dissipating. He tried to sound business-like.

"So, where is it this time?"

"Same place, more or less." Haldred sighed. Karrig heard the weariness in his brother's voice. He put down his knife and fork and looked across the table once more, seeing the strain beneath the beetling brows. Haldred's eyes were red-rimmed, as if he'd hardly slept in days.

"You mean I've got to go through all that Spider-Man stuff again?"

Haldred wouldn't meet his eyes. "Sorry."

It was Karrig's turn to sigh, anger replaced by weariness. "Why? How did you get it so wrong?"

Haldred's eyes narrowed once more, but the fight had gone out of them. "I don't know. I just don't know. Do you think I haven't asked myself that?" He stared at his plate, but didn't eat. "I don't think I was wrong, but I can't exactly accuse him of having memory failure, can I? I wouldn't make it out of the cave." His eyes searched the table. "It must have been the trail of clues." He gave Karrig a brief account of his encounter with Corpse Swallower and then the call from Yuri, and his visit.

Karrig tried a different tack.

"What does he want with all this artwork? Has he stopped with the political instability stuff? Great if he has, but I don't get it. A few decades ago, it was books. Then it seemed he wanted to bring down the whole world in one continual revolution. I thought it was because he was bored. Liked hearing about the chaos up above. Wanted to set up an apocalypse. But why change tack now when it looks like it's working? Makes little sense to me."

"No, me neither. I tried asking him." Haldred looked up. "But it was no good. He just threatened me if I dared question him again. You should have seen it. His rage! The earth shook. I thought he was going to bring the roof down on top of us. He's a psycho." Haldred kept his voice low, but he sounded more urgent now; a fire had rekindled in his eyes. "I can't read his thoughts. No one can. But if we don't get the right painting for him, we're toast. I know that much. He's got agents out there. Who knows how many? They may be spying on us now, for all I know."

Karrig glanced around the bar. The fear in his brother's voice was sobering. He wasn't making it up. Although Karrig had steered as well clear of Loki as he could since Haldred's tenure had begun, he'd always been tainted by association, while protected from Mótsognir's retribution. Nothing made sense, apart from Haldred's fear of Loki's followers. Perhaps he should pay more attention to that. If he'd slipped over onto the god's bad side, the future could be dangerous. The thought sent a chill down the dwarf's spine. He'd been above ground far too long; they both had. As a race they were long-lived, but he had to admit, their lifespan seemed unnaturally long. Was Mótsognir still king? Were they still wanted? Karrig had no desire to venture back down to Nidavellir to find out.

His thoughts reverted to his brother. Was the mistake an age thing? Had Haldred's memory suddenly failed him? It was a worrying thought.

"You should leave me out of it. I don't want any part of his games anymore."

Haldred looked shocked. "What do you mean? I can't. We're in this together, remember? You vowed to help."

"God knows what I was thinking. You're hopeless. I must have been feeling sorry for you."

Haldred gave him a calculating look. "We're in this together. You know that. I go down, so do you. There's no walking away."

Karrig felt helpless. He couldn't deny it, but the sense of injustice still burned. If anything, it was growing. His jaw clenched so tight it was difficult to get the words out. "It's not my fault. It's yours."

"Crap."

"Yes, it is. This is all on you." Karrig's temper was rising once more. "You were the one who couldn't let things lie. Couldn't just take your punishment and wait until we could go home. You had to rise to the bait. You couldn't resist it, could you?"

Haldred's voice rose in response, unable to let the accusation lie. "You'd have done the same. I should never have been exiled in the first place."

"Yeah, but it wasn't me who made that stupid wager. It wasn't me who pissed off his daughter."

"I was set up. Anyway, it wasn't me who tried to push our claim to grandfather's gold."

Karrig snorted, and his face twisted. He leaned across the table, his voice an angry hiss. "That gold is mine. Ours. With that ring, we could overthrow Mótsognir and his whole corrupt and feeble rabble. We could take the throne ourselves." Gold lust burned in his veins, his eyes wide. He felt a pulse throbbing in his temple and froze. There was no point following that train of thought, no matter the extent of the injustice he felt. Karrig pinched the bridge of his nose and tried to calm the torrent in his head. He took a deep breath, then turned his hostility back towards his brother. He'd heard all the denials many times, and Haldred's refusal to accept fault always infuriated him, almost as much as his refusal to throw his weight behind his push to reclaim Hreidmar's gold. He folded his arms, scowling, his appetite gone.

Amid the background hubbub of the bar, an uneasy silence settled between them. Haldred was first to break it, calmer now. He placed his hands on the table, either side of his plate, his voice quiet.

"Leave it. If we get Loki off our backs, we can chase the gold, if you like. I'll be happy to stand with you on that. But first things first. Like I said, I need your help. I can't do this without you."

"Piss off."

"I mean it. Look, I'll make it up to you. I'll even give you a bigger share of the money."

Karrig paused, suspicious. He knew he should just walk out. Leave and never look back. Try to avoid Haldred for the rest of his life. But he wondered how long that might be. Without Haldred, he had no one to watch his back. No one to protect him from the Trickster's devious servants, the truth-twisting vermin that poisoned discourse, plotted against the truth and tracked down the enemies of the warped god beneath. Nor would there be any protection from the dwarf king's spies.

He weighed the options in his mind, but there were no good solutions. If he walked out and his brother let it slip that he was no longer onboard, he'd be a wanted man. If he stayed in their mutually antagonistic relationship, he'd hate every hour, day, year it kept him away from his rightful inheritance, and the titles and power that went with it. But at least he'd be able to fill the empty days with earthly distractions, transient as they were. He drummed his fingers on the table top, unaware he was doing so.

Haldred appeared to sense his dilemma. For the first time, he sounded conciliatory, although also weary and resigned. "It was a long time ago. How was I to know she had an allergy to were-gold?"

Instead of soothing Karrig, his brother's words poured petrol on the flame. Incensed, and seeking someone else to blame, he leaned forwards again, his voice little more than an anguished hiss.

"It was an allergy to the spell you put on it. Not the gold itself."

Haldred looked uncomfortable. Karrig pressed on, beside himself in his rage.

"I can't believe you were so stupid." He tapped a finger on the side of his head. "I mean, are you fucking mental or what? Trying to trap her with a love charm. Her, of all people?" His face lit up with righteous anger, his own struggle with greed forgotten in the joy of scoring points.

"It wasn't a love charm. It was a Makers Spell. For the Fire Serpent itself. But what would you know?"

Despite his fury, Karrig didn't have a response. He suspected it was a lie, but even he felt the fierce love of craft intrinsic to all of their kind: the desire to imbue the items they made with a life force of their own; a life force forged in possessiveness, beauty, the avaricious love of everything precious, and above all, the desire to be adored. The allure of dwarf gold needed no further explanation. It burned in his heart alongside that long-standing sense of injustice.

They both knew the rest; it didn't need saying. They'd been forced to leave Nidavellir and flee to Midgard following Karrig's failed attempt to plead for their mother's inheritance: the cursed hoard. Any chance of returning from exile was finally sabotaged by Haldred's fateful pact. Each was guilty in his own way. Neither accepted it was his fault: they both blamed the other, but here in Midgard, they were forced to rely on each other to survive. Their symbiosis was founded on a poison that infected both of them.

Behind it all, beneath the greed, plots and counter-plots, Karrig yearned for his home, but who was there to listen to any plea for clemency? Odin and Co. had forsaken these parts for centuries now, and there was no one left to appeal to. No one whose mercy he could rely on. He was lost. They both were.

At least Haldred looked equally miserable. With a sigh, Karrig relented.

"Okay, so hit me with it. What's the target?"

Haldred brightened. "Haven't you been listening? Like I said, it's another icon. It's a repeat. Varlaam monastery again; we were so close. You know the way in this time, and they'll never expect a second theft just a few weeks after the first. *Saint Nicolas of Myra*, like I said. You're good at this. It'll be a piece of cake." Karrig stared blankly as the words finally sank in, leaving a cold dread in their wake.

The sulky waitress reappeared and dumped a small plate containing a chocolate cupcake on the table between them, a single red and white candle alight on its crown.

"Happy birthday," she said in a sullen voice, before departing.

Haldred looked after her for a moment, then back to his brother, a stupid grin on his face.

"Result," he exclaimed.

Karrig hid his head in his hands.

CHAPTER 17
HEALTHCARE

Another day, another vehicle. This time Agent 73 crouched beneath a red four-door Nissan Micra, reflecting on his conversation with the large grey cat. She had certainly been persuasive. In fact, when she was speaking, everything seemed to make sense. Yes, of course, he was proud of Greece's cultural heritage. He absolutely wanted to protect and defend it and save precious artefacts from falling into the wrong hands, whatever they were. How could she doubt him? But now, forty-eight hours later, in broad daylight, he couldn't remember what culture meant, or what an artefact was. His horizons had shrunk back to the car park and its immediate vicinity and the valley below the monastery, down between the steep walls of rock.

His thoughts wandered there now. He should practise his hunting technique again, perhaps this evening. Without warning, but in all too familiar a fashion, his stomach rumbled. It growled at him, a twinge of discomfort intruding into his thoughts. Agent 73 shifted his position under the car and tried to ignore it.

What else had she said? Something about the village? Oh, yes. Food was on offer. Somewhere. He'd never ventured into the human settlement before. He'd always stayed up on the hill where it was safe. Did he feel brave enough to explore the warren of houses and buildings on some foolhardy mission to find food he could actually eat, rather than scraps flung in his direction or accidentally dropped? It seemed a preposterous idea, but then his stomach lurched again and the hunger pangs intensified. His body was doing its best to persuade him. Perhaps he should go. Soon. Today, even. But not right now. Something might turn up. Scraps from another careless human or maybe a kind one. It didn't really matter as long as it was edible.

Three hours and several cars later, he'd been given nothing. The afternoon was dragging on, and he couldn't concentrate on anything. He felt so hungry. He crawled out from under the latest vehicle – an Opel hatchback, metallic powder blue – and stretched to relieve the stiffness along his spine. An observer would have regarded him as pitifully thin. For Agent 73, however, it was just a normal day. Feeling lackadaisical was nothing new.

Come on. This was no good. He had to overcome his fear of the village sometime.

A short hop onto the wall, and a bigger leap down the far side, and to his surprise he found he'd made a decision. He descended the steep, rugged slope to the valley below using his favoured path. Summoning his courage, he turned his nose towards the town and set off.

All the way, a debate raged in his head. Did he dare? But… food!

What if he was attacked? Surely they all hated outsiders down there? But… food!

But he might die.

But he might get a full belly.

That would be no good if he was dead, although at least he'd die full and happy.

On it went: the argument between the opposing camps in his head. Call and response rattling around his brain, and before he'd reached any resolution, he had passed the first few houses.

The black cat sought shelter beneath a bush to scope out his surroundings. It all appeared quiet now, but where was everybody? He knew dogs lived here; he could often hear them when up in the hills. And he knew there were cats. He sometimes saw them venturing tentatively into his valley, but where were they? Agent 73 considered the type of cat that would put up with living so close to dogs and shuddered. They must be very forgiving, strong, brave, or just plain stupid. He hated dogs and always stayed well away from them; they could be unpredictable, but what about the local cats? He wasn't sure he wanted to meet any of them, either. Everyone he met up in the hills always said townies were selfish bastards. Smug, to boot, and even more territorial than usual. They didn't share. They could also be aggressive. Devious scum. He'd have to be on his guard every step of the way from here. It had been a stupid idea to come. Was he deluding himself to think there was readily available food down here? Doubts clouded his mind, and he almost turned back to go home.

He sat there for a while, dangling between the horns of his dilemma. Around him, shadows lengthened.

This was silly; he was talking himself out of it. He was an agent, for heaven's sake.

As if on cue, his stomach rumbled again, dispelling any remaining doubts. It was time to do something. After one last scan for danger signs, he ventured out from his hiding place, and onward into town. It was, perhaps, the bravest thing he'd ever done. By now, in late afternoon, the temperature was dropping, as was the sun. Agent 73 tried, but failed to remember the grey cat's directions. As he'd never ventured this far before, they hadn't made much sense in the first place. She said something about turning off the road to go between buildings, and a garden, whatever that was.

He despaired; the buildings looked confusing. They nearly all had gaps between them. What could she have meant? In growing desperation, he took the first side street he came to and followed it, hoping not to get lost. Thankfully, it was quiet. Too quiet for his liking; if there were enemies nearby, and he was pretty sure there were, he'd rather he could see them. His heart sank further when he realised this road was quite short. It ended not far ahead, where a large building blocked his path, matching those on either side. Nonplussed, he looked about him. This urban jungle felt too intense; too much. He'd only been here a few minutes and already he couldn't wait to get back into the hills. What a fool he'd been. He looked left and right. The buildings in this part of town all looked the same to him. On a whim, he took the first one on his right and squeezed through a narrow gap in the fence.

Agent 73 found himself in a small and tidy front garden, little more than a patch of grass surrounded by a few straggling shrubs, with a couple of low trees (or tall bushes, he couldn't really tell) alongside a wall to his right. He stopped in his tracks. There, part hidden by jutting branches set down on a bare patch of earth, were two huge silver bowls, one filled with interestingly scented food pellets, the other with water. Agent 73 paused for a moment to once more scan his surroundings for potential hostiles. He couldn't quite believe his luck. Turning back to the food, he set aside his doubts and delayed no more. For the first time in his life, Agent 73 tucked into a hearty square meal.

He ate and drank to his heart's content and then sat back, bloated. It was an unusual feeling and somewhat unpleasant; not at all what he had expected. There was nothing to be gained from setting off up into the hills straight away; he really wanted a nap. As he examined his feelings further, Agent 73 decided that being excessively full was far better than being empty. Another scan of the garden revealed no sign of interlopers who might try to steal his newfound treasure. It would be nice to keep this secret to himself. He wondered if he should do some scent marking to declare possession and claim territorial rights. The small black cat rose to his feet, slowly walked to the gate and gave it a quick spray of urine. He repeated the act on the corner of the house and once again on its doorstep, just to be sure. To be on the safe side, he marked the wall at the back of the garden – his new personal Eden – as well.

As he circumnavigated his domain, looking for a suitable sleeping place, he wondered if he really needed to live up in the hills. Perhaps he should relocate. This place seemed to have everything he needed. A vehicle drew up outside the property, causing Agent 73 to dart beneath the hedge alongside the front fence and hide, keeping as still as possible. A large human emerged and strode purposefully up the path to the front door, then went inside.

Good. It hadn't seen him. But it had taken no notice of his carefully laid territorial markers, either. Although from what little knowledge he'd gleaned about humans from his observations in the car park, such rude behaviour came as no surprise.

After a minute or two, he began to relax and think about that snooze, but then a second vehicle arrived and another human marched up to the door. Agent 73 raised his head slightly and watched it warily. This one didn't go inside but banged on the door, and when it opened, said something before retreating to the car. He watched it leave, but noticed that the door hadn't closed. Instead, the first human appeared, heading straight for him. He stood, prepared to flee, when it stopped a couple of metres away and crouched down making peculiar noises. Curiosity got the better of him, and he studied the face. Human facial expressions remained something of a mystery, but this one seemed to be trying to be friendly, holding its hand out towards him. He ignored the stupid sounds it was making and focused on the hand. It didn't contain any food, or anything useful, but he realised this human might be the one who filled the bowls, so perhaps it had some treats hidden on its person somewhere. He edged out from his hiding place and vectored towards it, one slow step at a time, sniffing and glancing up at its face, wary of any sudden change of expression or movement.

It could have been a beautiful moment, like the first encounter with aliens from another planet. The gradual emergence of trust, to be followed by some initial tentative efforts at communication and building understanding. Instead, his world went dark as a blanket was thrown over him from behind.

Infuriated, Agent 73 struggled to free himself, but became more entangled as his claws caught in threads of the material. He was scooped up and deposited into some kind of box. Thankfully, the blanket was removed, but before he could react and free himself, the lid of the box was slammed shut and locked. His protesting mew was ignored. He berated himself; what an idiot to trust these monsters. He had been far too complacent. Never, never, never trust a human! But for all his anger at his own stupidity, his outrage was about to be raised several notches.

The box was deposited in the rear mouth of the car, but at least there was some light coming in. He had time to briefly register it: a RAV4 off-roader, silver with black trim, now muddy. He'd sat underneath these things for most of his life, but this was the first time he'd had a ride in one, and he didn't like it. Excitement at the unexpected experience was low on his list of emotions, behind fear and anxiety, followed by more fear, mixed with a healthy dose of dread and a dollop of horror. It was a heady brew and had adrenaline pumping around his system in no time. On top of the biggest meal he'd ever had, it made him feel sick, a sensation exacerbated by the unexpected changes of direction.

Agent 73's inaugural car journey was, thankfully, a brief one. His box was picked up and taken into another building through a large, heavy door, then another, and finally a third, before being deposited on some kind of table. Then the horror started. The next few minutes were the worst of his life, and would remain etched into memory forever, or at least until the next such encounter.

The box was opened, but all trust had now gone and he stayed put. A gloved hand intruded into his space, and he attacked it before it could grab him. But his world tilted on its axis as the box was tipped up and gravity extracted him. Damn.

There were two of them, and the moment he appeared, the second oaf pinned him down by the back of his neck. He wriggled for all he was worth, but couldn't break the two-handed grip. The other one removed the box, and to Agent 73's horror, he was inspected. With two of them, he had no chance. One restrained him with appalling strength, the other systematically invaded his personal space in ways he couldn't begin to describe. He wriggled, bit, hissed and struggled, but his torturers were too strong. Twice he thought he'd broken free, only to be recaptured and held even more tightly. The small cat had no choice but to endure the ignominy of a full, highly personal examination. He was squeezed and prodded in his most private places, then had his mouth forcibly opened and his teeth studied and even scraped a little. He was briefly picked up and confusingly placed into a large stainless-steel basin, then held tightly once more and fiercely groomed with a vicious-looking metal comb. He looked on, aghast at the sight of all the fur the awful specimen of a human took from the contraption. That was *his* fur! His torturers inspected it in the way a seer might study entrails. They exchanged messages; were they egging each other on?

Worse was to come. With no warning, his tail was lifted and something cold shoved into his anus. Agent 73 snarled and told them what he'd do to them, their children and their children's children, but they ignored him. Even that didn't satisfy them. Still held in their deadly grip, something sharp was jabbed into the scruff of his neck and he felt a cold substance trickle into his body. It was an unpleasant sensation, but whatever it was immediately began to dissipate. What had they done to him? Something was dabbed onto the back of his neck, and again there was an injection, but this one was different. Less painful, but it left something there permanently. What was it? One of them held some kind of device a few centimetres above his head and once more spoke in their strange babbling language.

"Alpha, gamma, epsilon…"

Then it made some marks in a book, while he looked on in helpless frustration. Finally, his head was tilted up, his lips and teeth parted, and something dropped down his throat. Poison? A sleeping draught? He tried, but couldn't regurgitate; the fiends held him close while one of them stroked his throat until he swallowed.

At long last, the box reappeared, and he could retreat into its dark interior to gather his thoughts and forge plans for devastating revenge upon the entire human race. What sort of sorcery and evil magic was practised in this hideous place? The intelligence he'd gathered through this ordeal was important, he felt certain. If he survived, he should tell someone. He'd have to get the news out before anyone else was made to suffer such an awful fate.

Beyond the confines of his portable prison cell, the two human witches discussed his treatment for a few minutes more, then he was taken back through the multiple doors to the car. For the first time in a while, a glimmer of hope sparked. Perhaps he would survive. His heart rate slowed.

Finally, to his intense relief, he was returned to the garden and released. He looked around, blinking in the brighter light and wary of the tall humans standing above him. He was about to run for cover when he spotted a calico cat lounging on the small patch of grass to his right. She didn't seem to appreciate the danger she was in.

"Watch out," hissed Agent 73 as he darted past it in search of cover. "Get away from them. Escape while you can. Quick, or they'll get you. They're vicious. I only just survived." The other animal didn't move or display any signs of alarm. Beneath some overhanging vegetation, Agent 73 turned and hesitated, unsure how to mount a rescue of the poor dumb beast in the face of apparently insurmountable odds. Townies really were thick. The humans stepped back, then turned away. While he was pondering his next move, the other cat spoke to him.

"Hi, I'm Frederica, Agent 49. But you can call me Freddie." Agent 73 stared, dumbfounded. "They're not so bad when you get to know them. They have lots of food." Her eyes flicked to the silver bowls.

Agent 73 was now thoroughly confused. Was this creature a stooge? Part of their evil web of intrigue? Had she been in on the abduction from the start? Freddie calmly studied the scenery while Agent 73 vented his spleen over the vicious treatment to which he'd been subjected. After he'd run out of expletives, he calmed down a little.

"Relax," the other animal told him. "It's all part of the induction process. Didn't she warn you there was a health plan?"

CHAPTER 18
CAPTURED

Senses were tuned to the max, eyes fixed on the long grass beneath the dark foliage of the dimly outlined bush three metres in front of him. Ears were pricked, focused forward and straining to interpret and locate every sound, whiskers fanned to either side of his face, sensitive to any vibration in the still night air that might indicate movement. He had it covered. It was in there, somewhere. Any minute now it would be his, and his alone. Competition, an unwelcome thought, crept into a dark corner of his mind. Where did they come from, these annoying intruders? He didn't need anything clogging up his mental machinery right now, just as he was preparing to pounce. Nevertheless, that pesky inkling wouldn't let him be; it nagged at his conscious thought until he was forced to look. He was not going to look. He was staring with laser-like precision on the patch of vegetation in front of him, here in the valley on this moonlit night. But what if there was a competitor up there, biding its time and waiting to swoop and steal his prey from under his nose?

Damn, he'd have to check. He had no choice. Get it out of the way. Then he could concentrate properly. An imperceptible sigh, a glance up and to the right. A quick check of the branches of the nearby tree. Any owl-shaped shadows against the dark starlit sky? No. Good. Back to…

He wasn't the only one checking for movement. Simultaneously, the vole sensed its slim remaining chance to break for freedom and took it. Agent 73 reacted, pounced, missed. Just. He changed direction, anticipating his prey's zig-zag trajectory, and leaped. His target changed direction, too, but so did he, in mid-air. And again, he missed. A brief, desperate chase ensued, but longer legs and a lack of cover told, and he was victorious. He crunched down on bone; the vole was dead.

Agent 73 was slowly getting the hang of this hunting malarky. It still wasn't easy, but he was gradually perfecting his technique. The extra muscle power helped. Since discovering the food source at the edge of town – a cross between a restaurant for cats and the meeting place of the local agents of the CIT – he'd bulked up a bit. Enough to cover his ribs, at least. Hunger no longer maintained such a powerful hold on his daily routine; but there was, he had to admit, no real substitute for the thrill and satisfaction of the chase.

The small black cat settled down on the flattened patch of grass to enjoy his meal. But after only a few mouthfuls, he was distracted by movement and sound above. No owl this time, but the sound of someone trying to be quiet; the clink of metal, and slither of rope and slap of shoes on rock that identified another dangling human, swinging on the end of another of those long strings. He was closer than last time, although descending from a similar place. Perhaps this was a regular occurrence? The cat watched distractedly, fascinated by the way the man used his legs to walk backward down the cliff face, occasionally bouncing away from it. It was another baffling facet of human behaviour. Did they do this in the daytime as well?

A memory snagged at the back of his mind; he was meant to look out for something. What was it the big grey cat had been so interested in? Oh, yes. Bags. Was the human carrying a bag? He studied the silhouette of the descending figure afresh. It was hard to tell, although the figure's back was unusually shaped. It seemed to bulge outward. Was that a bag? It might be. Yes, definitely. It was a bag. Maybe. Why did she think it was important? What was in it? Driven by a combination of orders and his own natural curiosity, he stood and craned his neck to view the creature's landing, then edged forwards to get a better view.

Agent 73 paid close attention as the figure landed and began to disentangle itself from the string, then remove some sort of complicated strapping from its groin. Humans and their strange ways could be so fascinating sometimes, particularly when acting against type, like now in the middle of the night. This one was quite small, but perhaps the small ones were better at walking down cliff faces? It seemed strange that it tried to do so in the dark. Anyone knew they weren't a nocturnal species; not here in the countryside, anyway. He had no concept of what they got up to in their towns.

Meal forgotten, Agent 73 moved forwards, his attention now focused entirely on the human. It fussed around, patting itself, checking for something. The bag lay on the ground, momentarily unattended. What was in it that was so interesting to everyone? He crept closer, curiosity piqued. It was far too big for him to move, but it seemed to just have a loose flap at the top, and the opening was large enough for him to crawl inside. Perhaps a quick sniff and paw-prod to check out the contents? That would be good intelligence for his superiors. He might even get a commendation.

The man still seemed distracted, intent on pulling down the rope he'd just descended. Keeping half an eye on him, Agent 73 crept closer, crouching as flat against the ground as possible. Perhaps there was some food in there; something exotic but really tasty. That would be an unexpected bonus.

He couldn't think of anything better to keep in a bag, although the grey cat might not see it that way.

The noisy flapping of wings and rustling leaves to his left indicated a new arrival. Agent 73 stopped dead and twisted his head towards it. A huge black bird; a raven, perhaps. He'd seen such birds before, but not as big as this one.

"What do you think you're doing, shorty?"

The voice was cracked and harsh and loud in the quiet of the night, and the accent unfamiliar. Agent 73 froze, unable to move. This thing was easily big enough to pick him up in those hideous talons and carry him away to eat at leisure. He didn't consider that he could understand its speech. Never before had he paid attention to the strange squawks, caws and trills of birds. The cat looked for hiding places. Fortunately, the bird hadn't seen him yet.

"Don't call me shorty," snarled the man in a surprisingly abrasive voice, turning sharply to face the bird. "And keep your voice down. You don't know who might be watching." He glanced around, searching the edges of the clearing, but could see nothing in the shadows. Fortunately, his gaze swept across Agent 73 without noticing him.

"I'm watching, for one, and you'd better have a good explanation," said the raven.

"Well, it's none of your damn business, is it?"

"You can't take it to him. Give it to me."

With his eyes fixed on the bird, the short man stooped and extracted something from the bag. The cat, barely two metres away, froze, his body flat against the earth. The man swept a long bright metal thing from its enclosing sheath. It glistened in the moonlight. Agent 73 had never seen a sword before, and had no word to describe it, but this object looked dangerous, and he had an instinct it was sharp. His mouth was dry, but he couldn't take his eyes from it. The short man waved the sword at the raven, which sat on a branch, fixing him and the weapon with a dark, beady eye. There seemed to be a stand-off.

Agent 73 sensed a change in the air; a new scent, unfamiliar but potentially dangerous. He dared a glance behind. The shadows kept their secrets, but something was coming, panting and treading non-too silently. No escape would be possible in that direction. Where could he hide? The bag before him was the only option. He hoped it would mask his scent. With eyes focused upward on the sword-wielding man, and ears tilted behind towards the loud-breathing creature, the black cat crept closer, a centimetre at a time. He was no longer paying attention to the argument going on above him between the man and the raven; the greater threat was from behind. Why hadn't they heard it?

"You don't know the half of it. Anyway, it's not up to you to tell me what I do with my time."

At the lip of the bag, he paused, hypnotised by the tip of the sword as it described small circles in the air. The light of the moon was reflected many times over along the length of its blade, so much that it seemed infused with light. He saw intricate patterns that he had no words to describe; beautiful and strange. He swallowed, then recommenced his crawl towards the safety of the bag's interior. Above him, the debate continued. Behind him, the panting got louder, the scent more pungent.

"There will be consequences," was all the bird said.

"Oh, yes. I know all about them. I've lived with them for centuries."

By now, Agent 73 was beside the bag. He nosed beneath the flap and slipped into the inviting darkness, then burrowed underneath something hard and rectangular until he came up against softer material that smelled, not unpleasantly, of sweat and body odour. He tunnelled underneath this, too, and prayed he hadn't been spotted.

From his hiding place, Agent 73 wondered what was

happening, but he didn't dare move. He pondered the strange scents inside the bag, but couldn't identify them. Instead, he strained his ears to catch what he could of the continuing conversation.

"It's not too late. Talk to us, and we can help. He is sympathetic to your situation and can offer protection. Help to heal the anguish in your heart. Why give succour to your tormentor? He who destroyed your family all those years ago?"

There was a pause. When he spoke, the cat detected a raw edge to the man's voice.

"What does your master care of my family? What succour has he offered down the centuries of exile? If he was concerned about our welfare, why didn't he get in touch years ago? No. It's too late."

"It's never too late. Think. This is your chance to break the bonds of slavery. To be free once more. To break from he who brought doom to your family all those years ago." In the depths of the bag, Agent 73 strained his ears, but the man said nothing. The bird continued. "Be quick. His agents are closing in. Give me the bag before they get here, and I will distract them so you can escape."

The man seemed to consider his options.

"Which one are you?"

A longer pause. The bird seemed reluctant to reply. "Huginn."

"Well, you can tell your master it's too late. I've got a commission. Now, if you'll fly off, I can be on my way." The cat could detect anger and bitterness in the voice, subtleties he'd never detected in human speech. Why had he never paid attention to what they said until now? He chose not to dwell on the fact; he was grateful to be out of sight, and his bigger concern was staying alive.

· · ·

Down in town Haldred sat in the car, just like last time, and tried to keep his nerves in check. This one should be smoother. Karrig now knew what to expect. They'd been over the layout of the buildings on the summit several times, and his brother was certain that he could bypass the security system once again. Neither of them had detected any sign of an upgrade, and on his reconnaissance visit Haldred could not see any signs of work. They had checked and rechecked the plan and the timings, and it seemed straightforward enough for a burglar with Karrig's skills. He closed his eyes and forced himself to remain calm.

On the opposite side of the rock, a large wolf waited. She looked at the buildings on the summit, but could see nothing. The night was progressing. Surely the thief must be emerging by now. She wasn't here to intercept him; just to make sure the package was extracted and sent on the first leg of its journey safely. She would only be forced to intervene if the burglar and his accomplice did something unusual, or a third party intervened. The chances of that happening were extremely small.

Someone else would take over the next leg; most likely someone with wings. This theft was important to those at the top; it would be tracked every step of the way. The Supreme Pack Leader wouldn't allow another cock-up, or so she'd been told. Watch and report back, they'd said. Don't let them see you: stay out of sight. So far, nothing had happened. But it was too quiet. Doubt nagged at her thoughts. Perhaps she should have a look around…

Groping in the dark, sniffing out her route, she circumnavigated the monastery. The ground was uneven, and the vegetation dense, slowing her progress. She made her way north, then headed east, and heard raised voices. Suspicion drew her closer.

A large wolf is not the stealthiest of animals, and she was sufficiently self-aware to realise the fact. She had to maintain some distance if she was to remain undetected, but her eyes and ears were sharp. The wolf tried to pant more quietly as she edged forwards; sounds seemed somehow amplified in this narrow valley with its vertical rock walls. What she saw stopped her in her tracks. It was the thief, but what was he doing? He held a gleaming, bright sword, but seemed to be talking to someone. At his feet lay the equipment he'd used in his climb: rope, harness, his backpack. Then she saw it: an enormous raven, sitting on a low branch which bent under its weight. It was arguing with the dwarf.

There was movement at his feet. A small creature stealthily crawled into the bag. A cat, she realised with a sneer; one of those small, insufferably smug little parasites that hung around with humans, manipulating them with their so-called charm. The dwarf ignored it. What was it doing? Was it assisting him or just in the wrong place at the wrong time? The dwarf became agitated and brandished his sword at the bird. She recognised it and a knot of primeval fear took root in her stomach. The glint of the blade, shining in the gloom, reflected the thin light from the moon above, and she saw the patterns along its length. Moon Carver, it was called, and it was said to be sharp enough to draw blood from the wind. Many of her kind had tasted its steel in bitter disputes in the past, and she was not minded to join their number.

She watched as the dwarf clumsily shoved his gear into his bag with one hand, while his attention remained focused on the bird, his sword raised. He slung the bag over his shoulder and set off down the hillside. The raven continued to argue but also stayed well out of range of the blade. The wolf smelled treachery, but there was still a chance he was following orders. Staying a safe distance behind, she followed him down the track until he reached the road.

. . .

From the claustrophobic dark of the bag, Agent 73 wondered what was going on. There were a few metallic clinks and noises he couldn't place. Maybe the man was packing his things away. Had the argument stopped? The flap opened and a coiled rope was thrust on top of him, followed by some bits of metal and stiff wire. With a lurch, the bag was lifted and hoisted over a shoulder, and the items settled around him. There was a squeeze as the man patted it, checking the contents were in place. Then, to his horror, the flap opened once more, only for a pair of gloves to be dropped inside. He hardly dared to breathe. The cat was squashed between a large rectangular object, a smelly glove and the coiled rope, but one of the bits of metal was sticking into a leg, and it hurt. Agent 73 tried to free his paw while swinging on the man's shoulder and regularly crunching into his back. The rectangular thing was dusty; he sneezed. The pain in his leg began to subside and to his surprise he found the conversation outside was continuing. He strained his ears, but could only hear snatches.

"…taking it?"

"Better you don't…"

"You know I will tell him everything. He wants to know your… if you won't…"

"…got my orders."

"He can…"

"…trust you…"

The volume rose in line with tempers. It was clear these two were wary of each other. Agent 73 couldn't make out anything further. He lurched around some more as the man moved, apparently over uneven ground, and started to regret his hiding place. Feeling hot and nauseous, and repeatedly sandwiched between the man's back and the bag's contents, the journey became unbearable. Each sharp squish took his breath away. Fortunately his whimpering squeaks were inaudible to those outside.

With a pang of regret, he remembered his abandoned supper, but the thought of food made his stomach lurch. His thoughts, instead, turned to where he might be taken. Perhaps this hadn't been the best choice of hiding place.

The movement calmed down a little, and he could hear more snatches of conversation from outside.

"Shoo! Go away! I've told you; I'm not interested. Stop…"

"…peck your eye out…"

"…ever threaten me…"

"…better have a good excuse…"

"…owe him anything. Nobody follows him any… of touch… powerless… stronger elsewhere… irrelevant… when was the last time…"

"Now sod off."

There was a whooshing sound, as if something was being swung around quickly. The cat remembered the long, bright metal object. Was it being brandished? The bag swayed alarmingly on the man's shoulder as he moved.

"…tasted this before…"

A frustrated caw, then silence. Agent 73 felt momentarily weightless as the man swung the bag over his shoulder – then squashed, as it landed on a hard surface with the rectangular thing on top of him, taking his breath away. Momentarily winded, he let out a small squeak of pain and surprise, but fortunately no one seemed to hear. He was further pinned down as additional items were dumped on top of the bag, then a slamming sound cut off all exterior noise. After a moment, he dared to move, flexing his legs to try to free his body and get some room. Fortunately, the bag wasn't tied too tightly, so he poked his nose out, then his head, only to find to his dismay that he was in total darkness. He must be in some kind of container. He lurched sideways as it moved. A car! But a silent one. Different from those he knew from his car park or his previous journey down in town. He'd been kidnapped. Agent 73 lay down in the darkness and assessed the situation. Being a secret agent wasn't all fun and food. His career had taken a decidedly dangerous turn. Where was he being taken, and how long would he have to put up with this awful prison? Above all, what was a man doing talking to a raven, and how come he'd understood them?

After the car left, the raven flew away, and the wolf emerged onto the road. She watched the tail lights disappear around a bend, heading north into the hills. The dwarf had double-crossed his friend, waiting in his car down in the town. Something had gone wrong. Was he working with the cat? Was it delivering him new orders, or acting on its own? The way it had crept into the bag with the stolen object made her suspicious. No one had ever mentioned cats being involved in this, so what was it doing? It was imperative that she reported back as soon as possible. Her pack leader would know what to do.

Down in Kastraki, Haldred became more agitated by the minute. What had happened? He tried phoning his brother, but it just rang out. Where was he? As the eastern sky grew lighter, he began to despair. The scale of his problem dawning simultaneously with the new day.

CHAPTER 19
THE ORACLE OF ACHERON

Apollo was closer now. He could sense it, hear it, but still the river proved elusive. In this land of tall trees and trackless hills, progress was slow. What Apollo hoped would stem from this strange pilgrimage, he wasn't sure; he just felt compelled to try. He travelled mainly by night in an attempt to evade Zeus' many spies in the air and on the ground, and it seemed to have worked, although his success at avoiding detection left a lingering residue of concern. It had been too easy, and he was not yet ready for a confrontation with his father.

Early one morning, as daylight penetrated beneath the canopy, he spied his target below, at the bottom of a steep wooded slope, winding its way through the hills in search of the Adriatic. The Acheron, River of Woe, one of the great rivers of the Underworld, emerged above ground among the mountains of remote Epirus, and carved a deep canyon before bursting through to the flat lands on its way to the sea. Apollo stared at it and let the sound of rushing water seep into his consciousness. His nostrils flared to embrace the myriad scents of the wet rocks, mosses, ferns and trees, the flowers and grasses along the banks. He closed his eyes and allowed their fragrance to drown his senses.

What did he hope to discover? Now that he'd arrived, he couldn't really say why he had come. He had been acting on instinct, seeking absolution for sins too many to count; sins his fellows steadfastly ignored. As if proud of their guilt, they remained shame-free and defiant, rarely striving to attain the standards of civilised behaviour they valued in everyone else. Apollo could no longer bear the hypocrisy. He needed to find his own path to absolution. Perhaps this river was the starting point.

Standing on the riverbank, he looked along its length in each direction, then slowly, purposefully, stepped into the water, pushing against its strong tow, heading into the middle of the stream. At this point in its course, the Acheron was wide but not deep, although it was more than deep enough to cover him. The water was clear and cold, the riverbed stony, with many rocks breaking the surface. Half swimming, half walking across the uneven riverbed, his progress was slow.

At the midpoint, Apollo stopped and pointed his nose upstream – the water breaking around his chest just below his chin – oblivious to the piercing chill. He paused for a long moment, then ducked down and dived into the shallow pool before him. Below the surface, the sunlight reflected the trees lining the banks, and gave the water a greenish hue.

He tried to empty his mind of conscious thought. Would the cleansing flow erase his sorrow and wash it downstream behind him? On that, the river god stayed silent, avoided his clear-eyed stare and refused to engage.

After a long while, Apollo broke the surface and shook his head violently. He regained his footing and slowly made his way to the opposite bank. To his disappointment, he felt no different. The ennui and sadness remained etched into the fabric of his being; how could he ever escape it?

He looked up.

A small brown cat waited for him on the shore.

"I am the Oracle of Acheron," she announced. "Oracle of the Dead."

Apollo gave the cat a cursory glance, then shook himself from nose to tail, releasing the water in his fur. He walked past, almost brushing the other animal with his flank, and lay, sphinx-like, on a small green mound behind it.

He closed his eyes and tried to ignore the creature. To his annoyance, she didn't leave. If he wanted to get some time to himself, he would have to hear her out, or chase her away. Tempting though it was, the day was warm, and he was in no mood to run. Through narrowed eyes, he studied her: small, neat, well-groomed and far too relaxed in his company for his liking.

"What have you come to tell me?" he said, his golden eyes now focused.

The Oracle sat up, maintaining a respectful distance, but didn't answer his question directly.

"This is the River of Absolution, in which the dead bathe to relieve their pain. It helps them to ease their sorrows. Its power is diminished above ground. I can only hear a faint echo of their voices."

"I am aware of that."

"Then you must know it is only of benefit to the shadows of the dead. You are not dead."

He realised by now that immersing himself in the River of Woe had not worked; the dull ache in his heart was just the same as before, but he had no desire to be lectured on what he could or could not do. With eyes opened just a little wider, he continued to stare at the Oracle, and in a cold voice, changed the subject.

"Why have you waylaid me?"

"Your arrival was foreseen. I come to greet you, and share some news."

"Foreseen? By whom?"

The Oracle glanced over her shoulder, as if looking at something beneath the shadow of the trees. She turned back, hesitating. "I have some gift of foresight." The golden-eyed stare was more piercing now: she had Apollo's full attention.

"Explain."

Again, the faltering response. Oracle or not, her loyalties were apparently divided.

"I come from the Necromanteion of Acheron, not far from here. Maybe you have forgotten, but beneath the temple is a gateway to the Underworld, the realm of my Lord Hades and his queen."

Apollo said nothing. Any memory of the temple had long since been erased, but at the back of his mind, he was annoyed. This Oracle was far too independent of thought for his liking. He narrowed his eyes and pinned her with his stare, as if trying through willpower alone to see inside her head. The cat squirmed and gave a protesting squeak, but couldn't turn away.

"What did they tell you, the guardians of the dead?" he asked.

The Oracle uttered one last squeal, then became still. Its reply was delivered in a monotone. "I was sent to give you a warning." Apollo raised his head imperceptibly, his eyes boring into her. "In Hades' realm, rumours of change abound; the future, once fixed, is no longer certain. It is being remade." He waited while the other struggled to organise her thoughts. "But not by us." Having spoken, the cat became silent.

He refused to dismiss her. "Continue." Although gently delivered, it was a command. The Oracle shivered, hesitated, then spoke once more.

"I see a web shake as the spider awakes; the threads tremble as the pieces move. Unquiet spirits are shaken from slumber. I see a once-imprisoned giant walking free. Thought-weaver, lie-spinner, dream-twister. Grimólfr is his name.

And…" Her eyes closed, and she tried to swallow, unable to continue. Apollo held his breath, still fixated on the animal before him. After a moment, the Oracle stirred once more and looked him in the eye.

"I see a dynasty brought low by poison on the breath of the wind. One by one, alone they fall, each sundered from their kin. In their place reigns chaos. And from chaos comes the end of all gods. All this is yet to come, and some of it may still be averted, but there is greater peril ahead for you, Apollo, Son of Zeus." She faltered. An unnatural hush enveloped the glade while Apollo held her in his grip, staring deep into her soul.

"Continue," he said in a low growl.

"A taste that heralds destiny, you seek.

Down path foretold, a road forewarned,

Guarded, gated, dark, unlit.

The guardians? Those unjustly slain,

In pursuit of what?

Fair justice, or a jealous fit?

But know this, mighty lord of fate:

The lies you sowed, the lives destroyed,

Await you in the dark, ahead."

Finally he relented and released the spell, and the small animal collapsed onto her side, panting.

A minute passed, then another. Slowly, the Oracle rose to her feet, unsteady and with tail shaking. She looked around the clearing, her eyes stopping on the ginger and white cat before her. "Where am I? Who are you?"

"A friend," was all he said, then lowered his head onto his paws again and closed his eyes. The small brown cat gave him a fleeting glance, shook her head, then hurried away without looking back. Once more he gave his mind up to birdsong, insects and the sound of rushing water.

· · ·

"What are you doing here? Did you fancy a dip? I thought you'd know bathing in the Acheron doesn't work for immortals." A large white cat emerged from behind a tree close to the riverbank. Apollo yawned in irritation and scratched behind an ear. An hour's snooze was nowhere near enough to prepare for verbal jousting with Hermes. He gave the new arrival a small nod of greeting and looked the other way, unwilling to explain his motives; he didn't really understand them himself. The white cat drew closer and sat down on a comfortable patch of grass to admire their surroundings.

"It's very peaceful around here. Quite secluded." He gave his companion a sidelong glance. "At least you've escaped the hustle and bustle of real life for a while. What a good place to recharge your batteries."

Apollo could never quite tell if the messanger god was being sarcastic or not. He tried to ignore him, letting the sound of the water and the creatures of the forest wash over him once more. Hermes broke the spell, sounding a little more business-like.

"Trouble is, you can't hide here forever. You'll be spotted eventually, and apart from that, Athena's got a job for you." He gave the ginger-and-white cat an apologetic glance. "If you're willing, of course," he added.

"What does she want?"

The white cat shifted its position and resumed. "The Meteora, Thessaly. The place with all the monasteries perched on clifftops." He glanced across to check the other animal was paying attention. "They've had a spate of robberies recently. Artworks. Icons. Portraits of Him or his followers." He still couldn't bring himself to utter the name Jesus. "Anyway, they're priceless cultural treasures stolen, presumably, to order. But by who? We don't know."

Apollo studied his companion, still struggling to concentrate. "Does it matter?"

"Maybe. Maybe not. We need to work that out. But in the

meantime, we need to find out what's happening and where they are being taken. If we can follow the trail, we can find out why, and put a stop to it."

The ginger cat looked across the river again. "Does she want me to go on a wild goose chase?" He sounded distracted, his thoughts still elsewhere.

"No. She'd like you to go over and talk to our local agents, help organise them a bit, motivate them. She's recruited a decent local network, but they're probably in need of guidance. They're all raw, and she fears they might have missed some clues. What do you say?" He looked at his friend expectantly.

Apollo met his eyes. "I don't mind going, but it's a long way just to deliver a pep talk."

"Do you have anything more pressing right now?"

Apollo said nothing. Hermes stood, ready to leave. "Oh, one more thing. Olympia's had her litter. They're bright, lively little things. A couple of them even have your colouring: they're inseparable. I think she's called them Ion and Delphos. She said to say hi."

Apollo stared into the distance for a moment. Olympia hadn't entered his thoughts for a long time; the antics of the Athenian gangs seemed to distant now, both trivial and inconsequential, but just for a moment a ray of light broke through to lift his mood.

"*Ion and Delphos*. I like that." He forced himself to move. "Okay, I'll get moving after dark. See what I can find." He set off deeper into the woods to find somewhere to sleep where he wouldn't be disturbed.

CHAPTER 20
BETRAYED

Fear, worry and fury combined with a feeling of helplessness. It all gnawed at Haldred's insides and fogged his thoughts. He sat in the car, next to a wall at the side of Memorial Park in Kastraki, staring out of the windscreen but not seeing anything; a seething mass of indecision. The eastern sky grew brighter, adding to his dismay. Something had gone wrong. He needed to act, but what should he do?

Haldred got out of the car, closing the door as quietly as he could, and walked up the road towards the towering pillars of rock, and the Monastery of Varlaam. He left the last houses of the village behind and strode on in the gloom another few hundred metres. He was close to the monastery now. The path climbed steadily to the main road that snaked between the rock towers. Opposite, the ground was steeper and more rugged, and the path narrower, but he was close now; only a hundred metres from the target. Where was Karrig? Craning his neck, Haldred could see the walls of the monastery against the lightening sky, but could detect no sign of movement. He paused and listened. The dawn chorus had begun, but there were no other sounds. No footsteps, heavy or otherwise, no crunch of loose gravel underfoot, or rustle of backpack or metallic clink of climbing gear. Nothing apart from the birds.

Anxiety knotting his stomach, he turned back, descending into the village. Before he arrived, he held onto the brief hope that he would find Karrig waiting impatiently by the car, armed with a sarcastic barb or two, but he had no such luck. Haldred's heart sank. By now the sun was illuminating the peaks, and it crept down the rock face, the town below basking in a reflective glow. Shutters were being opened, and people would soon emerge, ready for work or school. Haldred felt exposed. It was time to move the car. His hands clammy on the steering wheel, he drove to the main street in neighbouring Kalabaka. At least he felt more anonymous here, the battered Dacia at home amid other similarly dusty, rusty vehicles with their chipped and dented paintwork: the scars of automotive life.

Haldred pondered his next moves. His insides churned, but not with hunger. Dread had killed his appetite. What could have happened? Either his brother had stolen the painting, or he hadn't. If he'd succeeded, where was he? If not, had he been apprehended and turned over to the authorities, or had he fallen to his death while trying to flee? Haldred took out his phone and searched through the mapping system to try and locate the nearest police station. He should try to get close, to observe and spot any unusual activity. This was a quiet agricultural community, not a hotbed of crime, so any arrest for theft up at one of the monasteries should surely be a major operation for them? Equally, if Karrig had fallen, there would be some sign of emergency response teams scouring the area? Unless no one had yet noticed. He'd heard no sirens, which, he supposed, was a good thing.

He put the car in gear and followed the directions on his phone. It proved tricky to find a suitable place for quiet observation of the front entrance, but fortunately he had binoculars in the back of the car. He parked down the street and retrieved his pack from the trunk. For the next hour, he alternated between observing the police station and probing his laptop for information, searching local news items, or trying to find messages containing relevant keywords. For good measure, he searched for news of any activity by the emergency services overnight. The whole process was painfully slow. Across the course of his overlong life, he'd become fluent in seven major languages, but Greek was not one of them, and he was forced to rely on patchy translation software.

The search proved to be a dead end, and the inactivity at the police station began to get to him. When did the monastery open to tourists? He needed to get up there and have a look for himself. A quick check online told him he still had forty-five minutes to wait. It seemed longer. He gritted his teeth and slumped in his seat. After an interminable wait, he finally judged the time right to drive up to the monastery; he didn't want to get there too early.

When he arrived, he was the second vehicle in the car park. Ahead of him was a blue and white police car. From the wall, a mangy brown cat eyed him. There was no other sign of activity. The police car was empty, its occupants up on the rock. It was the first sign he'd seen that something had happened. Would they delay opening?

After a few minutes a large tour bus arrived, disgorging thirty or more tourists, cameras at the ready. They busied themselves wandering around, teasing the cats, who appeared as if by magic, and photographing each other standing before the monastery and the surrounding hills. A tour leader finally got their attention, and they congregated at the far end of the path leading to the monastery. Haldred decided there was safety in numbers, and joined the back of the group.

Once inside the complex, he made a beeline for the

church, where he found a policeman and monk deep in conversation. Both looked up in exasperation. He was obviously not welcome. The policeman walked towards him, ushering him out. Haldred pretended not to understand, and the policeman addressed him in English.

"You must leave. The church is closed to visitors."

"But..."

"No exceptions. A sign should have been put up." He moved closer, arms outstretched, shepherding him to the door. Looking past him, Haldred could make out a gap at the lower corner of the iconostasis, where a painting should have been.

"Why?" he managed.

Behind the policeman, the monk confirmed what he already knew. "We have suffered a theft." He looked mournful. "This is a sad day."

Haldred gave in and retreated outside. So, his brother had, at least, obtained the painting, and had got away. The news didn't make him feel any better. Where was he? He hurried down the rock-cut stairs back to the lower level. Then, on a whim, he made a detour off the path to explore the ground below the monastery. He had no real idea what he was looking for, but after a while he found a small clearing where the ground seemed to have been disturbed, a low shrub flattened and a branch of a small tree broken off. There were a few footprints on the soft earth. Haldred looked up. It was close to the rock face; a credible landing area. More worryingly, he noticed, it was not far above the road he'd crossed earlier, and he could see the path snaking back towards Kastraki. Why had his brother not taken it?

He descended to the road and stood there, looking along in both directions. A horrible thought grew at the back of his mind. Had he been picked up by someone? Had he left a car here, waiting? No way. He'd been in Karrig's company for days in the lead-up to this. They'd spent a lot of time meticulously planning and organising the theft, and for the last forty-eight hours, they'd been virtually inseparable.

Except for yesterday afternoon.

Haldred stood rooted to the spot as it came back to him. A car tooted as it sped by. He realised he was standing halfway into the road and pulled back. In the middle of the afternoon, Karrig had told him he needed to stretch his legs and get some air. He'd been gone over two hours.

The thought of betrayal almost choked him. Ice fire flowed in his veins, and his anger exploded. He let back his head and howled in rage, not caring who might be in earshot. Then he turned back to the hillside track and retraced his steps to the car, the effort of climbing soaking up some of the venom. In his pack, he had a large paper map of this part of the country. He unfolded it across the hood and tried to calm down. Now was not a time to vent his anger; he needed a cool head. Where would Karrig have gone? What were his options? He felt it likely he'd choose a different escape route to last time, so that probably ruled out Albania. Would he dare a long ferry trip with the police, potentially paying more attention to passengers? Unlikely. He'd probably head north and try to cross the border somewhere quiet. With a six- or seven-hour start, he'd be close by now, or maybe already abroad? There was a flapping of wings and the largest black bird he'd ever seen skidded to a halt on the roof of the car with a loud *kark*.

Haldred stood up and waved his arms at it, but the bird stood its ground then shuffled sideways, struggling for purchase on the smooth metal, fixing him with a sideways look. Its size was intimidating, and at eye level, its sharp beak merely added to Haldred's unease. As it shuffled forwards, he took a step back.

"You'll be wanting directions."

Haldred frowned and stepped back. "Clear off." He looked about the car park, but it was sparsely populated.

News of the theft had apparently put visitors off. He gave the bird a suspicious look. "How come you can speak?"

"Your brother was quicker on the uptake."

Haldred glared at it. "What do you know? Have you seen him?"

"He was here last night."

Haldred looked around again, now more concerned that there might be eavesdroppers; but they were alone. "What do you know?"

The bird shuffled sideways, claws scratching the roof. "I am Huginn. I make it my business to know. And I know he's heading north. He must have crossed the border by now. You have no time to lose."

"Which border? Where?"

The raven spread its wings, preparing to depart. "North Macedonia." He rose into the air. Before Haldred could say anything, the raven was nothing but a distant dot on the horizon.

Haldred stared after it, then scanned the map, looking for the nearest border crossing and his brother's likely route. He scrunched it up and threw it into the car, climbed in behind the wheel and set off for North Macedonia, his mind in a whirl as he tried to understand what had just happened. Everything that came to mind just made his situation worse. Huginn was bound to Odin. Haldred's knuckles whitened as he gripped the wheel. He felt sick, his breathing shallow. What did Odin know of his mission? How long had he been under observation? If the bird was to be trusted, he had a direction, at least, but his pursuit still felt futile, and the last thing he wanted was to become a pawn in a contest between two such dangerous gods.

CHAPTER 21
A JOURNEY IN THE DARK

Agent 73 had expected noise, but he was surprised at how quiet it was in the womb-like interior of the car's boot. The vehicle rattled and squeaked as metal ground against metal or plastic, or the suspension cracked over potholes. But there was no engine noise. He was surprised. He couldn't work it out.

Having spent a large proportion of his waking life beneath cars of all shapes and sizes, 73 was familiar with the roaring, rumbling sound they made when turned on. This one was different. Was it magic of some kind? He chose not to dwell on it. Instead, he felt out his surroundings with the senses available to him, sight being useless in this impenetrable dark. The first task was to escape from the bag in which he'd been hiding. Fortunately, he could easily push his way out. A thought struck him, and he nosed his way back inside, burrowing in the dark to find the outline of the rectangular object he'd been sitting on. He felt it important to scent mark the thing, just in case. A quick squirt here and a rub of his chin and forehead there, and it was done. If he came across it anytime in the next few weeks he'd recognise it instantly, even though he'd not yet seen it.

Satisfied, he re-emerged from the claustrophobic enclosure to the darker-than-night luggage compartment. At least there was a little more air in here. The sudden changes of direction left him momentarily unbalanced, so he learned to crouch next to the bag and react as the vehicle swung back and forth on twisty roads and sharp bends. As he adjusted to the movement, he wondered how long this journey in the dark would last. But he didn't want to think about where he would end up. He told himself it was too far in the future to contemplate. Instead, he tried to get as comfortable as possible amid the various items surrounding him.

It was difficult to relax among the chunky coils of rope, karabiner clips, nylon harness and a canvas bag that littered the trunk, but his wriggling created a moderately comfortable space, sufficient for him to curl up, head on paws and try to rest.

He closed his eyes, but sleep was impossible. Instead, his mind wandered, reminiscing on his lovely car park, his precious hunting zone in the valley between the towering cliffs, and whether he would ever see it again. Why had he agreed to take part in this foolish scheme? The huge raven loomed, unbidden, into his thoughts, his mouth suddenly dry at the recollection. Subconsciously, his claws flexed, though they would have been next to useless against that monster. It was the most frightening bird he'd ever seen. He hoped there weren't any more at his destination, wherever that proved to be. He tried to put the thought out of his mind as he drifted into uneasy sleep. Visions of raking talons and a harsh stabbing beak punctuated his dreams.

At long last, the sense of motion ceased. Agent 73 tensed, just as he had the time before, and the time before that. But this felt different. A siren wailed, getting closer. He'd occasionally heard sirens near his car park at home, but this one was higher in pitch, more urgent. It cut out, but 73 could still hear the roar of an engine; a normal growling engine of the kind he was used to. It seemed to be idling; not approaching or passing by, but keeping its distance.

A door slammed. Footsteps. Then a voice. Crouching in the dark, he heard the humans talk. He couldn't hear what they were saying, but the conversation seemed to be getting heated; an argument brewing.

A loud explosion made him jump, then freeze with fright. Outside he was dimly aware of shouts and a groan. Something heavy bumped against the car from the side, making it roll slightly. 73's claws clutched at the carpet lining the boot.

There was a second bang, not quite so loud, a little further away, and more shouting. Then more explosions behind him. Whatever was happening out there felt very dangerous. More shots. Then he heard a dull *thunk* just above his head and something whizzed by, far too close for comfort. Instinctively, he flattened his body against the floor. Light penetrated his prison, momentarily blinding him. 73 blinked a few times as his eyes adjusted. Outside, yet more loud shots fired. He shrank back as far as he could, as if an extra few centimetres would save him.

He heard glass shattering, a muffled shriek, one final bang, then silence. Was it over? He waited for further shots, but there were none. Instead, he heard footsteps as someone moved around outside. A car door opening and closing caused the car to shake again, then he felt movement. They were leaving.

Feeling braver, Agent 73 sniffed at the nearest hole, scenting cooling metal and traces of something else that wasn't familiar, but slightly acrid. He peeped through the hole and got the briefest glimpse of a man lying on the road, and, just before it disappeared round a bend, a brightly coloured car with blue lights flashing on its roof.

At least he now had some light entering his cell, and some fresh air. He could faintly detect the scent of pine trees and a hint of animals, probably goats. Where was he? How far from home? Was it still the same day? He suspected not, but he had no sense of how long he'd been imprisoned; it just felt like forever.

This section of his journey was more uncomfortable. The car sped up, and veered sharply from side to side as it twisted and turned along a narrow road, little wider than a track from what he could see to the rear. Clouds of dust obscured the view, and bumps lifted him off his feet. Agent 73 crouched, trying to regain some stability, and blinked his eyes against the particles. The road became even more bumpy, and he bounced up and down for quite a while. Then the terrain calmed down once more, and finally the car drew to a halt. The cat settled as far back in the luggage compartment as he could, fearing detection.

The light intensified as the car boot opened. Silhouetted against the glare, he initially sensed, rather than saw, a short man. At least he had an inkling what to expect. The man did not, and was startled to see a cat in the trunk of his car. He swore loudly and reached down towards 73, receiving a sharp bite on the finger as his reward. He shouted in pain and studied his hand; Agent 73 had drawn blood. Snarling, he balled his hand into a fist and jabbed down at the animal, but 73 was ready. He leaped sideways, bounced inelegantly off the side of the luggage compartment, then bounded for freedom, seeking the small gap between the edge of the car and the man's arms. His opponent was faster than 73 expected and adjusted his aim, trying to grab the stowaway, but the lunge merely caught his tail. It proved too sleek and slippery a rope to grip, and the cat was free, hurtling across the gravel for the cover of the nearest scrubby vegetation. He scrambled up a hillside, past low tangled bushes, gnarled trees and jutting rocks, and didn't stop until he was well clear of both the vehicle and its occupant.

From a safe vantage point, he turned and looked back, heart racing. Fortunately, the man seemed to have no thoughts of pursuit. Instead, he examined his hand and sucked his wounded finger. Agent 73 waited for his breathing to slow, staring all the while at his former captor.

The man studied the trunk of the car, apparently checking its contents. He pulled out the bag 73 had been hiding in, opened it and extracted the painting, examining it from all angles, relieved to see it in one piece.

Agent 73 got his first look at the mysterious object with the sharp corners that he'd been jammed against. Gold paint glinted in the light. He'd never seen anything so beautiful. Momentarily forgetting the danger he was in, he stepped out from his cover and peered more closely. It was a picture of a man, and over his shoulder a building on a hill, at the foot of which was a dark blob; a cave, perhaps. The cat was entranced; even from a distance the detail was captivating. A figure in the painting stared out boldly, as if challenging viewers to believe.

The short man wrinkled his nose, held the painting closer and sniffed it. Agent 73 felt pride that his scent marking had proved so successful. But what if they tracked him down? His marker was his calling card and highly distinctive. It said "Agent 73 was here" in big bold pheromone markers, as individual as any signature. At the time, he was proud to lay down a mark as a brave member of the Cat Intelligence Team; it seemed the heroic thing to do. Now, in the middle of nowhere, with no backup in sight, it felt naïve and foolish. He might be tracked down like a rabid dog and shot. The thought made him shudder. He refocused his attention on the man, and watched as he continued to study the painting, peering at it from close up and from different angles, and finally at arm's length, as if admiring the workmanship. After a while he put it down, examined the bag's interior, sniffing at it, and then, apparently satisfied, reached for another package in the trunk, took out some bubble wrap and covered the painting.

From the interior of the car he retrieved the long metal shiny thing and slotted it into a sheath that had been in the bag. He placed it carefully next to the painting. In the middle of the night he'd been careless in his haste, but now, Agent 73 noticed, the man took far more care to repack his bag. The last item to go in was the newly wrapped painting. Finally satisfied, the man slung to over his shoulder and slammed the lid of the trunk closed.

Agent 73 expected him to drive away, but he didn't. Instead he moved around to the far side of the vehicle, where the cat could only see his head and shoulders. The man opened the door and leaned in, appearing to rummage around inside for a while, then walked around the car once more, searching on the ground. Agent 73 saw him pick up a large rock, and take it back to the car. He bent down, out of sight, then stood back, and to Agent 73's surprise the car silently moved off of its own accord, tyres crunching over the gravel. The black cat tensed as the vehicle careered off the side of the road and down a steepening slope. It crashed through trees and bushes, before coming to an abrupt halt with a final smash into a narrow gorge down below, almost standing on end.

The cat turned his attention back to the man. What would he do? Was he going to chase him? To 73's intense relief, once the car had disappeared the short man set off away from him, along a dusty track across the moorland towards some distant mountains.

To be on the safe side, the cat watched him closely until he was out of sight, then sat back while the tension drained from his body. What an adventure. He felt exhilarated to have survived, but now he was both tired and hungry. What did an inexperienced predator do for food around here? He looked about him, and, anxious not to follow the strange man, set off uphill in the opposite direction in search of food.

. . .

As he walked, Karrig cursed his stowaway; its bite had been deep and painful. Around the shoulder of the mountain, he paused and scanned the view. The road he'd driven along was little more than a gravel track: rough and unmetalled, and best of all, untravelled. The ankh app had, to that extent, given him excellent guidance. In following it, he had risen some distance from the plains, and now, looking south, a wide treeless vista spread out before him. There was no sign of pursuit.

He considered the events of the past hour. The traffic cops who'd stopped him back near Prilep seemed to have been acting alone, rather than as part of a concerted search.

Nevertheless, paranoia framed his thoughts; he wondered what they'd relayed over their radio. No doubt their colleagues were scouring the scene around the car by now, but beyond the calibre of his gun, he hadn't left much evidence behind, and the road where they had pulled him over had been quiet. Still, it was better to abandon the vehicle: - Greek number plates, news filtering out of the theft of another priceless artwork from a location just a few hours' drive away… They may put two and two together and there would be road blocks ahead. How long before they found the abandoned car and followed him on foot? Maintaining a brisk pace along the track helped keep the nervous tension in check.

Karrig pulled out the phone and the mysterious ankh app woke up. The software seemed to have taken over the device, and was able to somehow anticipate his thoughts. He shuddered; it gave him the creeps. Was he under surveillance? He considered whether to throw it away, but it held too much valuable data to tie him back to the theft, as well as all his personal information. He was more wedded to it than ever.

A map filled the screen, overlaid with a green line indicating the direction he should follow. He scrolled to track the line, then zoomed out to get an idea of scale. It directed him over the mountains into nearby Albania, where he would be met at the small town of Peshkopi. Karrig scowled at the screen. He might have completed a theft as instructed, but he wasn't wet behind the ears. No way was he walking into a trap where he'd be forced to hand over his precious cargo to some nameless thugs in the middle of nowhere before he'd been paid. No. The handover would be arranged according to his own timetable.

He shut down the app and opened a different mapping application. It indicated that he was about twenty kilometres due south of Skopje, high in the mountains. It would be a tough hike, but he could make it in twenty-four hours or so. All he needed was to find a shepherd's hut or something similar to shelter in overnight. He set off, wondering if he knew anyone in Skopje. As he walked, he scrolled through his address book.

CHAPTER 22
A STRANGER ABROAD

Agent 73 didn't care to hang around on the upper slopes of the mountain as night drew in. It felt too exposed, and after his lengthy imprisonment, he kept scoping about for prying eyes. Laboriously, he climbed the hillside, zig-zagging his way higher despite the constant distraction of sudden noises, scents, and movement nearby: the call of goats; dry, dusty earth; gorse and ground-hugging flowers he couldn't name, and a beetle scurrying beneath a rock. Frequently, he paused to take in his surroundings and enjoy a brief catnap.

But evening was approaching, so he pressed on, trying to ignore his empty stomach. Would he find any prey this high up the mountainside? He was relieved to find the mountain top flatten into a broad whaleback ridge, speckled with occasional rocky outcrops and ground-hugging scrub.

As the evening darkened, he was still exploring this elevated plateau. He settled down for a rest in the lee of a small rock formation and watched the sun set before him, soaking up the last warmth of the day. Sleep was fitful; he was constantly disturbed by the chill wind whistling through gaps in the stones, constantly changing direction as if determined to keep him awake. It was a poor refuge; he resolved to find better.

Around midnight, he gave up any pretence of sleeping and stretched, arching his back. It was time to find food. He set off in what he hoped would be a promising direction, but try as he might, he found no prey. Here on the ridge, few creatures ventured out in the night. If any did, they were nowhere near him.

Agent 73 gave up in favour of just exploring, sniffing around to discover more about this strange landscape. All he detected were goats, gorse and myrtle, together with a few other plants he couldn't identify. There was nothing edible, at any rate. Nothing on his target list was dumb enough to live in such an exposed location, he supposed. He chewed at a few scant blades of grass, normally just a palate cleanser, but by now a way to stave off the hunger pangs that churned around in his stomach. It only made him feel even more hungry.

As the sun lent the eastern horizon a purple then pinkish glow, he found another hollow beneath a stunted tree and had another nap. This spot was at least better protected from the elements and now he had descended from the ridge, the wind was no longer so insistent or penetrating. While the sun climbed, he slept, the tension of the last few days seeping from his body and his mind.

He came to in mid-morning feeling more refreshed, and once again had a good look at his surroundings. He was high on the slopes of a broad valley. Some way below, he could see and faintly hear a small river bustling along southwards. He heard the tinkle of bells on the collars of goats roaming the hillside opposite, and watched them for a moment. For a brief instant, he envied their varied diet; they could eat almost anything. But then he shuddered with disgust at the thought of chewing leaves and berries for your whole life. Where was the pleasure in that? Despite the distance, he stiffened. Goats were not normally a threat; he'd come across one or two that roamed near Varlaam, but they were unpredictable and more than a little crazy. They lived in a world of their own; friendly one minute, then inexplicably hostile the next, and you could never have a sensible conversation with them. 73 didn't feel like wandering through a whole herd. Remaining stock still, despite the distance, he watched their slow progress along the hillside as they foraged from one clump of vegetation to the next.

He shook his head as if to stop his thoughts wandering too far off track and raised his sight above the level of the goats to peer further along the valley. To his satisfaction, there seemed to be a human settlement in the distance, nestling by the river. That looked more promising. Perhaps it was home to others of his kind? Maybe a member of the Cat Intelligence Team? There was only one way to find out.

CHAPTER 23
FOLLOWING A COLD TRAIL

The queue of vehicles at the crossing point was not moving. Behind Haldred, it lengthened by the minute. He got out and stood by the side of the road, squinting ahead and trying to work out what was going on. The border crossing seemed to be closed. Nothing passed through in either direction. Full of nervous energy, he wanted to kick something. Instead, he chewed his lip and tapped his foot.

A huge bear-like man walked back from the border checkpoint. He wore cowboy boots, and a denim shirt one size too small; the buttons strained, and there were sweat stains beneath his arms. His jeans were belted beneath an overhanging stomach.

Haldred tried to imagine the guy crossing the threshold of his gallery in fashionable SoHo; but it was too much of a stretch. Manhattan wasn't just in a distant country: it felt like a different universe. It was the first time Haldred had thought about his previous life in weeks. It no longer seemed real, as if it had been lived by someone else.

He set the thought aside as the man stopped by the truck immediately in front of Haldred's car and clambered into his cab. Haldred glanced at the plates. Germany. He walked forwards and hailed him in German.

"What's going on?"

The trucker closed the door and leaned out, wiping a hand across his forehead. He looked back in the direction of the crossing.

"It is open, but very, very slow. They're giving everyone the treatment. The rumour is there's been some incident up ahead."

"What sort of incident?"

The man shrugged and leaned out of his window and looked back down the growing line. "I don't know." He put the truck into gear. "Hey, we're moving a bit. Small mercies."

Haldred stepped back as the huge rig advanced twenty metres, then stopped in a hiss and squeal of air brakes. He shook his head and went back to his car. This could take all day.

Behind the wheel once more, Haldred pondered his alternatives. The day was drawing on, and with few other crossing points, a detour wouldn't save any time. It may even be worse. He rested his head on the steering wheel and closed his eyes. The stress was getting to him. All the time he was stuck here, Karrig was making progress, putting distance between them. He realised his hands were cramping from gripping the steering wheel too hard, and consciously tried to relax. There was no other option than to sit it out. At least, this time, he didn't have a priceless painting in the trunk.

The thought made him sit up. Was that it? Was the theft the reason vehicles were getting the treatment? Had his brother made it through safely? He must have done, otherwise they'd stop looking. Haldred groaned and slumped back in the seat, resigned to a long wait.

He finally entered North Macedonia at 4 p.m., as the sun was descending to the western horizon, shadows lengthening. He had maybe four to five hours of light in which to search for clues as to Karrig's whereabouts. The country was smaller than he'd anticipated.

By 7 p.m., he was driving into the outskirts of the capital, Skopje, along the Boulevard Alexander the Great, and engulfed by a growing sense of futility. What was it with the red buses? Were they pretending to be London? He turned off the highway, heading, he thought, towards the centre. Immediately the streets became quieter, traffic lighter. Low-rise housing gave way to taller apartment buildings and the occasional tower block, adorned with graffiti he couldn't understand.

In desperation, he pulled into a side street and found a place to park. Standing beside the car, he retrieved the map and stared at it once more, trying to understand where his brother would be heading. The scale was far too large to be meaningful, and Haldred was engulfed with a sense of futility. What was the point? He chewed his lip again, and tried to think, but the map no longer made any sense.

A screech from a nearby lamppost made him look up. From its exalted perch, the raven stared down at him.

"Yes?" It was impossible to keep the frustration from his voice, despite his relief at seeing the bird.

"They're looking for him."

"So am I."

"Is that what you call it?"

Haldred swallowed a retort and puffed out his cheeks. He took another breath. "Who's looking for him?"

"Surely you can guess."

He'd been so intent on his own chase that he hadn't thought his master's wider network might also be on his brother's trail. The thought that they might find him first almost choked him.

"Where do I find him?"

"He's in the mountains, somewhere south of here. On

foot, but he's hiding right now, and I can't track him in the dark without moonlight."

"He ditched the car?"

The raven said nothing, just switched position and looked down at him from the other eye.

"Where did he get rid of the car?" said Haldred.

"Near a place called Dolna Belitsa. But you'd better be quick." Huginn took wing once more and sped away. Haldred stared after it, clenching and unclenching his fists. How he'd love to get them around that bird's neck. At least he had a name. Providing he could find it. Once more he pored over the map, his head moving back and forth as he tried to find his new target. After a few minutes, he realised it was useless this far beyond Greece. With a snarl, he screwed it up and threw it in the gutter, and resorted to his phone. He'd have to retrace much of his journey before he could pick up the trail again, and most of it would be in the dark. With a grunt, he realised his map might be useful after all, and retrieved it from where he'd thrown it, then set off once more, back the way he'd come.

At Prilep, he slowed, driving cautiously until he was sure he was on the correct road. But after a few kilometres, he was forced to stop. A couple of workmen were winching what looked like a broken-down police car onto a flatbed truck. He passed by slowly, and in the rapidly fading dusk he thought he saw windows pierced by bullet holes. Could it be…?

Several kilometres further on, he came to a bend in the road, and his phone announced he had arrived at his destination. By now, night had fallen, and his task seemed impossible. The light of his headlamps picked out a gravel track that wove off to the right. It looked close to impassable, but it was the only lead he had, providing the bird was correct. Cautiously, at little more than walking pace, Haldred proceeded along it, as it wound up the slope ahead. *This is crazy*, he told himself. *What am I doing?* The pursuit in pitch-dark was nigh impossible.

He slowed down and looked for somewhere to stop. About a kilometre down the track, the verge was broad enough for him to pull over without blocking it. Here was a good enough place to leave the vehicle. It was out of sight of any police car that might pass along the main road behind him, and if they came up here... well, it was a chance he'd just have to take.

Dusk had descended into darkness as Haldred shouldered his pack and set off along the rugged, dusty path. He crossed a small ravine and climbed the steep slope opposite, panting for breath, his boots struggling for purchase on the loose surface. Clouds moved sluggishly across the sky, but his route ahead was mostly clear enough with no torch. Dark or dim environments were familiar for a dwarf and his night vision was better than a human's. Haldred paused to take note of his surroundings and let his eyes roam the terrain ahead. Up the hillside, he could see a couple of people on what must be the gravel track, torches sweeping back and forth as they examined their surroundings. The police must have already arrived.

He advanced more cautiously now, trying to place his feet as quietly as possible. The two figures were deep in conversation, gesturing between the road behind and something further along the track. They appeared to agree and set off back towards the main road and the waiting policemen. Haldred stepped behind a low gnarled tree and waited until they were safely past and out of sight, then made his way to where he'd first seen them. Even with his excellent night vision, it was difficult to make out any features in the terrain. Slowly, he edged forwards around the next bend. The track appeared to carry on, following the same contour for kilometres. Why had the investigators been so animated?

Haldred stopped and looked around, searching the slope below.

Then he saw it. Easy to spot. A car was wedged into a narrow gap between rocks, perhaps fifty metres down the hillside. It was nose down, the trunk and rear wheels in the air. Haldred scrambled down to it, and tried to open the driver's door, but it was jammed, deformed by the collision, and wedged shut. The other side of the car was caught against the hillside. He stood on the slope above, and leaned across to try the trunk, barely able to reach it. He felt, then noticed, the jagged edge of bullet holes, and, with an effort, unfastened the latch. It swung open. He pulled himself up until he could look inside, but as he suspected, it was empty. His weight made the car unstable, and the metal creaked. Haldred jumped aside and watched it settle lower into the gorge, but it gave no further clues. He knew this was the car Karrig had used for his escape. He scratched his head in contemplation and looked around once more. The ground below sloped gently down into a broad valley, from what he could make out.

At some distance, he could see the lights of a settlement; only a village. He must have passed it before he came across the police car. It seemed that shots had been exchanged, and Karrig had decided he'd be safer abandoning his vehicle. Where had he gone? Haldred turned away from the village lights and set his face to the darkness, shadows of mountains blocking out the stars. In the intermittent moonlight they loomed large; a forbidding obstacle. That must be where his brother had gone, he reasoned. But how much of a lead did he have?

With a sigh, he pulled the shoulder straps on his pack tighter, and walked on into the night.

CHAPTER 24
DESERTED VILLAGE

As Agent 73 passed a remote farm building, a large black dog chased him up the hillside, wheezing and panting. Fortunately, 73 had both age and a good head start on his side, so outpacing the psychotic mutt was hardly a problem. After a couple of hundred metres or so, it gave up and slunk back home.

Dispirited, the cat turned his back on the hateful animal and headed on up the valley. Carving out a territory with neighbours like that might be difficult. He ignored the hunger pangs, and pressed on, following the south-facing slopes, to let the sun warm him. It proved a longer slog than he'd expected. As a cat, Agent 73 wasn't used to route marches. Lounging around in the shade expending minimum effort was more his thing, but a reluctance to spend another night on the open mountainside drove him on. Hopefully, his destination would be more accommodating with a few good resting spots and hunting grounds. A place to rest and recuperate, and maybe find a home.

As the day drew on, the power of the sun waned, and the sky became a featureless grey-white backdrop. A chilly wind flowed down the valley, ruffling his fur. He kept a lookout for other creatures, both edible and non-edible, but saw and smelled none. The lack of animal scent was strange, as if they avoided this part of the valley, but that made little sense to the black cat. Surely there would be some sheep or goats roaming these hills? Perhaps his sense of smell was waning? He shuddered at the thought.

As he trudged along, he reflected on the past week. Being a secret agent hadn't turned out to be such fun. He'd been captured, rudely poked and prodded, only just avoided becoming victim to a nasty-looking raven and a wolf, captured again by another human, imprisoned in the dark, shot at, narrowly escaped, abandoned in the middle of nowhere, and finally chased out of the first human habitation he'd come to by a four-legged xenophobic rustic. He wasn't happy. In fact, if he saw that stuck-up grey cat again, he'd give her a piece of his mind.

Composing his resignation speech occupied his thoughts for much of the morning as he plodded along the hillside. At least it diverted his attention from the growing sense of loneliness and the silence of this strange valley.

After a long time, he came to a rocky outcrop jutting from the valley side and stopped. It looked like the kind of place rodents might live. He spent a few minutes exploring and sniffing around the base of the rocks, but found nothing, then jumped on top, to see the land around, but saw no sign of warren or hole or hideout. With a sigh, he raised his eyes towards the horizon and stiffened. The village he'd been aiming for was close now, near the end of the valley as it narrowed and wound into the mountainside behind.

Shelter, and hopefully comfort, lay ahead, and with a bit of luck, company. The small cat narrowed his eyes against the light and studied it more closely. There were buildings, but they looked different. Abandoned. Most of them had no roof, and some walls seemed to have holes or gaps. He raised his nose slightly and sniffed the air. At this distance, even with a perfect sense of smell, he would have trouble detecting the scent of human or other animals, so he wasn't surprised when he sensed nothing. He would need to get nearer to take a meaningful reading, but something about the place seemed wrong.

Agent 73 thought for a while. At least it may provide shelter, and if abandoned, it would be just the kind of place where mice and other small animals might live. And he was a secret agent, despite his misgivings about his employer, he should investigate. He leaped down, delicately, and recommenced his slow walk, now taking a straighter course and paying more attention to his destination.

Drawing closer, 73 felt the valley sides encroaching on him. Here it was much narrower and its sides steeper. The landscape seemed to herd him towards the narrow winding track that ran beside the bustling stream on the valley floor. Stony bluffs and stunted trees obscured the view along its length, and the settlement ahead often disappeared from view. It had seemed not too far away when he'd first set eyes on it, but it seemed to take a long time to get there.

He turned a corner and finally there it was, just ahead and now slightly above him. He was surprised he'd dropped so far down the hillside. A shallow slope lay before him, up which the narrow gravel road twisted then plunged between the buildings. At his left, a narrow water meadow lay on the other side of the stream, but there was no sign of any animals grazing; the hay was tall and untouched.

The first building looked larger than he'd originally thought. A high stone wall faced him with just two small windows, one above the other, and no sign of a door. He supposed the entrance must be round the corner. Above it glowered the dark, steep slopes of a large mountain, barren and rocky. The sky overhead was now a dull grey, sucking any joy out of the day. The air seemed thick, and the village silent. Listening.

Agent 73 paused, uncertain. He looked over his shoulder but could see no further than the bend in the track and its overhanging tree. He surveyed the slopes on either side, rugged and unwelcoming, and took a deep breath. He'd come this far, he might as well go on, though he didn't much like the look of the place. He advanced cautiously, eschewing the long grass verge in favour of the gravel road, despite the sharp-edged pebbles that sometimes caught under his pads.

The first house loomed over him, then he was past it and onto a level, though overgrown, cobbled street. Silent doorways stood on either side, some contained firmly shut doors, as if the owners had just popped out for a couple of hours, but most were hanging off their hinges, or broken, or missing entirely.

He paused in front of a single-storey cottage with no roof and space where windows should have fitted. A rotting wooden door, once painted green, hung off a single rusting hinge at the top. 73 slowly walked past, glancing inside nervously.

He walked on into the heart of the deserted village, past more empty buildings on either side. Here, in what passed for the centre, the houses were more substantial, usually two storeys, occasionally with a pane of cracked or broken glass still retained by a crumbling frame. Curiosity piqued, he realised how much there was to explore here, and surely among the ruins he'd be able to find some prey animals?

The uneasy feeling that had grown steadily inside him dissipated a little. He entered one building through a large hole at the base of its door. The room inside was silent and gloomy. Two windows, one of which contained some glass, let some light in, but the ceiling was largely intact apart from a few holes, and a broken flight of stairs rose to the rear, leaving a dark void beneath. He sniffed around, but caught nothing other than dust, stone and weeds. An upturned table and collapsed broken chair comprised the only furnishings, although when he jumped up, he found a thickened pyramid of candle wax on one windowsill, cold and gathering dust.

From his perch, he looked down the valley back in the direction he'd come. There were few signs of human activity. No fields dotted this rugged landscape. The valley floor was too narrow at this point. The scene outside looked unchanged and unchanging, unwelcoming even to that most persistent of species: humanity. For a fleeting moment, Agent 73 wondered what had brought them to this place, but as he neither knew nor cared about human activity, he found no answers. Not for the first time he longed for his car park, safely in the shadow of Varlaam Monastery, and the familiar scents and sights of home.

Curiosity drove him to explore the upper floor, but he found the staircase treacherous. Several steps were missing or smashed, and one tilted alarmingly when he stepped onto it, making him instantly jump to the next. The floor of the upper room was barren apart from an ancient-looking cupboard against one wall. It had no doors, and its shelves were empty. The floor looked dangerous. In some places, there were holes where he could glimpse the room below. Above him, rafters were still intact, supporting most of a corrugated iron roof, although this too was rusting and had many gaps. 73 paced around carefully. Some floorboards seemed scarcely able to hold his weight. The walls still held some of the whitewash that would once have made this a bright and cheerful abode, the only sign that someone might have once cared about the place. But now the plasterwork was cracked and split, revealing bare masonry behind.

None of this meant anything to the cat. He knew nothing about human habitations or building techniques. He just wanted somewhere to shelter for the night and this place might just do. He felt a draft flowing through a crack in the wall, bringing with it the myriad scents of the outside world. It detracted from the smell of the room, and as he explored, his nostrils detected a faint whiff of decaying organic matter; the echo of an animal's faecal deposits. It unsettled him. He had no idea what sort of creature would have defecated here; it was more disturbing than reassuring.

Still, it had been some time ago, and he took comfort from the fact there was no sign of recent activity. Crouching, he looked around once more. There was nothing up here to provide shelter or comfort, but the ground floor had possibilities, at least beneath the stairs.

Gingerly, he made his way down again. The boards creaked alarmingly beneath his feet, a noise that felt almost like a physical presence in the confines of the house, and sent a chill down his spine. He froze, regretting his decision to explore. Perhaps this place was not meant to be examined? Did he really want to stay here? Once more he looked around but saw nothing to spook him, and slowly his heartbeat returned to normal. Agent 73 resumed his descent, every sense on alert. There was a definite feeling he was being watched. It made him uncomfortable and added to a sense of melancholy that fed his unease. He told himself not to be so silly, and returned to the road outside, putting off the decision on where to shelter for the night until later.

The air was chillier now and the light beginning to fade. The day was waning, but his spirits rose once he was beneath an open sky again. A rumble in his stomach reminded him of the reason he had come here. It had looked like good hunting ground for rodents, although now that he saw the state of the village, he was no longer so certain. 73 scanned the shells of the nearer buildings. Most of them were derelict, without roof or floors. A small cluster of buildings further along the main street from the house he'd explored seemed to offer some hope. Carefully picking his way towards them, he stayed close to the wall, as if to remain out of sight of any potential occupants.

Evening shadows lengthened, and the looming mountain beyond the end of the street lent an oppressive air, blocking out much of the evening light. Night would come early in this place.

Agent 73 pressed on, and was finally rewarded with the faintest sound of scrabbling mice feet. Focusing intently, ears pricked and eyes alert to any sudden movement, he saw it, running between fallen stone blocks that littered a narrow alley between empty buildings. He pounced just a moment too soon, missed, and the chase began. His target sought refuge in a crack at the base of a wall, but a combination of anticipation and desperation ensured that the cat got there first. The hapless creature turned left, then right, in an attempt to shake off pursuit, but 73's reactions were better and he caught it quickly. He was in no mood to play with his prey. Hunger drove him to despatch it quickly and wolf it down. His hunger pangs were finally sated, at least for a while. As he finished his meal, he looked up, realising how gloomy it had become. Dusk had arrived, and the sky was growing dark.

There was a rustle of vegetation behind him. Agent 73 jumped and swivelled around in the air just in time to see a rat dart away from the empty window above him. He paused. Having just eaten, he wasn't inclined to start another chase immediately, but he looked to find an entrance to the building to see where it had come from. Immediately he thought better of it: exploration could wait. Normally he was at his most active at this time of day, but for once he felt reluctant to go exploring in the dark; this place gave him the creeps. A wave of weariness swept over him. It was time to find somewhere to rest.

The rest of the village proved disappointing. The best-looking place was boarded up, with no entrance he could find. Beyond that, the other former houses were little more than shells comprising four walls surrounding rugged patches of ground. The wind increased in strength, bringing cold air down from the mountain, sighing through the empty buildings, and the temperature dropped. Above him, clouds thickened and moved more quickly across the sky. He felt a drop of rain, then another. It was going to be a stormy night. The few remaining doors and windows in the houses nearby rattled, readying themselves to defy the forces of nature in one more unequal fight. The wind whistled and moaned through innumerable cracks and holes in the masonry, as if the whole village were complaining about the injustice of it all.

Agent 73 hastened his search for somewhere dry and out of the wind where he could sleep for the next few hours. The only building that could offer decent shelter was the first one he'd explored. He found himself on the threshold once more, but reluctant to enter. A sudden squall of rain made up his mind, and he stepped back inside, shivering.

The room downstairs was now dark. It felt oppressive. The gloomy atmosphere he'd previously encountered had deepened. He told himself he would find better lodgings as soon as the rain stopped, and made for the pool of darkness beneath the stairs. The cat now had the uncomfortable sense that the house was watching him, and reprimanded himself once again for his stupidity, shaking his head to dispel the thought. Curling up with his back to the wall, he faced the entrance and tried to sleep. He was weary after his long journey, but the events of the past few days rattled in his brain, and he could do nothing other than lie there wide awake.

Through cracked and grimy windows he watched ragged clouds scud across the sky. At least the strengthening wind had broken them up, allowing occasional moonbeams to cut through and shed some light on the floor in front of him. It was little comfort. Floorboards creaked, as if some unseen creature was pacing back and forth, and leaves rustled on the trees and bushes outside. The rain kept up a steady thrum on the cobbles and the corrugated sheeting of the roof.

The oppressive atmosphere was getting to him. Nervous exhaustion left 73 feeling drained, but still he couldn't sleep. This place felt wrong. He couldn't wait to get away. Why had he come here? He thought about making a break for it, but the rainwater outside had turned the street into a makeshift stream, and through the bare windows he could see branches whipping back and forth alarmingly in the howling gale. This was going to be a long night.

A strange aroma hit his nostrils. What was it, and why hadn't he noticed it earlier? Was it delivered to him by this malignant wind? A wild doggy smell, but more powerful than any hound he'd ever met. He'd come across it before, recently, beneath the cliffs that supported Varlaam Monastery, and it awoke a primeval fear deep within. In his imagination he saw monsters and huge evil birds, and told himself to calm down; it was just a playful wind delivering the stench of the town midden. Then he remembered no humans lived here; there was no dump. Outside he thought he heard a branch crack, but he couldn't be sure. His stomach turned over at the thought something might be out there, and the fur stood up along his back.

A sudden shaft of moonlight from a break in the cloud illuminated the interior of his shelter, giving a clear view of the cracked walls, the empty floor with its upturned table, and the half door that continued to dangle on its one remaining hinge, defying the wind. How long could it remain like that, banging against the door jamb? Darkness returned as new clouds snatched the moonlight away. Another crack: where from? The scent in his nostrils was stronger now, and more alien. *It's coming*, he thought, fighting to stay calm. Every fibre of Agent 73's being wanted to run as fast and as far away from this dreadful place as possible.

A flash of light and thunder cracked overhead, louder than any that he'd ever heard, and he saw it, there in the doorway. A wolf, huge and strong. Agent 73 was paralysed with fear. It was blocking his only escape route. Lightning flashed again, and it had gone. The cat looked around wildly. Where was it?

CHAPTER 25
FREDDIE

T he large ginger-and-white cat casually stepped off the bus, apparently unnoticed, and without a care in the world. He crossed the main square and made for the northern edge of town. A short while later, he approached the side road where the local coordinator was said to live. Agent 49 was in the small garden, hard at work as usual, napping. Apollo eyed the narrow gap in the fence, but chose to hurdle it instead, landing with delicate precision close to the other cat.

Freddie, startled at the unexpected intrusion, jerked awake, blinking and trying to get a proper look at her visitor.

"Er, hello?"

"Calm down. I mean no harm." The visitor circled the lawn, studying his surroundings, before turning to his host once more. Freddie tried to recover her composure and an essence of dignity. She sat upright, as if to attention, wondering if there was enough time for a quick wash. With right front paw halfway to her mouth, the ginger cat turned towards her, so she satisfied herself with a quick scratch behind the ear.

"Can I help?" Freddie pretended to study the hedge,

keeping her visitor in her peripheral vision, but was unable to prevent her tail twitching nervously.

If Apollo was amused, he didn't show it. One more perambulation around the garden, a sniff at the food, then he returned to lounge on the grass, a couple of metres away from the Cat Intelligence Team's local coordinator. It was time to get down to business.

"I'm from HQ," he offered. "How about you give me an update on this recent incident you reported?"

Freddie had never had to deliver a report to one of the big cheeses before and she'd have liked more time to practise. To buy herself time to think, she embarked on a more thorough scratch, hoping she didn't forget anything.

"Well…" she began, suddenly aware of her heart beating faster. "Last night. No, the night before last. Two nights ago." She was getting flustered. This must sound dreadful. With head bowed, she tried to collect her thoughts.

Apollo lay on his side, the epitome of calm relaxation. "It's okay. Take your time. Start from the beginning."

The calico glanced at the newcomer. He'd only just arrived, but he looked as if he owned the place. Freddie closed her eyes for a moment, then began again.

"I wasn't there, you understand." She ventured a quick glance at her companion to check he did. "But there was an owl. She told me everything."

"Everything?"

"Well…" This was awkward, had she really told her everything? "…as much as she could." She paused, trying to recollect the detail of the bird's story. "She said she was just out hunting as normal, but she spotted one of the Varlaam cats down in one of her usual hunting grounds. She said it was black all over. I think it was our local agent up there; Agent 73. She had her eye on a vole, but he got to it first, and she was annoyed, so she perched in a nearby tree to watch it, and maybe steal it."

Freddie took a couple of breaths while she continued to organise her thoughts. It was difficult getting them all in order. What happened next? Oh yes… "Then she saw the cat looking up at something. She followed its gaze and spotted a man hanging from the cliff by a rope. He was coming down. This is what was really weird; she said he was walking down the rock." Freddie faced Apollo, eyes wide in incredulity, but the ginger cat showed no reaction. She went on.

"She watched him until he reached the ground, but when she turned her attention back to the cat, it had gone. It was halfway to where the man was standing."

She stopped, lost in thought, trying to picture what a man would look like walking down a cliff face, but without any frame of reference she gave up. The ginger cat was still patiently waiting. Freddie gathered her thoughts once more; where had she got to? Oh, yes.

"There was a bird. A big black one. She didn't see it arrive, but there it was, arguing with the man. How strange is that?" She glanced once more at her visitor, who remained impassive. "Mmm? Well, yes. Most unusual. I mean, who talks to humans? Er, where was I?" The ginger cat yawned. "Then it got even stranger. The man pulled out a long shiny metal thing and waved it at the bird. It shone in the moonlight. It looked dangerous, and the bird didn't like it." Once more she let her thoughts drift while she tried to picture the scene. "Anyway, that was about it. They argued. Then the man picked up his things and walked down to the road." Another thought occurred to her. "Oh yes, she said there was a wolf!"

The ginger cat raised his head. "A wolf?"

Pleased to have got a reaction, at last, Freddie elaborated. "That's what she said. She said it was hanging back in the shadows, but watching the man and the black bird. Then it followed them."

"What happened to the cat?"

"Agent 73? Oh, I don't know. She lost sight of him in all the excitement. No one knows."

"Where is he now?"

"No one knows that, either. He hasn't been seen." Freddie stopped. She stared at the other cat. "You don't think he…? I mean, he wouldn't? Would he?"

Her report complete, Freddie sat, unsure what to do next. She studied the ginger cat for a reaction. She'd thought it terribly important when she first sent a message to Athens, but seeing the lack of a reaction from her visitor, she felt deflated.

Apollo rolled over, then back again, stretching. He yawned.

"Can you show me where all this took place?"

"I think so."

Freddie would have preferred the owl as a guide, but she should have enough to go on. Hesitantly at first, she led the way out of town and up the path into the hills to what she believed to be the approximate site of the incident.

An hour later, they were there, or as near as she understood. She looked around, hoping for a sign that she was right, and stood feeling helpless while the other animal began to investigate. The ginger cat sniffed around, spending a long time searching the edges of the clearing and beyond. Freddie bent her snout to the earth, in unconscious imitation, but failed to detect anything out of the ordinary. What was so interesting. It was just earth and vegetation; a few droppings here and there, so what? She sat down and waited.

Searching the ground nearby, Apollo was immediately convinced this was the place the owl had witnessed the encounter. The lingering aroma of wolf – a pungent scent unlike any other – was easy to pick out. With his nose a little closer to the ground, he retraced his steps across the middle of the clearing, where the ground was most disturbed.

Mingled with wolf essence was another scent, partially masked. It was one he'd not encountered before; not in this body, at any rate. He struggled, but failed to place it. It was human-like, but not quite; the difference so subtle as to be easily missed by even a talented tracker. But if he concentrated, it was definitely there. What did it remind him of? Caverns, maybe; places deep underground; rocks; mud; damp, dripping stone; clay; fire and smoke? Definitely subterranean. The human seemed to have some connection with the underworld, and that alone made him unusual.

Apollo studied the ground for other signs. The vegetation had been trampled where the man had landed. Grass blades were bent and mashed into the earth. Twigs were broken, and the paw prints of the wolf still clear; it wasn't even trying to hide its tracks. How far could he follow it? He sniffed the ground more closely and thought he could detect, faintly, the signature of a cat, a small one, and asked his companion for verification. Freddie, visibly delighted to have something useful to do, acknowledged that, yes, there appeared to be the scent, however faint, of Agent 73.

"But at this point it disappears," said Apollo, momentarily stumped. The trail was clear until it reached the middle of the flattened grass, then it vanished. They searched the nearby area, systematically circling around, gradually further from the epicentre. But there was no other sign. It was a mystery. Agent 49 looked baffled, and said so. Apollo caught her eye.

"Perhaps he was beamed up by aliens?" he suggested. His companion looked blank. "Or maybe he was abducted from this point, knowingly or unknowingly." Freddie looked around suspiciously. "He wasn't eaten at any rate," Apollo concluded. "At least, not here. There's no blood or bone fragments or other scraps, so hopefully he's still alive."

Freddie stared back, trying to join the dots, but struggled to keep up with the ginger cat's detective work.

"Let's follow them down to the road," Apollo commanded, setting off without waiting for his colleague. They followed the strong scent of wolf and more subtle aroma of near-human down the steep hillside to where it met the road. This was the point at which Apollo could no longer find any trace of the man-creature. There was no sign of a struggle, just the lingering scent of the wolf following the road towards the west. Apollo turned to his companion, searching for something encouraging to say.

"Better see if you can recruit another agent to watch the car park and the valley," he suggested. Freddie looked crestfallen.

"It was bad enough in town," she mumbled. "Up here, well, they're hardly the sharpest claw in the paw."

The ginger cat gave her a reassuring look. "You've been very helpful. Well done. Make sure you keep up the good work, but we need to maintain a watch. Greece will thank you for this." At the back of his mind, Apollo wondered why he was coming out with this nonsense, but it seemed to do the trick. Freddie appeared thrilled with the recognition.

"See you round." With that, Apollo turned his nose to the north and pursued the pungent odour of wolf. His curiosity had been piqued. He needed to find a crow or raven of his own to question, and he had to track down that wolf. Agent 49 wasn't the only one with renewed purpose.

CHAPTER 26
NO ESCAPE

A flash of lightning blinded him, and when he could see again, the wolf had gone. Had he imagined it? Every nerve fibre of 73's body was on high alert. He felt so tense he could almost taste it. The fur on his back was on end. Quickly he scanned the room, doorway, empty windows, and wished with all his heart that he was far away from this awful place.

Outside, the rain intensified. He listened to it hammering on the corrugated iron above, and tried to detect the sound of large animals prowling around. Through the holes in the roof and ceiling above, some of the rain drops stabbed down into the floor in front of him, spattering in the dirt. The storm was the least of his worries. Had he imagined the evil-looking beast, or was it still out there, prowling somewhere, waiting for him to make a move? Fear glued him to the spot. Unable to move, his head swam in a sea of indecision. Had it seen him? When would it make its move?

As if in response, over the noise of the whistling wind and insistent rain, came a sound that froze his blood: a full-throated wolf howl, a sound so primeval that even though he'd never heard it before, Agent 73 instantly knew its portent. An icy arrow of terror pierced his heart. There was no more doubt; the wolf was real and out there. The only question was, did it know he was here? He clung on to a thin hope: perhaps the rain and squalling wind had masked his scent? Lightning flashed again and this time, to his utter horror, he saw it again, inside the room and to his right. Agent 73 had no time to wonder how it had moved so fast; he bolted for the exit, and from the corner of his eye saw it move to intercept him. He made it through the empty portal by a hair's breadth, blind to what might be outside, and landed in the middle of the rough, part-cobbled street. Instinctively, he turned to his right, towards the heart of the dark settlement, the bigger beast on his tail.

Fortunately for 73, the wolf's turning circle was wider, and it careened off the wall of the building opposite before resuming the chase, giving him a couple of metres lead. Agent 73 was young, fast, had excellent night vision and adrenaline coursing through every vein. But he was alone and in unfamiliar territory with no knowledge of possible hiding places. Rain, rodding down, soaked his body and splashed in front of him, forcing him to squint and making it difficult to see. He ran on instinct. Could he give the big brute the slip? It seemed, for a moment, possible.

As he ran down the winding, uneven street, he looked for potential escape routes where his agility and smaller size might offer him an edge, but to his horror, a second wolf appeared from a narrow alley to his left as he passed it, then a third emerged from a building ahead. It stood there, waiting for him, heedless of the storm, tongue lolling from the side of its jaw in anticipation. There was only one escape route: a narrow gap between houses to the left, barely visible in the gloom; black depths outlined by deep grey shadows. He took it, panic driving him on. In this dark passageway there was barely any light, and it was almost impossible to see, even for an animal with good night vision. He raked his shins on a large stone block in his path and tumbled over, rising to his feet again in a single movement. In his desperation, he barely noticed the pain; that would come later, assuming he could still feel anything. Pure fear was driving him on. His leading pursuer hurdled the block with ease, gaining ground.

At least he was heading downhill slightly, and out of the ghostly deserted settlement, but he now had three wolves in close pursuit, and little chance of outrunning them. The alley became a track, and the track turned into a path, diving between low prickly bushes and dark, twisted trees. Now the ground rose ahead of him, and on either side, unnoticed, the valley sides drew closer and steeper. Lungs burning, he turned a corner and the narrow path ended at the mouth of a cave at the base of a high cliff, a void of deeper black amid the surrounding darkness.

Without thinking, he dived in, then slowed, confused, temporarily blinded. At least he was free of rain splashing in his face, but immediately his nostrils detected a foul stench. Something dead lay at the back of this cave, and it had been there for a while. He heard another howl behind him, this time of victory, and with sickening certainty the cat knew he was trapped. Terrified, but strangely resigned, he turned to face his pursuers and meet his fate.

They stood at the entrance of the cave; three silhouettes of menace. Behind them, the storm appeared to be moving down the valley. Lightning flashed further away, the thunderclap taking longer to be heard. The three were panting, but confident in their victory. In a small corner of his confused brain, Agent 73 was surprised by that. Surely he was only modest prey for such large animals? He'd give them only a mouthful or two apiece. He supposed times were hard here in these unforgiving mountains. The middle wolf took a step forward and leered down at him. It was all over. Agent 73 knew his fate; to be torn limb from limb by these monsters, who might go on to fight among themselves over his small body. He just hoped they ended it quickly for him first.

"We've been looking for you," said the first wolf, the apparent leader of this little pack.

Agent 73 wondered why it was talking to him; inexperienced though he was, he'd never been inclined to chat with his prey. Perhaps it was part of the mental torture they practised around here?

"Caught us unawares, you did," the big wolf continued. "Or, at least, caught Freda out. Took her a while to realise who you were. You look smaller than we'd been told. Mind you, if you'd been as big as she said, you'd never have fitted in your mate's bag." He had been slowly advancing while speaking, but now stopped barely a metre in front of the cat. 73 was almost overwhelmed by the smell: vaguely dog-like, but wilder and far stronger. Now that he'd stopped running, he was fully aware of the jagged pain in his forelegs, but visceral fear still kept the full impact at bay. He said nothing, just stared up at the bigger animal, waiting for the pounce.

"I don't know what they want with you. You're so puny, you're hardly worth our while." The long face and slavering tongue were almost close enough for Agent 73 to swipe at, if he'd dared.

A second wolf spoke from the cave entrance. "Should we beat it up a little? Loosen its tongue?"

The first wolf looked over its shoulder. "No. Orders were to bring him in for interrogation intact." He looked down at the black cat between his paws, and could barely keep the gloating from his voice. "We can have a little fun later." He made a show of looking the cat up and down. "Not that he looks capable of putting up much of a fight."

73 stood rooted to the ground, trying to work out what was going on. He trawled his memories, but drew a blank. So much had happened since he'd left home, it seemed like a different life. But wolves hadn't been part of it, he was

certain. Unless… He remembered the strange scent that had driven him to hide in the first place. A pang of regret hit him; why had he tried to investigate?

He was puzzled, though. How come these animals had heard about that incident, if it was indeed what they meant? How had they tracked him here? It made no sense. He realised he was being spoken to once more.

"Right, you little runt. Let's get moving."

Agent 73 looked around but could see nowhere to go. With exaggerated patience, as if talking to a small cub, the leader addressed him once more.

"I assume you've got a sense of smell? Just follow Rolf, and no funny business. I'm right behind you."

Rolf stepped forwards, and to 73's surprise headed further into the cave. Surely there was no way out? Still, he obeyed orders and followed, sidestepping the ageing remains of what he assumed was a deer or ibex. How deep was this cave? At least he found it easy to follow the scent of the animal in front; it was almost overpowering in its intensity. He didn't stop to wonder how the wolf kept going in the pitch-dark; that was the least of his concerns, but it moved ahead confidently at an even pace, veering only occasionally to sidestep some unseen obstacle.

As far as Agent 73 could tell, their route led straight into the mountainside, descending at an even gradient. He wondered how long they could continue like this, in the dark, but to his surprise found he could see the outline of the animal ahead, and dimly perceive the rugged walls of the passage on either side. The light grew steadily brighter as they descended.

After a while, their path crossed another, much wider. It was level and paved, and went straight in either direction, as far as 73 could make out. It was dimly lit by blue-tinted globes that seemed to nestle against the uneven roof like balloons illuminated from within. Agent 73 stared at the nearest one, trying to understand it, and wondered who, or what, had put it there. As if reading his thoughts, his chief tormentor spoke.

"Dwarf lights. Put here centuries ago by the traitorous snivellers. Don't trust them an inch, dwarves, but at least the little fuckers can dig." He looked at his companions. "Right, let's pick up the pace a little. Off we go."

They turned to the left and followed the path at a slow trot, a pace that the shorter-legged 73 could just about keep up with, although after a while he found it a strain. He wasn't used to this type of endurance exercise. His kind didn't track ibex to caribou across mountains or frozen wastes for days on end. He was an ambush predator. Short sprints and long rests were his forte. The constant pace, right at the edge of his ability, developed into a new form of torture. He longed for a break, but as soon as he slowed, he received a sharp nip to his rear or tail, as extra motivation. Finally, he couldn't help but slow to a walk, receiving a nasty bump as his reward. The leader snarled at his weakness.

"Keep going, you scrawny rat. No slacking."

"I can't go on," pleaded 73. "I need something to eat."

The wolf sneered once again. "No food for prisoners."

73 tried to get going again, but broke down a few minutes later. "Please, I've got to rest. I can't keep going like this." His foreleg was throbbing.

His taskmaster snarled once more in frustration, nipped at the cat's flank and yelped a few times as his prisoner collapsed in pain.

"God, you're pathetic. What a feeble little species you are. Call yourselves predators? I'll be kind. We'll walk for a while. Enjoy it while you can, while you've still got legs."

In a strange mixture of relief and despair, Agent 73 scrambled to his feet and plodded on behind Rolf, his tormentor at his side.

CHAPTER 27
HALDRED AND THE WOLVES

"It seems we have a stalemate."

The words spoken in the harsh tongue of the wargs grated on his ears like the clash of an iron bar on metal railings, but there was no denying the truth of them.

"Perhaps we do," Haldred admitted, eyeing his adversaries warily, and trying to think how to escape.

"Except there are more of us," the wolf went on, "and we don't tire easily. Whereas you cannot stay awake forever." The huge beast's tongue lolled from the side of its long snout, saliva dripping from the tip. Hostility filled his yellow eyes, mingled with the certainty of victory. There was a pause. Haldred considered the truth behind the threat. His immediate future did look bleak. Still, he brandished the Heckler & Koch pistol before him, waving it from side to side as a warning. The wolves eyed it with fear bordering on dread. Their discomfort bought him confidence. Still, with odds of six to one, if they held position, surely their leader was right; he would tire and weaken. They just had to wait. In the meantime, they took care to keep moving in and out of his peripheral vision, so he couldn't see all of them at once.

Haldred had travelled just a few hundred metres from his

car before they emerged from the hillside above and below, surrounding him. They must have been watching him from the moment he arrived to investigate the abandoned vehicle. He cursed himself for not checking his surroundings more carefully when he'd arrived, but in the pitch-dark, what could he have done?

Another hour passed and the Mexican stand-off continued. Haldred dared not move away from the rock face at his back, for fear of attack from the rear. He couldn't risk being surrounded. It was difficult enough to keep his eyes on them as it was, and their persistence bothered him. Why were they so powerfully motivated? There could be only one answer, and he didn't like that thought. He licked his dry lips. What he would give for a sip of water right now? He carried a bottle in his pack, but he doubted he'd have the time to reach for it, remove it and unscrew the top and sip before they were on him, like a pack of hounds overpowering a fox. He tried a different approach.

"What do you want with me? I'm no threat."

A gargling sound greeted his words. He suspected the leader was laughing at him.

"We don't want anything," came the response, "but our leader would certainly like a word."

"Who? What do you mean?" Haldred fumbled for understanding, although he feared he knew the answer only too well.

"Let us take you there, and you can answer for yourself."

"I'm not going anywhere. Not now. I'm in the middle of my mission. I have more to do. Tell him it's not finished yet."

There was a pause while the wolf leader digested his words. "I speak for no 'him'. I serve our queen, the alpha female and matriarch of our pack. She has a few words of encouragement to set you on your way." As he spoke, the great wolf paced back and forth, drawing Haldred's eyes away from the others who stood between them. Their retinas glinted as they caught scraps of dim moonlight. As his attention flicked from one to another, they took turns to dart forwards, testing his reactions. It was difficult to maintain focus on the leader. A trickle of sweat ran down the dwarf's face. He brushed it away with a hasty swipe of his free hand.

"Queen? I am not aware of any queen among your kind, now or ever."

"Then you have little knowledge of our society."

"What does she want from me?"

"She does not share all of her plans. Find out yourself. Ask her."

Haldred's thoughts raced. He was trapped here in a remote valley in the mountains, trying to search for a sign that his brother had previously passed this way and hidden a painting, but it felt like a forlorn hope. Why would anyone leave something valuable in a forsaken place like this? Of more immediate concern were these slavering beasts before him. They could tear him apart in an instant if he let his guard down. He couldn't see a way out other than by killing them all, but the odds were stacked against him. He might get two or three before the rest were on him, and he knew they would be merciless.

Reluctantly, Haldred had to admit that he had no option other than to go with them and meet their queen. The only sliver of comfort was that it was not to Loki's cave. Not yet. Did the queen know of his mission, or did she have some other agenda? He lowered his weapon.

"Alright, then. I'll come with you. But I want safe passage there and away again. Is that clear?" He wasn't really in a position to make demands, but respect for his gun seemed to count for something. The wolves backed off slightly, and several bowed their heads in acknowledgement.

"I'm glad you saw sense," said the leader. He glanced at his companions. "Follow them. I'll be behind you." He barked an order to one of his subordinates, who set off up the hillside behind. Haldred followed, ill at ease, but relieved to be moving. The proximity of the enormous beasts was unnerving, and their unpleasant smell – wet earth mingled with rotting carpet – filled his nostrils. In the confined space of underground passages, he knew it would be worse, and he was certain their destination lay somewhere beneath these mountains. Haldred cursed his rash stupidity for venturing so far into wolf territory, the natural domain of Loki's loyal servants.

Normally his spirits rose whenever he was beneath ground, but on this occasion it would be different. In a warren of unfamiliar passages filled with others of their kind, escape would be tricky. Haldred knew he would have to strike a deal of some kind. How else could he be sure they would let him go?

Into the deepening shadow they plodded, six large wolves with a dwarf in their midst, strung along a narrow path in single file. Gloom engulfed them the further they went, but for Haldred, it started within.

CHAPTER 28
DREAM TWISTER

Agent 73 knew, the moment he saw it enter the cavernous hall, that this animal was different. The mere sight of it made his skin crawl beneath his fur. Although huge, it looked as if it could barely be alive. Skin hung in folds from its skeletal frame, every rib visible. Its coat was matted and its fur seemed to be falling out, revealing flaky, scabby skin beneath. How old could this creature be? A foul smell of decay preceded its approach, and when it drew close, the cat couldn't help but recoil from the fetid stench of its breath. It looked like a walking corpse, but the eyes were fiercely alive, and as it approached, they were boring into the small cat with malice.

They stood in the centre of a huge cave where the wolves had deposited him, with dire warnings not to move, then retreated to keep watch from a distance in the shadows. He'd been here for some time. The newcomer stopped uncomfortably close, towering above the small black cat. Agent 73 couldn't prevent his legs from trembling, but he said nothing. Rather than crane his neck to look at its face, he was absorbed by the animal's scarred and blistered paws. This creature had endured great pain, he suspected, and knew how to inflict it on others. A wrong word would most likely lead to a bite, cuff, or worse. He wished he was bigger, but even the largest of his relatives would be no match for this monster. From the corner of his eye, he noticed his captors, the other wolf guardians, moving further away, as if they too were wary of the newcomer. They hovered in Agent 73's peripheral vision, pacing the fringes of the hall, hugging the walls, tense and vigilant.

The large wolf appeared to be waiting for him to make some move. Agent 73 risked a glance up at its face and wished he hadn't. The wolf's eyes, yellow and bloodshot, seemed to be sunk deep into its skull, and around them its fur was thinning. He caught its hateful breath; an image of maggots, and dung, bloated flies and filth crowded his thoughts. So overpowering was the scent, the cat tried to breathe through his mouth.

Satisfied it had got his attention, the wolf spoke, its voice a whispering oily croak, swathed in layers of phlegm. It was deeper than the other wolves he'd met, but far more sinister, and it made the cat's skin crawl. He wanted to wash, to try to get that smell out of his nostrils, but such was his dread that he dared not move a muscle.

"And they tell me you are dangerous. An enemy of our Lord, and one who seeks to vaunt his ambitions. Our ambition. Our plans. You look far too feeble to have caused this much trouble." The newcomer looked down at the cat, turning its head slightly as if a different angle would reveal new insights. "Still, this won't take long, then we can move on to more pressing matters." The beast stopped, pinning the cat with his stare. He resumed in almost conversational tones that served only to deepen Agent 73's terror. "This is what will happen. First, I will enter your thoughts, delve into your deepmost sanctuary, then take your mind apart, thought by thought, one mental strand at a time. I will find pleasure in that act; it satisfies me. It is a special skill, honed over centuries."

Agent 73's eyes were wide; two dark windows into his soul. His tormentor seemed to relish the fact. The beast continued, but the cat barely heard what it said; he was still trying to comprehend what he'd just heard.

"In doing so I will discover all your innermost secrets and plans. Then I will tear your body to pieces, finally ending your predicament. But I get ahead of myself. Let us go back to the start and take it one step at a time and consider the journey that brought you here. Tell me about that pretty little picture you and your devious friend stole? Where is he, by the way?"

Agent 73's body trembled with fear, but he barely registered the fact, so absorbed was he with the monster standing above him. His jaw clamped shut, locked by terror. He had no idea how to respond. With his eyes wide and fixed on his torturer, he couldn't move.

The gigantic wolf regarded the cat for a while, then continued. "You seem to be a little tongue-tied. No matter. We'll get on to that in due course, once you've loosened up. Along with the little matter of your betrayal." Another pause. Agent 73 still stared back, foolishly and helplessly. He had no idea what his tormentor was talking about.

Abruptly, the wolf lay down on its stomach, placing its face closer to 73's eyeline. It was as if he were held in a hypnotic embrace.

"It wasn't really worth it, was it? This detour of yours. But I'm curious. Was it your idea or his? Who was it who forced you onto a different course? Are you a decoy, or did you genuinely fall out?"

At last, 73 felt able to speak, his body still shivering. "I don't know what you mean."

"Of course you don't. Nobody does at the start, but before long, you'll be begging to get it all off your chest. That's the way it goes. Avoidance, denial, incomprehension, then resentful acceptance, sorrowful admission, and at the end, imploring me to release you into comforting oblivion. I've seen it all before."

The cat tried to swallow, but his mouth was too dry. "Who are you?" he whimpered.

A wheezing rumble originated somewhere deep in the wolf's throat. Apparently, it was laughing.

"Touché. Well done, my little friend. A reminder that, no matter how experienced I may be, it is never too late for manners. Forgive me. I forgot to inform you who I am. It is only polite to let your victim know who is about to dismember it, mind and body. I'm sure it is courtesy you extend to your own small victims? Well, let me put you at ease." The mockery in the wolf's voice only amplified Agent 73's sense of futility. The cat said nothing, his wide eyes, unwavering attention and the fur on his back standing on end were sufficient betrayal of his feelings.

The creature before him looked old beyond his ken, and decrepit beyond measure, but possessed of a power he could only guess at. Any hope of escape vanished; he would die here, and there was nothing he could do about it.

To his surprise, the elderly wolf averted his eyes, staring into the dark at the edge of the cave, apparently lost in reverie, his voice initially hesitant.

"I am a Jotun in wolf form. They called me Grimólfr. Yes, that was it." The massive head swivelled back towards the black cat, his voice growing stronger. "Grimólfr, the Terror of the Tundra. Once, I roamed at the head of my pack, circumnavigated the world in eternal winter, pursued my enemies across the endless frozen dark. But that was long ago. And for a long time, I slept. But his lieutenants awoke me. The Lord of Wolves, Master of the Wild Hunt, sire of Fenris, the cunning father of our kind. And to his service I joyfully returned. I have a new name now; a new name for an old skill. I manipulate minds, disentangle dreams, eviscerate thoughts and obliterate my enemies from the inside, one idea at a time. They call me Dream Twister." He paused as if expecting a response, but Agent 73, rooted to the spot with fear, said nothing.

Dream Twister rose ponderously to his feet, and made a leisurely circumnavigation of the cat, observing him minutely from all angles, as if looking for a weak spot. Rooted to the spot and unable to move, 73 followed the wolf with his head as far as he could, feeling exposed and uncomfortable. He almost preferred it when he could see his interrogator properly. In the shadows towards the fringes of the hall, more wolves had arrived, drawn by the spectacle. Agent 73 had never previously been the centre of so much attention, and preferred his customary anonymity. Although he suspected a desire to see the demonic creature in action had drawn them, rather than the reputation of his potential victim. He was not surprised to see that they maintained a respectful distance. 73 would dearly have liked to have done the same, but he didn't have the option.

At the epicentre of the unequal contest, the small black cat crouched as still as possible, rigid with fear, every moment expecting the worst. All his muscles were clenched so tight he could barely have moved if he'd wanted to.

"Look at me."

Despite the situation, the command caught Agent 73 by surprise. He looked up at the sharply angled face before him, noting the grey flecks around the animal's snout, and the ragged ears that no longer fitted a perfectly triangular profile. None of the creature's monologue had made any sense to him. He wondered how old it could be. The stench of foul breath was stronger than ever, but he steeled himself against it and tried as he might, feeble though he felt, to resist the other animal's overwhelming aura of power. A quiver of fear ran through his small body. Was this it? The end?

"You messed up our plans." Agent 73 blinked in

surprise. The wolf continued. "Caused things to go awry. Without your intervention, the painting would be ours. You owe us."

Dream Twister stared at him for a long time. If he was expecting a response, none was forthcoming. Agent 73 was still trying to work out what it was talking about. He felt confused; thoughts came slowly. His memories seemed tangled up. He tried to make sense of the jumble of recollections swirling around his mind.

"He had a big sharp steel thing. It was scary. Your friend the bird feared it." Agent 73 was barely aware of speaking; he had a strong urge to tell the large wolf everything he'd seen. It felt important. Dream Twister looked down at him for a long moment, then to Agent 73's surprise, lay down in front of him as if relaxing on a nice hearth rug in front of a crackling fire. The wolf's eyes never wavered from the cat.

"Go on."

Agent 73 paused, trying to order his thoughts. He felt it was important to get this right. He spoke slowly. "Your colleague… was late." He stopped, unsure, but held by the fixed blank stare of the wolf, went on. "He, the man that is, had climbed down his string."

"Rope."

"Rope. He was on the ground. Then he appeared. Your friend, that is."

"Tell me about this colleague."

Surely they must know who was on their side. "A huge bird. Black. Like a crow, but bigger. A lot bigger." Agent 73 really didn't want to elaborate further.

"And what did he have to say for himself, this colleague of ours?" The words seemed mild enough, but the cat sensed something more than just curiosity hanging on his response. He floundered for a moment, trying to recollect what was said.

"He started off being rude to the man." His interrogator

stayed silent. More was expected. "Told him there would be consequences."

"Consequences?"

Agent 73 racked his brains. Snatches of conversation came back to him.

"Yes. He said he couldn't give it to him."

"Who?"

"I don't know. Just 'him'. Then the bird said he should take it himself. The man got cross. Took this sharp metal thing out of his bag and waved it around."

"So, you were there with an angry man brandishing a deadly sword at a large agitated bird. How did you escape?" The question seemed mild enough, but 73 detected more than a hint of sarcasm behind it.

"I hid. In a bag. The bag the man had brought."

"You hid."

"Yes."

"That's all."

"Yes."

"And he just carried you away. Just like that? How very convenient."

The cat was instantly aware how feeble that sounded. He blinked his eyes and stared back into his tormentor's face, doubting his memories. What had he forgotten? Could he be sure of anything anymore?

"Now, let's get down to the real truth, shall we?"

CHAPTER 29
DEPOSIT

Berlin was grey. It was one of those days where there seemed barely enough light to reach ground level. Persistent drizzle soaked the city's inhabitants as they went about their business, silent and resigned. In their midst, overlooked and anonymous, Karrig navigated the crowds. He alone seemed to have his eyes on the horizon. Everyone else was looking down, heads shrouded beneath hoods or hats. Being of smaller stature gave him one advantage: there was less danger of losing an eye on the end of one of those damn umbrellas they all carried.

He'd exited from the U-Bahn station at Unter den Linden and then turned into Friedrichstrasse and zig-zagged through the grid-iron pattern of streets until he saw his destination. Arriving at the heavy plate-glass door, he entered the foyer of an anonymous office building and, ignoring the reception desk, turned to his left to approach a second heavy door. On the wall to the side was a keypad beneath a card slot. Karrig fished for his wallet in the inside pocket of his jacket and produced a card. He punched a five-digit PIN into the keypad and was rewarded with the satisfying click of a lock opening.

The room beyond was carpeted and marginally more

welcoming. A slightly overweight male member of staff, squeezed into a suit one size too small for him, sat behind a desk opposite, a veneer of sweat glistening on his forehead despite the constant 18°C temperature. He looked up from his screen as Karrig approached.

"I'd like access to my vault."

"Of course, sir." The man produced a key and handed it over. It was the master key, which, along with Karrig's private key, would open his own individual deposit box. He took it without proffering thanks and strode to the door at the far end of the room. The officer returned to his work.

Next to the door was a small rectangular recessed opening. Karrig slid his hand in and held it still for a couple of seconds while a scanner assessed the vein pattern on the back, and then released the lock to allow him entry. He entered a spacious circular corridor, carpeted and lit by recessed LEDs in the ceiling. Interspersed at regular intervals between the lights were security camera bubbles. Each wall was lined from just below the ceiling to just above the floor with silver doors in a brushed aluminium finish, each numbered and containing a double keyhole lock. Most were of uniform size, but occasionally he would come to a set of larger-sized doors where bigger items could be stored.

Karrig reached into his trouser pocket for a matchbox-sized device and, without removing it, pressed the single button on its exterior. The surveillance cameras would cease recording until he pressed it again. Confident he was no longer being observed, the dwarf held his deposit box key in the palm of his hand, but continued past the numbered door in search of another. He halted further on, confident of his new choice, then with eyes half closed, in a trance-like state, murmured a runic charm. He approached the silver door of the compartment he'd selected, and inserted both keys into their respective locks. Twisting both keys simultaneously, he opened it and removed the long metal box inside. This he carried into the room to his right, in the centre of the circular corridor.

The ceiling held two further security cameras, but these he could now safely ignore. The room was empty apart from a large table, on which Karrig placed the box, and next to it, his bag. He removed the painting from the bag, still in bubble wrap, and gently placed it into the box. It fitted neatly, with little room to spare. He closed the lid and returned to the corridor, slid the box back into its compartment and locked the door, then retraced his steps to the exit. Just before he left, he clicked the button on his device once again.

Karrig strode across to the reception desk and handed back the master key with a cursory nod, then departed. Once safely under cover of the rain again, he felt the weight lift from his shoulders. He turned up the collar of his coat and whistled tunelessly as he made his way back to the U-Bahn station and from there to the Hauptbahnhof. He selected one of the left luggage lockers, and placed the safety deposit key inside. With a smile he wondered how long it would take them to work out the number of the box he'd used. Perhaps he'd save them some effort, once he was sure the funds had landed in his account.

Satisfied he'd completed his task, he made his way to the airport, already looking forward some much-needed, hedonistic rest and relaxation. He'd selected somewhere warm, and near the sea. Somewhere with a bit of nightlife, music, booze and lively company, male or female. And he knew just the place. Only when he'd arrived would he'd switch that sinister phone back on again, demand payment, and ask where his new patron would like him to post the key to the left luggage locker before informing him of the painting's location. All once payment was safely residing in his account, of course. Then, for a few days – or with a bit of luck, several months – the old gods could go to hell.

CHAPTER 30
THE WOLF QUEEN

Haldred stood before the wolf pack's self-appointed queen, their alpha female and head, feeling wrong-footed. He was cautious and determined to give away as little as possible. He knew enough about wolves and their societies to realise that this was an unusual arrangement. What had happened to her mate? His absence didn't alter his situation, though. Her followers gave her due reverence and obeyed without question. That much was normal. Whatever reservations they might have harboured, they kept them to themselves.

The queen stood on a prominent rock in the middle of a large cave. Haldred looked around, counting at least thirty other beasts, all waiting to hear what he had to say. They'd let him take some water, but his mouth was still dry. She addressed the dwarf.

"You must know you have been under surveillance for some time. I don't know what you've done to anger our lord, but that is of no importance to us. Suffice to say we are happy to carry out his orders." Haldred's face was blank. "A web of associates has tracked you across the continent, including my extended family, and it is our good fortune to have apprehended a traitor. Whether you like it or not, you bring us honour. Soon you will be escorted to our lord to answer for your crimes. You can pray he will be lenient, but I think that unlikely. Hopefully, he will give us your bones to gnaw on as reward."

His restraint snapped, and before he knew it, he was pleading for his life. "No, no. You can't." He gesticulated helplessly, arms flailing.

"I think you'll find we can."

"No, it's… I'm no traitor. I'm trying to retrieve the item. Can't you see, I'm working with you, not against you."

The queen ignored his protestations. "Your partner might have escaped, though I'm sure he'll be tracked down before long. In the meantime, you must answer for both of you."

"We're not partners."

"No matter."

"He betrayed me." Haldred's voice rose as he tried to defend himself, overwhelmed with exasperation. This was all a misunderstanding. He wasn't going to be held to account for crimes his brother had committed. He wondered if Loki would see it that way.

"Just excuses."

"I can resolve this. I'm trying to find him, if you'll just let me do my job. Every hour you keep me here makes that more difficult."

The wolf queen focused on him in a way that may have been designed to make him feel insignificant and vulnerable, but Haldred wasn't going to let one of Loki's pet puppies intimidate him. He paused to collect his thoughts, hand on hip, pinching the bridge of his nose with the other as he tried to keep his temper under control. How to explain himself to imbeciles? He continued with exaggerated patience, his voice a little calmer. "I'm trying to find him so I can retrieve the package. Then I'll take it to him. Myself. In person. It will be through *my* efforts the traitor will be caught."

Silence filled the hall.

"Explain that to our master."

Haldred sighed. "I won't be able to get it back if you take me straight to him. It'll be too late. Loki would prefer to get his painting rather than hear some tired excuses." He knew full well that Loki would not be remotely satisfied with excuses, and his contract would most likely be terminated with prejudice, but he chose not to labour the point. "You must see the logic in that." His eyes hardened, a sly grin touching his mouth. "But among the excuses, you can be sure that I'll inform him how obstructive you were. How your delays made capturing him impossible."

There was a pause while the queen chewed over this unpleasant possibility. "He has no doubt already completed his task, so your speeches will have no bearing. Or maybe our leader's other servants will intercept your colleague. For all I know, they may already have done so and your protestations will be irrelevant."

"He's not my colleague! He betrayed me. *Us*." Haldred was shouting now, his frustration getting the better of him. Some wolves moved closer, within touching distance, their threat real, their proximity disconcerting. From the nearby growls, several appeared to be upset that he was taking such an aggressive tone of voice with their queen. Haldred looked around and raised his hands, palms outstretched, then took another breath and tried again.

"He won't have had time to take it anywhere yet. I can find him. I know I can. Then, when I've got the item back, we can share the glory." He tried to smile. "You can come with me. We'll deliver it together." He caught something of her mood from the look she gave him. "You can have all the credit, of course. All the fame. He likes his wolves, doesn't he? Think of the affection he'll pour down on you. Think of the praise, the fuss. The privileges. You could be his guard of honour when he's free. You'd like that, wouldn't you?"

Haldred couldn't help but think his pleading was in danger of sounding patronising, but if there was one gap in the canine armour, it was the archetypal desire for acknowledgement and praise from their superiors. It was a long shot, and if he'd made the wrong call, he'd know about it soon enough.

Looking down from her pedestal, the wolf queen paused.

"If this object is going to be delivered, we shall do the delivering. You will just accompany us to watch and answer his questions."

Haldred bowed low. "Of course, your majesty. Given your status, I would expect nothing more."

"In the meantime," she continued, "we are about to witness the interrogation of a foreign agent. Someone we believe has been acting on behalf of this unknown party. Maybe you should come along. If his story tallies with what you've said, so much the better. If not, we will deal with you then."

Haldred's heart sank. Escaping from the pack would be more difficult than he had hoped. Idly, he wondered who they had in mind. Would they corroborate or undermine his story?

CHAPTER 31
INTERROGATION

Thoughts chased each other lazily around 73's head, but many of them returned to the same starting point again and again: when would the nasty bit start, and how much would it hurt? Fantasies briefly floated past. "Look into my eyes," he imagined himself saying, turning the tables on his opponent, who would melt before his stern gaze. A separate part of his brain wondered what had sparked a thought like that at a time like this? Shouldn't he be terrified and rooted to the spot, rigid with fear? Terror was strangely lacking, or at least it didn't consume every part of his body and soul. Not yet, anyway. Maybe it would come. That took him full circle to where this train of thought originated; when would the horrible questioning start, and how bad would the torture be? For the moment, a strange detachment came over him. *You are not alone.*

Agent 73 wanted to move, but also felt a strong urge to stay exactly where he was and take the game to his opposite number. His bravery surprised him, and as he thought about it, he realised he wasn't afraid. He was a predator, huge and powerful. The biggest and baddest there'd ever been. In these parts, at least. In his imagination, it was his enemy quaking with fear before him, trembling and uncertain of everything except for imminent death. Inwardly, he chuckled, another fragment of his fractured mind assessing it as mirthless, yet another as merciless. What was happening to him?

"Hadn't we better start then?"

Had he just spoken? He must be feeling incredibly confident.

"*We already have*," said a voice in his head.

Strange sensations floated around his consciousness. He felt himself under scrutiny from the inside, at the same time realising that was impossible, but by now he wasn't confident about what was real and what was not. He looked up, and his brain froze. The wolf transformed before his eyes. Above, perilously close, was an enormous triangular insect head. From the narrow mouth immediately before him, he was drawn to large hemispherical compound eyes at the back of the head, multifaceted but predominantly green. Behind them he guessed was a narrow neck that connected the head to a distant bulbous body, mostly in shadow. No ears were visible. Two enormous insectoid legs were splayed on either side of the cat, dwarfing him.

Agent 73's stomach turned over and a sense of dread enveloped him. He expected a sudden dart forwards from that terrible head and the legs to either side, and the impact of a sharp bite followed by the probing tubular tongue that would penetrate his body and mulch his insides. A cold shiver ran down his spine.

Anticipating his thought, the head looming above him tilted to one side and turned. A pause, and a sharp, sudden pounce produced a catch; a fly caught between pincers. With horrible sluggishness, the mantis began to eat, feasting on the fat, hairy abdomen, the juice of the entrails dripping from its mandibles even while the unfortunate victim's legs flailed in its face. The flailing lessened as the creature died, and was consumed from the inside out before the cat's eyes.

A warning, perhaps, and effective. Agent 73's insides turned to jelly, a desire to flee all-consuming. But he was still incapable of movement. He'd never had an instinctive revulsion towards insects; he found them fascinating, especially beetles, as he'd been by far the larger entity and there was no sense of threat. With the tables turned, he was appallingly vulnerable. He cowered before the inscrutable eyes and waited while the beast continued its meal in a leisurely fashion. When at last its grisly repast was over, the head turned back to the cat, the juices of the fly's innards still dripping from its chin, and studied him once more. The demonstration, if that was what it was, had succeeded. Exposed and terrified, Agent 73 shook with terror.

The creature spoke. Again, the cat sensed the words in his head, rather than via his ears.

"Now, where were we?" There was a pause. "Ah, yes. Time for a little chat about you, isn't it? Yes, it's time to find out a little bit more about our small visitor. I must admit you're very brave to come up into the mountains, right outside our lair. It's almost as if you wanted to observe our movements; report our comings and goings, to spy on us, to put it bluntly."

The faux friendliness did not fool the cat. It was as convincing as a human with some food in one hand and a big stick in the other. He waited.

"Tell me where you come from." The face hovered over him, bobbing slightly.

"I come from the car park."

"A car park? How interesting. Tell me, do you like cars, or is there another reason to live there?"

The mantis was frightening, but the condescending tone irritated Agent 73, and deposited a tiny nugget of resistance among his thoughts. But he did wonder where all this was leading.

"I just like to sit under them on hot days." He'd like to say something crushingly witty, but he couldn't think of anything clever to fire back. The mantis remained inscrutable, waiting for its subject to continue.

"I get things to eat," the cat added. "From the humans. Well," he considered, "some of them, anyway. Others aren't very nice." He still felt himself pinned by those eyes, and hoped desperately that he'd said the right thing. He didn't want to end up like the fly, whose wing lay just to the right, on the edge of his peripheral vision.

"And does the car park have a name?"

For a moment, Agent 73 was baffled. Of course not. Who, in their right mind, would name a car park?

"Varlaam Monastery," he blurted out, the idea having suddenly popped into his head. "Yes, that's it. Varlaam Monastery Car Park." He'd always known that, of course. Agent 73 chastised himself for forgetting something so basic. The mantis remained still.

"Varlaam Monastery," the giant head repeated. "And what did you do at Varlaam Monastery?" The tone had changed from condescending to something harder edged, more searching.

"I've been watching for signs of criminal activity." Agent 73 felt pleased to talk about something he knew. He wondered why this other creature was so interested in how he spent his days. In fact, why was it interested in anything to do with his mundane life. He was just a cat, and an ordinary one at that. He harboured no delusions. *Don't do yourself down so much*, came a thought in his head. *No cats are ordinary. Have some respect for yourself and your species.*

From above, the condescending tone returned. "That seems like quite an important job. Did you think it up all by yourself?"

Agent 73 paused, uncertain. "No."

"Mmm?" came the reply.

"Yes," he said.

"Oh, how interesting. No, then yes. Which one is it? It's not that hard, surely?"

Even in this parlous state, the cat was aware of the dripping sarcasm. Agent 73 suddenly felt hot under his fur, but he was also aware it was important to get the answer right.

"I didn't have to. It was my decision." The assertiveness in his answer surprised him.

"Oh, you decided? Well done. You must have a very high opinion of yourself. Are you expecting a medal?"

Agent 73 didn't know what a medal was, but if this creature thought it a good thing, he definitely didn't want one. His reply was testy. "I didn't have to."

"You had the chance to say no? To turn down this job that you invented for yourself, then didn't? So, it seems someone did ask you to perform this task. What did you say it was? 'Watching for signs of criminal activity'. Well now, who would you have turned down? They can't have been very persuasive, or frightening."

"Nobody." The cat felt both irritated and defensive, but strangely proud of having made such a decision by himself, of his own free will. It was an unfamiliar emotion, but it comforted him to think he'd done the right thing. His thoughts returned to the strange conversation with the grey cat, and he decided he wouldn't have changed anything, even though it had led him to this perilous situation. He didn't want to share any of the details of the conversation with his terrible interrogator. "It was my choice."

"You sound a little touchy." The cat looked down, trying to take his mind off the terrible head in front of him. "That makes me suspicious. I think you may just be trying to hide something from me. Something about a person or creature who gives you instructions, yes? That's what I think, at any rate, that you are nothing but their pawn. A little pet who got ideas above his station and ended up completely out of his depth. Am I right?"

Agent 73 said nothing, uncertainty clouding his mind. Out of nowhere, he had the sensation of warmth and comfort. A strange voice murmured encouragement inside his head, gentle but distant.

You are not alone.

"I don't know," was all he could reply.

"Someone must have said something, even if only in passing? Put yourself in my position, and tell me, is it really likely that a small, innocuous animal – a mere feline, and a simple one at that – could have dreamed up some ingenious plan to try to identify criminal activity all by yourself? Hmm? You agree that sounds suspicious, no?"

The hideous head towering above him, with its syrupy sarcastic voice made him shudder, but still he could not move. The other voice murmured at the back of his mind once more.

Just tell him as much as you need.

"I didn't have to help. I wanted to." Searching his memories, he wasn't sure he was telling the truth, but if he'd been dismissive at the time, his decision felt right now. He liked the thought of helping the grey cat; she'd been his friend.

The mantis's head just looked at him then tilted slightly. The cat braced himself for attack, but it didn't come.

Instead, the face before him changed, softening and becoming less angular. It morphed into something more familiar: another feline. Young, appealing and sensual. Provocative, even. He searched this new image and became lost in its haunting beauty. He could glimpse appealing hindquarters, and the casual lie of her tail. Her whole stance was inviting. He was no longer rooted in rock, but rather than relief, he was overwhelmed with desire for this divine creature before him.

The emotion grew instantly, with all other thoughts dispelled, even the icy fear that had gripped him just moments ago. Now, confronted by this lithe, stunning creature, an intense yearning overwhelmed him; an emotion more powerful than he'd ever known. The primitive urge to mate, old as life itself, consumed him.

Small and insignificant though he was, he desperately wanted to impress her. His breathing quickened, and he could feel his impatient heart beating in his chest. The apparition before him was so real, he could think of nothing else. With tunnel vision, his focus increased until he could see nothing apart from her face and her eyes, beckoning silently with the subtlest of signs. Her musky scent soaked his senses, powering his lust; a silky soft forehead bunted against his own. 73 bowed his head and closed his eyes, overcome with desire.

"You must realise how silly your story sounds?" Purring filled his ears, flowed into and through his body in wave after wave of sensuous vibration. "Now, let me tell you what I think," she breathed, "then you can tell me I'm right, and we can all move on. Wouldn't you like that? I might even let you..." she whispered, her voice no louder than the beat of butterfly wings in the thick air between them. "I see how much you'd like that." She let the thought hang. The room felt hot and airless, the link between them almost physical. Around the edges of his peripheral vision, the light assumed a pinkish fuzzy neon glow, all he could do was concentrate on her eyes.

"Oh, yes." He could say no more. All the pent-up fervour of his young life filled the space between them, fulfilment balanced on invisible scales, waiting for her next word. He was hers. He would do whatever she wanted.

"Now what I think is this," she purred. "I think you and your little friend, the one dangling on the end of the rope, are acting together. He steals the painting, you keep watch for observers, and give him warning. And together, you're acting on behalf of that big, bad black bird? He's the one that's really giving the orders, am I right?" She paused, examining his face in minute detail, looking for signs of a response.

"It's easy," she breathed. "Just admit it and get past the lie, then you can relax and tell me everything, just like I know you want to." Her voice dropped. "Whisper it to me." A slow blink almost drove him insane. His breathing was ragged, his body taut as a coiled spring. He looked deep into those eyes, swimming in desire, happy to confess all; anything he'd ever known. He'd even make things up just so he could confess them, so he could consummate his desire. But the deeper he looked, the more he saw. And what he saw was darkness: eternal, without warmth or love. Only emptiness, devoid of feeling. The urge to confess vanished, evaporating in his fear of the void. His body relaxed, and he shivered in the sudden chill as the dank atmosphere of the cave returned. Rather than falling in love, he realised he was cold and alone. Isolated. A different kind of fear returned. The face before him assumed a cold, resentful look, then changed. He closed his eyes.

After a while, he cautiously opened them and found that he was alone in a dark place, lying in a pool of dim light which extended only a metre beyond his body. He couldn't sense any walls, and guessed that this must be a large, cavernous space. Any sense of relief at being free to move was instantly extinguished. He felt ancient beyond the normal span allocated to his kind. Every muscle ached, and every joint throbbed with arthritic pain. Moving was an effort and his breathing was laboured. Weariness soaked through every fibre of his body and into the stone beneath. Any vestige of hope evaporated. He flopped onto his side, knowing that there was no way he could ever get up again. From this agony, death would be an escape.

On the edge of the light circle, as it faded into black, he saw a gigantic reptilian head, and a forked tongue flicked out, tasting the air. Above it, two protruding eyes studied him as if he were an annoying puzzle to be solved. Behind the head, a long snake-like body disappeared into the gloom. As the tongue darted forth, Agent 73 noticed rows of sharp triangular teeth behind thin, bloodless lips. The creature was dispassionate in its appraisal of him.

"I must admit you have surprised me," it said, in a quiet, hissing voice. "One barrier after another. Whoever sent you was truly ingenious, if cold and heartless. They trained you well." The cat had no idea what the creature meant. He was here alone. Everything he'd done since the night he ventured down into the valley had been his own initiative. No one had "sent" him. Amid the weariness pervading his body, that was his least concern, and probably his last. He had no desire to understand what his questioner wanted. He was past caring. He heard the voice again.

"But your secrets will be revealed in due course. You cannot shield your deepest thoughts from me, and once we know who your masters are, we can examine their motivation, and together we can search for meaning. Oh yes, my not-so-innocent little friend. There is always meaning, always a purpose, and behind all that stands one great truth: knowledge is power. We have much to explore, you and I. Either voluntarily, with your help, or against your will. To me, it's immaterial. Remember this: somewhere between your darkest fear and your brightest hope lies the truth. That is all I seek. That is what we will find, you and I. First, tell me what you saw."

He'd hoped it might be over, but it was clear there was to be no respite. Thinking took all his energy. Agent 73 struggled to organise his recollections.

"I've told you. There was a man."

"No. The thing that was stolen." An increase in volume betrayed the creature's impatience. "The painting. Tell me about it."

There was a pause while Agent 73 tried to ignore the pain

that clouded his thoughts, struggled against it, and failed. He closed his eyes.

"Perhaps this will help," the hissing voice prompted. The cat opened his eyes and saw a dark shape approaching across the floor; a worm, moving with a horrible concertina shuffle. He tried to focus before it got too close. What he saw made him shudder in horror, causing a vibration of agony to sweep across his body. The worm was smooth-skinned, eyeless, segmented and moving with purpose. The segments of its body stretched and contracted as it moved. A small circular mouth seemed to sniff him out. Agent 73 wanted to move, to roll away, to stand up and leave. But gravity welded his frame to the floor.

The thing, approaching with purpose, slithered across his neck, up towards his ear. He couldn't stop it. Without pause it burrowed in, and the cat experienced a sharp but fleeting pain as it broke some membrane or other and slithered down inside him. Then, nothing. The lack of further pain worried him. Ahead, he focused once more on the lizard before him.

"That is one of my pets. A Mind Worm. Such a pretty creature, don't you think?" There was a hint of triumph in the voice now.

"What's it doing?" Agent 73 was close to panic; unsurprising given the circumstances. The inscrutable reptilian eyes blinked, and its forked tongue made another foray.

"Why, it's doing what all worms do. Chewing through your grey matter, mulching, analysing and regurgitating, then sifting through the debris. It's just the usual composting process. Makes those thoughts of yours nice and friable, so I can watch all your little memories germinate and grow, then pluck out the ones I want." The head retracted slightly, as if to consider its answer. Apparently satisfied, it tried to justify itself. "I have to do this because you're refusing to divulge what I want to know. Acting dumb and all that. Your plan is so transparent. Don't think you've fooled me for an instant.

But it won't work. Not with me. Not against Dream Twister." The creature could not hide its arrogance.

Agent 73 could only listen and try to understand, but as his thoughts fractured and broke apart, even that was proving tricky. What had he been blocking? He wasn't aware of trying to obstruct or obscure anything. He was just a simple animal that had ended up in this extraordinary situation. His first instinct was usually to be helpful. Well, okay, his second instinct; the first was usually to stay well out of anything approaching an argument, but that was no longer an option. Idly, as if he had all the time in the world to explore his feelings, the cat wondered how long his predicament might last. It wouldn't have a nice outcome; he was now absolutely positive about that. But surely his tormentor didn't have any reason to prolong the agony.

Thoughts chased one another around his head like butterflies around flowers. Names? What names? If he could, he would have laughed at the absurdity of it. What did he know of names, who never even had a proper one of his own? A nuzzling comforting sensation encroached on the fringes of his scattered consciousness. *Don't panic. Everything will be alright.*

In the midst of his torment, a sense of detachment took him. In his imagination his thoughts took the form of bees buzzing around a bougainvillea.

He had no time to relax. A burst of images from memory splashed across his consciousness with bewildering speed. They seemed wrong: scenes from his life that he could only witness, not organise. The intrusion was alarming. Something or someone was sifting his thoughts, and he had no say. The images flitting across his mind's eye were all jumbled up. Some felt unfamiliar, he presumed they were, from early kittenhood. Scenes of the mother he only vaguely remembered, terrifyingly thin and with the haunted look of one who'd suffered too many beatings. There were pictures of life in the car park; encounters and arguments with his rivals; the visit to Freddie and the meeting with the wolf. But some things were missing. He found he couldn't bring to mind the grey cat at all, or the moment he hid in the short man's backpack, or the discussion that was going on. He only dimly recalled the horrible imprisonment in the back of the car. He saw the creepy deserted village and the dreary valley leading up to it, but not his escape from the car. Nor could he picture the driver, other than a vague outline. His treasure, the item he'd been slammed against in the backpack was nothing more than a blur.

The cat witnessed all this with an air of detachment, as if these episodes in his past belonged to someone else. His life was being independently curated, and he had no say in the exhibition. Throughout the process, he periodically experienced sharp jabbing pains that made him wince, as if the invisible librarian was sorting through some particularly painful episodes. Fortunately, as he was young, there weren't too many.

The lizard morphed into something larger, harder, and more frightening. The face was still reptilian but elongated and knobbly with far larger teeth, which it struggled to contain in its long jaw. A single ridge of hard scales rose from its back, and in the distance the cat was aware of a massive heavy tail that thrashed impatiently. In the shadows to the side, Agent 73 watched as enormous leathery wings unfolded. The creature snarled, and the cat caught a whiff of bitumen and charcoal on the beast's breath and a draft of hot air. He had no reference point for dragons; he'd never seen one before. But even in his innocence the thing looked alarming. The questioning was angry now.

"How did you learn to shield your thoughts? A pathetic creature like you? Stop hiding them. Give me their names, or I'll burn you to a crisp." Demonic yellow eyes glared at him.

"What names?" the cat pleaded, realising that exasperation was likely to be his last emotion.

The reply came as a growling snarl and a short puff of flame that passed close to his head, singeing his whiskers. Agent 73 tried one last time.

"I don't know what you want!"

The dragon rose, clumsy and cumbersome in its size, until it stood on massive legs, towering over the feeble cat that lay prone and exhausted on the ground.

"Trying to play the hero, eh? Trying to obstruct me? You simple fool."

So, he thinks I'm a hero? Despite his predicament, the cat experienced a secret surge of pleasure and satisfaction that reached to the tip of his tail and the end of his claws. But an appreciation of the danger extinguished any lingering self-congratulatory feelings, and for a moment he couldn't think of anything to say.

"Someone asked me if I wanted to be a hero once, and I said no." He barely knew where he was, or what was happening. His breathing was ragged and his throat sore, but he found the defiance to go on. "I don't remember anything about my mother except for one thing." Agent 73's voice faltered. The dragon stared at him. "But that one thing she told me was this: never give in to bullies."

He closed his eyes and waited for the fearsome blast that would destroy him. In his pain-wracked mind, it was all over. He hoped it would be quick. Instead, a bewildering flood of images exploded in his brain as if his entire life's experiences were swirling and tumbling together simultaneously. Across them came a flash of light, searing and scattering everything else to the shadows, and then putting the shadows to flight.

Fragments of incoherent thought struggled to link and make sense of it all, but failed. A monstrous creature of light was in the cave, so bright it was impossible to properly look at. He caught the fleeting impression of a cat, but much bigger. The dragon's head moved quickly, darting from side to side, trying to locate the intruder, but dazzled by the sudden glare. Agent 73 felt a burden lift, but it was replaced by woozy fatigue. Unconsciousness was coming. Through half-closed eyes and with a sense of exhausted detachment, he observed his interrogator's sudden moves.

Blinded, the dragon twisted back and forth, searching. Enraged, it shrieked; an unearthly and ear-splitting squeal of fear and desperation. Shadowy wings stretched from wall to wall but were peeled away by the light. The cat felt the searing heat as a bolt of flame jetted from the dragon's mouth, double the length of its body. But against a creature made of light, it was like trying to melt a glacier with a torch. Once more, the dragon tried to fry its unseen opponent, but to no avail. Taking its time, the newcomer advanced steadily. To his surprise, 73 could now make out eyes amid the wider glow. Focused, golden, and filled with merciless detachment.

The newcomer pounced like a gigantic cat on a mouse. His senses fading, Agent 73 saw Dream Twister change shape ever more rapidly as it tried to escape. Briefly, it held the form of a giant spider, but its legs were too feeble to stab or hold its enemy. A paw made of light seemed to bat it away like a paper toy, only to be pounced on with renewed ferocity as it landed, and was gripped between enormous jaws. The spider became a bull, a vulture, a hyena. All to no avail; it could not break free. The images flooded the small cat's befuddled mind, but none of it made sense. With his last sight, it was hurled into the air in the form of an enormous wolf, and he thought he saw a man – nothing more than an outline of shimmering gold – draw a mighty bow and shoot an arrow of bright white light through its heart. He knew no more.

CHAPTER 32
MYKONOS

Blinded by the sudden flash of lights, and deafened by squealing and yelping, Haldred hurled himself to the ground, his eyes shut tight, his hands clamped over his ears. Pressure waves rolled over him, scattering and tearing at all in their path and rendering him unconscious.

When he came to, it was dark but his head was spit with pain. He lay there trying to work out what had happened. Faint light allowed him to make out the rough walls of the cave once more. There was no sound. A minute passed, two, before he dared to move. Satisfied it was safe, he rose unsteadily to his feet, staggering until he regained his balance, then tentatively reached for the back of his head. Wincing in pain, he detected the crustiness of dried blood in his hair, but at least the wound seemed to have stopped bleeding. He felt sick.

Cautiously, Haldred squinted about him until his eyes properly adjusted to the dim blue of dwarf-light and he was able to stand upright and stretch his aching back. He closed his eyes again, to try and calm his throbbing head, and come to terms with the dull ringing in his ears. It took a while before he was able to open them again and take in the surrounding devastation.

No one else was alive; he was surrounded by the bodies of many wolves. They made grotesque shapes, scattered about the floor. Haldred wondered how he'd survived when so many had not. Was it luck that he had been close to the entrance, partially shielded from the blast of whatever had killed them? His eyes were drawn to the formidable body of Dream Twister himself, much larger than he'd remembered and in death even more repulsive.

The body was covered with deep scars that still oozed black blood that was still congealing as it was exposed to the air. Haldred guessed he hadn't been unconscious as long as he'd first thought. He stared at the enormous corpse, transfixed. The gigantic carcass held a brooding presence, but as Haldred watched, it began to dissolve as if eaten away from within. In horrible fascination, he witnessed it crumble to dust, leaving only an outline on the floor.

Freed from his nightmare vision, he looked around. Of the cat there was no sign. It must have been blown to atoms. Nor was there any evidence of the queen amid the dead. He presumed she, at least, and some of her entourage had escaped. Whatever or whoever had made the dramatic intervention was also gone.

Haldred suffered a moment of indecision. Here was his chance to escape. But which way should he go? There were at least three exits from this cave; which one led away from the wolves to freedom? As he considered the options, movement attracted his attention. Something was slithering across the floor: the Mind Worm. Somehow, it must have escaped from the target's body. Where was it going? Absorbed, and a little repulsed, Haldred followed the creature's slow progress across the floor as it sought sanctuary. At the back of his mind, a madcap plan formed. What if…?

Frantically, he searched for a way to capture it, then

spotted his pack against the wall and hobbled over to retrieve it. Biting down his fear of what the worm might do to him if he mishandled it, he attempted to pick it up. It was like trying to catch a quicksilver slug; repeatedly, it slipped through his fingers. Finally, he placed the pack on the ground before the thing and ushered it into a side pocket, then closed the zip.

He stood once more and winced. Looking down, through a rip in his trousers, he saw a large gash above his knee, and felt the warm wetness of blood trickling down his leg. No wonder he was struggling to walk. Yet walk he must. He had no desire to be here when his captors finally recovered their courage and returned.

An inherent familiarity with underground locations enabled him to pick a good escape route from the wolves' lair. Letting his instincts guide him, Haldred followed the streams of fresher, cleaner air flowing down into the labyrinth, and avoided those entrances that he suspected contained hidden dangers. But the pain in his leg prevented him from moving fast. Several hours passed before he emerged into bright sunshine, high on a mountainside. Below him, not far away, was a large lake. He had no idea where he was.

Grimacing with every step, he negotiated the steep, untracked slope to the valley floor, and the thin ribbon of tarmac he'd spotted weaving between fields and farms. Once down, he waited by the roadside until he saw a tractor arriving, and held out his thumb. The farmer took a long look at his dishevelled appearance, and jerked his head at the empty trailer he was towing. The journey to the nearest small town was uncomfortable but mercifully short. Once there, Haldred was able to let his credit card work some magic of its own.

The beauty of small airports is that you can leave them quickly, and within twenty minutes of landing, Karrig was in the back of a taxi on the short journey to the luxurious beachside property he'd rented. Nestling in a secluded spot on a rocky promontory overlooking the sea, it even had a small private beach, but more importantly, for his liking, it was just a few minutes stagger from a complex of beach bars and nightclubs that would test his stamina and satiate his appetite for partying for the next week or two.

Less than an hour after landing, he was floating on his back in the pool, enjoying the late afternoon sun, relaxing. He'd earned this break, and he was going to make the most of it. His brow furrowed momentarily, as his memory flicked across the circumstances that had led him here. But he dismissed the negative thoughts. Competition was part and parcel of the trade they were in. Haldred would get over it.

The one-storey house sprawling across this jagged headland was architect-designed to unobtrusively meld with the scenery. It fitted in and around the outcrops and was partly built into the hillside behind, rather than dominating the landscape. Its seclusion made it a triumph of concealment, although that had been a secondary concern when Karrig made the booking. But now, lounging by the pool, he was grateful for the solitude. He would have company aplenty later on.

Thirst took him through the large open patio doors and across the cool open-plan living and dining area to the kitchen beyond. He slammed cupboard doors until he found what he was looking for: some glassware and the beverages the owner had assured him were present. He poured himself a generous gin and tonic, then detoured into the bedroom to retrieve a paperback from his bag.

He was struck by how much the room resembled a cave, but the granite that formed the wall and roof had been smoothly polished so that the crystals glistened, reflecting the glow from recessed lighting and giving a cool ambience. It was as if the architect had lived underground. Thoughts of his long-lost home flooded his mind, catching him by surprise. Karrig tried to avoid such recollections normally, but here he was reminded anew of what he'd been forced to abandon. A wave of regret washed over him. He ran his hand lightly over the surface of the rock and closed his eyes, feeling the pulse of crystalline granite through his fingers. The bones of the earth felt good here. He muttered a prayer to Yggdrasil, the World Tree which held Midgard in its embrace. Not normally prone to acts of piety, he switched his attention to more mundane matters, grabbed his book and returned to the patio.

Sipping his drink, he pondered the evening ahead. A short walk away lay his evening's entertainment; two or three nightclubs where he could while away a few hours, part with a significant amount of cash and in the process make some new temporary best friends. Perhaps he could entice a few of them back here to continue the party? All in due course; no need to overdo it on the first night.

The phone with the sinister app floated once more into his thoughts. When should he make contact? He frowned and absently rubbed his forearm, as if trying to brush away an itch. There was time enough. He'd just completed a tricky job on behalf of an extremely dangerous deity. He needed to unwind before making contact again. The memory of that earlier encounter still made his skin crawl and, despite wanting payment, Karrig was in no hurry for a repeat. If others of his kind knew what he'd done, they would be horrified with his behaviour all over again. He would never free himself of this stain on his character. An eternal outcast. Unclean. A cultural traitor at the very least.

He closed his eyes and tried to empty his mind of such thoughts and release the tension in his shoulders. A few minutes later he opened his eyes and looked about him afresh. He may have been an outcast and a crook, but as he basked in his immediate surroundings, he had to admit he enjoyed the lifestyle the proceeds allowed. However, he desperately wanted it to be a one-off; he had no desire to become trapped in an endlessly repeating cycle like his miserable brother. It might be worthwhile doing some research on Set, his friends and enemies. How dangerous was he, and what was Karrig dealing with? Whether he could arm himself against something similar happening in the future was a different matter. Karrig pushed the paperback aside, reached for his laptop and started reading.

A short distance away, a long-haired red tabby cat strolled among the rocks of the promontory, sniffing the afternoon air. He hadn't been awake for long, and with the sun already descending quickly towards the horizon, the evening's revelries were drawing closer. In just a few hours, he would be back at his favourite beach-side haunt: the bar and nightclub by the shore. Dionysus enjoyed life on Mykonos. The long summer months made it the perfect place to hang out, and he enjoyed the attention he got from the clubbers. Winter was another matter; perhaps he should retreat to the mainland during the colder months, as he once used to, but that could wait for now. The season was not yet over, and there were still plenty of long nights of hedonistic fun ahead.

Before the club opened and the partying commenced, he needed to stretch his legs and get a little air. A regular daily stroll took him across the rocky headland at the western tip of the bay. It was quiet here, and he could enjoy the warmth of the afternoon and find a comfy spot to lounge and enjoy views of the sea for a while. He would stay to watch the sunset before heading back to meet this evening's worshippers. Dionysus always waited until the place was in full swing before entering. It wouldn't do to appear needy.

Walking past the house to his favourite perch, he glanced

at the short figure sitting on the patio, absorbed in his computer. Humanity never failed to disappoint; why come to such a wonderful location and sit staring at a screen when below him was a perfect small cove and secluded beach, and only two metres to his right, a relaxing pool?

CHAPTER 33
DECISION TIME

It took twenty-four hours to get back to Prague, but there was little sanctuary to be found back at his apartment. Haldred shut the door behind him, and leaned against it for a moment, eyes closed, trying to block out the world. It was impossible. Immediately, the incessant hissing chatter began to intrude on his thoughts. *Give me freedom. I deserve to be set free. Now. You owe me; you don't own me. Traitor. Release, release, release me.*

"Shut up."

In the kitchen cupboards he found the paracetamol and swallowed a couple, washing them down with the dregs of the vodka. Then he showered, re-dressed the wound on his leg, and found a change of clothes. Another quick search of the kitchen uncovered a plastic box with a sealed lid. He pondered briefly. Did the thing need to breathe? Or did it live entirely off the brainwave energy of its host? He couldn't take any risk, so with a sharp knife, he ground a couple of tiny holes in the lid, and coaxed the Mind Worm into its new prison. That would have to do. In daylight it seemed diminished, somehow, its movements slow and sluggish. Maybe it was hungry to feed. He would need to give it some fresh meat soon.

In Bratislava, Anja had established a lookout post on the roof of the building opposite the apartment of the fake dwarf. She was sure he was the key, but the rest of the clue still baffled her. Why was he twice fake? Why couldn't her handlers ever be direct? She finished the vegan wrap and turned to her small range finder on its little tripod. He was still there. Occasionally she would see his bald head scuttling past the window, usually carrying something: a mug, a glass, a paintbrush, a palette board. He must fancy himself as an artist.

The only art Anja cared for was crunching, powerful drumbeats underpinning jagged guitar chords. As for painting, the darker the better; anything that hinted at the world's impending gloomy fate. The sooner they got used to the idea, the better.

She glugged down some mineral water, grimaced at its sodium flavour, and checked the label. Where was the source? Coming from Iceland's overlaid realm, she knew all about volcanic springs, but this one tasted rank. She made a face, and threw the bottle aside, then returned to her vigil. At her side was the sniper rifle with its telescopic sight that she'd removed from the hard-shell case and assembled when she got up here. It was far enough back from the parapet to be invisible from below.

Yuri was making good progress. His painting was almost ready. For the zillionth time, he stood back and cast a critical eye over his efforts and compared them to the high-resolution digital rendering he'd printed, pasted to a board and placed next to it. He peered at the photo, fished a pair of glasses from a pocket and peered at it more closely. Had he replicated the brush strokes well enough? The original was an exquisite example of the period. Stylistic perfection itself, and bore very few marks of wear, despite its age. It was critical to get the imperfections right. Yuri noted the blemishes and set to work to recreate them. The whole process had taken far longer than he'd hoped, but it was nearly finished. He was aware of being in a race against time and dreaded the next visit from his client: the tall olive-skinned stranger and his terrifying friend. He absolutely had to be ready for them whenever they called. These past few days, he had lived in fear of…

A knock at the door. Yuri froze. He put down his brush and sidled to the window at the far side of his studio apartment; the only one that looked out from the rear of the building. Inconveniently it was above the kitchen sink, but as an emergency measure he'd acquired and fixed a long rope ladder there for eventualities such as this. The knock became louder, more insistent.

"Open up. I know you're in there."

Yuri threw the ladder out and leaned forward to watch it unroll. His stomach lurched. He feared heights, but extreme circumstances demanded extreme measures.

"It's me. Haldred. I want to talk."

He frowned. Haldred? What was he doing here?

"Just a minute." He stood by the sink, his thoughts racing. "Who's with you?"

"No one."

"How did you get in?" The pause was just long enough to give him doubt.

"I got lucky. Someone came out just as I arrived."

Yuri doubted it, but he approached his door, anyway.

"What do you want?"

"I've got something for you. Something important."

"What is it?"

"Open the door and I'll show you." Haldred sounded impatient. Yuri unlocked, but kept the chain on. He opened the door a crack and peered out. He could only see Haldred. He closed the door again and unfastened the chain, then stood back to let his friend in.

Standing in the hall, Haldred's impatience grew. Of course he hadn't needed anyone else to let him in. He was a dwarf. His skill with locks and spells enabled him to open it easily, but it would destroy all trust if he repeated the trick with Yuri's door, and for the moment, he still wanted him onside. He put the thought of what he was about to do to the back of his mind.

As soon as he entered the apartment, he recognised the signs of someone under pressure. Fast-food wrappers littered the floor, alongside empty beer bottles. Coffee mugs littered the table alongside an overflowing ashtray and crumpled magazines. Dirty plates were stacked in the sink, and the detritus of an artist lay all around: empty paint tubes, jars of brush cleanser, sketches and notes, palette knives. The open window with the ropes dangling out was unexpected. Was that Yuri's escape route? The fresh air had made little impression on the fuggy atmosphere. His eye was drawn to the easel in the centre of the room on which sat a pristine version of the icon of Nikita the Martyr. Lovely, but pointless. *What a waste of time*, he thought, and suppressed a spasm of anger at the misunderstanding that had led him on that pointless exercise. And he still believed it? Oh well, that was Yuri's problem. Right now, he had more urgent matters to deal with.

On the rooftop opposite, drops of rain fell. Anja swore and grimaced at the grey skies above. The last thing she wanted was to be lying here in a puddle all day, waiting for her target. For a moment she considered abandoning the vigil for the day, but then she peered over the parapet again and put the thought aside. Downstairs, at the front of the building opposite, a short, bearded man stood at the door; he appeared to be studying the lock intently. A resident?

He entered the building, turning sideways to close the door, and in that moment she realised how short he was relative to the door handle, and caught sight of his long, forked beard. He was no man. He was Svartalfar: a dark elf, that species commonly referred to as dwarves. The real thing.

The cryptic instruction began to make sense. *The non-dark will lead you to your answer*. The fake dwarf upstairs had led her to the real thing, his dark elf contact. Her target. She turned her attention back to the windows of the apartment, saw the fake dwarf's confusion, and watched as he moved to the shadows at the back of the room, then out of sight. After a while, she saw the newcomer enter then swiftly move across the room to study something out of sight in the other direction. *It would be nice to just blow the whole apartment to pieces*, she thought, *and do the job properly*. Anja pulled her rifle closer and continued watching through the telescopic sight. Her finger reached slowly for the trigger.

Haldred scanned the forger's face. Yuri seemed paranoid. He made scarcely any more sense than at their last meeting.

"I've got something for you. A new commission."

"Can't. I've got to finish this."

"It looks finished to me. But this one can't wait."

Yuri was ready to argue. Haldred tried to placate him. "It's really easy. It'll take you no time at all. You just have to go with the flow and paint what the creature tells you, or shows you."

Even in his distracted state, Yuri's fractured thoughts coalesced in confusion. "What creature?"

Haldred dropped his pack and extracted a plastic box, trying not to think about what he intended to do to his friend.

He advanced towards the artist; his mouth dry. "This," he said.

Yuri looked at the black snake-like thing wriggling feebly inside the box and backed away. He tripped over a chair and fell to the floor. Immediately, Haldred was on top of him, pinning him down with his knees. He ripped open the box and tipped the contents onto Yuri's face. He screamed, but to no avail. The Mind Worm, sensing fresh feeding material, worked its way into his nostril, in search of nourishment. Haldred watched as its body elongated and stretched to enter the narrow space. Within moments, it had disappeared into its target's sinuses and the soft tissue behind.

Yuri screamed some more, and a trickle of blood ran out of his nose in the creature's wake. His body bucked, nearly throwing the dwarf aside, then went still. His eyes opened, a wild and frenzied look in them. Haldred felt sick to the core of his being, but he moved aside to let the artist stand.

"Now, paint what you see."

It was a desperate throw of the die, and for a moment it appeared to work. Yuri sat, then started babbling.

"So beautiful. So fresh, it could have been painted yesterday. The features, very refined for an artist of that era. And the setting, the positioning. How delicate is the hillside town? The cave is crude, but overall, what a fine example of the era."

Still muttering to himself, the forger staggered to his feet, his eyes staring wildly but seeing visions far away. He stumbled like a blind man, bumping into furniture, hands outstretched, trying to grasp for materials, searching for an easel. Haldred was delighted. For a moment, he put his guilt to one side. His gamble seemed to have worked. It just might save him. He would make it up to Yuri later; something lavish from his gallery in New York. It would all work out fine.

"Where are my brushes?"

Haldred selected an appropriate clean brush, and pressed

it into his friend's hands. He steered him towards the easel and swapped the canvas for a blank one. Yuri dropped the brush. Haldred leaned down to pick it up and heard a sharp crack. Still bent over, he looked aside and saw a hole in the window, glass splintering and fracturing around it. Behind him, Yuri toppled over sideways. In horror, Haldred saw the spray of blood and brain matter on the wall behind, and looking down, the hole in the side of his friend's face, above the ear.

"No!"

As he moved closer, there was another crack, and something flew past so close he could feel the air move. He threw himself flat and crawled to the back of the room, trying to take in what was happening. For more years than he could remember, he'd lived with the fear of assassination, but now an attempt was being made, he struggled to absorb it. Finally, a survival instinct kicked in, and he crawled towards the door. Cautiously, he stood, hoping he was out of sight of the sniper. His first thought was to run down the stairs, but whoever was out there was probably expecting that, so he needed another way out. Was there a fire escape? Maybe, but he didn't want to risk the stairwell for the same reason. His gaze returned to the rope ladder Yuri had dangled out of the kitchen window.

Haldred checked he was still out of sight of the assassin, and crept towards it. He was in luck. He tested the fastenings, then risked a quick look over the edge and felt sick. So, it came to this: wait here like a rat in a trap, or risk falling to his death via this flimsy-looking ladder. With his heart in his mouth, he climbed into the sink, trampling on broken crockery, and edged backwards out of the window, trying not to think of the drop. Part way out, the thought crossed his mind that there might be an accomplice watching the rear of the building, but it was too late now. He reached for a rung with his foot, panicking until he found it. It seemed far too narrow to take his weight, but it held. Step by fearful step, he edged down, almost frozen in fear.

What if someone entered the flat and cut the rope? Or looked down and shot him from above? Terror lent him greater speed, and as soon as he was a manageable distance from the ground, he jumped.

The landing winded him, and sharp pain shot up from ankle to knee, but he was otherwise unharmed. Adrenaline flowing, he had enough energy to scramble over a high wall, then half ran, half hobbled on his wounded leg as fast as he could through the maze of alleyways. Plan A had died with Yuri. What now? He'd have to find his brother.

CHAPTER 34
MOON CARVER

"I'm going down to the beach for a swim."

"What's wrong with the pool?"

"Nothing. I just want to feel sand beneath my feet. Coming?"

"Later. I've just got—"

"Okay. Don't be too long." With that, the girl swept out of the wide patio door and flip-flopped across the slabs and down the short rocky path to the beach. Karrig watched her go, bikini-clad with a loose white shirt flapping in the breeze. He anticipated their next coupling, perhaps in the surf. The little beach that lay below the house was virtually their own private space, hidden between two short promontories that jutted into the sea. He thought about getting changed and following her, but he had to check in first. Make sure the payment was on the way. The delay was making him nervous.

He stretched, yawned and went to get his phone from the bedroom. It rang as he reached for it.

"Hello?"

"Has the parcel been delivered?"

"Yes. Just as you said." There was the slightest of pauses.

Karrig felt his heart beating more forcefully beneath his ribs. The voice at the other end of the line was smooth.

"Good."

"About payment."

"All in good time. I need to verify the delivery first. And of course, it's vulgar to discuss pecuniary matters on the phone, don't you think?"

"Yes, but…"

"You will be amply rewarded. My lord recognises loyalty from his servants."

"Hey, I'm not his servant."

The speaker cut across him, smooth as silk, just as he had been in the car. "Just a figure of speech. Perhaps my ear is not so well attuned to the modern idiom. We all serve in some capacity or other, I'm sure you agree."

Karrig didn't have the energy to argue. "Okay, no problem. I just…" The line went dead. He glared at the phone in frustration. Servant or not, he just wanted to be paid. Working for a new client always raised questions of trust, and until he saw the evidence in his account balance, there was always a nagging doubt. Usually, however, he didn't fear his clients.

"No problem, eh?" The voice came from behind the door. Karrig looked up, startled. Framed by the doorway was his brother, holding a gun levelled at his chest. He didn't look happy.

"How did you get in?" It was a stupid question; the patio door was wide open, but with the shock of seeing his brother standing there, Karrig wasn't thinking clearly. A dwarf with a key and a few simple charms could open any locked door. What really flustered him was that Haldred was the last person he wanted to see right now, or for quite a considerable time. He should have been more careful to cover his tracks. Too late now. As he silently chastised himself, Karrig mentally measured the distance between his right hand and his backpack. Three metres, roughly. Too much to cover before being shot, unfortunately, and he knew his brother wouldn't hesitate to pull the trigger. There was little love between them in the first place, but a broken oath on top of that amounted to a huge additional grievance, and would give him cause on its own. If their positions were reversed, he would feel the same.

"We had a deal. We had a contract."

Karrig raised his arms, palms out, dropping the phone. It clattered to the floor next to the bed.

"Look, I had no choice. I'll sort it out." He didn't know how, but hopefully, he could defuse the situation. Buy some time at least.

"Why? Just tell me that. Why?" Haldred sounded hurt as much as angry. The change of tone gave Karrig a pang of guilt. He wondered what he could say that would convince his brother, but came up with nothing.

Haldred continued. "Apart from leaving me in the lurch, with half of his hungry puppies on my tail, what did you do it for? What was going through your tiny mind that was so important you broke the trust of a god? For fuck's sake, what kind of idiot are you?"

Karrig looked at him, red-faced, almost spluttering in anger, and realised with a shock he'd never seen his brother so close to losing it before. He was so tense, the gun trembled in his hand.

Haldred edged forwards. As he raged, the weapon in his hand became part of the conversation, his gesticulations waving it back and forth as he made his point. It occupied all of Karrig's attention. It became still once more as his brother stopped.

"I was compromised," said Karrig.

"Compromised? What's that supposed to mean?" Haldred held his arms wide as if to emphasise the question. Karrig caught him on the jaw with an uppercut, sent him staggering backwards. Before his brother could recover his balance, Karrig grabbed his gun hand and slammed it against the edge of the long alabaster shelf that ran along the wall. The weapon clattered out of Haldred's grip, but before Karrig could grab it, a fist caught him on the temple, hard enough to make his head ring. He crumpled to his knees. Haldred scrambled to retrieve his gun, and had just about reached it when Karrig's head caught him in the side, just beneath the ribs, and sent him slamming into the wall. The gun skittered away across the smooth surface, further out of reach. The brothers grappled with each other. Neither was an expert fighter, but both were strong and tough. They rolled on the floor, seeking a move that would render the other helpless.

Karrig broke the hold his brother had on his wrist and clubbed him on the side of the head with a flailing haymaker, which Haldred could only partly block. It had the desired effect; he wriggled partly free, scrambling towards his pack with his right hand while his left was still pinned down. In a desperate move, he reached in and felt the comforting handle of Moon Carver, wrenching it free in one sweeping move. Just in time, Haldred caught the gleam of silver light and pushed him away. The arcing blow missed Haldred's head by millimetres, as the blade sliced the marble tile in half, and sank deep into the underlay. It shocked Karrig, that the venom behind it could have easily cleft his brother's head in two, but it also took him time to wrench the sword free, so deeply had it cut into the floor. By the time he'd pulled it out, Haldred was on his feet and pointing the gun at him again, more wary now. They looked at each other.

"That should be mine," Haldred said, nodding at the sword.

"Father bequeathed it to me."

"Bequeathed, my arse. You stole it while he was on his deathbed." Haldred's fury was rekindled by another betrayal, almost but not quite forgotten. The troubled blade had long brought enmity between them. Both had coveted it: a fabled sword of ancient renown. Legend said its edge was so fine it could draw blood from the wind. They had long ago agreed never to speak of it, to keep it locked away, but that was then. Now he held it, Karrig saw the envy rekindled in his brother's eyes. He pressed his claim, gleefully reopening old wounds in this fey mood, everything else forgotten except for points scoring.

"Yes, *bequeathed*. With his dying breath. And where were you in his hour of need? Off on some pointless errand for your paymaster, the Trickster." He tilted his head, narrowed his eyes. "You should never trust them. They'll be the death of you."

"Like you should know. He's been good to me."

"Shifted a few coins into your piggy bank, you mean."

"And you're so different? Plenty of that went your way. You've become rich thanks to him. And me. You were happy to take his gold not so long ago."

Karrig paused, a sly look on his face. He turned his head and spat on the floor. "I had the choice, though. I was never his slave. And you were just desperate for help." His voice was loaded with meaning. Haldred just looked at him.

"We had a deal. A deal bound in blood: I need help, and you give it. A family's bond. More sacred even than to the gods. It was an unbreakable oath. A contract."

"Let's just say I got a better offer."

They stood facing each other. Some of the heat left Haldred's voice. He held the gun steady while he scanned the room. "Where did you stash it?"

"What."

"You know."

Karrig sniggered in triumph. "Ha, so that's what this is all about, is it?"

Haldred stared back. "Quit screwing around. Where is it?" He pushed the gun forwards, as if closing the distance would increase the threat. Karrig snarled; a primeval sound from the back of his larynx.

"Piss off while you can. You're never going to get hold of it." He slashed out with the sword, aiming wildly. Haldred pulled back, but not before Moon Carver sliced through his handgun as if it were made of cheap plastic. With horror, he saw he was holding just a trigger and handle, and little else. He threw it at his brother and darted back through the doorway into the open-plan living room. Karrig ran after him, relishing the sight of his brother fleeing, the long suppressed bitterness between them driving him on.

Haldred made the wrong choice and retreated into the kitchen, realising his escape route via the entrance passageway was blocked by a locked door. He veered left, around the island unit, looking for objects to throw. Karrig followed more slowly now, dodging, but still advancing, still menacing. He was consumed with fury. All the guilt he'd felt in betraying his brother back in Prague had hardened into resentment and self-justification. There was a nasty grin on his face as he saw his brother cornered, and he moved in for the kill. All reason had left him; blood lust alone drove him on, the legacy of the blade he held.

Haldred was cornered, there was no escape, but as he advanced he pushed two tall bar stools over to block Karrig's path. It was a desperate play; they made a feeble barricade. Karrig grinned and advanced. It was time to resolve their feud for good.

He vaulted the first set of long chrome legs blocking his path, but miscalculated, and caught a toe on the second set, and stumbled headlong into the cabinet beyond. Moon Carver, thrust out in front of him, stabbed into the cabinet as Karrig crashed face first to the floor. His fall wrenched the sword handle from his grip, but it remained embedded in expensive kitchenware, like a latter-day sword in the stone. Seeing his chance, Haldred grabbed the hilt with both hands and pulled; an opportunist, undeserving Arthur. It came free more easily than he'd expected, and in one movement, before he could think, he stabbed down at the figure beneath him, trying to rise. The blade passed through the middle of his brother's back, sheathing itself in bone and muscle, tendon and gore, pinning him to the floor. A gout of blood from his dying brother's mouth splashed the toecap of Haldred's loafers.

Haldred let go and stood back as the magnitude of his action sank in. For a long moment, he could do nothing other than stare in horror at the fruit of his anger. An appalling puddle formed around his feet, and he stepped back, unable to think clearly. The hilt stood proud from his brother's back as if to taunt him, the amethyst set in the pommel glinting in a hideous appeal to the jewel lust in his dwarfish soul. Haldred tore his eyes away, and stared down at his hands as if to disown them, purveyors of the ultimate crime: kin-slaying. He was forever an outcast now, among his kind. Unclean and forsaken. At the back of his head, the pounding pulse imposed its rhythm once more. Suddenly, a kind of madness took over, and he stomped around the kitchen, all reason gone. Sordid self-justification was the only refuge he had left.

"Shit, shit, *shit*." He glared at the corpse. "What did you do that for? You stupid wanker. I only came to talk." He kicked the leg below him, but it offered no resistance, just the dull acceptance of his blow. Haldred covered his face with his hands, trembling, trying to get a grip once more on reason, then walked around the room, a fading set of bloody footprints marking his progress. Finally, he sat on the sofa, head in hands.

How long he stayed there he couldn't tell, but gradually the madness left him. In its wake, an aching weariness took root. With reddened eyes, he looked around the room. Calmer now, but burdened with a weight that stretched his sanity to its limit. Just one tiny strand of reason kept his soul from plunging into unplumbed depths. He knew with awful certainty he could never rid himself of this crime, but for now, there were things he had to do.

Feeling numb and still trembling, he clambered to his feet and scanned the room, seeking clues to the whereabouts of the thing he'd come for. He didn't expect for an instant that the painting would be here, but he had to find out where his brother had stashed it. There must be a laptop or a phone; he could worry about breaking the password later. He had to get away.

There was no sign of anything in the living room. He bit his lip and looked towards the patio to the place where the path descended to the beach. His insides churned; how long before the girl would come back? With greater urgency, he returned to the bedroom and stopped in amazement. A large, long-haired red tabby lounged on the double bed. Wine-dark eyes met the dwarf's in a steady, unflinching gaze.

Haldred struggled to comprehend what it would be doing here. Hadn't it heard them fighting? Had it been attracted to the noise? He felt a little dazed, but there was no time for contemplating the motives of cats. He quickly scanned the room. The remains of his gun lay on the long shelf. By the foot of the bed was his brother's pack. That would be it. Haldred grabbed it and shooed the cat from the bed, tipping the contents onto the duvet cover in its place. A few clothes, wallet, some money, the sword's scabbard with ancient dwarfish symbols engraved down its length. No phone or computer. With increasing urgency, he searched the innards of the bag once more. But it held no secrets. He knelt and searched the floor, then lay flat to peer under the bed. Behind him, Dionysus, the phone held firmly in his mouth, walked slowly from the bedroom, across the living room, and the patio beyond, before leaping up onto the rocks at the far side of the pool.

Haldred's frustration intensified. He felt beneath the bed

to no avail, then stood once more, and vented his feelings by throwing an ornamental ceramic jug against the wall. He tried to think, but the torrent in his head held back any clarity. Massaging his temples with his fingers couldn't restore calm, either. In desperation, he returned to the living room, but movement caught his eye; the top of a head bobbing up the path from the beach. It was time to leave. For an instant, he entertained thoughts of a double murder to allow more time to search, but by now the blood lust had left him. He knew he couldn't carry it through.

In haste, he scooped whatever he could of his brother's possessions into the bag – wallet, keys, notebook – then retreated to the kitchen on the way to the front door. He paused and forced himself to look. Karrig's body still lay there, inert, the blade and hilt protruding from his back. Haldred knew he couldn't leave the sword there, but he no longer wanted it or anything to do with it. He wished he'd never seen the damn thing. It should have been buried with their father. The sound of feet crunching on gravel outside made up his mind. Tentatively, he touched the pommel, then gripped the sword and, with a grimace, wrenched it free. It took more effort than he expected. The blade gleamed in the dull light, blood dripping from the tip. "Sorry," he mouthed, uselessly, and wiped the flat of the blade on his brother's backside, then returned it to the scabbard in the pack. With relief, he made it to the front door and, as he closed it quietly behind him, he heard the girl calling from the patio.

"I thought you said you were coming? Where are you?"

Haldred walked out past the gate and down the road, trying to appear calm and unhurried, even as he heard the screams behind him.

CHAPTER 35
GOD OF ECSTASY AND TERROR

On the flat roof of the one-storey building, ignoring events below, Dionysus contemplated the phone. The pretty little coloured rectangles, while appealing, were trivial, he suspected. Instead, he recomposed his inner sight and looked beyond them, with the focus only the divine can summon, past the internal components that made up the device to the base matter of the universe itself. He observed the flow of electrons between tiny sections of the innermost storage chip: to power the screen, to transmit via the antenna and dissipate until they reached the nearest mast. He knew it represented information to be distilled into knowledge, but what kind of knowledge? And for something that was supposedly inert, there was a surprising amount of activity.

Behind the screen, a hidden security app with no associated icon stared back via the camera, detecting whiskers, fur and half a face. As Dionysus stepped back slightly, STUBBINS got a clearer look, and captured several still images, forwarding them to its servers stamped with the date, time and location data.

Dionysus stared back with an intensity beyond mere

curiosity, scrutinising the compartmented programs on their tiny chip. He watched data ride in and out in bursts, dissipating via the antenna, scrolled through millions of lines of code – a language he sensed, rather than read – registering images and words until he arrived at a curious void at the heart of the device. Strange to find emptiness amid so much sub-atomic activity; a hole in the electromagnetic field.

He observed input ports and exit gateways, but behind and between, in the invisible nothingness, something absorbed information and held it. Dionysus couldn't see what. A shiver ran along his spine; he was certain he was being observed, maybe evaluated. Could it see through his present disguise? He had no way of telling, and his ignorance of who or what could be doing so disturbed him to his core. What exactly was it, and who put it there? What was its purpose?

Crouched on the rooftop, he considered anew the activities of the dwarf. He was a recent arrival. What had brought him here? Had he known about the contents of his phone? Dionysus suspected not. He turned his head to the sea while his thoughts remained deep within the inner workings of the device, touching and examining it from different viewpoints. As a god who still moved among the planet's inhabitants and took an interest in their deeds, there shouldn't be anything beyond his ken. But apparently there was, and he'd found it. The thought of some potential new player in the game was both thrilling and concerning in equal measure.

He felt like laughing out loud, but frustratingly, his present set of vocal cords did not allow it, so instead he took silent pleasure in the irony. He, Dionysus, on the surface the most frivolous and misunderstood deity, with the least apparent gravity, and worst case of attention deficit, was confronted by a conundrum potentially beyond them all. But little about this god was trivial. Within Dionysus, danger lurked; he nurtured both friendships and enmities that had endured for millennia, never to be erased. That was one reason the others usually gave him a wide berth. Even his father's consort, Hera. Had he just made a new enemy? It was too early to tell, but the idea was delicious. The mere fact he could not yet penetrate the void at the heart of this thing made him suspect so.

His attention shifted and perception retreated to his normal visual senses, and he noticed the sea. His thoughts switched from excitement and curiosity to ice-cold analysis. Dionysus considered his findings. The void was part of the device, but not of it; presumably a minor facet of a much greater whole that resided elsewhere. A modern-day Hydra. It was inert, yet apparently watchful, and, he assumed, calculating; all of which implied sober assessment driven by intelligence. But whose?

Sober assessment. He turned the phrase over in his mind and examined its chilling implications. He lived by the opposite creed: *in vino veritas*. The fruit of the grape was subtle and sublime, made to be celebrated and appreciated, as well as for joyous release and inebriation. It was the invention of his creative mind; his gift to the world. It also opened a handy window into men's souls, loosening their tongues, laying bare their secrets; something he'd used to his advantage repeatedly.

Wine. At once both sacred and profane. He was its master and its muse. To spurn the pleasure of occasional inebriation was... lamentable. Disdaining a gift from the gods was dangerous. Foolhardy, even. Dionysus intrinsically distrusted anyone, or anything, that masked their true nature behind a cloak of sobriety. Yes, he decided. He had a new enemy.

CHAPTER 36
ADRIFT

Back on the boat, Haldred stowed the pack in the space beneath his berth and prepared to depart. He couldn't leave the island fast enough, but a wave of irritation washed over him as he reviewed his provisions. He had scarcely any food left, and little water. The thought of heading back into town in search of a shop was appalling, but so was the thought of leaving without food or drink. Reluctantly, he retraced his steps along the jetty to the small town beyond. He felt the eyes of everyone scrutinising him as he passed, and half expected to hear shouts of pursuers behind him, or sirens fast approaching, hunting him down. The rational part of his brain suspected he looked shiftier than ever, so he made a conscious effort to straighten his back and lift his head. All it did was make him realise how tense his body felt. At the counter, with shopping under his arm, he thrust a handful of notes towards the shopkeeper.

"That's too much."

"It's okay. Keep the change." He couldn't wait to get outside, away from security cameras, away from suspicious eyes. Only when he was out on the open sea, holding the wheel of his sailing boat, did he feel the burden shift a little.

The wind washing over him eased his mind, and the afternoon sun warmed his back. He closed his eyes and listened to the plaintive calls of the gulls, the sound of the hull crashing through the swell.

The incongruity struck him: he, a dwarf, a creature of the underground, of caves and tunnels, mining and making, seeking solace on the sea with its endless horizons and constantly changing weather. But it was the only place he felt able to think. The only place where he could still the constant thunder in his head. Need he ever go back? Couldn't he just stay here? Sail the globe forever? He let the thought marinate for a while as the wind snapped the sail and doused him in spindrift. Running would be futile. The vengeance of the gods might wait, but somewhere, sometime, it would catch him. It was inevitable.

That evening, he lowered the anchor in a quiet sheltered cove and lay on his bunk, hoping the motion of the waves would lull him to sleep. But it was futile. He might be in better control of his emotions, but unpleasant images from the day still churned through his mind. With a sigh, he realised he'd better have another look through the scant materials he'd salvaged from the beach house. He tipped them out once more.

The wallet was useless to him; it contained no hidden slips of paper with passwords or messages. Just a few bank and loyalty cards, and a driving license. He turned over the cards. Most were from organisations he knew, but one was different. The silver chip on the front made it look like any other bank card, but there was no account number or signature strip, no lettering or name. Nothing, in fact, apart from a logo, which he didn't recognise. He pocketed it, and placed the rest aside for disposal, then turned to the passport. It was standard issue, nothing special. The photo looked back at him accusingly. Haldred closed it, decided he'd better destroy it, and tried to rip it apart, but the plastic pages defied even his strength. Teeth gritted, he looked around the small galley for something to chop it up. There was, of course, one blade that could do the job effectively, and would slice it into salami if he desired. But the thought made him shudder. He laid the passport next to the discarded wallet and turned to the notebook. There surely had to be something of use in there.

Instead, as he leafed through the pages, he was overtaken by renewed feelings of despair. Most of the book was blank, and the pages at the front contained only the mundane details of flight numbers and schedules, car hire booking references, and the contact details for cheap hotels. Leafing through the pages more slowly told him something about his brother's itinerary after the theft at the monastery, but he'd guessed most of that, anyway. One page listed the climbing gear he'd need and gave details of the places he could buy it. Haldred found himself comparing it with his own preparations from the first effort. The second time around he'd left it to Karrig, but where he'd got the car in which he escaped, there were no clues. Was it really only a month since their first misguided heist? So much had happened since then.

He turned the page and stopped. Two pieces of information stared up at him: an address and a hand-drawn image. The address: Werner Strasse. The image: an Egyptian hieroglyph. He frowned at it. He was no expert on the country or its past, but to his untutored eye it looked like the Eye of Horus.

CHAPTER 37
NIGHT CLUB

All Haldred wanted was the warm, wet comfort of another body. It didn't matter whose. She was so inviting, grinding her pelvis to the beat, dressed in a skirt so short he'd barely have to duck to look up it. It shouldn't be allowed: pumping her hips like that. The pounding in his head increased, out of sync with the music, following a rhythm of its own, dull and incessant. It was getting worse; he needed release. He needed some action but an innate reticence kept him ogling like a goggle-eyed fool while around him the nightclub crowd continued to party, oblivious to his silent anguish, oblivious to everything except their hedonism, the joy of intoxication and anticipation of an impending climax. Everyone except him.

He'd never felt comfortable around women, whether dwarfish or of any other variety. Something about being in their presence tied his tongue in knots, made him feel foolish and clumsy. They sapped his confidence. In that, he was the diametric opposite of his brother. The thought lingered for a while, distracting him. He let it drop. Tonight, he was searching for confidence in the bottom of a glass, but it wasn't yet working.

That was why he preferred to get his kicks via commercial channels under normal circumstances. It was quick, easy, and meant he didn't have to indulge in meaningless conversation or foreplay. Most of the time, at any rate. Above all, there was no commitment. But that wouldn't do tonight. With a faceless assassin on his trail – maybe more than one – he needed to hide, and the anonymity of a crowd lent him some sense of security at least.

He'd abandoned the boat at a marina on Naxos, then bought a seat on the next available plane out: a low-cost flight to Frankfurt. From there, he'd caught a train back to Prague. He wasn't sure why; he had nowhere else to go. Tense as a coiled spring, he took refuge in alcohol. Huge quantities of alcohol. Haldred had never been a big drinker, but right now, as his options and his world closed in around him, it felt like embracing an old friend. Drink was fast becoming the only way he could hush the aching and banging in his head, and the circular negative thoughts. Every waking hour they nagged him, gnawed at his subconscious, dragged him closer until he felt himself on the brink of the abyss.

Permanently on edge and guilt-ridden, he missed Karrig's jibes, his grumbling. He had always been ready with a sharp response, but he got the job done, time after time, efficiently and cleanly. How would he cope alone? It was impossible to stay in his apartment; he kept seeing ghosts in the shadows, hearing assassins in the stairwell, spies on the landing. Loki's agents were everywhere; how long before they tracked him down and exacted revenge?

Tonight, in desperation, he'd wandered the streets from bar to bar until he got swept up in a crowd queueing for this nightclub. Safety in numbers. He could hide here. And just maybe find some company to kill another few hours while he bought himself time to think.

Haldred closed his eyes and tried to sway to the beat, but dizziness overtook him, accompanied by nausea. He opened them again, not sure in that instant whether he was still upright. Relieved to find he was, he decided the best solution to his balance problem was another drink, and lurched back to the booth where he'd been sitting. The vodka and tonic was still there, amid a sea of glasses, empty or partially full. He knocked it back and slumped against the back of the cheap leatherette banquet seats, trying to recover his thoughts. He ought to be doing something to get out of this mess, but right now he couldn't see how. It would have to wait. The act of remembering his failed mission caused the alcohol in his bloated stomach to reel and roil. He swallowed back a sudden urge to regurgitate and closed his eyes. The pounding in his head grew worse. Pressure. Fear. Anguish. No. Not now. There had to be some way out, somewhere to go, someone to spend some time with, a one-night stand, anything.

With a sly glance, he watched her gyrate on the dance floor again, and imagined them gyrating together in her bed. A lecherous grin turned the corner of his mouth. She'd been friendly enough until now. Friendly, but a little cool. It was time to remove her inhibitions. He'd brought her another vodka back from the bar; the more the merrier. With a little luck, he'd be able to steer her tipsy steps home, arm in arm like a helpful hero, then accept the grateful thanks she'd be sure to give him. They'd need to shake off her friends, though.

The table was littered with glassware of different designs and sizes. Which one was hers? Swaying slightly, he tried to focus his mind and remember, but the effort was too great. He sat back and belched loudly; the sound system rendered it inaudible. Where had she been sitting? Which glass was nearest? He lasered in on a likely culprit. That one. Still half full. Surely hers. He topped it up and placed the glass down on the table a little too hard. Something was wrong. He was in danger of overstepping the invisible line between drunk-and-convivial and drunk-and-incapable, but he was still possessed of just enough self-awareness to know it. He should be careful. Haldred closed his eyes for a moment to steady himself, then resumed his lecherous surveillance of the dance floor. She was still there, amid her friends, swaying enticingly and, in his warped imagination, luring him on.

From the raised walkway, Anja scanned the dance floor below. Puffs from the smoke machine wreathed about the dancers and were lacerated by sharp-angled beams from the coloured lights above and to the side. The relentless beat drove them on. Beneath their feet, floor panels flashed periodically in time with the music. She'd followed her target in here. It didn't seem like the place you'd find a fifteen-hundred-year-old dwarf, but then she regarded all of that species as beyond her powers of understanding. Cunning and avaricious, yes; twenty-first-century disco bunnies? Not as far as she was aware.

As she searched the seething mass of bodies below, she mused further on his motivation. Had he seen her? He'd run from Bratislava fast enough, so he knew he was a hunted man, but did he know who was hunting him? Had he ventured in here hoping that safety in numbers would save him? Or was it he just didn't care anymore, like some latter-day Winston Smith waiting for one of Big Brother's followers to shoot him up with love? Well, she didn't love him, and followed a different god, but she was keen to shoot him, or in the present circumstances, slide the knife she'd tucked into the top of her boot between his ribs. First, she had to find him.

Trailing him to this middle-of-the-road nightspot had been easier than she'd expected, although she felt wrongly dressed for the occasion. Still in black from head to foot, she'd swapped the T-shirt for a long corset with elaborate fastenings down the front. It had a practical use: the hidden sheath held two short throwing knives. Below this she wore a leather mini skirt and over-the-knee boots, with a longer knife slipped into the top of the right boot. An altogether flimsier version replaced her heavy coat; only a slip of fabric that hung from her shoulders and floated nicely as she walked, and left her arms free for any fight moves she needed to make. All told, her look was more appropriate for a fetish club than this place, with its Day-Glo and neon, but she didn't care. Let them gawp. She just wanted to find the dwarf and put him out of his misery.

Anja took another sip of her drink – a sweet-tasting, blue-tinged cocktail – aware that the moron approaching from her right was about to make a pass. What witty banter passed for a chat-up line here in Prague? At first she ignored him, but he tried again in English, yelling in her ear.

"You look like you need a dance partner."

"Fuck off." She turned towards him and gave him a mock smile that didn't extend as far as her darkly shadowed eyes, and packaged it with a scowl. He took the hint and raised his hand in mock surrender. She watched his eyes slide off to the side in search of a new target as he brushed past. Her attention returned to the dance floor below. One tune morphed into another, but the pulsating rhythm of the beat stayed the same. It wouldn't have been her choice of mission, but she was determined to succeed and worm her way further into the organisation. If she was to get closer to the top of the hierarchy, she couldn't afford to fail.

If left to her own devices, she'd be in a dark, smoky backstreet dive playing air guitar to some local metal band. Retro house and disco, mixed with the odd cheesy hit from yesteryear wasn't her thing at all, but the worst thing was the punters. Shallow and needy; office workers and students. What did they know of the real world? Were they even aware of the games being played out there? She viewed them with contempt. They remained wilfully ignorant of the destruction, desecration and decay all around. There was hate, and there was despair out there in the real world, and unspeakable things happening every day. But they closed their minds and stayed safe in their little bubble, along with their one-inch thoughts and their pathetic Barbie and Ken look-a-life. They hadn't even the faintest inkling of the approaching endgame. When it arrived, as it soon would, it would blow their tiny minds. Literally, if she had anything to do with it.

Her attention wandered. With an automatic and a full magazine, she could do some serious damage in here, and the pathetic attention-seekers below would deserve it. For a moment she followed her fantasy, in her mind's eye seeing them jerk and fall as the bullets hit, spraying jets of blood across the DJ booth and dance floor. Shocked and surprised faces and bullet-riddled bodies bucking and tumbling in slow-mo. One day.

Her glass was empty. She pushed towards the bar, squeezing her way to the front.

"Anja, hi. What are you doing here?" The shout from the guy next to her jolted her out of her reverie. Dan, one of the road crew. She was momentarily lost for words.

"We're over there," he said, jerking a thumb to the far end of the bar. "Some of us in the road crew and a couple of the band." She looked past him and saw Rudi, the drummer, deep in conversation with the lighting crew rigger. Dan shouted over the noise. "What can I get you?"

Anja was flustered. She was here for a hit. How could she escape from them now? And what would they think of her coming here by herself? But, Rudi…

"I'll just have a beer," she yelled. Perhaps she should be sociable for a while, before she resumed her deadly hunt for the dwarf. As she looked along the bar, Rudi glanced up and caught her eye. He smiled and her heart leaped. All thought of work vanished as she pushed towards him through the throng. But, a Bee Gees t-shirt? How clever, how retro, how hokey, and how good it looked on him.

Haldred's attention was still on his target. After a while, the girl and her friend returned to the booth. She nodded brightly to him and sat down, edging round the seating in his direction. They picked up their drinks and began talking to one another. Haldred sat back and waited for an opportunity to get into the conversation. He grew tired of waiting and tapped her on the shoulder.

"How 'bout we go back to mine?"

"What?"

He leaned closer. "Go back. To my place. To party. 'snot far."

The look of disgust caught him by surprise. "No offence, mate, but piss off." She turned away again.

Anger and embarrassment coloured his cheeks. She'd pay. She and her poisonous friend. The girl turned her back to him, tried to resume her conversation, drank. A sly, knowing smile crossed his lips as he sat back and watched.

The night dragged, or at least that's how it felt to him. He decided on a different approach. Talk to her friend first, wheedle his way in. He leaned forwards, trying to eavesdrop, but his mind wandered. She was visibly drunk. So much so that getting her home might prove tricky, but he was strong enough to carry her if need be. It was just a case of manoeuvring her to the exit. He waited.

Two young men approached. One of them eyed Haldred and the space between him and the girl. Haldred stared back defiantly and shuffled closer to her. The newcomer scowled at him and sat down anyway, then spoke across him.

"Evening, ladies. Couldn't help but admire that lovely pendant you're wearing. It looks beautiful. Someone's been treating you?"

Haldred couldn't believe such a cheesy, obvious line would get her interested, but she began talking, laughing and responding. He looked down at the item itself, nestling in her cleavage. *What a beautiful setting for something so cheap*, he thought. There, on the end of a chain, was a piece of tat; a knotted Celtic design. He could knock together something like that in half an hour. Less, probably. He looked up. Annoyingly, the conversation became more animated as they talked past him.

"Yeah, it was from my last boyfriend. Wanna closer look?" She leaned in and thrust her tits towards her admirer. They wobbled enticingly close to Haldred's face.

"Well, I would do, but old grandad here's in the way. What'd you say we dance, and I can get a proper look?" They started to move.

"What did you call me?" Somewhere in the back of his mind, he knew he shouldn't rise to the bait, but he couldn't resist. Humans and their pathetic jokes… But Haldred was past caring. The throbbing at his temples redoubled, but a flash of fury overrode it.

"Keep yer hair on, mate. Just a little joke." The young man was dismissive. Haldred felt like lashing out, but something held him back; maybe the knowledge that he'd lose any chance with the girl if he did. In some deluded corner of his mind, he still felt he'd be able to win her over. The men and women parted, shuffling around the curved bench seating to the open side. The girl tried to stand, but her ankle twisted sideways, and she fell. Haldred watched the scene unfold in front of him with a strange sense of detachment; he'd misjudged her capacity for vodka. They dragged her to her feet.

"Whass up?" It was her friend, with a concerned look on her face.

"Don' feel well," was all the girl could manage. She slumped backwards onto the curved benches.

Another newcomer arrived, anxious to have his say. "It was him," he accused, pointing at Haldred. "He was topping up her glass. I saw him." He looked around as if seeking confirmation. The group turned to the dwarf. One of them reached out and grabbed the front of his shirt, and pushed his face forwards. Feeling the hands on him and seeing the man mouthing something broke Haldred's trance. He took tight hold of the man's wrists and pulled them apart, bursting a couple of buttons. But he didn't let go. Instead, he jerked the man closer and butted him savagely, feeling satisfaction at his opponent's crushed nose and the spatter of blood down his shirt. He threw the startled human backwards with a snarl and looked for an escape route. But he was surrounded.

The fight that followed was brief. Punches flailed towards him from drunken clubbers on all sides, but the blows barely registered. Haldred was no warrior, but a life of crime and his years as a smith lent him a natural strength beyond them all. Still, he was heavily outnumbered, and eventually the blows began to tell. A glass smashed nearby and someone tried to thrust the jagged edge into his face. He ducked aside, but it caught his ear, leaving a nasty deep cut. All of his energy and pain went into a savage uppercut into the man's groin, doubling him over with a yell.

The music played on, masking the sounds of the assault, but the disturbance caught the attention of the DJ and bar staff. Burly bouncers swam towards them through the crowd. In the end it took three of them, but eventually Haldred was subdued and dragged, kicking and squirming, to a rear exit. Out of sight of the revellers, they laid into the dwarf with relish, kicking and punching until he could no longer stand. Then they opened a fire escape and threw him into the alley beyond. He landed on his face in a puddle, battered and bloody. The door slammed behind him, and he was alone.

Haldred rolled onto his back and lay there unmoving, staring up at the dark sky. How pathetic humans were. It had taken three of them – big ones – to eject him. They were feeble and nothing to fear. No, they were nothing to worry about. Not when you had a god on your tail.

He laughed at the absurdity of it all. A phrase from some foreign bard popped into his head. *I'm lying in the gutter looking at the stars*, he thought, and in those stars his future was written. He giggled uncontrollably. His body shook as the laughter became more manic.

Above him, beyond the edges of the tall buildings on either side, the stars revolved, swooped and whirled. Haldred's stomach gave an unpleasant lurch. He rolled over and threw up.

CHAPTER 38
A RESOLUTION OF SORTS

The raven swooped out of the sky and landed on the ground barely a metre away. Its sudden arrival caught Apollo by surprise. He dropped Agent 73 on the ground, and crouched, ready to pounce, until he saw who it was.

"You shouldn't sneak up like that," he said.

"Sorry."

The ginger-and-white cat narrowed his eyes and shot the bird a murderous look. It took a couple of steps sideways and backwards, and apologised once more. On the ground between them, Agent 73 rolled over and gave a squeak that passed for a groan. He was still unconscious. Apollo glanced down at his charge, then back to the bird.

"A little less drama next time, huh?" The raven shuffled sideways once again, and cawed another apology. "Anyway," the cat continued, "good to see you after all this time. Although I doubt you're here to bring me any happy news."

The bird's head bobbed up and down in what passed for a formal greeting. "The Allfather requests an audience with you, my lord."

"What about?"

"The… other one. The troublemaker."

"Loki?"

"Yes. Him. He's getting restless, we believe. He has agents abroad, causing trouble and leaving chaos in their wake. The Allfather is worried that matters are getting out of hand. It will affect all of us, even here."

Apollo studied the bird, trying to recollect its name. "You are Huginn?" The bird nodded in acknowledgement. "How do you know this?"

"We gather intelligence all the time, my brother and me. So do Geri and Freki. They report turmoil among their kind."

"That I know only too well," Apollo said. "Alright. Tell him I'll come. Where is he?"

The raven looked relieved. "Geneva." He hesitated. "I could…"

"No." Apollo's response was firm. "I'll make my own way."

"So be it. I will tell him to expect you." Enormous wings flapped, and it took to the air, and away. Apollo watched it depart, rapidly shrinking to a spot in the sky.

At his feet, the small black cat appeared to be coming to. "Jeneeva, Jeneeva," it said, rolling over once more, eyes still closed. It began to make a chattering noise, as if conversing with someone Apollo could not see. "Just tell me everything. Everything you know. For he's a jolly good fellow… The cat sat on the mat. I sat on the mat next to a frog on a log, and a dragon in a bog." It chattered on, not making any sense. Apollo wondered whether the poor animal's fractured mind would ever recover from his ordeal. He bent down and grabbed him by the scruff of the neck once more, and set off for somewhere safe. *At least that'll shut him up.*

His destination was Arnissa, a sleepy small town by a lake. It was the sort of peaceful place where, he hoped, Agent 73 could recover. They arrived in late afternoon. Apollo found his way to a quiet meadow between the lake and the town.

The black cat was still groggy, but at least he was silent now, lost in his own web of memories. Apollo watched him with paternal concern. He could see the other animal had sustained no permanent physical damage, but his healing skills didn't extend to his mind. For that, he needed Psyche; if only he knew where to find her. Instead, he gave out reassuring purrs, and lounged nearby, trying to help his charge to sleep.

"I never knew her. I never even knew her name." It was still dark, at least an hour before dawn. Agent 73 had woken up. How long he'd sat there, head bowed, nose almost on the ground, Apollo couldn't say. But he was the picture of misery. The large ginger cat hesitated. This was the first sane thing the black cat had said since his ordeal, but he sounded in the depths of despair. For a moment, he wondered how to answer.

"Who do you mean?"

His companion was silent for a while. "He taunted me. He... he said she didn't care. My mother." The misery was clear in every word. "I can't remember her. Not really. Nothing much."

Apollo stared into the dark, thinking. "She had a name," he said, finally. "She had a hard life. You should not judge her so easily." For a moment, he wondered if the black cat had heard him; it remained immobile for a long time.

"What was it?"

"She was called Nina."

Silence.

The small black cat's eyes opened to a tiny slit. "Tell me about her."

Apollo turned his head to look directly at his companion. "She didn't want to leave you. She had no choice. The so-called leader of your community terrorised her."

"The one who died? Petros?"

"Yes."

"I never liked him. He was always nasty to me." Apollo stayed silent. "Makes sense, I suppose," the small cat continued, "but she could have tried."

Apollo observed the bodily signs of his companion's discomfort, noting the tension that filled his frame. "Don't be too hard on her. She had so many problems."

"But she abandoned me. She ran. She never even said goodbye." 73's voice was thick with emotion.

"She couldn't. A car struck her. Not fatally, but enough to damage her brain. She could move physically, but she was damaged mentally. Unable to think clearly. She lashed out, and no one could reason with her. Finally, they drove her away. None of it was her fault."

Agent 73 bowed his head and closed his eyes tight against the news. It all made sense, but it was no comfort. If anything, knowing her pain and suffering and the sadness and isolation of her inevitable end made his inner turmoil worse. To his surprise, the other cat purred. It was a parental purr: comforting, soothing. Agent 73's anger ebbed, to be replaced by a different kind of pain and sorrow: the hurt of missed opportunities, and chances denied. An outpouring of grief for someone he'd never known. For himself and what might have been. The eastern sky was lightening, the dawn chorus in full voice. The black cat looked up, able to meet the eyes of his saviour for the first time. "Thank you."

"For what?"

"For telling me about her. For giving me a past."

Apollo looked away, still keeping his attention on his charge. It had been the smallest of gifts, and a painful one to receive. Agent 73 staggered to his feet, still unsteady after his ordeal. He trembled, emotion coursing through his small body. After a moment, he gave Apollo a brief, grateful glance and walked away towards the lake shore, needing to be alone with his thoughts.

Apollo rolled onto his side and let him depart.

"I didn't know you knew her."

He didn't really need to look up; Hermes' voice was distinctive enough. Resigned to having to sharpen his wits, he suppressed an irritable growl and sat up. His colleague strolled towards him, stopped at a respectable distance, and flopped down, satisfied with his entrance. Apollo washed a paw in as leisurely a fashion as possible and avoided giving Hermes the attention he always craved. He was in no hurry. After paying suitable consideration to his appearance for a few minutes, he paused, paw hovering mid-air.

"What now?" he said. For a while, the white cat sat silent, as if pondering what to say.

"I hear they call you Hyperborean Apollo?"

Apollo gave him a sharp look, then turned away again. He didn't want any scrutiny of his extra-curricular activities. That was a side of his nature that he preferred to keep only to himself. "What of it?"

"Apparently, they want to talk to you. Well, the one who calls himself Odin does, at any rate."

"I know. For once, you're behind the times."

The white cat shook his head, scratched behind his ear. "I don't know what you see in them."

"I've known them for a long time. They're alright. Bit strange, but who isn't?"

"They're aliens. Barbarians, from what I hear." Apollo was surprised to hear his colleague talk like this. He thought he was more open-minded.

"We're distantly related, you do realise?"

The white cat stayed silent for a while. "Well, I'm just here to pass on the news. It's up to you what you do with it. But don't go native." He cast his bright blue eyes in Apollo's direction. "Remember, civilisation started here."

The ginger cat's thoughts drifted. "How did you know?"

"We are in Greece. These peculiar foreigners and their disciples can't expect to get away with coming here and not being noticed."

"Apart from when they steal our artworks," Apollo reminded him. "That precious heritage Athena's always on about?" Hermes gave an almost imperceptible, dismissive nod of his head.

"Anyway. She just asked me to check in on you and our mutual friend." He looked towards the lake shore where Agent 73 was walking, still lost in thought. "He did well. It seems she wants to declare him a hero of the Cat Intelligence Team. He'd be our first one."

"I'll tell him." Apollo wondered if such news would be enough to revive the small cat's spirits.

Hermes paused, then spoke again. "You took a bit of a risk, didn't you? To help a mortal, I mean." Apollo stared at him, eyes narrowed. Hermes continued. "Usually, we leave them to get out of their scrapes by themselves, or let them die trying." His blue eyes returned Apollo's stare, but gave nothing away. The silence between them stretched, before the ginger cat broke the tension.

"It was necessary." He glanced at the now-distant black animal.

"Explain."

"He might have revealed our current situation. Named names and inadvertently given the game away. He might have revealed more about our status than we'd like." His head turned back to his companion. "Not deliberately, of course. In the end, he proved more resilient than I expected."

"Perhaps you underestimated him?"

"Yes, it seems that even the least of mortals has the capacity to surprise you."

Apollo continued to search his companion's impassive face, then gave up. Silence resumed, this time more companionable, as both looked across the lake. Eventually, Hermes spoke again.

"Speaking of revelations, Athena's more keen than ever to find the whereabouts of the tree. She asked me to remind you to keep an eye out for clues. Anything."

"The Tree of Demeter?"

"Yes, that one. She's determined to find it." Hermes looked directly at Apollo, now silhouetted against the brightening eastern sky. "In view of the rumours from the north, it might be no bad thing." The ginger cat's thoughts drifted to his recent conversation with his sister. He said nothing. "Well, I must be going."

Apollo stirred. "Oh, there is one thing."

"Yes?"

"Where's Geneva?"

He lingered by the lake shore well into the following day, reluctant to depart. Agent 73 was still subdued. Apollo kept his distance, watching over his small charge. They had wandered a little closer to the town now, still by the lake, but next to a park with a children's play area. A mother had brought her small daughter to burn off some energy before teatime, and he watched as the little girl used the slide several times, then went on the swings. Across the park, Agent 73 approached cautiously, drawn by his natural curiosity for unusual human behaviour. He was spotted. The girl emitted a squeal of delight and jumped from the swing, heading straight for the cat. Apollo saw him rise to his feet, and hesitate, looking over his shoulder for cover. *No*, he thought. *Not this time.*

The girl sensed the nervousness in the black cat, and instinctively slowed down, keen to make friends. Apollo watched from the other side of the park as she drew close. He could tell that Agent 73 wasn't sure what to make of this one, and guessed she may be a lot smaller than most of the humans he'd met. He admired the fact that the small cat's fear seemed to fade, and a little of his confidence returned. It was no real surprise when Agent 73 allowed himself to be stroked. He seemed to be developing a connection with the girl. It was more surprising that he let her pick him up; a novel experience for a cat previously used to fleeing from excitable humans. Apollo watched closely as the girl walked slowly back to her mother, her small charge nestled in her arms.

"Can we keep him?" she asked, excited.

He noticed the mother's interest, and sensed her instinctive response was to say no. But he saw her relent, as she too tickled Agent 73 between the ears.

"We'll have to check he already hasn't got a home."

"I found him here. He's a stray, I'm sure of it. Look how thin he is."

The exchange continued for a while, the black cat snug in the girl's arms. The mother gathered her things, slung her bag over her shoulder, and the three of them made ready to depart.

"What are you going to call him?"

The girl thought for a minute. "Markos. I'm going to call him Markos."

Agent 73, Hero of the Cat Intelligence Team, finally had a name.

CHAPTER 39
THE NOTE

Dawn broke piercingly bright, spearing through his windows. In his barely conscious state, Haldred could only groan and try to turn his head away, but found his face glued to the sheet. A combination of blood, vomit and spittle held him there. With a grimace, he finally managed the turn, reopening the cut by his ear. He had no idea where he was. His eyes refused to focus, and his mouth felt like sandpaper. At least he recognised that he was face down, but where? Maybe his bedroom? He would ponder how he made it home another time.

An hour passed, and the pain cleaving his skull in two got worse. What day was it? At last, he could move, but his command over arms and legs was intermittent. Invariably, another close-up view of the unsavoury porcelain interior of his toilet bowl was his first excursion. He indulged in another period of barely conscious reflection while he lay on the cold tiled floor of his bathroom. The constant chitter-chatter cut through the pain and sickness, leaving its own trail of desecration across his soul; a steady drizzle of bitterness and wheedling manipulation. He tried to shut his mind to it.

As the morning progressed, Haldred re-emerged like some warped and malign larva from a chrysalis. His memory was faulty. Plans had come to naught, that much was obvious. Otherwise, he'd have woken up with company, and probably some explaining to do. He reckoned the empty feeling inside would be the same, regardless.

From his sofa, staring at the blank wall opposite, he wondered what to do. Everything had gone wrong. His mission was a failure. His brother had betrayed him and sold the painting to a rival. Who? Why? He had no idea where to even start if he was to try to recover it. His brother… A picture of the scene in the house on Mykonos flashed before him. He closed his eyes. Tried to bite back the anguish. *Failed*.

He was finished. If he could not fulfil his master's tasks, he would be of no use. There were many stories of what happened to those who broke their oath or failed to comply. Haldred shook his head, unable to remove the awful images that crowded his thoughts.

In misery, he scanned the room. It was devoid of clutter; he kept little furniture here, other than the detritus of the last few days. The debris from yesterday's carry-out meal littered the coffee table; the polystyrene box that had held his kebab lay open, the remains of side salad spilled on the table and the floor nearby, intermingled with a few fries. Plastic sauce sachets, squeezed and mostly emptied, littered the spaces between empty beer bottles and cans, several of which lay on the floor. Some of the content had leaked onto the rug, leaving stains and an accompanying beery smell. Plates from breakfast and earlier meals piled on the seats nearby or perched precariously on the far edge of the table. He should clear up, but what was the point? Still, he needed more. Something to dull the pain and maybe deaden the terrible shock to come. The thought was unnerving; it turned his insides to liquid.

Haldred's eyes wandered towards the door. There lay his

pants, in a crumpled tangle, where he'd apparently stripped last night. Coins and keys had spilled out of the pockets, and what was that in their midst? A screwed-up piece of paper. He reached out and picked it up. It was a handwritten note with an address. He frowned. Where had that come from? For a moment, his memory flatlined, as his head swam.

He sat still and closed his eyes tight until he was back in the room. Focusing enough to read was still a problem. With an effort, he opened his eyes as wide as he could, and moved his hand back and forth until he found an appropriate distance.

He mouthed the words as he read them. *Secrets of the Urdarbrunnr, The Wharf, Trondheim.* Some antique dealer? A new-age mystic? What?

Then it came back to him.

The man on the plane. The interminable bore, Valley.

What a vacuous twat he'd been. The hint of a grimace turned down the corners of his mouth at the memory. It seemed a lifetime ago. He was sure he'd thrown the stupid note away, but here it was. He must have jammed it deep into his pocket. Haldred slumped back onto the sofa, staring at the ceiling, while his head continued to throb. He closed his eyes. How long? There could be a knock at the door any minute. While he remained here, he was vulnerable; a rat in a trap. There was no other way of escape, other than hurling himself through the window. Perhaps even that horrible fate might be better than what else awaited him.

Snatches of conversation drifted across his consciousness. *"I think you'd find it illuminating. Enlightening, even."* Trondheim? Enlightening? At least it would get him away from this death trap. But it was in the heart of his master's domain. There would be spies and agents everywhere. Every move he made would be watched. *"They say it has magical properties,"* Valley had told him. A likely story. What was the thing he'd been prattling on about? An old kettle or something? Would it make a gift for an angry god? Something to appease him? The idea was crazy, but he had no other leads, and no idea what else to do, and he hated the idea of just waiting to be caught. Might as well lead them on a merry chase, at least. He had nothing to lose.

Still feeling dreadful, he showered and found a few cleanish items in his wardrobe. He shoved the last few presentable things into his backpack and paused. His hand had brushed against Moon Carver's hilt, untouched since he returned from Mykonos. Cautiously, he unsheathed it and held it up. The blade gleamed blue-white in the gloom. Haldred swallowed, as he looked once more at the sword that had done for his brother, the weapon his father had forged and wielded many long years ago, the weapon he'd used to threaten Mótsognir. Along its length were intricate Nordic carvings, knotted serpents and other creatures. Their outlines glowed. He'd never paid them due attention before, and the intricacy and detail fascinated him. It was a superb example of the craft of his people. Equally, he felt repulsed to be holding the weapon that had done so much harm, heirloom or not. A trickle of sweat ran down his spine. With a shudder, he returned it to its scabbard and threw it on the bed. Then he had second thoughts, picked it up and thrust it into his backpack once again. It wouldn't provide him with much protection against a gun, but it might be useful if he needed to threaten someone, he supposed. After a quick scan of his debris-strewn apartment, he checked he still had the address in his pocket, then left.

The one saving grace was that he still had money in the bank. At the car hire office, he sourced a luxury four-by-four and waited impatiently while it was brought around from the lot. It took him some time to adjust the seat and the position of the steering wheel to make it bearable for a thousand-mile drive. Why couldn't the bastards ever make things for smaller races? With a grunt, he experimented until he reached the best combination of settings available, then settled behind the wheel, his pack thrown on the seat beside him, and set off for the north.

CHAPTER 40
SECRETS OF THE URDABRUNNR

The last time Haldred was in Trondheim, raw sewage was running down the street, and ragged children chased clucking chickens, played games of tag and tried to pick his pockets, while their filthy, pock-marked, bent and misshapen elders tried to rob him blind. He had no love of the place, and it took a week to get the stench of the middens out of his nostrils. He was forced to admit the city had changed a bit in the intervening years, and it took him a while to get his bearings. The wharves that lined the rivers were long ago claimed and subdivided among the merchants, and each had built long, pitched-roof warehouses next to one another, so they could unload ships at one end and sell their goods to the public at the other, storing it in between. Every metre of wharf was now occupied by the descendants of those original warehouses, now housing restaurants, shops and more, and rendering the river invisible except for a few places.

Haldred scowled at the crumpled note once again. *Kjopmannsgata*, it said, but he couldn't see it anywhere. Frustration increasing, he walked along the street once again, peering at each building.

Then he saw it: a narrow building, nestled between two larger stores. *Secrets of the Urdarbrunnr*. The window facing the street was large, but the interior dark, as if daylight feared to penetrate. Stepping across the threshold was like entering a folk museum. Antique farm equipment filled almost all available floor space, and old implements were stacked against the walls. Scythes, hammers, axes, tools for woodworking, heavy rustic tables, butter churns, milking stools, implements from old farm kitchens, and more.

The aroma of ageing timber was all-encompassing and the old wooden items on display seemed to suck the light from the dim lamps that hung from the rafters and adorned the walls. Little of what he saw was metal. He wondered if he'd been led here under false pretence.

A woman emerged from behind a desk at the back of the store. Tall and elegant, with an ageless face, she looked like a Victorian governess: prim and formal. A high-collared blouse decorated with lace frills matched her high-waisted ankle-length skirt in a darker colour. The severity of her dress found an echo in the look she gave him.

"Can I help?"

Haldred looked around, unable to see anything that might be an ancient kettle. "I was told you might have an antique of interest. An old kettle." Even as he said it, he knew his trip was in vain. There would be nothing of the kind in this resting place for nineteenth-century farming equipment. She looked down her long, straight nose at him, as if weighing her response.

"Follow me," she said.

She led him to the rear corner of her gallery, where a large, battered, age-blackened iron kettle hung by a handle from a long hook at the apex of a tall iron tripod. It looked ancient indeed. Haldred walked around it, squinting in the gloom. There were rust spots around the join between the handle and the vessel itself, and in places the iron looked to be barely retaining its shape. He wondered if it could still hold water.

"Can I touch it?"

She shrugged. "If you buy it, you can do whatever you want."

He looked up at her. "How much?"

She gave him a shrewd look. "One of Idunn's Apples might suffice."

Haldred chuckled. The famous mythical apples that proffered eternal youth to the ageing gods, according to legend. "Seriously. How much?"

"What price do you attach to enlightenment?" For a moment Haldred wondered if she were mocking him.

He avoided her face and examined the kettle once more. Could this be the real thing? A relic from the age of wonders. The thought of being within touching distance of something so old made his mouth feel dry. Without thinking, he reached out a hand.

"No touching," came the stern reprimand. He withdrew, guiltily. Was this really likely to enlighten him? Haldred's thoughts whirled, as they had done continuously these past few days. At the back of his head, the throb of his ever-present headache pounded more insistently. Right now, he could use a drink, and he reached for the flask in his inside pocket. Not now. Later. He forced his hand back and felt a bead of sweat prick his brow. He licked his dry lips. All of his negotiating skills seemed redundant. The only thing that mattered was to find out if this thing lived up to Valley's claims. The nagging doubt that this was just a wild goose chase remained.

"Money's no object. I can give you whatever you like. Name your price." He was past caring. He just wanted this ancient kettle, wanted to fill it with mead and experience whatever visions it would reveal. He had nothing more to lose. He'd lost the painting, broken the terms of his engagement, and his master was not prone to mercy. Yuri's fate had made that clear. Haldred was certain his life would be over as soon as they caught up with him, and he couldn't run forever. If he was to bear witness to the ancient past, it was now or never.

The woman looked at him, appearing to revel in his discomfort. "Give me that which you hold most dear. The thing you poured yourself into. The object you failed to give away."

Haldred recoiled. What did she know? Suspicion clouded his mind. "It's not for you."

Her smile widened. She inclined her head. "Not for me?" she purred. "Why might you say that? You should be grateful someone is willing to take it off your hands."

He took a step forwards, his hands clenching into fists. "It's not for anyone." For a moment they stared at each other, the tall woman and the dwarf, locked in a battle of wills. Then she relented and stepped back. Her features softened.

"Ah, well. It was worth a try." She retreated to the chair beside her desk.

Haldred felt wrong-footed, as if he'd won, but secretly lost some intangible game he'd never realised he was playing. "I just wanted to drink from it."

She looked at him. "Why didn't you say? Just wait here." With that, she stood again and retreated into the back room, reappearing a minute later with a large pitcher and a cup. She poured the content of the pitcher into the kettle and handed Haldred the cup. "Here. Drink whenever you are ready, but do not take too much. You must drain the cup." He found the look on her face unreadable, but her voice held an authority he could not ignore.

With hand trembling, he took the cup from her, and turned to the kettle hanging from its tripod stand, then took a scoop of water, careful to only take half a cup. Haldred held it to his lips and paused. The tall woman stood at his side, watching closely. He found her presence unsettling, but put his doubts aside and drank. He drank and drank, but still there seemed to be more within. A horrible nagging doubt formed at the back of his mind. What strange magic was this? He tilted his head further back and strove to drain the cup. He'd only taken a small amount. Barely a mouthful. What was going on? It was with an enormous sense of relief that he finally finished. He stood straight with a loud burp, and looked at the cup, dumbfounded at how small it seemed in relation to the amount of water he'd just drunk. *Water*. How disappointing. Just water. All of his hopes vanished, and he felt crushed. There was no dramatic revelation of a secret escape, a way to break free from his ordeal. He handed the cup back, and promptly fell over, his body going into spasm, his eyes staring wildly at things not in the room. Finally, he fell still.

Haldred opened his eyes to a different room: his old shack, sometime after his exile. With a shock, he saw a heated argument taking place between two dwarves, himself and his brother, over the cause of their exile. Karrig swore at him and stormed off. He sighed. It had taken decades before he could smooth it over. He saw himself working on basic implements for local farms and villages, then his throat tightened as he saw a crooked man walking up the road. This was like revisiting his memories. He knew it all too well: the forge, the challenge and the oath. This wasn't showing him anything new. He felt he'd been cheated. Then the vision took him deeper.

There were no excuses. Everything he'd requested had been provided. To hang him, a neutral observer might have said, but Haldred had no such objectivity. He was committed. With care and precision, he pored over his books of lore, late into the night, night after night, bringing forth the ancient knowledge of his people, and blending it with his own perception. He scribbled notes in margins, took astronomical readings, weighed impossible objects on his scales and measured the unmeasurable. His planning was meticulous.

At last, the allotted hour of the most propitious day arrived. At first there was meditation, a reconnection with the natural world and, in particular, the base materials of the earth; the foundation of his trade. Being above ground made it more difficult than if he still resided in his former home, but it was possible. Within his trance, he called forth the spirits of his ancestors for advice and guidance, conversing in thought and debating with them, seeking to tease out their secrets, the revelations they sought to hide in their precious metallic hearts. After many hours of such wrangling, he was satisfied he'd gathered the knowledge he required.

Then he began.

For thirty hours straight he toiled in his workshop, the world outside his door a distant memory. He toiled in search of perfection, at the pinnacle of his skill. Never had he poured so much of himself into his work; the distillation of the essence of his crafty people mixed with his own jealous, fractured mind.

The gold – pure and of the highest quality – he wrought and moulded into a serpentine form, sinuous and strong. It hovered in his thoughts. With care and precision, he drilled the core of a spine along its length, and into it he placed a single strand of hair from the tail of Hrimfaxi, the horse of the night goddess, Nott, platted with two strands of hair from Arvak and Alsvid, the horses that pull the sun chariot across the sky, and a strand from the tail of Skoll, the great wolf that chases the sun and will devour it on the last day. The work was detailed and meticulous, and precise.

He spent a lot of time crafting the scales along the body of the snake and, finally, its head – finished apart from the empty eye sockets. Haldred stepped back, blinked his eyes to clear his sight and looked at what he had wrought, sitting there on his bench.

It shone, infused with a subtle inner glow. The red light of the forge and his lamps emphasised the supple movement and elegant sinuosity moulded into every element of the body. It seemed to hum with inner vibrancy, as if waiting. The head he had fashioned with extra care: fangs, red-gold and sharp, protruded from the upper jaw in miniature homage to Jormungandr, the monster that encircled the world, a creature he'd only had the fortune to meet in his imagination. But the final touch was missing. He still needed to give it sight. For that, he had another plan.

The stranger had presented him with a pair of fire rubies: red flame-infused gemstones. Beguiling and mysterious. He polished and cut the stones until they were of the right size: multifaceted, and ready for the penultimate stage of the journey.

The work had been meticulous and the process lengthy. Now he rested, and after a lengthy sleep he locked the serpent away and set off on a journey, taking with him the twin stones and a carefully adapted Astrolabe. He journeyed along the coast until he was opposite Torghatten, the island mountain with a hole piercing its heart that lay to the west. There, on the afternoon of the Autumn Equinox, he waited, hoping against hope for clear skies. It looked as if his plans might be foiled, but at last, the setting sun emerged from beneath the roof of the clouds and cast a rosy glow on their underside as it dipped beneath the sea in a spectacular sunset.

Haldred took out his device and placed the two rubies in the clasp prepared for them. He measured the position with care and precision, aiming at the aperture within the mountain. A system of prisms built into the device directed the last rays of the setting sun through the hole in the mountain, into the Astrolabe, then down to suffuse the precious stones within.

He had captured the last rays of summer light as the world turned, for half a year, to the dark. Ever afterwards they would glint, deep in their heart, with the foreboding of eternal night and the restless spirits that reside there, in that night without stars. They were, Haldred considered, a suitable gift for the pale-faced Queen of the Dead in her dread realm.

He rushed home, eager to complete his work, and without resting, set aside his pack and took out the stones. With great care, he fixed each one into the eye socket of the serpent, then performed one last ritual. Standing over them, he muttered a spell of his own devising in the ancient secret tongue of his people.

Finished at last, he placed the Fire Serpent in an inlaid box prepared for it, and locked it away for safety, then hid it in a secret place. Then he retired to his bed and slept for two days and one night. Painstakingly, over the next twenty-four hours, he emerged from his trance, and back into the normal waking world, but he felt drained. He had poured a large part of his creative life force into that object, and now he felt empty and devoid of feeling.

Never again would he manufacture anything so beautiful, so ornate, or of such power. Haldred realised he had not eaten for days, and ransacked his cupboards for anything and everything he could get; but it wasn't enough. He slaked his thirst with beer and mead from his stores as his energy returned. Finally, it was time to take a look at the result of his endeavours, but he was almost afraid of the prospect. With trembling fingers, he released the catch of the box and prised the lid open. There lay the Fire Serpent, coiled and pliant, an ornate piece of jewellery fit for any princess, queen, or goddess.

He had fashioned it as a bracelet, the long sinuous body

able to wrap around its wearer's arm three times, head towards the wrist, tail pointing to the elbow. Supple and flexible, it would adapt to the wearer, whoever they were, but it could also be worn as a necklace, the head and tail linking like a miniature Jormungandr to adorn the wearer's throat.

Haldred gazed in awe at his creation. It was beautiful indeed. Who could resist its charms? Then he looked at those ruby eyes and a shadow of disquiet crossed his soul. Was that a dangerous glint deep within? An independent spirit looking back at him, coiled and threatening?

He slammed the lid shut and passed a trembling hand across his brow. What had he done? He persuaded himself he was dreaming still; a hangover from his creative trance. It was just the life force of the gold itself, a blend of desire and longing, the simple power of beauty mixed with craft. That would be it, he told himself. He'd sunk so much into this challenge, and he'd created an artefact of stunning complexity and beauty befitting of his skill It was a credit to his creativity and power, and a possessive pride surged through him. It would mark his fame like nothing else. Of course, the serpent desired to be worn and adored, on full display to the world. It was the not-so-hidden aim of every beautiful object ever made by his people, and among their craftsmen, he was supreme. The Fire Serpent was the pinnacle of his achievement.

His sight returned to his lonely shack, next to his forge. He saw the crooked man return to take him to see the Queen of the Dead, and fulfil the challenge, but with surprise, he saw he was not at home. When had this visit taken place? Rather than leave again, the visitor entered further into Haldred's meagre cottage, rummaging among the boxed items on the shelves against the back wall. He concluded his search and pulled down the box containing the serpent. Haldred couldn't breathe. How had he known?

Spoken enchantments opened the box. There lay the serpent, docile and eyeless, awaiting his final gift. The man took it out. With a strange relief, Haldred noticed the reverence with which he held it. But then he placed it onto the palm of his left hand, and held it at eye level. As Haldred watched, he spoke words of magic in a strange language, and, giving them shape with his right hand, wove them around the snake. To his horror the serpent responded, raising its head like a golden cobra above the coils of its body to defer to its new master. He heard its hissed response.

"I am yours forever."

For a long moment the man watched it move, then, with a command, he put it to sleep, placed it carefully back in the box, spoke more words of enchantment over it, closed the lid and placed it back on the shelf where it had been. He departed, leaving no sign of his visit.

The scene changed again, and with a horrible sinking feeling, Haldred knew what was coming next. He and the crooked man were deep underground, far deeper than Nidavellir, home of the dwarves. This was Hel, the realm of the dead. Even in his disembodied state, he shivered at the chill in the air. Ice flows and frozen lakes they passed. Along cold, lonely valleys they trudged, passing occasional camp fires lit by the dead in their struggle to find any warmth. Joyless, dreary towns punctuated their journey, filled with empty windows, closed doors and silent streets. Finally, they arrived at a larger settlement, around a vast hall, its roof high and distant. Around them gathered some inhabitants of this realm: the old and the lame, the sick of all ages, never to recover, slow to heal. About the queen herself was a bodyguard of young, well-muscled warriors, cloaked in furs and animal hide. They were the unlucky ones, Haldred realised. Those lost overboard, who fell from high crags, or became victims of sudden illness. Not everyone had the chance to reach Valhalla. Behind them, and in their midst, enthroned upon cold polished stone sat the queen of this realm. Hel herself.

She wasn't quite what Haldred had expected. Her complexion, though pale, was healthier than he'd been led to believe, although when he bowed before her, he noticed her legs beneath her skirts looked greenish-black and diseased. She wore garments of fine linen, and a cloak of furs, a simple silver circlet on her head inlaid with fine white diamonds. It looked nothing special.

Hel peered down from her throne with a bored and sullen expression. He wasn't quite sure whether to speak or stay silent. Next to him the crooked man removed his hat, bowed low, then stood straight, catching Haldred by surprise. He took his lead, and bowed once more, then returned his gaze to the queen.

"To what do I owe this visit?"

Before Haldred could speak, his fellow traveller stepped forwards. "Greetings, my lady. We have come to ask you to settle a little wager. A matter of pride and expediency, if you will."

The dwarf looked at him askance, but moved alongside his companion, and knelt on the lowest step of the dais. He opened the wooden box and held it out.

"I bring you a gift, most noble Queen. A trinket of my own design. Something which I sincerely hope will bring you a little happiness."

Intrigued, she leaned forwards and picked up the Fire Serpent, then brought it close to her face. Its ruby eyes sparked and gleamed in the dim firelight that flickered in the hall. She looked at it, turned it around to examine the serpent from another perspective, then stared into its sparkling ruby eyes, absorbed. Haldred held his breath. Whatever broke that spell, he never understood, but with a shriek of fear and outrage she threw it far across the hall and followed it with a curse. Then she stood, towering above the dwarf, tall beyond measure, glaring down at him. Dead or not, her eyes held menace that pierced him to the core.

"What is the meaning of this? What gave you to think that foul thing would win my affections? Begone, lest I imprison you here now. But know this, dear dwarf, that when your time comes, you will find a cold and bitter welcome in my halls."

Haldred scrambled to his feet, and bowed, then bowed again, fumbling for an apology. He was beside himself; what had gone wrong? Next to him, the man who had once been crooked stood tall, smiled, gave the queen a brief nod of the head and turned smartly on his heel.

"Come, master dwarf," he said. "We must have a conversation, you and I." He set off at a brisk pace. Haldred followed. Glinting in the shadows at the far end of the hall, he spied the Fire Serpent, detoured to scoop it up and return it to his box, then scurried after his new master.

The vision faded, and with a jolt, Haldred was back in the antique shop in Trondheim once more. His head was spinning. It took a minute or more to return to his senses. He sat up, then stood, rubbing the tender spot on the back of his head from his fall. He didn't know whether to laugh or cry. The god had deceived him. After all these years, and everything that had happened, he saw that he'd been tricked. He was always doomed to lose his bet. He'd been set up, trapped in a web of lies. By any token of justice, the oath he'd sworn was invalid. He was free, a burden removed from his shoulders. If only he could prove it.

But he was burning with fury. Dwarves are vengeful creatures by nature, and now he wanted to even the score. A desire for revenge pulsed through him, but where could he start? How do you seek vengeance upon a god?

The gallery owner stood close by, observing him closely.

"What was in that kettle?" he asked, suspicion clouding his mind. She smiled.

"Only water. Water from the Well of Urd."

Haldred frowned. "Well of Urd?"

"Of course. Where else could you find such purity and clarity from the past?" She beamed at him. "Shop!" she called, clapping her hands. Through the door at the rear, two figures appeared, and Haldred experienced shock anew. Fellow dwarves. They halted before him, one on either side, and bowed low in traditional greeting.

"I am Anarr," the first said.

"And I am Ginnarr," the other added.

Haldred's face darkened. "I know those faithless names," he growled. "Your foul deeds have long besmirched our race. Begone."

They ignored him. "We have new employment these days," said Anarr.

"We are bounty hunters," added his brother. With that, they grabbed Haldred and snapped handcuffs around his wrists. "You're coming with us, back to Nidavellir," said Anarr.

"It's time to answer for your crimes," said Ginnarr, sounding prim.

Haldred looked up at the tall woman, searching her face for answers. "What treachery is this?"

She gave him a cool, appraising look. "You should know enough about us to work that out for yourself."

Haldred struggled against the pull of his captors, and stared at her, uncomprehending. She saw the look. "Come on, master dwarf. Surely you've seen a Norn before? After all, there are quite a few of us about." His eyes widened in recognition. He was bundled into the stockroom at the back, then down a flight of stairs to a jetty beneath the building, and into a waiting speedboat. She followed, apparently revelling in his surprise. "How did you think I could draw water for your kettle from the well my cousins carefully guard?"

"Why?" was all he could think of asking, standing his ground briefly against his captor's pull. She shrugged.

"Messing with fate is what we do. It's nothing personal. We alter the fate of many to a lesser or greater extent. Most of them never notice."

CHAPTER 41
THE APARTMENT

Still feeling very much worse for wear, but with an inner-secret glow, Anja strode through the Old Town for a showdown with Haldred. She'd messed up in Bratislava, and allowed herself to be side-tracked last night; there could be no more mistakes. A smile curved the corner of her mouth; it had, at least, been worth it. A wild night of excess, spent in Rudi's company, and later in his arms, on the floor of some place on the other side of town, at the party they'd gone to when the club closed. It was unprofessional, but it felt good, and at last she'd got her man. But she'd deviated from her path, and, fun though it had been, she still had a job to do.

The address was familiar; she'd already been. It was just a few minutes' walk from the Old Town Square on a quiet street, unremarkable and lined only with residential blocks rather than shops.

His apartment was on the fourth floor. Up one last flight of steps, and she was standing at Haldred's door. It, too, was unremarkable. In need of a fresh coat of paint like all the others she'd passed, but quite normal. She decided to surprise him, so she took out her little tool wallet from a deep pocket in her coat, and expertly picked the lock.

The door opened silently, but the apartment was a mess. Her opinion of him fell; who would allow themselves to live in such slovenly conditions? Only a complete wastrel and deviant, she was sure. No wonder her masters had decided to eliminate him. She would be doing everyone a favour.

Anja crept through the debris on the living room floor to the bedroom, but it was empty. The kitchen, bathroom and spare room the same. She cursed herself for being too late. Where had he gone?

With a growl, she ripped blinds and curtains open to let some light into the place, and search for clues. Frustration mounted as she found nothing of use, and her unease at being here grew. It wasn't just the cloying air, and the smell of stale food, but something else: a feeling of dread that tingled down her spine and made her shiver as if she were cold. She began to sense a presence, and not a friendly one.

She dismissed the thought, and renewed her search, looking for a laptop, anything to indicate where he might be, and what he had done with the painting. There was no immediate sign of the computer, and she had a horrible feeling he'd taken it with him. She began a thorough room by room search.

The sixth-sense tingle was strongest in the spare bedroom. Driven by curiosity, she rummaged through drawers – all empty – and underneath the bed. Finally, she opened the wardrobe and saw cardboard boxes, clothes and a suitcase. The feeling was stronger here. This must be the source of the horrible tingling sensation. She began to feel, rather than hear, a strange voice in her head, manipulative and insistent: *Set me free, set me free*. Her search intensified. At the back of the shelf at the top, she found a wooden box and placed it on the bed. Scratches grooved its surface, and judging from the dark colour, it was extremely old.

The lid was closed and locked. She tried her tools, but nothing worked. Then she inserted the blade of one of her knives to try to lever it open, but that failed as well. Finally, she took it through to the kitchen, found a hammer in a drawer under the sink, and smashed the lock, then prised open the lid.

She stood back and looked; her eyes wide in wonder. The Fire Serpent, beguiling, coiled and patient, stared back, its ruby eyes glinting faintly in the light. Anja gasped in delight, and smiled, her frustration gone. Instead, she was enraptured by this most beautiful item of jewellery.

In wonder, she picked the necklace from the box and held it closer, examining the fine detail and supreme quality of its manufacture. It was stunning in its complexity, each individual scale along the body separately created and fitted into place with utmost precision. Anja had no thought of ever giving it up again. She tried it on her wrist, marvelling at the way it coiled about her forearm. Then she put it to her neck. It fitted her perfectly, wrapping around with sufficient length to spare so that the head grasped onto the tail.

She had to see the effect for herself.

In the bathroom, she stared awestruck at the beautiful, precious object that adorned her neck. The snake's head twisted slightly and tilted so that it appeared to be staring at her reflection in the mirror. *How clever*, she thought. But those eyes – ruby red at the edge – had a centre that was blacker than black, and she felt as if she were falling down a well. The Fire Serpent became hot, painfully hot, and the skin of her fingers sizzled. Anja scrabbled to remove it, tearing at it with her hands, but it became tighter, asphyxiating her. Choking, she collapsed on the floor, wildly thrashing as the serpent tightened its grip. It sank deeper into her neck until it penetrated within, disappearing beneath her skin, leaving no outward mark. Anja gave one last spasm, and lay still and lifeless, sprawled on the bathroom floor, arms and legs splayed at odd angles, eyes staring out, unseeing.

"Is that you, my little girl, my precious child?"

What?

"How clever of you to find me."

Where?

"Reunited at last. It's been so long. Do you remember our secret? Our precious time? We can make this our new secret, just you and me. We can do great things when you set me free. We can be together again, forever."

Who?

"Do you remember how to kiss your father? Good. Then get on your knees to worship."

NO!

Slowly, steadily, with a patience born of a thousand years, the serpent wormed into her brain, sucked at her thoughts, chewed on her soul, consumed her from within. What remained the serpent locked away in a tiny distant corner of its mind, to be consciously forgotten. On the bathroom floor, Anja's outward appearance was unchanged. For a long time, she lay there dead. Then she began to shake, from head to foot, violently crashing against porcelain, against the walls, against the side of the bath, before falling still. She closed her eyes, and coming to, as if from a long sleep, passed a hand across them, wiping out a memory.

She sat, then stood, gripping the handbasin until she felt steady. The body that was Anja opened her ruby-red eyes and stared at the world anew.

"Daddy!"

CHAPTER 42
THE HOUSE ON THE LAKE

The security system recognised the number plate of the approaching BMW and the electronic gates opened smoothly and silently. Without stopping, the four-by-four swept past and navigated the long drive, coming to a halt before the door with an expensive crunch of gravel. The driver emerged, dressed in black from head to toe as if in homage to the car. From the trunk, he retrieved a large briefcase, then placed a homburg hat on his hairless scalp and stepped back, looking towards the house.

He stood before an elegant eighteenth-century mansion, built on a simple rectangular footprint, but thoroughly modernised to exacting standards by its present owner. No expense had been spared on refurbishment, and the attention to detail was meticulous, from the marble-tiled hallways and painstakingly restored plasterwork, to the luxurious furniture and state-of-the-art appliances. Elegance and refinement merged effortlessly with comfort and convenience; it was a home to live in, as well as to impress. To either side of the house, and beyond, manicured lawns with sculpted flowerbeds led through a small orchard, past tennis courts and a maze, to the private jetty and boathouse by the shore of Lac Leman.

The house was thirty kilometres from Geneva, on the Swiss side of the lake. It was a tranquil haven, a calm oasis, a world away from the bustle of everyday life beyond its boundaries. The owner of the property was known to those in local high society as Max Stürme, a philanthropist and investor of unimaginable wealth but with a discreet lifestyle. He was not a total recluse; he hosted at least one charity event each summer, usually a garden party attended by several well-known celebrities. He was also a regular visitor to the opera, hosting guests in his private box. However, to an entirely different circle, he had another alias. Those who traded in stolen, often highly valued, works of art knew him only as The Collector, and from others in that business, he maintained a strict distance, operating solely through intermediaries. Stürme cultivated both personas, and was careful to maintain a suitable distance between them, but neither was an accurate reflection of his true identity.

As the man in black approached, the front door opened, and The Collector stepped forth; expensively, if casually dressed – a crisp white shirt, open at the neck, tucked into designer jeans. Black, tightly curled hair adorned an ageless face which was framed by a neatly trimmed beard.

"Was your mission successful, Antef?"

Antef removed his hat and bowed deeply. "Sire, I have the illustration you desired." He held out the case. The Collector glanced at it, then stepped forwards and grasped his servant's shoulders, a generous smile touching the corners of his mouth.

"You have done well, my friend. Come. Let us talk inside and you can show me your prize."

They entered the hall, stepping past the housekeeper who held the door open, then turned right into a refined living room. The Collector gestured to an antique coffee table and settled down on a luxuriously upholstered sofa, which he seemed to fill.

"Come. Sit."

Antef placed the case carefully on the table, the catches facing his master, and perched on the edge of the seat opposite, his normally confident demeanour slipping as if the briefcase might no longer contain what he thought it did. The Collector noted the nuances in his behaviour and smiled. It would never do to let one's servants be too comfortable in their own skin.

"I'm being rude. You've had a long journey. Please remove your coat and make yourself comfortable. I'll get us some tea." As if on cue, a housemaid appeared, took Antef's coat and hat, and swept out again. The Collector smoothly continued speaking, ignoring the case on the table.

"Tell me all about it."

Antef tried not to look at the briefcase and appear relaxed, but it was never easy in this company. Not when you had been brought up all your life to serve. The mere act of sitting in his master's presence was a rare honour, and one which he didn't feel he deserved.

He recounted his journey to Berlin, his uneventful retrieval of the object from the safe deposit facility of the Sparkasse Brandenburg, and, following inspection of the goods, completion of the thief's remuneration from an anonymous, untraceable account. He assured The Collector that the dwarf was satisfied with his commission and had performed his task satisfactorily. He neglected to mention the additional threats and counter-threats they had exchanged before he was given the correct deposit box number. It wouldn't do to appear to have been outwitted by a dwarf, even temporarily.

The Collector sat with his arms spread wide along the back of the sofa, legs crossed, grimacing. "You may not have heard the news, my friend. He seems to have come to an unfortunate end."

Antef sat just a little straighter. "Surely nothing to do with us?"

"Oh, no. Fear not. No one is aware of any connection to us." The Collector gave his servant a reassuring smile. "It appears to have been a little family dispute. A falling out. An argument that went too far in the heat of the moment. You know how these things happen. They seem to be naturally argumentative creatures, these dwarves." He stopped talking, his eyes fixed on Antef while the door opened once more and the housemaid placed a tray of tea and biscuits on the table between them next to the case. A brief word, and she placed a cup and saucer before each of them. Antef waited until the door closed before speaking, only too well aware of the consequences of family disputes.

"How unfortunate. Still, I am relieved to hear it. A loose end appears to have been tied up."

The Collector let the comment hang, then leaned forwards to pick up his cup and saucer and sit back again, sipping the tea. "Biscuit?"

"Oh, no. Thank you." Antef sipped his tea, but eating in the presence of his master was a step too far for his deeply ingrained sense of service. He kept his eyes lowered, the habit of a lifetime. The Collector allowed the silence to extend for a while, then placed his cup and saucer down and sat forward once more.

"Well, I suppose we'd better have a look at it, then?" He sounded relaxed and friendly, but Antef's mouth was dry, despite the tea.

The Collector took hold of the catches and glanced up at his servant once more, a teasing glint in his eye. He paused for dramatic effect, then opened the case. Fitting snugly inside, mummified in bubble wrap, was the icon from Varlaam Monastery. He took it out and removed the wrap, then held it out at arm's length, appreciatively. With a critic's frown, he tilted his head and inspected it from a different angle, then placed it on top of the case, apparently satisfied. He became more business-like.

"You have done well, Antef. I am pleased. I shall make sure you are rewarded."

Antef bowed his head and murmured his thanks. The Collector leaned forwards, poring over the painting. Antef watched him, anxious that there was nothing wrong. Instead, his mentor started conversing about the artwork before him.

"It's fascinating, isn't it, the skill of these medieval painters? Just look at the brushwork." He glanced up. "Nicolas was an interesting one. Very early saint. Fourth century, I believe. But I sense a bit of a hybrid, if this is anything to go by?"

Antef's glance veered between the painting and his master, his eyebrows raised. The Collector gave him a beneficent smile and pointed to some detail on the bishop's garb. "Look, here on his cope, woven into the pattern of the fabric. An ankh. An ancient Egyptian symbol, apparently appropriated by early Christians. And here, his ring. Is that in the style of the Ouroboros? The serpent that encircles the world and eats its tail? Sacred to both Greeks and Egyptians. Beliefs were more fluid in those days."

He pored over the rest of the painting. In the upper right quadrant was a depiction of a walled hilltop town, and in the lower right quarter, a cave. The Collector mused further, as if giving a lecture.

"This is where we get the really interesting clues, though. The town seems straightforward enough: Myra. You can tell by the flag. It was famous for several caves in the hillside beneath." He gestured to the lower corner of the painting, and leaned closer once more, studying it intently. "But look here. The paint seems to be much thicker, the brushstrokes cruder, probably by a different hand. As if an additional layer of paint has been applied to conceal something." He looked up again. "That's interesting, isn't it?"

Antef could only nod, pleased that his master was satisfied. The Collector sat back once more.

"You may go." The instruction was curt.

The servant sprang to his feet, nodded and headed to the door. After opening it, he turned towards his mentor and bowed more deeply. "My lord." He left.

The Collector waited a few moments, then stood. Picking up the painting, he made his way out of another set of double doors to the rear of the room, crossed a smaller sitting room, then walked along a short corridor before turning into a book-lined library. At the far corner, he selected a slim volume from the third shelf down and angled it downwards. A section of bookcases opened silently, revealing a short alcove with silver doors ahead. The Collector pressed the call button and entered the elevator. Once inside, he selected -2 and waited. The elevator descended far below the house, further underground than any normal basement might be found, deep into bedrock. The doors opened onto pitch-dark.

"Lights," he commanded. The house security system obeyed and the system came to life, illuminating a long room. Cones of light spread downwards, spotlighting objects in cases and on stands along its length. From a recess by the wall, floor-level lighting cast a glow upward and across, marking the carpeted walkway. The main hall was large, comprising a central rectangular space with anterooms branching off on each side, and yet more angled off from them. Taken together, they formed a significant labyrinth: a modern-day tomb lined with treasures fit for any Pharaoh. The walls were covered in floor-to-ceiling paintings depicting the life and adventures of a mighty deity; the god of storms and disorder, and true pharaoh of Egypt, and his veneration by obsequious followers.

Temperature and humidity were carefully maintained throughout the subterranean complex, and the air recycled and filtered to remove dust and other impurities. Three of the side rooms, and the main space, contained exhibits. A fourth, which could be sealed off when in use, held advanced analytical equipment and materials. Set made his way towards it, past a display stand specifically prepared for his new acquisition, and a treasure hoard more fabulous and storied than ever any dragon had guarded.

Behind glass, and beautifully illuminated was the Aegis of Athena, a mighty golden shield engraved with the head of a gorgon. On the other side of the aisle stood Flidais' chariot from Ireland, while down the length of the hall were displayed the Book of Thoth, the real Stone of Scone, Odin's arm ring Draupnir and several ancient reliefs of the Green Man and rare variants thereon, such as the Green Demon. On a velvet cushion sat the necklace Brisingamen, next to the mistletoe dart used to kill Baldur. A quiver of Apollo's arrows and Merlin's staff were in a display case in the corner. Nearby lay Roland's sword, Durendal, among a display of other famous weapons. The items were interspersed with many examples of fabulous statuary from Greece, Rome and Luxor, and other places, including a Gorgon's head and a large-scale replica of the Hydra. In a case at the far end of the hall was the antique prow of a ship. In contrast to the other pieces, it did not seem well preserved. Recovered after centuries buried in silt beneath the sea, the wood was fragile and seemed to barely have the integrity to hold together, or to contain the large knot of denser wood in its midst. It was the prow of a ship, the Argo, which once pronounced prophesies; though to Set's frustration, it had not yet spoken.

Set walked past his fabulous collection, entered a passageway to the left, then into a laboratory – brightly lit and well equipped – to the side. He laid his new acquisition flat on a table and peered at it intently. With his carefully attuned sight, he scrutinised it. The saint, positioned to the left-hand side of the image, held little real interest for him. Instead, he focused on the two smaller elements to the right.

At the top was a medieval interpretation of a fortified hilltop town, with walls and a keep, a flag flying proudly from it. Below this, in the bottom right-hand corner, was a cave, its contents clumsily concealed beneath a later layer of black paint.

He retrieved some materials from cabinets against a side wall, and returned. Then, with delicate precision, painstakingly removed that layer using a cotton bud and an appropriate solvent. The process took some time, but when finally satisfied he was finished, he stood back and admired what lay beneath.

It was a creature; a monster of some kind. No wonder they had wanted it removed from this Christian icon. What the original artist had painted appeared to be the head and shoulders of a bull emerging from the mouth of a cave. The forelegs were clearly displayed, but the body behind was unusual. The portion that was shown, before it disappeared into the cavernous depths, was elongated and appeared scaled and sinuous, unlike that of any normal mammal. Set pored over it for a long time.

Over his shoulder, via one of many security cameras positioned in the ceiling, STUBBINS also observed the painting. Via sensitive chemical detectors, the intelligent security system picked up a faint acidic aroma. It performed a multi-wavelength full spectrum scan and assembled the evidence. The object gave faint but detectable traces of cat urine, which was noteworthy in itself, given his superior's interests. The revelation of the Ophiotaurus was interesting, but beneath the surface coating was a more ancient image. It showed two female figures of indeterminate age, one with what might have been lighter coloured hair and an open, friendly face, her companion darker and more intense, and staring out of the canvas with, according to sophisticated pigment residue analysis, piercing grey-green eyes.

The figures stood either side of a small tree, each holding a fruit resembling an apple. The tree appeared to be growing on a rocky outcrop overlooking the sea.

STUBBINS recorded the image together with accompanying chemical and other relevant data, including suspected artistic provenance, dimensions, unusual and noteworthy pigments used and more. It time-stamped and packaged its analysis with comprehensive quantum-level encryption, and forwarded it to its master, marked *URGENT*.

THE END

FREE PREQUEL

To find out more about the series, join my mailing list and download a free prequel, click on the image or visit Andrew-Rylands.com
If you enjoyed The Accidental Hero, I would very much appreciate a review.

ACKNOWLEDGMENTS

It takes a number of people to produce a book of any quality, and I am extremely grateful for all of the talented professionals who have assisted me in preparing this book. They include Andrew Lowe, who provided superb editorial judgement and input, Lottie Clemens was an excellent proofreader, and Stuart Bache produced a marvellous cover. Others have chipped in with advice and comment along the way, foremost of whom has been my son Alex. His enthusiasm for the project has been invaluable.

ABOUT THE AUTHOR

Andrew lives near Edinburgh with a cat who insists on auditioning for a part in a future story. When he's not writing, or thinking about writing, he enjoys exploring both the UK, and the rest of the world, and planning his next trip. Greece, the inspiration for these tales, is always a favourite destination. There is nothing quite like standing among the ancient stones and listening for an echo of the stories they once witnessed. That was what started him down this road in the first place.

www.andrewrylands.com

Printed in Great Britain
by Amazon